John Henry Eaton, Jerome Van C. Smith

The Complete Memoirs of Andrew Jackson

seventh president of the United States - containing a full account of his military life

and achievements, with his career as president

John Henry Eaton, Jerome Van C. Smith

The Complete Memoirs of Andrew Jackson
seventh president of the United States - containing a full account of his military life and achievements, with his career as president

ISBN/EAN: 9783337403591

Printed in Europe, USA, Canada, Australia, Japan

Cover: Foto ©Andreas Hilbeck / pixelio.de

More available books at **www.hansebooks.com**

THE

COMPLETE MEMOIRS

OF

ANDREW JACKSON,

SEVENTH PRESIDENT OF THE UNITED STATES.

CONTAINING A FULL ACCOUNT OF HIS MILITARY
LIFE AND ACHIEVEMENTS, WITH HIS
CAREER AS PRESIDENT.

NEW YORK
HURST & CO., Publishers
122 Nassau Street

PREFACE.

IT is not the intention of the compiler of the following Memoirs to present his readers with a prolix preface, because it constitutes that portion of a book which is seldom honored with a reading.

When high party feelings were fully developed, in relation to a presidential candidate, the engines of abuse brought into operation on the one hand, and on the other the fulsome adulation exhibited towards the distinguished patriot whose life is here delineated, induced the compiler to undertake an investigation of the subject in order to bring to light a true statement of facts.

With this object constantly in view, there has been a careful examination of the official documents which relate to his public acts. His talents as a military commander, as a civilian, and, lastly, his moral character, are open to the inspection of all.

When the community entertain different views of the conduct or motives of an individual who has acted in a highly responsible capacity, it is exceedingly difficult to concentrate opinion by presenting a series of truths. Prejudice operates with peculiar force on the minds of one class, while the other, however well convinced of their error, are unwilling to be thought inconsistent, and therefore never acknowledge the falsity of the course of reasoning which they have once adopted.

Although this compilation has been attended with considerable anxiety in reducing the materials to an orderly arrangement, a hope is indulged that the reader will admit, from a candid examination of the whole, that the intention has not been to make the work subservient to party purposes: on the contrary, it is intended to be a plain record of events in the life of an illustrious American citizen.

The compiler of these Memoirs makes no claim to novelty or originality. He hopes, notwithstanding, that they will not be found uninteresting. It has been his aim to be strictly impartial. The materials that compose his works have accordingly been derived alike from the enemies and friends of the hero, whose public and private character he has endeavored faithfully to delineate.

Unaccustomed to eulogy, and unacquainted with the chicanery of political life, the compiler submits the result of his inquiries to the impartial tribunal of the public.

S.

CONTENTS.

CHAPTER I.

CHAPTER II.

CHAPTER III.

v

CHAPTER IV.

CHAPTER V.

CHAPTER VI.

CHAPTER VII.

CHAPTER VIII.

CHAPTER IX.

1*

CONTENTS.

CHAPTER X.

CHAPTER XI.

CHAPTER XII.

LIFE

OF

ANDREW JACKSON.

CHAPTER I.

His birth, parentage, family, and education.—Engages in the American Revolution, and is shortly after, with his brother made a prisoner.—Their treatment and sufferings.—Commences the study of law.—His removal to the Western country —Anecdote.—Becomes a member of the Tennessee Convention, and afterwards a Senator in the United States' Congress.—Retires, and is appointed a Judge of the State Courts.—Declaration of war.—Tenders the services of 2500 volunteers to the President.—Ordered to the lower country.—His descent and return, and discharge of the troops.

ANDREW JACKSON was born on the 15th day of March, 1767. His father, (Andrew,) the youngest son of his family, emigrated to America from Ireland during the year 1765, bringing with him two sons, Hugh and Robert, both very young. Landing at Charleston, in South Carolina, he afterwards purchased a tract of land, in what was then called the Waxsaw settlement, about forty-five miles above Camden ; at which place the subject of this history was born. Shortly after his birth, his father died, leaving three sons to be provided for by their mother. She appears to have been an exemplary woman, and to have executed the arduous duties which had devolved on her, with great

faithfulness and success. To the lessons she in
culcated on the youthful minds of her sons, was
no doubt, owing, in a great measure, that fixed opposition to British oppression, which afterwards so
much distinguished them. Often would she spend
the winter's evenings in recounting to them the
sufferings of their grandfather at the siege of Car-
sickfergus, and the oppression exercised by the no-
bility of Ireland over the labouring poor ; impressing it upon them, as a first duty, to expend their
lives, if it should become necessary, in defending
and supporting the rights of man.

Inheriting but a small patrimony from their father, it was impossible that all the sons could receive
an expensive education. The two eldest were,
therefore, only taught the rudiments of their mother
tongue, at a common country school. But Andrew, being intended by his mother for the minis-
try, was sent to a flourishing academy at the Waxsaw meeting-house, superintended by Mr. Hum-
phries. Here he was placed on the study of the
dead languages, and continued until the revolutionary war, extending its ravages into that section
of South Carolina where he then was, rendered
it necessary that every one should betake himself
to the American standard, seek protection with the
enemy, or flee his country. It was not an alternative that admitted of tedious deliberation. The
natural ardour of his temper, deriving encouragement from the recommendations of his mother,
whose feelings were excited by those sentiments in
favour of liberty, with which, by her conversation,
his mind had been early imbued, quickly deter
mined him in the course to be pursued ; and, at the
tender age of fourteen, accompanied by his brother

Robert, he hastened to the American camp, and engaged actively in the service of his country His eldest brother, who had previously joined the army, had lost his life at the battle of Stono, from the excessive heat of the weather and the fatigues of the day.

Both Andrew and Robert were, at this period, pretty well acquainted with the manual exercise, and had some idea of the different evolutions of the field, having been indulged by their mother in attending the drill and general musters of the neighbourhood.

The Americans being unequal, as well from the inferiority of their numbers, as their discipline, to engage the British army in battle, had retired before it into the interior of North Carolina; but, when they learned that Lord Cornwallis had crossed the Yadkin, they returned in small detachments to their native state. On their arrival, they found Lord Rawdon in possession of Camden, and the whole country around in a state of desolation. The British commander being advised of the return of the settlers of Waxsaw, Major Coffin was immediately despatched thither, with a corps of light dragoons, a company of infantry, and a considerable number of tories, for their capture and destruction. Hearing of their approach, the settlers, without delay, appointed the Waxsaw meeting-house as a place of rendezvous, that they might the better collect their scattered strength, and concert some system of operations. About forty of them had accordingly assembled at this point, when the enemy approached, keeping the tories, who were dressed in the common garb of the country, in front, whereby this little band of patriots was completely

deceived, having taken them for Captain Nis-
bet's company, in expectation of which they had
been waiting. Eleven of them were taken prison
r ; the rest with difficulty fled, betaking them
s   s to the woods for concealment. Of those
who thus escaped, though closely pursued, were
Andrew Jackson and his brother, who, entering a
 ret bend in a creek, that was close at hand,
o ained a momentary respite from danger, and
avoided, for the night, the pursuit of the enemy.
The next day, however, having gone to a neighbouring house, for the purpose of procuring something to eat, they were broken in upon, and made
prisoners, by Coffin's dragoons, and a party of tories who accompanied them. Those young men,
with a view to security, had placed their horses in
the wood, on the margin of a small creek, and posted, on the road which led by the house, a senti-
nel, that they might have information of any approach, and in time to be able to elude it. But
the tories, who were well acquainted with the country and the passes through the forest, had, unfortunately, passed the creek at the very point where
the horses and baggage of our young soldiers were
deposited, and taken possession of them. Having
done this, they approached, cautiously, the house,
and were almost at the door before they were discovered. To escape was impossible, and both
were made prisoners. Being placed under guard,
Andrew was ordered, in a very imperious tone, by a
British officer, to clean his boots. This order he
positively and peremptorily refused to obey ; alleg
ing that he looked for such treatment as a pris
oner of war had a right to expect. Incensed at
his refusal, the officer aimed a blow at his head

with a drawn sword, which would, very probably
have terminated his existence, had he not parried
its effects by throwing up his left hand, on which
he received a severe wound, the mark of which he
bears to this hour. His brother, at the same time,
for a similar offence, received a deep cut on the
head, which subsequently occasioned his death.
They were both now taken to jail, where, sepa
rated and confined, they were treated with marked
severity, until a few days after the battle before
Camden, when, in consequence of a partial exchange, effected by the intercessions and exertions of their mother, and Captain Walker, of the
militia, they were both released from confinement
Robert, during his confinement in prison, had suffered greatly; the wound on his head, all this time,
having never been dressed, was followed by an in-
flammation of the brain, which, in a few days after
his liberation, brought him to the grave. To add
to the afflictions of Andrew, his mother, worn
down by grief, and her incessant exertions to pro
vide clothing and other comforts for the suffering
prisoners, who had been taken from her neighbourhood, expired in a few weeks after her son,
near the lines of the enemy, in the vicinity of
Charleston. Andrew, the last and only surviving
child, confined to a bed of sickness, occasioned by
the sufferings he had been compelled to undergo
whilst a prisoner, and by getting wet, on his return
from captivity, was thus left in the wide world,
without a human being with whom he could claim
a near relationship. The small pox, about the
same time, having made its appearance upon him
had well nigh terminated his sorrows and his ex
istence.

Having at length recovered from his complicated afflictions, he entered upon the enjoyment of his estate, which, although small, would have been sufficient, under prudent management, to have completed his education, on the liberal scale which his mother had designed. Unfortunately, however, he, like too many young men, sacrificing future prospects to present gratification, expended it with rather too profuse a hand. Foreseeing that he should be finally obliged to rely on his own exertions, for support and success in life, he again betook himself to his studies with increased industry. He recommenced under Mr. M'Culloch, in that part of Carolina which was then called the New Acquisition, near Hill's iron works. Here he revised the languages, devoting a portion of his time to a desultory course of studies.

His education being now completed, so far as his wasted patrimony, and the limited opportunities then afforded in that section of the country, would permit, at the age of eighteen, he turned his attention to acquiring a profession, and in preparing himself to enter on the busy scenes of life. The pulpit, for which he had been designed by his mother, was now abandoned for the bar; and, in the winter of 1784, he repaired to Salisbury, in North Carolina, and commenced the study of law under Spruce M'Cay, Esq., (afterwards one of the judges of that state,) and subsequently continued it under Colonel John Stokes. Having remained at Salisbury until the winter of 1786, he obtained a license from the judges to practise law, and continued in the state until the spring of 1788.

The western parts of the state of Tennessee were, about this time, often spoken of, as presenting flattering prospects to adventurers. He immediately determined to accompany Judge M'Nairy thither, who had been appointed, and was going out to hold the first supreme court that had ever sat in the state. Having reached the Holston, they ascertained it would be impossible to arrive at the time appointed for the session of the court; and therefore determined to remain in that section of country until fall. They reached Nashville in October. It had not been Jackson's intention, certainly, to make Tennessee the place of his future residence; his visit was merely experimental, and his stay remained to be determined by the advantages that might be disclosed; but finding, soon after his arrival, that a considerable opening was offered for the success of a young attorney, he determined to remain, though the prospect before him was, certainly, not of an encouraging cast. As in all newly settled countries must be the case, society was loosely formed, and united by but few of those ties which have a tendency to enforce the performance of moral duty, and the right execution of justice. The young men of the place, adventurers from different sections of the country, had become indebted to the merchants; there was but one lawyer in the country, and they had so contrived, as to retain him in their business; the consequence was, that the merchants were entirely deprived of the means of enforcing against those gentlemen the execution of their contracts. In this state of things Jackson made his appearance at Nashville, and while the creditor class looked to it with great satisfaction, the debtors were sorely displeased. Applications were immediately made to him for his professional services, and on the morning after his

2*

arrival he issued seventy writs. To those prodi-
gal gentlemen, it was an alarming circumstance
their former security was impaired; but, that it
might not wholly depart, they determined to force
him, in some way or other, to leave the country;
and, to effect this, broils and quarrels with him
were to be resorted to. This, however, was soon
abandoned, satisfied by the first controversy in
which they had involved him, that his decision and
firmness were such as to leave no hope of effecting
any thing through this channel. Disregarding the
opposition raised to him, he continued, with care
and industry, to press forward in his professional
course, and his attention soon brought him forward,
and introduced him to a profitable practice. He
was subsequently appointed attorney-general for
the district, in which capacity he continued to act
for several years.

Indian depredations being then frequent on the
Cumberland, every man, of necessity, became a
soldier Unassisted by the government, the settlers were forced to rely for security on their own
bravery and exertions. Although young, no per
son was more distinguished than Andrew Jackson, in defending the country against these preda-
tory incursions of the savages, who continually
harassed the frontiers, and not unfrequently approached the heart of the settlements, which were
thin, but not widely extended. He aided alike in
garrisoning the forts, and in pursuing and chastis-
ing the enemy.

In the year 1796, having, by his patriotism, firmness and talents, secured to himself a distinguished
standing, he was chosen one of the members of the
convention for establishing a constitution for the

state. His good conduct and zeal brought him more prominently to view; and, without proposing or soliciting, he was, in the same year, elected a member of the house of representatives, in congress, for the state of Tennessee. The following year, his reputation continuing to increase, he was chosen a senator of the United States' congress, and took his seat on the 22d day of November, 1797. About the middle of April, business of an important and private nature imposed on him the necessity of asking leave of absence, and returning home. Leave was granted, and before the next session he resigned his seat. He was but a little more than thirty years of age, and hence, scarcely eligible, by the constitution, at the time he was elected. The sedition law was introduced into the senate, by Mr. Lloyd, of Maryland, in June, and passed that body on the 4th of July following; hence the name of Jackson, owing to the leave of absence which had been granted him in April, does not appear on the journals. On the alien law, however, and the effort to repeal the stamp act, he was present, resting in the minority.

The state of Tennessee, on its admission into the Union, comprising but one military division, and General Conway, who commanded it, as major-general, dying about this time, Jackson, without being consulted on the subject, was, as the constitution of the state directs, chosen by the field officers to succeed him; which appointment he continued to hold until May, 1814, when he was constituted a major-general in the United States' service.

Becoming tired of political life, for the intrigues of which he declared himself unqualified, and having for two years voted in the minority in congress, he resigned, after the first session, his seat in the senate. To this measure he was strongly induced, from a desire to make way for General Smith, who, he conjectured, would, in that capacity, be able to render more important services to the government than himself. His country, unwilling that his talents should remain inactive and unemployed, again demanded his services. Immediately after his resignation, he was appointed one of the judges of the supreme court of the state. He advanced to the office with reluctance, and in a short time resigned, leaving it open for those, who, he believed, were better qualified than himself, to discharge its intricate and important duties. Unambitious of those distinctions and honours which young men are usually proud to possess; finding, too, that his circumstances and condition in life were not such as to permit his time and attention to be devoted to public matters, he determined to yield them into others' hands, and to devote himself to agricultural pursuits; and accordingly settled himself on an excellent farm, ten miles from Nashville, on the Cumberland river; where, for several years, he enjoyed all the comforts of domestic and social intercourse. Abstracted from the busy scenes of public life, pleased with retirement, surrounded by friends whom he loved, and who entertained for him the highest veneration and respect, and blessed with an amiable and affectionate consort, nothing seemed wanting to the completion of that happiness which he so anxiously desired whilst in office.

Great Britain, by multiplied outrages on our rights, as an independent and neutral nation, has provoked from our government a declaration of war against her. This measure, though founded in abundant cause, had been long forborne, and every attempt at reconciliation made, without effect; when, at length, it was resorted to, as the only alternative that could preserve the honour and dignity of the nation, General Jackson, ever devoted to the interests of his country, from the moment of the declaration, knew no wish so strong as that of entering into her service, against a power, which, independent of public considerations, he had many private reasons for disliking. In her, he could trace sufferings and injuries received, and the efficient cause, why, in early life, he had been left forlorn and wretched, without a single relation in the world. His proud and inflexible mind, however, could not venture to solicit an appointment in the army, which was about to be raised. He accordingly remained wholly unknown, until, at the head of the militia, employed against the Creek Indians, his constant vigilance, and the splendour of his victories, apprized the general government of those great military talents which he so eminently possessed, and conspicuously displayed, when opportunities for exerting them were afforded.

The acts of congress of the 6th of February and July, 1812, afforded the means of bringing in to view a display of those powers, which, being unknown, under other circumstances, unfortunately, might have slumbered in inaction. Under the authority of these acts, authorizing the president to accept the services of fifty thousand volunteers, he addressed the citizens of his division, and twenty-five hundred flocked to his standard. A

tender of them having been made, and the offer accepted, in November he received orders to place
himself at their head and to descend the Mississippi, for the defence of the lower country, which
was then supposed to be in danger. On the 10th
of December, those troops rendezvoused at Nashville, prepared to advance to the place of their des
tination; and, although the weather was then ex-
cessively severe, and the ground covered with
snow, no troops could have displayed greater firmness. The general was every where with them, inspiring them with the ardour that animated his
own bosom.

Having procured supplies, and made the necessary arrangements for an active campaign, they proceeded, the 7th of January, on their journey; and,
descending the Ohio and Mississippi, through cold
and ice, arrived, and halted at Natchez. Here
Jackson had been instructed to remain, until he
should receive further orders. Having chosen a
healthy site for the encampment of his troops,
about two miles from Washington, he devoted his
time, with the utmost industry, to training and preparing them for active service. The clouds of
war, however, in that quarter, having blown over,
an order was received from the secretary of war,
dated the 5th of January, directing him, on the re-
ceipt thereof, to dismiss those under his command
from service, and to take measures for delivering
over every article of public property, in his pos
session, to Brigadier-General Wilkinson. When
this order reached his camp, there were one hundred and fifty on the sick report, fifty-six of whom
were unable to raise their heads, and almost the
whole of them destitute of the means of defrav-

ing the expenses of their return. The consequence of a strict compliance with the secretary's order inevitably would have been, that many of the sick must have perished, whilst most of the others, from their destitute condition, would, of necessity, have been compelled to enlist in the regular army, under General Wilkinson. Such alternatives were neither congenial with their general's wishes, nor such as they had expected, on adventuring with him in the service of their country; he had carried them from home, and, the fate of war and disease apart, it was his duty, he believed, to bring them back. To have abandoned them, therefore, at such a time, and under such circumstances, would have drawn on him the merited censure of the most deserving part of his fellow-citizens, and sensibly wounded his own generous feelings. Add to this, those young men who were confined by sickness, learning the nature of the order he had received, implored him, with tears in their eyes, not to abandon them in so great an extremity, reminding him, at the same time, of his assurances, that he would be to them as a father, and of the implicit confidence they had placed in his word This was an appeal, which it would have been difficult for the feelings of Jackson to have resisted, had it been without the support of other weighty considerations; but, influenced by them all, he had no hesitation in coming to a determination.

Having made known his resolution to the field-officers of his division, it met, apparently, their approbation; but, after retiring from his presence, they assembled late at night, in secret caucus, and proceeded to recommend to him an abandonment of his purpose, and an immediate discharge of his troops. Great as was the astonishment, which this measure excited in the general, it produced a still higher sentiment of indignation. In reply, he urged the duplicity of their conduct, and reminded them, that, although to those who possessed funds and health, such a course could produce no inconvenience, yet to the unfortunate soldier, who was alike destitute of both, no measure could be more calamitous. He concluded by telling them, that his resolution, not having been hastily concluded on, nor bottomed on light considerations, was unalterably fixed; and that immediate preparations must be made for carrying into execution the determination he had formed.

He lost no time in making known to the secretary of war the resolution he had adopted; to disregard the order he had given, and to return his army to the place where he had received it. He painted in strong terms the evils which the course pursued by the government was calculated to produce, and expressed the astonishment he felt, that it should have originated with the famous author of the "Newburg Letters," the once redoubted advocate of soldiers' rights.

General Wilkinson, to whom the public property was directed to be delivered, learning the determination which had been taken by Jackson, to march his troops back, and to take with them so much of that property as should be necessary to their return, in a letter of solemn and mysterious import, admonished him of the consequences which were before him, and of the awful and dangerous responsibility he was taking on himself, by so bold a measure. General Jackson replied, that his conduct, and the consequences to which it might lead,

had been well considered, and that he was prepared
to abide the result, whatever it might be. Wilkinson had previously given orders to his officers to
recruit from Jackson's army; they were advised,
however, on their first appearance, that those troops
were already in the service of the United States,
and that, thus situated, they should not be enlisted;
and that he would arrest and confine the first officer who dared to enter his encampment with any
such object in view.

The quarter-master, having been ordered to
furnish the necessary transportation for the con
veyance of the sick and the baggage to Tennes
see, immediately set about the performance of the
task; but, as the event proved, with not the least
intention of executing it. Still, he continued to
keep up the semblance of exertion; and, the better to deceive, the very day before that which had
been appointed for breaking up the encampment,
and commencing the return march, eleven wagons
arrived there by his order. The next morning,
however, when every thing was about to be packed
up, acting doubtless from orders, and intending to
produce embarrassment, the quarter-master entered
the encampment, and discharged the whole. He
was grossly mistaken in the man he had to deal
with, and had now played his tricks too far to be
able to accomplish the object which he had, no
doubt, been instructed to effect. Disregarding
their dismissal, so evidently designed to prevent
his marching back his men, General Jackson seized upon these wagons, yet within his lines, and compelled them to proceed to the transportation of his
sick. It deserves to be recollected, that this quarter-master, so soon as he received directions for

furnishing transportation, had despatched an express to General Wilkinson; and there can be but
little doubt, that the course of duplicity he afterwards pursued, was a concerted plan between him
and that general, to defeat the design of Jackson ;
compel him to abandon the course he had adopted ;
and, in this way, draw to the regular army many
of the soldiers, who, from necessity, would be driv-
en to enlist.   In this attempt they were fortunately
disappointed.   Adhering to his original purpose
he successfully resisted every stratagem of Wilkinson, and marched the whole of his division to the
section of country whence they had been drawn,
and dismissed them from service, as he had beer
instructed.

To present an example that might buoy up the
sinking spirits of his troops in the arduous march,
he yielded up his horses to the sick, and, trudging
on foot, encountered all the hardships that were
met by the soldiers.   It was at a time of the year,
when the roads were extremely bad, and the
swamps, lying in their passage, deep and full; yet,
under these circumstances, he placed before his
troops an example of patience and hardship, that
lulled to silence all complaints, and won to him,
still stronger than before, the esteem and respect
of every one.   On arriving at Nashville, he communicated to the president of the United States
the course he had pursued, and the reasons that
had induced it.   If it had become necessary, he
had sufficient grounds on which he could have jus
tified his conduct.   Had he suffered General Wilkinson to have accomplished what was clearly his
intention, although it was an event which might,
at the moment, have benefited the service, by add

ing an increased strength to the army, yet the example would have been of so serious and exceptionable a character, that injury would have been the final and unavoidable result. His conduct, terrible as it first appeared, was in the end approved, and the expenses incurred directed to be paid by the government.

CHAPTER II.

Indian preparation for hostilities.—Tecumseh arrives amongst the southern tribes; his intrigues.—Civil wars of the Creeks.—Destruction of, and butchery at Fort Mimms.—Expedition against the Indians.—Jackson unites with the army, and enters the enemy's country.—Scarcity of supplies in his camp.—Learns the savages are imbodied.—Seeks to form a junction with the East Tennessee division.—Detaches General Coffee across the Coosa. —Battle of Tallushatchee.

THE volunteers, who had descended the river, having been discharged early in May, there was little expectation that they would again be called for.   Tennessee was too remotely situated in the interior of the country to expect their services would be required for her defence, and hitherto the British had discovered no serious intention of waging operations against any part of Louisiana. Their repose, however, was not of long duration. The Creek Indians, inhabiting the country lying between the Chatahochee and Tombigbee, and extending from the Tennessee River to the Florida line, had lately manifested strong symptoms of hostility towards the United States, from which they had received yearly pensions, and every assistance which the most liberal policy could bestow. This disposition was greatly strengthened, through means used by the northern Indians, who were then making preparations for a war against the United States, and who wished to engage the southern tribes in the same enterprise.

An artful impostor had, about this time, sprung up amongst the Shawnees, who, by passing for a prophet, commissioned by the "Great Spirit" to communicate his mandates to his red children, had acquired, among his own and the neighbouring tribes, astonishing influence. Clothed, as they believed him to be, with such high powers, they listened to his extravagant doctrines, and in them fully confided. He succeeded in kindling a rage against the Anglo-Americans, which soon after burst forth in acts of destructive violence. His brother, Tecumseh, who became so famous during the war, and who was killed subsequently, at the battle of the Thames, was despatched to the southern tribes, to excite in them the same temper. To the Creeks, by far the most numerous and powerful, he directed his principal attention. Having entered their nation, some time in the spring of 1812, he repaired to Tookaubatcha, where he had repeated conferences with the chiefs; but, not meeting with the encouragement he expected, returned to the Alabama, which he had previously visited, and there commenced operations.

Finding there several leaders of great influence, who entered into his views, he was enabled to carry on his schemes with greater success. Deriving his powers from his brother, *the Prophet*, whose extraordinary commission and endowments were well understood by all the neighbouring tribes in the south, his authority was regarded with the highest veneration. He strongly interdicted all intercourse with the whites, and prevailed on the greater part of the Alabama Indians to throw aside the implements and clothing which that intercourse had furnished, and return again to their savage state, from which he represented them as highly culpable for having suffered themselves to be estranged. In

3 *

a word, no means were left untried to excite them
to the most deadly animosity and cruel war. To
afford additional weight to his councils, this designing missionary gave assurances of aid and support from Great Britain; whose power and riches
he represented as almost without limits, and quite
sufficient for the subjugation of the United States.
So considerable an influence did his intrigues and
discourses obtain over the minds of many, that it
was with difficulty the most turbulent of them could
be restrained from running immediately to arms,
and committing depredations on the exposed frontiers. This hasty measure, however he represented as calculated to defeat the great plan of operations which he was labouring to concert; and enjoined the utmost secrecy and quietness, until the
moment should arrive, when, all their preparations
being ready, they might be able to strike a decisive blow; in the mean time, they were to be industriously employed in collecting arms and ammunition, and other necessary implements of war.

Having ordained a chief prophet, whose word
was to be regarded as infallible, and whose directions were to be implicitly followed, and established
a regular gradation of inferior dependants, to dis-
seminate his doctrines through the different parts
of the nation, Tecumseh set out to his own tribe,
accompanied by several of the natives.

From this time, a regular communication was
kept up between the Creeks and the northern
tribes, in relation to the great enterprise which
they were concerting together; whilst the parties
carrying it on committed frequent depredations on
the frontier settlers. By one of these, in the summer of 1812, several families had been murdered

in a shocking manner, near the mouth of the Ohio and, shortly afterwards, another party, entering the limits of Tennessee, under circumstances of still greater barbarity, butchered two families of women and children. Similar outrages were committed on the frontiers of Georgia, and were continued, at intervals, on the inhabitants of Tennessee, along her southern boundary.

These multiplied outrages, at length, attracted the attention of the general government, and application was made, through their agent, (Colonel Hawkins,) to the principal chiefs of the nation, who, desirous of preserving their friendly relation with the United States, resolved to punish the murderers with death; and immediately appointed a party of warriors to carry their determination into execution. No sooner was this done, than the spirit of the greater part of the nation, which, from policy, had been kept, in a considerable degree, dormant, suddenly burst into a flame, and kindled into civil war.

It was not difficult for the friends of those mur derers, who had been put to death, to prevail on others, who secretly applauded the acts for which they suffered, to enter warmly into their resent ments against those who had been concerned in bringing them to punishment. An occasion as they believed, was now presented which fully au- thorized them to throw aside all those injunctions of secrecy imposed on them by Tecumseh and their prophets. They now resolved to lay aside all restraint, and execute at once their insatiate and long-projected vengeance, not only on the white people, but on those of their own nation, who, by

this last act of retaliatory justice, had unequivocally
shown a disposition to preserve their friendship
with the former. The war clubs* were immediately seen in every section of the nation; but more
particularly among the numerous hordes residing
near Alabama. Brandishing these in their hands
they rushed, in the first instance, on those of their
own countrymen who had shown a disposition to
preserve their relations with the United States, and
obliged them to retire towards the white settlements, and place themselves in forts, to escape the
first ebullition of their rage. Encouraged by this
success, and their numbers, which hourly increased, and infatuated to the highest degree by the
predictions of their prophets, who assured them that
the "Great Spirit" was on their side, and would
enable them to triumph over all their enemies, they
began to make immediate preparations for extending their ravages to the white settlements. Fort
Mimms, situated in the Tensaw settlement, in the
Mississippi territory, was the first point destined to
satiate their vengeance. It contained, at that time,
about one hundred and fifty men, under the command
of Major Beasley, besides a considerable number of
women and children, who had betaken themselves
to it for security Having collected a supply of
ammunition from the Spaniards at Pensacola, and
assembled their warriors, to the number of six or

---

* Instruments used by the Indian tribes on commencing hostilities; and which, when painted red, they consider a declaration
of war. They are formed of a stick, about eighteen inches in
length, with a strong piece of sharp iron affixed at the end, and
resemble a hatchet. They use them principally in pursuit, and
after they have been able to introduce confusion into the ranks
of an enemy

seven hundred, the war party, commanded by Weatherford, a distinguished chief of the nation, on the 30th of August, commenced their assault on the fort; and, having succeeded in carrying it, put to death nearly three hundred persons, including women and children, with the most savage barbarity. The slaughter was indiscriminate; mercy was extended to none; and the tomahawk, at the same stroke, often cleft the mother and the child. But seventeen of the whole number in the fort escaped, to bring intelligence of the dreadful catastrophe. This monstrous and unprovoked outrage was no sooner known in Tennessee, than the whole state was thrown into a ferment. Considerable excitement had already been produced by brutalities of earlier date, and measures had been adopted by the governor, in conformity with instructions from the secretary of war, for commencing a campaign against them; but the massacre at Fort Mimms, which threatened to be followed by the entire destruction of the Mobile and Tombigbee settlements, inspired a deep and universal sentiment of solicitude, and an earnest wish for speedy and effectual operations. The anxiety felt on the occasion was greatly increased from an apprehension that General Jackson would not be able to command. He was the only man, known in the state, who was believed qualified to discharge the arduous duties of the station, and who could carry with him the complete confidence of his soldiers. He was at this time seriously indisposed, and confined to his room, with a fractured arm; but, although this apprehension was seriously indulged, arrangements were in progress, and measures industriously taken.

to prepare and press the expedition with every possible despatch.

A numerous collection of respectable citizens, who convened at Nashville on the 18th of September, for the purpose of devising the most effectual ways and means of affording protection to their brethren in distress, after conferring with the governor and General Jackson, who was still confined to his room, strongly advised the propriety of marching a sufficient army into the heart of the Creek nation; and accordingly recommended this measure, with great earnestness, to the legislature, which, in a few days afterwards, commenced its session. That body, penetrated with the same sentiments which animated the whole country, immediately enacted a law, authorizing the executive to call into the field thirty-five hundred of the militia, to be marched against the Indians; and, to guard against all difficulties, in the event the general government should omit to adopt them into their service, three hundred thousand dollars were voted for their support.

The settlers were fleeing to the interior, and every day brought intelligence that the Creeks, collected in considerable force, were bending their course towards the frontiers of Tennessee. The governor now issued an order to General Jackson, who, notwithstanding the state of his health, had determined to assume the command, requiring him to call out, and rendezvous at Fayetteville, in the shortest possible time, two thousand of the militia and volunteers of his division, to repel any invasion that might be contemplated. Colonel Coffee, in addition to five hundred cavalry, already raised, under his command, was authorized to organize and receive into his regiment any mounted riflemen that might make a tender of their services.

Having received these orders, Jackson hastened to give them effect; and with this object appealed to those volunteers, who, with him, had heretofore descended the Mississippi to Natchez. He urged them to appear at the rendezvous, on the 4th of October, equipped for active service. He pointed out the imperious necessity which demanded their services, and urged them to be punctual; for their frontiers were threatened by a savage foe. In the mean time, until this force could be collected and organized, Colonel Coffee, with the force then under his command, and such additional mounted riflemen as could be attached at a short notice, was directed to hasten forward to the neighbourhood of Huntsville, and occupy some eligible position for the defence of the frontier, until the infantry should arrive; when it was contemplated, by the nearest possible route, to press on to Fort St. Stephen, with a view to the protection and defence of Mississippi.

Every exertion was now made to hasten the prep· arations for a vigorous campaign. Orders were given to the quarter-master, to furnish the necessary munitions, with the proper transportation; and to the contractors, to provide ample supplies of provisions. The day of their rendezvous being arrived, and the general not being sufficiently recovered to attend in person, he forwarded by his aid-de-camp, Major Reid, an address, to be read to the troops, accompanied by an order for the establishment of the police of the camp.

For the police of his camp, he announced the following order :

"The chain of sentinels will be marked, and the sentries posted, precisely at ten o'clock to-day.

"No sutler will be suffered to sell spirituous liquors to any soldier, without permission, in writing, from a commissioned officer, under the penalties prescribed by the rules and articles of war.

"No citizen will be permitted to pass the chain of sentinels, after retreat beat in the evening, until reveille in the morning. Drunkenness, the bane of all orderly encampments, is positively forbidden, both in officers and privates: officers, under the penalty of immediate arrest; and privates, of being placed under guard, there to remain until liberated by a court martial.

"At reveille beat, all officers and soldiers are to appear on parade, with their arms and accoutrements in proper order.

"On parade, silence, the duty of a soldier, is positively commanded.

"No officer or soldier is to sleep out of camp, but by permission obtained."

These rules, to those who had scarcely yet passed the line that separates the citizen from the soldier, and who had not yet laid aside the notions of self-sovereignty, had the appearance of too much rigour; but the general well knew, that the expedition in which they were embarked involved much hazard; and that, although such lively feelings were manifested now, yet, when hardships pressed, these might cease.

Impatient to join his division, although his health was far from being restored, his arm only beginning to heal, the general, in a few days afterwards, set out for the encampment, and reached it on the th Finding, on his arrival, that the requisition was not complete, either in the number of men, or the necessary equipments, measures were instantly taken to remedy the deficiency. Orders were di rected to the several brigadiers in his division, to hasten immediately their respective quotas, fully equipped for active operations.

Circumstances did not permit him to remain at this place long enough to have the delinquencies complained of remedied, and the ranks of his army filled. Colonel Coffee had proceeded with his mounted volunteers to cover Huntsville, and give security to the frontiers, where alarm greatly prevailed. On the night of the 8th, a letter was received from him, dated two days before, advising, that two Indians, belonging to the peace party, had just arrived at the Tennessee River, from Chinnaby's Fort, on the Coosa, with information that the war party had despatched eight hundred or a thousand of their warriors to attack the frontiers of Georgia; and, with the remainder of their forces, were marching against Huntsville, or Fort Hampton. In consequence of this intelligence, exertions were made to hasten a movement. Late on the following night, another express arrived, confirming the former statement, and representing the enemy, in great force, to be rapidly approaching the Tennessee. Orders were now given for preparing the line of march, and by nine o'clock the next day the whole division was in motion. They had not proceeded many miles, when they were met with in telligence that Colonel Gibson, who had been sent out by Coffee to reconnoitre the movements of the enemy, had been killed by their advance. A strong desire had been manifested to be led forward: that

4

desire was now strengthened by the information just received; and it was with difficulty their emotions could be restrained. They accelerated their pace and before eight o'clock at night arrived at Huntsville, a distance of thirty-two miles. Learning nere. that the information was erroneous which had occasioned so hasty a movement, the general encamped his troops; having intended to march them that night to the Tennessee River had it been confirmed. The next day the line of march was resumed. The influence of the late excitement was now visible in the lassitude which followed its removal. Proceeding slowly, they crossed the Tennessee, at Ditto's Landing, and united in the evening with Colonel Coffee's regiment, which had previously occupied a commanding bluff, on the south bank of the river. From this place, in a few days afterwards, Jackson detached Colonel Coffee, with seven hundred men, to scour the Black Warrior, a stream running from the north-east, and emptying into the Tombigbee; on which were supposed to be settled several populous villages of the enemy. He himself remained at this encampment a week, using the utmost pains in training his troops for service, and labouring incessantly to procure the necessary supplies for a campaign, which he had determined to carry directly into the heart of the enemy's country.

With General Cocke, who commanded the division of East Tennessee militia, an arrangement had been made the preceding month, in which he had engaged to furnish large quantities of bread stuff, at Ditto's Landing. The facility of procuring it in that quarter. and the convenient transportation afforded by the river, left no doubt on the mind o

Jackson but that the engagement would be punctually complied with. To provide, however, against the bare possibility of a failure, and to be guarded against all contingencies that might happen, he had addressed his applications to various other sources. He had, on the same subject, written in the most pressing manner to the governor of Georgia, with whose forces it was proposed to act in concert; to Colorel Meigs, agent to the Cherokee nation of Indians, and to General White, who commanded the advance of the East Tennessee troops. Previously to his arrival at Huntsville, he had received assurances from the two latter, that a considerable supply of flour, for the use of his army, had been procured, and was then at Hiwassee, where boats were ready to transport it. From General Cocke, about the same time, a letter was received; stating that a hundred and fifty barrels of flour were then on the way to his encampment; and expressing a belief, that he should be able to procure, and forward on immediately, a thousand barrels more. With pressing importunity, he had addressed himself to the contractors, and they had given him assurances, that, on his crossing the Tennessee, they would be prepared with twenty days' rations for his whole command; but finding, on his arrival at Ditto's, that their preparations were not in such forwardness as he had been led to expect, he was compelled, for a time, to suspend any active and general operations. Calculating, however, with great confidence or exertions, which, he had been promised, should be unremitting, and on the speedy arrival of those supplies descending the river, which had been already unaccountably delayed, he hoped, in a few days, to be placed in a situation to act efficiently. Whilst

he was encouraged by these expectations, and only
waiting their fulfilment, that he might advance,
Shelocta, the son of Chinnaby, a principal chief
among the friendly Creeks, arrived at his camp,
to solicit his speedy movement for the relief of his
father's fort, which was then threatened by a considerable body of the war party, who had advanced
to the neighbourhood of the Ten Islands, on the
Coosa. Influenced by his representations, and
anxious to extend relief, Jackson, on the 18th, gave
orders for taking up the line of march on the fol
lowing day, and notified the contractors of this arrangement, that they might be prepared to issue,
immediately, such supplies as they had on hand;
but, to his great astonishment, he then, for the first
time, was apprized of their entire inability to supply him whilst on his march. Having drawn what
they had in their power to furnish, amounting to
only a few days' rations, they were deposed from
office, and others appointed, on whose industry and
performance, he believed, he might more safely
rely. The scarcity of his provisions, however, at a
moment like the present, when there was every appearance that the enemy might be met, and a blow
stricken to advantage, was not sufficient to wave
his determination. The route he would have to
make, to gain the fort, lay, for a considerable distance, up the river. He determined to proceed;
and, having passed his army and baggage wagons
over several mountains of stupendous size, and
such as were thought almost impassable by foot
passengers, he arrived, on the 22d of October, at
Thompson's Creek, which empties into the Tennessee, twenty-four miles above Ditto's. At this place
he proposed the establishment of a permanent de-

pot, for the reception of supplies, to be sent either up or down the river. Disappointed in the hopes with which he had adventured on his march, he remained here several days, in expectation of the boats that were coming to his relief. Thus harassed at the first onset, by difficulties wholly unexpected, and which, from the numerous and strong assurances received, he could by no means have calculated on; fearing, too, that the same disregard of duty might induce a continuance, he lost no time in opening every avenue to expedient, that the chances of future failure might be diminished. To General Flournoy, who commanded at Mobile, he applied, urging him to procure bread stuff, and have it forwarded up the Alabama by the time he should arrive on that river. The agent of the Choctaws Colonel M'Kee, who was then on the Tombigbee, was addressed in the same style of entreaty. Expresses were despatched to General White, who, with the advance of the East Tennessee division, had arrived at the Look-out Mountain, in the Cherokee nation, urging him, by all means, to hasten on the supplies. The assistance of the governor of Tennessee was also earnestly besought. To facilitate exertion, and to assure success, every thing within his reach was attempted: several persons of wealth and patriotism, in Madison county, were solicited to afford the contractors all the aid in their power; and, to induce them more readily to extend it, their deep interest, immediately at stake, was pointed to, and their deplorable and dangerous situation. should necessity compel him to withdraw his army, and leave them exposed to the mercy of the savages.

4*

Whilst these measures were taking, two run
ners, from Turkey town, an Indian village, des
patched by Path-killer, a chief of the Cherokees,
arrived at the camp. They brought information,
that the enemy, from nine of the hostile towns,
were assembling in great force near the Ten
Islands; and solicited that immediate assistance
should be afforded the friendly Creeks and Cherokees, in their neighbourhood, who were exposed to
such imminent danger. His want of provisions
was not yet remedied; but, distributing the partia.
supply that was on hand, he resolved to proceed, in
expectation that the relief he had so earnestly
looked for, would, in a little while, arrive, and be
forwarded to him.

He instructed General White to form a junction
with him, and to hasten on all the supplies in his
power to command; with about six days' rations
of meat, and less than two of meal, he again put
his army in motion to meet the enemy. Although
there was some hazard in advancing into a country
where relief was not to be expected with such
limited preparation, yet, believing that his contractors, lately installed, would exert themselves to the
utmost to forward supplies, and that, amidst the va-
riety of arrangements made, all could not fail, and
well aware that his delaying longer might be productive of many disadvantages, his determination
was taken to set out immediately in quest of the
enemy. He replied to the Path-killer, by his runners, that he should proceed directly for the Coosa
and solicited him to be diligent in making discove-
ries of the situation, and collected forces of the
savages, and to give him, as early as possible the
result of his inquiries.

" The hostile Creeks," he remarked to him, " will
not attack you until they have had a brush with me,
and that, I think, will put them out of the notion of
fighting for some time." He requested, if he had
or could any how procure, provisions for his army
that he would send them, or advise where they
might be had : " You shall be well paid, and have
my thanks into the barguin. I shall stand most in
need of corn meal, but shall be thankful for any
kind of provisions; and, indeed, for whatever will
support life."

The army had advanced but a short distance
when unexpected embarrassments were again presented. Information was received, by which it
was clearly ascertained, that the present contractors, who had been so certainly relied on, could
not, with all their exertions, procure the necessary
supplies. Major Rose, in the quarter-master's department, who had been sent into Madison county,
o aid them in their endeavours, having satisfied
himself, as well from their own admissions as from
evidence, that their want of funds, and consequen'
want of credit, rendered them a very unsafe dependence, had returned, and disclosed the facts to
the general. He stated, that there were there
persons of fortune and industry, who might be
confided in, and who would be willing to contract
for the army if it were necessary. Jackson lost
no time in embracing this plan, and gave the contract to Mr. Pope, upon whose exertions, he hoped,
every reliance might be safely reposed. To the
other contractors he wrote, informing them of the
change that had been made.

" I am advised," said he, " that you have candidly acknowledged you have it not in your power

to execute the contract in which you have engaged.
Do not think I mean to cast any reflection—very
far from it. I am exceedingly pleased with the
exertions you have made, and feel myself under
many obligations of gratitude for them. From the
admissions you have been candid enough to make,
the scarcity which already begins to appear in
camp, and the difficulties you are likely to encounter, in effecting your engagements, I am apprehensive I should be doing injustice to the army I command, were I to rely for support on your exertions—
great as I know them to be. Whatever concerns
myself, I may manage with any generosity or
indulgence I please ; but in acting for my country,
I have no such discretion."

This arrangement being made, the army continued its march, and, having arrived within a few
miles of the Ten Islands, was met by old Chinnaby,
a leading chief of the Creek nation, and sternly opposed to the war party. He brought with him, and
surrendered up, two of the hostile Creeks, who had
been lately made prisoners by his party. At this
place, it was represented, that they were within
sixteen miles of the enemy, who were collected, to
the number of a thousand, to oppose their passage.
This information was little relied on, and afterwards
proved untrue. Jackson continued his route, and
in a few days reached the islands of the Coosa,
having been detained a day on the way, for the
purpose of obtaining small supplies of corn from
the neighbouring Indians. This acquisition to the
scanty stock on hand, whilst it afforded subsistence
for the present, encouraged his hopes for the future,
as a mean of temporary resort, should his other
resources fail

On the 28th of October, Colonel Dyer, who, on the march to the Ten Islands, had been detached from the main body, with two hundred cavalry, to attack Littafutchee town, on the head of Canoe Creek, which empties into the Coosa from the west, returned, bringing with him twenty-nine prisoners, men, women, and children, having destroyed the village.

The sanguine expectations indulged, on leaving Thompson's Creek, that the advance of the East Tennessee militia would hasten to unite with him, was not yet realized. The express heretofore directed to General White had not returned. Jackson, on the 31st, despatched another, again urging him to effect a speedy junction, and to bring with him all the bread stuff in his power to procure; feelingly suggesting to him, at the same time, the great inconvenience and hazard, to which he had been already exposed, for the want of punctuality in himself and his commanding general. Owing to that cause, and the late failures of his contractors, he represented his army as placed in a very precarious situation, dependent, in a great measure, for support, on the exertions which they might be pleased to make; but assured him, he would still, at every risk, endeavour to effect his purpose; and, at all events, was resolved to hasten to the accomplishment of the object, for which he had set out. Believing the co-operation of the East Tennessee troops essential to this end, they were again instructed to join him without delay; for he could not conceive it to be correct policy, that troops from the same state, pursuing the same object, should constitute separate and distinct armies, and act without concert, and independently of each other. He entertained no doubt but that his order would be promptly obeyed.

The next evening, a detachment, which had been sent out the day before, returned to camp, bringing with them, besides some corn and beeves, severa. negroes and prisoners of the war party.

Learning now that a considerable body of the enemy had posted themselves at Tallushatchee, on the south side of the Coosa, about thirteen miles distant, General Coffee was detached, with nine hundred men, to attack and disperse them. With this force he was enabled, through the direction of an Indian pilot, to ford the Coosa, at the Fish-dams, about four miles above the islands; and, having encamped beyond it, very early the next morning proceeded to the execution of his order. Having arrived within a mile and a half, he formed his detachment into two divisions, and directed them to march so as to encircle the town, by uniting their fronts beyond it. The enemy, hearing of his approach, began to prepare for action, announced by beating of drums, mingled with savage yells and war-whoops. An hour after sun-rise, the action was commenced by Captain Hammon's and Lieutenant Patterson s companies of spies, who had gone within the circle of alignement, for the purpose of drawing the Indians from their buildings. No sooner had these companies given a few scattering shot, than the enemy made a violent charge. Compelled to give way, the advance guards were pursued until they reached the main body of the army, which immediately charged in turn. The Indians retreated, firing and fighting as long as they could stand or sit, without manifesting fear, or soliciting quarter. Their loss was a hundred and eighty-six killed; among whom were a few women and children. Eighty-four women and children were taken prisoners, towards whom the utmost humanity was shown. Of the Americans, five were killed, and forty-one wounded. Two were killed with arrows, which, on this occasion, formed a principal part of the arms of the Indians; each one having a bow and quiver, which he used after the first fire of his gun, until an opportunity occurred for re-loading.

Having buried his dead, and provided for his wounded, General Coffee, the evening of the same day, united with the main army, bringing with him about forty prisoners. Of the residue, a part were too badly wounded to be removed, and were therefore left, with a sufficient number to take care of them.

From the manner in which the enemy fought, the killing and wounding others than their warriors, was not to be avoided. On their retreat to their village, after the commencement of the battle, they resorted to their block houses, and strong log dwellings, whence they kept up resistance, and resolutely maintained the fight. Mingled with their women and children, it was impossible they should not be exposed to the general danger; and thus many were injured, notwithstanding every possible precaution. Many of the women united with their warriors, and contended in the battle with fearless bravory.

CHAPTER III.

General Jackson endeavours to unite with the East Tennessee troops.—Establishment of Fort Strother.—Learns the enemy are imbodied.—Marches to meet them.—Battle of Talladega.— Is compelled to return to his encampment, for want of supplies.— Anecdote.—Discontents of his army.—Militia and volunteers mutiny.—Address to the officers.—Is compelled to abandon Fort Strother.—Hillabee clans sue for peace.—Letter from the Rev. Mr. Blackburn.—Answer.—The volunteers claim to be discharged.—Mutiny.—Address to them.—General Cocke arrives with part of his division.—General Coffee's brigade petitions for a discharge.—General Jackson's answer.—They abandon the service, and go home.

MEASURES were now taken to establish a pe manent depot on the north bank of the river, the Ten Islands, to be protected by strong picketting and block houses. It was desirable to unite, as soon as possible, with the troops from the East of Tennessee; to effect this, Jackson, on the 4th, despatched an express to General White, urging him to unite with him as soon as possible, and again entreating him on the subject of provisions ; to bring with him such as he had on hand, or could procure ; and, if possible, to form some certain arrangement that might ensure a supply in future.

Anxious to proceed, and have his army active, he again, on the morning of the 7th, renewed his application to General White, who still remained at Turkey town.

The army was busily engaged in fortifying the site fixed on for a depot, to which the name of Fort Strother had been given. On the evening of the 7th, a runner arrived from Talladega, a fort of

the friendly Indians, thirty miles below, with in
formation, that the enemy had that morning en
camped before it in great numbers, and would
certainly destroy it, unless immediate assistance
could be afforded. Jackson, confiding in the statement, determined to lose no time in extending the
relief which was solicited. Understanding that
General White was on his way to join him, he
despatched a messenger, directing him to reach
his encampment in the course of the ensuing night,
and to protect it in his absence. He now gave
orders for taking up the line of march, with twelve
hundred infantry, and eight hundred cavalry and
mounted gun-men; leaving behind the sick, the
wounded, and all his baggage, with a force which
was deemed sufficient for their protection, until the
reinforcement from Turkey town should arrive.

The friendly Indians, who had taken refuge in
this besieged fort, had involved themselves in their
present perilous situation, from a disposition to
preserve their amicable relations with the United
States. To suffer them to fall a sacrifice, from any
tardiness of movement, would have been unpar
donable; and, unless relief were immediately ex
tended, it might arrive too late. Acting under
these impressions, the general concluded to move
instantly forward to their assistance. By twelve
o'clock at night, every thing was in readiness; and
in an hour afterwards, the army commenced crossing the river, about a mile above the camp; each
of the mounted men carrying one of the infantry
behind him. The river, at this place, was six hundred yards wide, and, it being necessary to send
back the horses for the remainder of the infantry
several hours were consumed before a passage of

all the troops could be effected. Nevertheless, though greatly fatigued, and deprived of sleep, they continued the march with animation, and by evening had arrived within six miles of the enemy. In this march, Jackson used the utmost precaution to prevent surprise; marching his army, as was his constant custom, in three columns, so that, by a speedy manœuvre, they might be thrown into such a situation as to be capable of resisting an attack from any quarter. Having judiciously encamped his men on an eligible piece of ground, he sent forward two of the friendly Indians, and a white man, who had, for many years, been detained a captive in the nation, and was now acting as interpreter, to reconnoitre the position of the enemy. About eleven o'clock at night, they returned with information that the savages were posted within a quarter of a mile of the fort, and appeared to be in great force; but that they had not been able to approach near enough to ascertain either their numbers or precise situation. Within an hour after this, a runner arrived from Turkey town, with a letter from General White, stating, that, after having taken up the line of march, to unite at Fort Strother, he had received orders from General Cocke to change his course, and proceed to the mouth of Chatauga Creek. It was most distressing intelligence; the sick and wounded had been left with no other calculation for their safety, than that this detachment of the army, agreeably to his request, would, by advancing upon Fort Strother, serve the double purpose of protecting his rear, and enable him to advance still further into the enemy's country. The information proved that all those salutary anticipations were at an end, and

that evils of the worst kind might be the consequence. Intelligence so disagreeable filled the
mind of Jackson with apprehension. Orders were
accordingly given to the adjutant-general to prepare the line, and by four o'clock in the morning,
the army was again in motion. The infantry proceeded in three columns; the cavalry in the same
order, in the rear, with flankers on each wing.
The advance, consisting of a company of artillerists, with muskets, two companies of riflemen,
and one of spies, marched about four hundred yards
in front, under the command of Colonel Carroll,
inspector-general, with orders, after commencing
the action, to fall back on the centre, so as to
draw the enemy after them. At seven o'clock.
having arrived within a mile of the position they
occupied, the columns were displayed in order of
battle. Two hundred and fifty of the cavalry,
under Lieutenant-Colonel Dyer, were placed in
the rear of the centre, as a corps de reserve.
The remainder of the mounted troops were directed to advance on the right and left, and, after
encircling the enemy, by uniting the fronts of their
columns, and keeping their rear rested on the infantry, to face and press towards the centre, so as
to leave them no possibility of escape. The remaining part of the army was ordered to move up
by heads of companies; General Hall's brigade
occupying the right, and General Roberts's the
left.

About eight o'clock, the advance having arrived within eighty yards of the enemy, who were
concealed in a thick shrubbery, received a heavy
fire, which they instantly returned with much spirit

Falling in with the enemy, agreeably to their in
structions, they retired towards the centre, but not
before they had dislodged them from their position.
The Indians, now screaming and yelling hideously,
rushed forward in the direction of General Roberts's
brigade, a few companies of which, alarmed by
their numbers and yells, gave way at the first
fire. Jackson, to fill the chasm which was thus
created, directed the regiment commanded by
Colonel Bradley to be moved up, which, from some
unaccountable cause, had failed to advance in a
line with the others, and now occupied a position
in rear of the centre: Bradley, however, to whom
this order was given by one of the staff, omitted to
execute it in time, alleging, he was determined to
remain on the eminence which he then possessed,
until he should be approached, and attacked by the
enemy. Owing to this failure in the volunteer
regiment, it became necessary to dismount the reserve, which, with great firmness, met the approach
of the enemy, who were rapidly moving in this
direction. The retreating militia, somewhat mor
tified at seeing their places so promptly supplied,
rallied, and, recovering their former position in the
line, aided in checking the advance of the savages. The action now became general along the
line, and in fifteen minutes the Indians were seen
fleeing in every direction. On the left, they were
met and repulsed by the mounted riflemen; but on
the right, owing to the halt of Bradley's regiment,
which was intended to occupy the extreme right,—
and to the circumstance of Colonel Allcorn, who
commanded one of the wings of the cavalry, hav
ing taken too large a circuit,—a considerable space

was left between the infantry and the cavalry, through which numbers escaped.

Jackson, in his report of this action, bestows ..gh commendation on the officers and soldiers.

In this battle the force of the enemy was one thousand and eighty, of whom two hundred and ninety-nine were left dead on the ground; and it is believed that many were killed in the flight, who were not found when the estimate was made Probably few escaped unhurt. Their loss on this occasion, as stated since by themselves, was not less than six hundred; that of the Americans was fifteen killed, and eighty wounded, several of whom afterwards died. Jackson, after collecting his dead and wounded, advanced his army beyond the fort, and encamped for the night. The Indians, who had been for several days shut up by the besiegers, thus fortunately liberated from the most dreadful apprehensions, and severest privations, having for some time been entirely without water, received the army with all the demonstrations of gratitude that savages could give. Their manifestations of joy for their deliverance presented an interesting and affecting spectacle. Their fears had been already greatly excited, for it was the very day when they were to have been assaulted, and when every soul within the fort must have perished. All the provisions they could spare from their scanty stock, they sold to the general who, purchasing with his own money, distributed them amongst the soldiers, who were almost destitute.

The condition of his posts in the rear, and the want of provisions, (having left his encampment at

5*

Fort Strother with little more than one day's re
tions,) compelled him to return; thus giving the
enemy time to recover.

The cause which prevented General White from
arriving at the Ten Islands at a moment when it
was so important, when it was so confidently expected, was as yet unknown. This mystery, hitherto inexplicable, was some time after explained,
by a view of the order of General Cocke, undei
which White, being a brigadier in his division,
chose to act, rather than under Jackson's. General Cocke stated to him, he had understood Jackson
had crossed the Coosa, and had an engagement
with the Indians. "I have formed a council of
officers here, and proposed these questions:—Shall
we follow him, or cross the river, and proceed to
the Creek settlements on the Tallapoosa? Both
were decided unanimously,—that he should not be
followed, but that we should proceed in the way
proposed!" He remarked, that the decision had
met his entire approbation; and directed White
forthwith to unite with him at his encampment,
where he should wait, fortifying it strongly for a
depot, until he should arrive. "If," said he, "we
follow General Jackson and his army, we must
suffer for supplies; nor can we expect to gain a
victory Let us then take a direction in which we
can share some of the dangers and glories of the
field. You will employ pilots, and advise me which
side of the river you will move up." In this, as in
every other measure, it seemed to be the studied
aim of Cocke to thwart the views and arrest the
successes of Jackson; and perhaps jealousy, in no
inconsiderable degree, was the moving spring to

his conduct. Both were majoi-generals, from the state of Tennessee, sent on the same important errand, to check an insolent foe.

Having buried his dead, and provided litters for the wounded, Jackson reluctantly commenced his return march on the morning succeeding the battle. He confidently hoped, from the previous assurances of the contractors, that, by the time of his return to Fort Strother, sufficient supplies would have arrived there; but, to his inexpressible uneasiness, he found that not a particle had been forwarded since his departure, and that what had been left was already consumed. Even his private stores, brought on at his own expense, and upon which he and his staff had hitherto wholly subsisted, had been, in his absence, distributed amongst the sick by the hospital surgeon, who had been previously instructed to do so, in the event their wants should require it. A few dozen biscuit, which remained on his return, were given to hungry applicants, without being tasted by himself or family, who were probably not less hungry than those who were thus relieved. A scanty supply of indifferent beef, taken from the enemy, or purchased of the Cherokees, was now the only support afforded. Thus left destitute, Jackson, with the utmost cheerfulness of temper, repaired to the bullock pen, and, of the offal there thrown away, provided for himself and staff, what he was pleased to call, a very comfortable repast. Tripes, however, hastily provided in a camp, without bread or seasoning, can only be palatable to an appetite very highly whetted; yet this constituted, for several days, the only diet at head-quarters; during which time. the general seemed entirely satisfied

with his fare. Neither this, nor the liberal dona
tions by which he disfurnished himself, to relieve
the suffering soldier, deserves to be ascribed to
ostentation or design: the one flowed from benevolence, the other from necessity, and a desire to
place before his men an example of patience and
suffering, which he felt might be necessary.

In this campaign, a soldier one morning, with a
wo-begone countenance, approached the general,
stating that he was nearly starved, that he had
nothing to eat, and could not imagine what he
should do. He was the more encouraged to complain, from perceiving that the general, who had
seated himself at the root of a tree, waiting the
coming up of the rear of the army, was busily engaged in eating something. The poor fellow was
impressed with the belief, from what he saw, that
want only attached to the soldiers, and that the
officers, particularly the general, were liberally
supplied. He accordingly approached him with
great confidence of being relieved. Jackson told
him, that it had always been a rule with him never
to turn away a hungry man when it was in his
power to relieve him. I will most cheerfully, said
he, divide with you what I have ; and, putting his
hand to his pocket, drew forth a few acorns, from
which he had been feasting, adding, it was the best
and only fare he had. The soldier seemed much
surprised, and forthwith circulated amongst his
comrades, that their general was actually subsisting
upon acorns, and that they ought no more to complain. From this circumstance was derived the
story heretofore published to the world, that Jackson, about the period of his greatest suffering, and
with a view to inspirit them, had invited his officers

o dine with him, and presented, for their repast, water, and a tray of acorns.

But discontents, and a desire to return home, arose, and presently spread through the camp; and these were still further augmented, by the arts of a few designing officers, who, believing that the campaign would now break up, hoped to make themselves popular on the return, by taking part in the complaints of the soldiery. It is a singular fact, that those officers who pretended, on this occasion, to feel most sensibly for the wants of the army, had never themselves been without provisions.

During this period of scarcity and discontent, small quantities of supplies were occasionally forwarded by the contractors, but not a sufficiency for present want, and still less to remove the apprehensions that were entertained for the future. At length revolt began to show itself openly. The officers and soldiers of the militia, collecting in their tents, and talking over their grievances, determined to yield up their patriotism, and to abandon the camp. To this measure there were good evidences for believing that several of the officers of the old volunteer corps exerted themselves clandestinely, and with great industry, to instigate them; looking upon themselves somewhat in the light of veterans, from the discipline they had acquired, they were unwilling to be seen foremost in setting an example of mutiny, and wished to make the defection of others a pretext for their own.

Jackson, apprized of their determination to abandon him, resolved to oppose it, and at all hazard. In the morning, when they were to carry their intentions into execution, he drew up the volunteers in front of them, with positive commands to prevent their progress, and compel them to return to their former position in the camp. The militia, seeing this, and fearing the consequences of persisting in their purpose, at once abandoned it, and returned to their quarters without further murmuring, extolling, in the highest terms, the unalterable firmness of the general.

The next day, however, presented a singulaɪ scene. The volunteers, who the day before had been the instruments for compelling the militia to return to their duty, seeing the destruction of those hopes on which they had lately built, in turn began, themselves, to mutiny. Their opposition to the departure of the militia was but a mere pretence, to escape suspicion, for they silently wished them success. They now determined to move off in a body, believing, from the known disaffection in the camp, that the general could find no means to prevent it. What was their surprise, when, on attempting to effectuate their resolves, they found the same men, whom they had so lately opposed, occupying the very position which they had done the day previous, for a similar purpose, and manifesting a fixed determination to obey the orders of their general! All they ventured to do was, to take the example through, and, like them, move back in peace and quietness to their quarters. This was a curious change of circumstances, when we consider in how short a time it happened; but the conduct of the militia, on this occasion, must be ascr'bed to the management of the general, and to the gratification they felt, in being able to de feat the views of those who had so lately thwarted

their own. To this may be also added, the consciousness all must have entertained, that the privations of which they complained, were far less
grievous than they had represented them ; by no
means sufficient to justify revolt, and not greater
than patriots might be expected to bear without a
murmur, when objects of such high consideration
were before them. But, anxious to return to their
families, wearied of their sufferings, they seized
with eagerness every pretext for exoneration, and
listened with too much docility to the representations of those, who were influenced by less honourable feelings. The militia continued to show
a much more patriotic disposition than the volunteers ; who, having adopted a course which they
discovered must finally involve them in dishonour
if it should fail, were exceedingly anxious for its
success. On this subject, the pretensions of the
cavalry were certainly much better established ; as
they were entirely without forage, and without the
prospect of speedily obtaining any. They pe-
titioned, therefore, to be permitted to return into the
settled parts of the country, pledging themselves,
by their platoon and field-officers, that, if sufficient
time were allowed to recruit the exhausted state of
their horses, and to procure their winter clothing,
they would return to the performance of their duty
whenever called on. The general, unable, from
many causes, to prosecute the campaign, and con
fiding in the assurance given, granted the prayer
of their petition, and they immediately set out on
their return.

About this time, General Jackson's prospect of
being able to maintain the conquests he had made
began to be cheered by letters just received from

the contractors and principal wagon-master, stating
that sufficient supplies for the army were then on
the road, and would shortly arrive: but discontents
to an alarming degree still prevailed in his camp.
To allay them, if possible, he hastened to lay before the division the information and letters he had
received, and, at the same time, invited the field
and platoon-officers to his quarters, to consult on
the measures proper to be pursued. He addressed
them in an animated speech, in which he extolled
their patriotism and achievements; lamented the
privations to which they had been exposed, and
endeavoured to reanimate them by the prospect of
speedy relief, which he expected with confidence
on the following day. He spoke of the immense
importance of the conquests they had already made,
and of the dreadful consequences that must result,
should they be now abandoned. "What," continued he, "is the present situation of our camp?
A number of our fellow soldiers are wounded, and
unable to help themselves. Shall it be said that
we are so lost to humanity as to leave them in
this condition? Can any one, under these circumstances, and under these prospects, consent to an
abandonment of the camp? of all that we have
acquired in the midst of so many difficulties, priva
tions, and dangers? of what it will cost us so much
to regain? of what we never can regain,—our
brave wounded companions, who will be murdered
by our unthinking, unfeeling inhumanity? Surely
there can be none such! No, we will take with
us, when we go, our wounded and sick. They
must not—shall not perish by our cold-blooded
indifference. But why should you despond? I
do not, and yet your wants are not greater than

mine. To be sure we do not live sumptuously; but no one has died of hunger, or is likely to die; and then, how animating are our prospects! Large supplies are at Deposit, and already are officers despatched to hasten them on. Wagons are on the way; a large number of beeves are in the neighbourhood; and detachments are out to bring them in.—All these resources surely cannot fail. I have no wish to starve you—none to deceive you. Stay contentedly; and, if supplies do not arrive in two days, we will all march back together, and throw the blame of our failure where it should properly lie; until then, we certainly have the means of subsisting; and if we are compelled to bear privations, let us remember that they are borne for our country, and are not greater than many, perhaps most armies, have been compelled to endure. I have called you together, to tell you my feelings and my wishes; this evening think on them seriously; and let me know yours in the morning."

Having retired to their tents, the officers of the volunteer brigade came to the conclusion, that " nothing short of marching the army immediately back to the settlements could prevent those difficulties and that disgrace, which must attend a forcible desertion of the camp by his soldiers." The officers of the militia determined differently, and reported a willingness to maintain the post a few days longer. "If provisions arrive, let us proceed with the campaign; if not, let us be marched back to where it can be procured." The general, who greatly preferred the latter opinion, to allay excitement, was disposed to gratify those who appeared unwilling to submit to further hardships· and with

6

this view ordered General Hall to march his orig
ade to Fort Deposit, and, after satisfying their
wants, to return and act as an escort to the provisions.   The second regiment, however, unwilling
to be outdone by the militia, consented to remain,
and the first proceeded alone.   On this occasion he
could not forbear to remark, that men for whom
he had ever cherished so warm an affection, and
for whom he would at all times have made any
sacrifice, desiring to abandon him at a moment
when their presence was so particularly necessary,
filled him with emotions which the strongest lan
guage was too feeble to express.   " I was prepared," continued the general, "to endure every evil
but disgrace; and this, as I never can submit to
myself, I can give no encouragement to in others.'

Two days had elapsed since the departure of the
volunteers, and supplies had not arrived.   The
militia, with great earnestness, now demanded a
performance of the pledge that had been given—
that they should be marched back to the settlements.   Jackson, on giving them an assurance that
they should return, if relief did not reach them
in two days, had indulged a confidence that it
would certainly arrive by that time; and now
from the information he had received, felt more
than ever certain that it could not be far distant.
Having, however, pledged himself, he could use no
arguments or entreaties to detain them any longer,
and immediately took measures for complying with
their wishes, and the promise he had made them.
This was, to him, a moment of the deepest dejection.   He foresaw how difficult it would be ever to
accomplish the object upon which his heart was so
devoutly fixed, should he lose the men who were

now with him; or even to regain the conquests he had made, if his present posts should fall into the hands of the enemy. While thus pondering on the gloomy prospect, he lifted up his hands, and exclaimed, with a look and manner which showed how much he felt, " If only two men will remain with me, I will never abandon this post." Captain Gordon, of the spies, facetiously replied, " you have one, general; let us look if we can't find another;" and immediately, with a zeal suited to the occasion, undertook, with some of the general staff, to raise volunteers; and in a little while succeeded in procuring one hundred and nine, who declared a determination to remain and protect the post. The general, greatly rejoiced that he would not be com pelled to an entire abandonment of his position, now set out towards Deposit, with the remainder of the army, who were given distinctly to understand, that on meeting supplies they were to return and prosecute the campaign. This was an event, which, as it had been expected and foretold, soon took place; they had not proceeded more than ten or twelve miles, when they met a hundred and fifty beeves; but a sight which gave to Jackson so much satisfaction, was to them the most unwelcome. Their faces being now turned towards home, no spectacle could be more hateful than one which was to change their destination. They were halted, and, having satisfied their appetites, the troops, with the exception of such as were necessary to proceed with the sick and wounded, were ordered to return to the encampment; he himself intending to see the contractors, and establish more effectual arrangements for the future. So great was their aversion to returning, that they preferred

a violation of their duty and their pledged honour
Low murmurings ran along the lines, and presently
broke out into open mutiny. In spite of the order
they had received, they began to revolt, and one
company was already moving off, in a direction
towards home. They had proceeded some distance,
before information of their departure was had by
Jackson. Irritated at their conduct, in attempting
to violate the promise they had given, the general
pursued, until he came near a part of his staff, and
a few soldiers, who, with General Coffee, had
halted about a quarter of a mile ahead. He or
dered them to form immediately across the road,
and to fire on the mutineers if they attempted to
proceed. Snatching up their arms, these faithful
adherents presented a front which threw the deserters into affright, and caused them to retreat
 recipitately to the main body. Here, it was hoped,
.he matter would end, and that no further opposition would be made to returning. This expectation was not realized; a mutinous temper began
presently to display itself throughout the whole
brigade. Jackson, having left his aid-de-camp,
Major Reid, engaged in making up some despatches, had gone out alone amongst his troops, who
were at some distance; on his arrival, he found a
much more extensive mutiny than that which had
just been quelled. Almost the whole brigade had
put itself into an attitude for moving forcibly off.
A crisis had arrived; and, feeling its importance,
ne determined to take no middle ground, but to
triumph or perish. He was still without the use of
his left arm; but, seizing a musket, and resting it
on the neck of his horse, he threw himself in front
of the column, and threatened to shoot the first

man who should attempt to advance. In this situation he was found by Major Reid and General
Coffee, who, fearing, from the length of his absence, that some disturbance had arisen, hastened
where he was, and, placing themselves by his side,
awaited the result in anxious expectation. For
many minutes the column preserved a sullen, yet
hesitating attitude, fearing to proceed in their purpose, and disliking to abandon it. In the mean time,
those who remained faithful to their duty, amounting to about two companies, were collected and
formed at a short distance in advance of the troops,
and in rear of the general, with positive directions
to imitate his example in firing, if they attempted
to proceed. At length, finding no one bold enough
to advance, and overtaken by those fears which in
the hour of peril always beset persons engaged in
what they know to be a bad cause, they abandoned
their purpose, and, turning quietly round, agreed to
return to their posts. It is very certain, that, but
for the firmness of the general, at this critical moment, the campaign would have been broken up,
and most probably not commenced again.

Shortly after the battle of Talladega, the Hillabee tribes applied to General Jackson for peace,
declaring their willingness to receive it on such
terms as he might be pleased to dictate. His decision had been already returned stating to them
that his government had taken up arms, to bring to
a proper sense of duty a people to whom she had
ever shown the utmost kindness, and who, never
theless, had committed against her citizens the
most unprovoked depredations; and that she would
lay them down only when certain that its object

6*

was attained. * " Upon those," continued he, " who
are disposed to become friendly, I neither wish nor
intend to make war; but they must afford evidences of the sincerity of their professions; the
prisoners and property they have taken from us,
and the friendly Creeks, must be restored; the instigators of the war, and the murderers of our
citizens, must be surrendered; the latter must and
will be made to feel the force of our resentment
Long shall they remember Fort Mimms in bitter
ness and tears."

Having stated to General Cocke, whose division
was acting in this section of the nation, the propositions that had been made by the Hillabee clans,
with the answer he had returned, he proceeded to
Deposit and Ditto's Landing, where the most effectual means in his power were taken with the contrac
tors, for obtaining regular supplies in future. They
were required to furnish, immediately, thirty days'
rations at Fort Strother, forty at Talladega, and as
many at the junction of the Coosa and Tallapoosa;
two hundred pack horses and forty wagons were
put in requisition to facilitate their transportation

---

* This communication did not arrive in time,—General White,
who had been detached for that purpose, having, the morning or
which it was written, destroyed their town, killed sixty, and
made two hundred and fifty-six prisoners. The event was un
fortunate; and in it may perhaps be found the reason why
these savages, in their after battles, fought with the desperation
they did, obstinately refusing to ask for quarter. They believed
themselves attacked by Jackson's army; they knew they had
asked peace upon his own terms. When, therefore, under these
circumstances, they saw themselves thus assailed, they no longer
considered that any pacific disposition they might manifest would
afford them protection from danger; and looked upon it as a
war of extermination. In their battles, afterwards, there is no
instance of their asking for quarter, or even manifesting a dis
position to receive it.

Understanding, now, that the whole detachment from Tennessee had, by the president, been re ceived into the service of the United States, he persuaded himself that the difficulties he had heretofore encountered would not recur.

The volunteers at Deposit began to manifest the same unwillingness to return to their duty that the militia had done, and were about to break out into the same spirit of mutiny and revolt ; but were restrained by an animated address by the general.

He now set out on his return to Fort Strother, and was delighted to find, by the progress of the works, the industry that had been used in his absence. But the satisfaction he felt was of short continuance ; although he had succeeded in stilling the tumult of the volunteers, and in prevailing on them to return to their posts, it was soon discovered he had not eradicated their deep-rooted aversion to a further prosecution of the war. The volunteers who had so lately clamoured about bread, when they were no longer hungry, began to clamour. with equal earnestness, about their term of service. Having lately made an effort to forsake the drudgery of the field, and failed, they were disposed to avail themselves of any pretexts, seemingly plausible, to obtain success. They insisted that the period, for which they had undertaken to act, would end on the 10th of December, that being the termination of a year from the day they had first entered into service , and, although they had been a greater part of the time unemployed, that recess was nevertheless to be taken into the computation. Jackson replied, that the law of congress, under which they had been accepted, requiring one year's service out of two, could contemplate nothing less than an actual service of three hundred and sixty-five days; and, until that were performed, he could not, unless specially authorized, undertake to discharge them. Ordering General Roberts to return, and fill up the deficiencies in his brigade, he now despatched Colonel Carroll, and Major Searcy, one of his aids-de-camp, into Tennessee, to raise volunteers for six months, or during the campaign, writing to many respectable characters, he exhorted them to contribute all their assistance to the accomplishment of this object. To a letter, just received from the Reverend Gideon Blackburn, assuring him that volunteers from Tennessee would eagerly hasten to his relief, if they knew their services were wanted, he replied, "Reverend Sir,—Your letter has been just received: I thank you for it; I thank you most sincerely. It arrived at a moment when my spirits needed such a support.

"I left Tennessee with an army, brave, I believe, as any general ever commanded. I have seen them in battle, and my opinion of their bravery is not changed. But their fortitude—on this too I relied—has been too severely tested. Perhaps I was wrong, in believing that nothing but death could conquer the spirits of brave men. I am sure I was; for my men, I know, are brave; yet privations have rendered them discontented:—that is enough. The expedition must, nevertheless, be prosecuted to a successful termination. New volunteers must be raised, to conclude what has been so auspiciously begun by the old ones. Gladly would I save these men from themselves, and en sure them a harvest which they have sown; but if they will abandon it to others, it must be so.

"You are good enough to say, if I need your assistance, it will be cheerfully afforded: I do need it greatly. The influence you possess over the minds of men is great and well-founded, and can never be better applied than in summoning volunteers to the defence of their country, their liberty, and their religion. While we fight the savage, who makes war only because he delights in blood, and who has gotten his booty, when he has scalped his victim, we are, through him, contending against an enemy of more inveterate character, and deeper design—who would demolish a fabric cemented by the blood of our fathers, and endeared to us by all the happiness we enjoy. So far as my exertions can contribute, the purposes, both of the savage and his instigator, shall be defeated; and, so far as yours can, I hope—I know, they will be employed. I have said enough.—I want men, and want them immediately."

He wrote to General Cocke, urging him to unite with him immediately, at the Ten Islands, with fifteen hundred men. He assured him that the mounted men, who had returned to the settlements for subsistence, and to recruit their horses, would arrive by the 12th of the month. He wished to commence his operations directly, "knowing they would be prepared for it, and well knowing they would require it." "I am astonished," he continued, "to hear that your supplies continue deficient In the name of God, what are the contractors doing? and about what are they engaged? Every letter I receive from Governor Blount assures me I am to receive plentiful supplies from them, and seems to

take for granted, notwithstanding all I have said to
the contrary, that they have been hitherto regularly
furnished. Considering the generous loan the
state has made for this purpose, and the facility of
procuring bread stuffs in East Tennessee, and of
transporting them by water to Fort Deposit, it is to
me wholly unaccountable that not a pound has ever
arrived at that place. This evil must continue no
longer—it must be remedied. I expect, therefore,
and through you must require, that in twenty days
they furnish at Deposit every necessary supply."*

Whilst these measures were taking, the volunteers, through several of their officers, were pressing on the consideration of the general, the expiration of their term of service, and claiming to
be discharged on the 10th of the month. From
the colonel, who commanded the second regiment.
he received a letter, dated the 4th, in which was
attempted to be detailed their whole ground of
complaint. He began by stating, that, painful as it
was, he, nevertheless, felt himself bound to disclose an important truth; that, on the 10th, the
service would be deprived of the regiment he commanded. He seemed to deplore, with great sensibility, the scene that would be exhibited on that
day, should opposition be made to their departure;
and still more sensibly, the consequences that would
result from a disorderly abandonment of the camp.
He stated they had all considered themselves finally
discharged on the 20th of April, and never knew
to the contrary, until they saw his order of the 24th
of September, requiring them to rendezvous at

____

* Independent of an advantageous contract made with the
government, the state of Tennessee had extended to this contractor a liberal loan, that immediate supplies might be forward
ed.

Fayetteville, on the 4th of October; for the first time, they then learned that they owed further services, their discharge to the contrary notwithstanding. "Thus situated, there was considerable opposition to the order; on which the officers generally, as I am advised, and I know myself in particular, gave it as an unequivocal opinion, that their term of service would terminate on the 10th of December.

"They therefore look to their general, who holds their confidence, for an honourable discharge on that day; and that, in every respect, he will see that justice be done them."

Although this communication announced the determination of only a part of the volunteer brigade, he had already abundant evidence that the defection was but too general.

"I know not," he observed, "what scenes will be exhibited on the 10th instant, nor what consequences are to flow from them here or elsewhere; but, as I shall have the consciousness that they are not imputable to any misconduct of mine, I trust I shall have the firmness not to shrink from a discharge of my duty.

"It will be well, however, for those who intend to become actors in those scenes, and who are about to hazard so much on the correctness of their opinions, to examine beforehand, with great caution and deliberation, the grounds on which their pretensions rest. Are they founded on any false assurances of mine, or upon any deception that has been practised towards them? Was not the act of congress, under which they are engaged, directed, by my general order, to be read and expounded to them before they enrolled themselves

That order will testify, and so will the recollection of every general officer of my division. It is not pretended that those who now claim to be discharged were not legally and fairly enrolled under the act of congress of the 6th of February, 1812. Have they performed the service required of them by that act, and which they then solemnly undertook to perform? That required one year's service out of two, to be computed from the day of rendezvous, unless they should be sooner discharged. Has one year's service been performed? This cannot be seriously pretended. Have they then been discharged? It is said they have, and by me. To account for so extraordinary a belief, it may be necessary to take a review of past circumstances."

*   *   *   *   *   *   *

To the platoon officers, who addressed him on the same subject, he replied with spirited feeling · but discontent was too deeply fastened, and, by designing men, had been too artfully fomented, to be removed by any thing like argument or entreaty At length, on the evening of the 9th, General Hall hastened to the tent of Jackson, with information that his whole brigade was in a state of mutiny, and making preparations to move forcibly off This was a measure which every consideration of policy, duty, and honour, required Jackson to oppose; and to this purpose he instantly applied all the means he possessed. He immediately issued the following general order:

"The commanding general being informed that an actual mutiny exists in his camp, all officers and soldiers are commanded to put it down.

"The officers and soldiers of the first brigade will, without delay, parade on the west side of the fort, and await further orders." The artillery company, with two small field-pieces, being posted in the front and rear, and the militia, under the command of Colonel Wynne, on the eminences in advance, were ordered to prevent any forcible departure of the volunteers.

The general rode along the line, which had been previously formed agreeably to his orders, and addressed them, by companies, in a strain of impassioned eloquence. He feelingly expatiated on their former good conduct, and the esteem and applause it had secured them; and pointed to the disgrace which they must heap upon themselves, their families, and country, by persisting, even if they could succeed, in their present mutiny. He told them, however, they should not succeed but by passing over his body; that even in opposing their mutinous spirit, he should perish honourably—by perishing at his post, and in the discharge of his duty. "Reenforcements," he continued, " are preparing to hasten to my assistance: it cannot be long before they will arrive. I am, too, in daily expectation of receiving information whether you may be discharged or not—until then, you must not, and shall not retire. I have done with entreaty,—it has been used long enough.—I will attempt it no more. You must now determine whether you will go or peaceably remain: if you still persist in your determination to move forcibly off, the point between us shall soon be decided." At first they hesitated;—he demanded an explicit and positive answer. They still hesitated, and he commanded the artillerists to prepare the match, he himself remaining in front of the volunteers, and within the line of fire, which he intended soon
7

to order. Alarmed at his apparent determination, and dreading the consequences involved in such a contest; "Let us return," was presently lisped along the line, and soon after determined upon. The officers now came forward, and pledged themselves for their men, who either nodded assent, or openly expressed a willingness to retire to their quarters, and remain without further tumult, until information were had, or the expected aid should arrive. Thus passed away a moment of the greatest peril, and pregnant with important consequences.

Although the immediate execution of their purpose was thus for the present prevented, it was presently ascertained not to be wholly abandoned, and that nothing could be expected from their future fidelity and services. Jackson, therefore, determined to rid himself, as soon as possible, of men whose presence answered no other end than to keep alive discontents in his camp. He accordingly prepared an order to General Hall, to march his brigade to Nashville, and to dispose of them as he should be directed by the governor of Tennessee. Previous to promulgating this, he resolved to make one further effort to retain them, and to make a last appeal to their honour and patriotism. For this purpose, having assembled them before the fort, on the 13th, he directed his aid-de-camp to read an address.

Warm and feeling as was the appeal, it failed of the desired effect. Captain Williamson alone agreed to remain. Finding that their determination to abandon the service could not be changed, and that every principle of patriotism was forgotten, the general communicated his order to General

Hall, and directed him to march his brigade to
Nashville, and await such instructions as he might
receive from the president, or the governor of Tennessee.

General Cocke, on the 12th, had arrived at Fort
Strother with fifteen hundred men; but it was
found from his report, that no part of his troops
had been brought into the field under the requisition
of the president of the United States; and that
the term of service of the greater portion of them
would expire in a few days, and of the whole
in a few weeks. In consequence of this, he
was ordered into his district, to comply with that
requisition, and to carry back with him, and to discharge near their homes, those of his troops, the
period of whose service was within a short time of
being ended. Colonel Lilliard's regiment, which
consisted of about eight hundred, and whose term
of service would not expire in less than four weeks,
was retained, to assist in defending the present
post, and in keeping open the communication with
Deposit, until the expected reenforcements should
arrive from Tennessee.

Meantime the cavalry and mounted riflemen,
who, under an express stipulation to return and
complete the campaign, had been permitted to retire into the settlements, had, at the time appointed
re-assembled in the neighbourhood of Huntsville
But, catching the infection of discontent from the
infantry, on their return march, they began now
to clamour with equal earnestness for a discharge.
The cavalry insisted that they were as well entitled
to it as the infantry; and the riflemen, that they
could not be held in service after the 24th, that
being three months from the time they had been

mustered ; and that, as that day was so near at hand, it was wholly useless to advance any farther.

General Coffee, who was confined at Huntsville by severe indisposition, employed all the means which his debilitated strength would allow, to remove the dangerous impressions they had so readily imbibed, and to reclaim them to a sense of honour and of duty ; but all his efforts proved unavailing. He immediately ordered his brigade to head-quarters : they had proceeded as far as Ditto's Ferry when the greater part of them, refusing to cross the river, returned in a tumultuous manner, committing on the route innumerable irregularities which there was no force sufficient to restrain. Not more than seven hundred of the brigade could be gotten over ; who, having marched to Deposit, were directed to be halted, until further orders could be obtained from General Jackson. At this place they committed the wildest extravagances : profusely wasting the' public grain, which, with much difficulty and labour, had been collected for the purpose of the campaign ; and indulging in every species of excess. Whilst thus rioting, they continued to clamour vociferously for their discharge. General Coffee, finding his utmost efforts ineffectual to restrain or to quiet them, wrote to Jackson, acquainting him with their conduct and demands, and enclosing a petition that had been addressed to him by the rifle regiment. In his letter he says, "I am of opinion the sooner they can be gotten clear of the better; they are consuming the forage that will be necessary for others, and I am satisfied they will do no more good. I have told them their petition would be submitted to you, who would decide upon it in the shortest

possible time." This was truly disagreeable news
to the general. On the brigade of Coffee he had
placed great reliance, and, from the pledges it had
given him, entertained no fears but that it would
return and act with him, as soon as he should be
ready to proceed.

The signers of that address, observes the general, commence by saying, "that jealousy is prevailing in our camp, with respect to the understanding between themselves and the government relative to the service required of them; and, believing
t to be its policy to act fairly, are of opinion that
a full explanation of their case will have a good
effect in promoting the cause in which they are
engaged."

There was but a single course left; to point
them to the pledge they had given, and appeal directly to their honour, believing that if this were
unsuccessful, there was "nothing by which he
could hope to hold them."

Jackson had just received a letter from the governor of Tennessee, in answer to his frequent and
pressing inquiries, as to the disposition which should
be made of the volunteers. It recommended what
had already, from necessity, been done; to dismiss—not discharge them, because the latter was
not in the power of either of them:—nor was
their dismission to be given because founded in
right; but because, under existing circumstances,
their presence could not prove beneficial, but highly
injurious. To induce them contentedly to remain,
the governor had suggested but one argument,
which had not already been unsuccessfully attempted; "that it was very doubtful if the government
would pay them for the services they had already

7 *

rendered, if abandoned without her authority." The letter was therefore enclosed for their inspection, accompanied with these remarks:—"I have just received a letter from Governor Blount, which I hasten to transmit, that you may avail yourselves of whatever benefits and privileges it holds out. You will perceive, that he does not consider he has any power to discharge you:—neither have I:—but you have my permission to retire from the service, if you are still desirous, and are prepared to risk the consequences."

These letters, so far from answering the desired end, had a contrary effect. The governor's was no sooner read, than they eagerly laid hold of it to support the resolution they had already formed, and, without further ceremony or delay, abandoned the campaign, with their colonel at their head, who, so far from having endeavoured to reconcile them, is believed, by secret artifices, to have fomented their discontents.

So general was the dissatisfaction of this brigade, and with such longing anxiety did they indulge the hope of a speedy return to their homes, that their impatience did not permit them to wait the return of the messenger from head-quarters. Before an answer could reach General Coffee, they had broken up their encampment at Deposit, re-crossed the river, and proceeded four miles beyond Huntsville. On receiving it, Coffee had the brigade drawn up in solid column, and the letters, together with the pledge they had given, read to them; after which the Reverend Mr. Blackburn endeavoured in an eloquent speech, in which he pointed out the ruinous consequences that were to be apprehended, if they persisted in their present purpose, to recall them to a sense of duty, and of honour : but they had formed their resolution too steadfastly, and had gone too extravagant lengths, to be influenced by the letter, the pledge, or the speech. As to the pledge, a few said they had not authorized it to be made ; others, that, as the general had not returned an immediate acceptance, they did not consider themselves bound by it; but the greater part candidly acknowledged, that they stood committed, and were without any justification for their present conduct. Thus, in a tumultuous manner, they abandoned their post and their duty, and, committing innumerable extravagances, re gardless alike of law and decency, continued their route to their respective homes.

CHAPTER IV

Discontents of the militia.—Governor Blount recommends an abandonment of the service.—Jackson's reply to his letter.—The governor takes measures for bringing out a sufficient force.—Conduct of General Roberts.—His brigade retires from service.—Lieutenant Kearley.—Arrival of additional forces.—Arrest of officers.—Expedition against the Indians.—His motives.—Battle of Emuckfaw.—General Coffee proceeds to destroy the enemy's fortifications.—Second battle of Emuckfaw.—Troops commence their return march.—Ambuscade formed by the Indians.—Battle of Enotichopco

But, whilst these unfortunate events were transpiring in the rear, matters were far from wearing an encouraging aspect at head-quarters. The brigade of West Tennessee militia, consisting of only about six hundred, imitating the evil examples of others, began to turn their attention towards home. Believing that three months constituted the tour of duty contemplated in the act under which they engaged, they insisted that it would terminate on the 4th of the ensuing month. It is true, the act had not defined the term of their engagement; but it had specified the object of calling them out, viz. to subdue the Indians;—and, as that object had not yet been attained, it was believed, that, at present, they were not entitled to a discharge. These troops, although raised by the state authorities, had been, by the particular recommendation of the legislature, received into the service of the general government, under the act of congress authorizing the president to call out a hundred thousand militia, to serve for six months, unless by his own order they should be previously dismissed. The militia of East Tennessee, having been specially mustered into service for three months, would, of course, be entitled to claim their dismissal at the expiration of that period; hence Colonel Lilliard's regiment, which constituted more than one half the present force at head-quarters, would be lost to the service on the 14th of the next month.

With the failure of General Cocke, to bring into the field the number and description of troops which he had been ordered to raise under the requisition of the president, as well as with the temper and demands of those who were in service, Jackson kept the governor of Tennessee correctly advised, and omitted no opportunity of entreating him, in the most pressing manner, to take the earliest measures for supplying by draft, or voluntary enlistment, the present deficiency, as well as that which, from every appearance, was soon to be expected. To these solicitations, he had now received the governor's answer, who stated, that, having given an order to bring into the field fifteen hundred of the detached militia, as was required by the secretary of war, and a thousand volunteers, under the act of the legislature of Tennessee of the 24th September, he did not feel himself authorized to grant any new mandate, although satisfied that the first had not been complied with; that he viewed the further prosecution of the campaign, attended as it was with so many embarrassments, as a fruitless endeavour; and concluded by recommending, as advisable, to withdraw the troops into the settlements, and suspend all active operations until the general government should provide more effectual means for conducting it to a favourable result. Jackson, far from having any intention to yield to this advice, determined to oppose it. Still. however, he was greatly concerned at the view the chief magistrate of his state seemed to take of a question of such vital importance ; and immediately proceeded to unfold himself fully, and to suggest the course, which, he believed, on the present occasion, it behooved them both to pursue : pointing out the ruinous consequences that might be expected to result from the adoption of the measure he had undertaken to recommend :—he continues :

"Had your wish, that I should discharge a part of my force, and retire, with the residue. into the settlements, assumed the form of a positive order, it might have furnished me some apology for pursuing such a course ; but by no means a full justification. As you would have no power to give such an order, I could not be inculpable in obeying, with my eyes open to the fatal consequences that would attend it. But a bare recommendation, founded, as I am satisfied it must be, on the artful suggestions of those fire-side patriots, who seek, in a failure of the expedition, an excuse for their own supineness,—and upon the misrepresentations of the discontented from the army, who wish it to be believed, that the difficulties which overcame their patriotism are wholly insurmountable—would afford me but a feeble shield against the reproaches of my country or my conscience. Believe me, my respected friend, the remarks I make proceed from the purest personal regard. If you would preserve your reputation, or that of the state over which you preside, you must take a straight-forward, determined course ; regardless of the applause or censure of the populace, and of the forebodings of that dastardly and designing crew who, at a time like this, may be expected to clamour continually in your ears. The very wretches who now beset you with evil counsel, will be the first, should the measures which they recommend eventuate in disaster, to call down imprecations on your head, and load you with reproaches. Your country is in danger:—apply its resources to its defence! Can any course be more plain? Do you, my friend, at such a moment as the present, sit with your arms folded, and your heart at ease, waiting a solution of your doubts, and a definition of your powers? Do you wait for special instructions from the secretary at war, which it is impossible for you to receive in time for the danger that threatens? How did the venerable Shelby act, under similar circumstances; or, rather, under circumstances by no means so critical? Did he wait for orders to do what every man of sense knew—what every patriot felt—to be right? He did not; and yet how highly and justly did the government extol his manly and energetic conduct! and how dear has his name become to every friend of his country!

"You say, that an order to bring the necessary quota of men into the field has been given, and that of course your power ceases; and, although you are made sensible that the order has been wholly neglected, you can take no measure to remedy the omission. Widely different, indeed, is my opinion. I consider it your imperious duty, when the men, called for by your authority, founded upon that of the government, are known not to be in the field, to see that they be brought there; and to take immediate measures with the officer, who, charged with the execution of your order, omits or neglects

to do it.   As the executive of the state, it is your
duty to see that the full quota of troops be constantly kept in the field, for the time they have
been required.   You are responsible to the government; your officer to you.   Of what avail is it, to
give an order, if it be never executed, and may be
disobeyed with impunity?   Is it by empty mandates that we can hope to conquer our enemies,
and save our defenceless frontiers from butchery
and devastation?   Believe me, my valued friend,
there are times when it is highly criminal to shrink
from responsibility, or scruple about the exercise
of our powers.   There are times when we must
disregard punctilious etiquette, and think only of
serving our country.   What is really our present
situation?   The enemy we have been sent to subdue may be said, if we stop at this, to be only exasperated.   The commander in chief, General Pinckney, who supposes me by this time prepared for
renewed operations, has ordered me to advance
and form a junction with the Georgia army ; and,
upon the expectation that I will do so, are all his
arrangements formed for the prosecution of the
campaign.   Will it do to defeat his plans, and jeopardize the safety of the Georgia army?   The general government, too, believe, and have a right to
believe, that we have now not less than five thousand men in the heart of the enemy's country, and
on this opinion are all their calculations bottomed;
and must they all be frustrated, and I become the
instrument by which it is done?   God forbid!

"You advise me to discharge or dismiss from ser
vice, until the will of the president can be known,
such portion of the militia as have rendered three
months' service.   This advice astonishes me, even

more than the former. I have no such discretiona-
ry power ; and if I had it would be impolitic and
ruinous to exercise it. I believed the militia, who
were not specially received for a shorter period.
were engaged for six months, unless the objects of
the expedition should be sooner attained ; and in
this opinion I was greatly strengthened by your
letter of the 15th, in which you say, when answering my inquiry upon this subject, ' the militia are
detached for six months' service ;' nor did I know
or suppose, you had a different opinion, until the
arrival of your last letter. This opinion must, 1
suppose, agreeably to your request, be made known
to General Roberts's brigade, and then the consequences are not difficult to be foreseen. Every
man belonging to it will abandon me on the 4th of
next month ; nor shall I have the means of preventing it, but by the application of force, which,
under such circumstances, I shall not be at liberty
to use. I have laboured hard to reconcile these men
to a continuance in service until they could be honourably discharged, and had hoped I had, in a great
measure, succeeded ; but your opinion, operating
with their own prejudices, will give a sanction to
their conduct, and render useless any further attempts. The, will go ; but I can neither discharge
nor dismiss them. Shall I be told, that, as they will
go, it may as well be peaceably permitted ? Can that
be any good reason why I should do an unauthorized act ? Is it a good reason why I should violate the order of my superior officer, and evince a
willingness to defeat the purposes of my government ? And wherein does the ' sound policy' of
the measures that have been recommended consist ?
o. in what way are they ' likely to promote the

public good ?'   Is it sound policy to abandon a conquest thus far made, and deliver up to havoc, or add
to the number of our enemies, those friendly Creeks
and Cherokees, who, relying on our protection, have
espoused our cause, and aided us with their arms ?
Is it good policy to turn loose upon our defenceless
frontiers five thousand exasperated savages, to reek
their hands once more in the blood of our citizens ?
What! retrograde under such circumstances !   I
will perish first.   No; I will do my duty: I will
hold the posts I have established, until ordered to
abandon them by the commanding general, or die
in the struggle ;—long since have I determined not
to seek the preservation of life at the sacrifice of
reputation.

"But our frontiers, it seems, are to be defended;
and by whom ?   By the very force that is now re
commended to be dismissed : for I am first told to
retire into the settlements and protect the frontiers,
next, to discharge my troops; and then, that no
measures can be taken for raising others.   No, my
friend, if troops be given me, it is not by loitering
on the frontiers that I will seek to give protection
—they are to be defended, if defended at all, in a
very different manner ;—by carrying the war into
the heart of the enemy's country.   All other hopes
of defence are more visionary than dreams.   What,
then, is to be done ?   I'll tell you what.   You have
only to act with the energy and decision the crisis
demands, and all will be well.   Send me a force
engaged for six months, and I will answer for the
result ;—but withhold it, and all is lost,—the reputation of the state, and your's, and mine along with
it."

This letter had considerable effect with the governor. On receiving it, he immediately determined on a course of greater efficiency, and ordered from the second division twenty-five hundred of the militia, for a tour of three months, to rendezvous at Fayetteville on the 28th of January. The command was given to Brigadier-General Johnston, with orders to proceed, without delay, to Fort Strother He instructed General Cocke to execute the order he had received from Jackson, for raising from his division his required quota of troops, and to bring them to the field as early as possible.

General Roberts, who had been ordered back to supply the deficiencies in his brigade, returned on the 27th with one hundred and ninety-one men, mustered for three months. Having halted them a few miles in rear of the camp, he proceeded thither himself, to learn of the commanding general, whether the troops he had brought on would be received for the term they had stipulated, as they were unwilling to advance farther until this point was settled. Jackson answered, that although he greatly preferred they should be engaged for six months, yet he had no wish to alter any engagement made with General Roberts, and would gladly receive them for that period. Notwithstanding this assurance, for some unknown cause, they suddenly formed the determination to return home, without gaining even a sight of the camp. To the misconduct of their general, was it justly to be attributed.

The careless indifference with which General Roberts had first treated the affair had subsided; and his fears took the alarm on receiving from General Jackson an order to parade immediately before the fort the men he had reported as brought into the field. He came forward to excuse what had happened, and to solicit permission to go in pursuit of the refugees. Overtaking them, at the distance of twenty miles, he endeavoured, in a very gentle manner, to soothe their discontents, and prevail on them to return; but, having been discharged, they laughed at the folly of his errand. Unable to effect his object, he remained with them during the night; and in the morning set out for camp, and his new recruits for home. On arriving at head-quarters, he ascribed his failure to the practices of certain officers, whom he named, and who, he said, had stirred up a spirit of mutiny and desertion among the men to such a degree, that all his efforts to retain them had proved unavailing. Jackson, who could not view this incident with the same indifference that Roberts did, immediately issued an order, directing him to proceed, forthwith, in pursuit of the deserters, and have them brought back. In the execution of this order, he was commanded to call to his aid any troops in the United States' service within the county of Madison, or in the state of Tennessee, and to exert all his power and authority, as a military officer, within his own brigade, and, in the event he should not be able to collect a sufficient force to march them safely to head-quarters, to confine them in jails, and make a report thereof without delay. This order was accompanied with an assurance, that all who should return willingly to their duty, except those officers who had been reported as the instigators, would be pardoned. Many of the men, and several of the officers, who had been charged as encouraging the revolt, learning the nature of the proceedings which were about to be enforced against them, returned of

their own accord to camp; and concurred in as-
cribing their late misconduct entirely to their general. He was afterwards arrested, and, upon this
and other charges exhibited against him, sentenced
by a court-martial to be cashiered.

The day arrived, when that portion of the militia,
which had continued in service, claimed to be discharged; and insisted that, whether this were given
to them or not, they would abandon the campaign,
and return home. Jackson believed them not entitled to it, and hence, that he had no right to give
it; but, since Governor Blount had said differently,
and his opinion had been promulgated, he felt it to
be improper that he should attempt the exercise of
authority to detain them. Nevertheless, believing
it to be his duty to keep them, he issued a general
order, commanding all persons in the service of the
United States, under his command, not to leave the
encampment without his written permission, under
the penalties annexed, by the rules and articles of
war, to the crime of desertion. This was accompanied by an address, in which they were exhorted
by all those motives which he supposed would be
most likely to have any influence, to remain at
their posts until they could be legally discharged
Neither the order nor the address availed any thing.
On the morning of the 4th of January, the officer
of the day reported, that on visiting his guard, half
after ten o'clock, he found neither the officer, (Lieutenant Kearley,) nor any of the sentinels at their
posts. Upon this information, General Jackson ordered the arrest of Kearley, who refused to surrender his sword, alleging it should protect him to
Tennessee; that he was a free man, and not subject
to the orders of General Jackson, or any body

8*

This being made known to the general, he issued, immediately, this order to the adjutant-general: "You will forthwith cause the guards to parade, with Captain Gordon's company of spies, and arrest Lieutenant Kearley; and, in case you shall be resisted in the execution of this order, you are commanded to oppose force to force, and arrest him at all hazards. Spare the effusion of blood, if possible; but mutiny must and shall be put down." Colonel Sitler, with the guards and Gordon's company, immediately proceeded in search, and found him at the head of his company, on the lines, which were formed, and about to be marched off. He was ordered to halt, but refused. The adjutant general, finding it necessary, directed the guards to stop him; and again demanded his sword, which he again refused to deliver. The guards were commanded to fire on him if he did not immediately deliver it, and had already cocked their guns. At this order, the lieutenant cocked his, and his men followed the example. General Jackson, informed of what was passing, had hastened to the scene, and, arriving at this moment, personally demanded of Kearley his sword, which he still obstinately re fused to deliver. Incensed at his conduct, and viewing the example as too dangerous to be passed in silence, he snatched a pistol from his holster and was already levelling it at the breast of Kear ley, when the adjutant-general, interposing between them, urged him to surrender his sword. At this moment, a friend of the lieutenant, who was present, drew it from the scabbard, and presented it to Colonel Sitler, who refused to receive it. It was then returned to Kearley, who now delivered it, and was placed under guard. During this crisis, both parties remained with their arms ready, and prepared for firing ; and a scene of bloodshed was narrowly escaped.

Kearley, confined, and placed under guard, be came exceedingly penitent, and supplicated the general for a pardon. He stated that the absence of the sentinels from their post had been owing to the advice of the brigade-major ; that not delivering his sword, when first demanded, was attributable to the influence of others, who had persuaded him it was not his duty to do so ; that he had afterwards come to the determination to surrender himself, but was dissuaded by those who assured him it would oe a sacrifice of character, and that they would share, and protect him, in the hour of danger ; why ne still resisted, in the presence of the general, was, that, being at the head of his company, and iaving undertaken to carry them home, he was re-strained, at the moment, by a false idea of honour. This application was aided by certificates of several of the most respectable officers then in camp, at-testing his previously uniform good behaviour, and expressing a belief that his late misconduct was wholly to be attributed to the interference of others. Influenced by these reasons, the general thought proper to order his liberation, and his sword to be restored. Never was a man more sensible of the favour he had received, or more devoted to his benefactor, than 'he afterwards became.

While these proceedings were taking place, the rest of the brigade, with the exception of Captain Willis's company, and twenty-nine of his men, con-tinued their march towards home, leaving behind, for the further prosecution of the campaign, and the defence of Fort Strother, a single regiment of militia, whose term of service was within a few weeks of expiring; two small companies of spies, and one of artillery.

Difficulties were constantly pressing; and whilst one moment gave birth to expectation, the next served but to destroy it. Jackson had been advised, and was buoyed by the hope, that adequate numbers would shortly come to his relief; and, until this could be accomplished, it was desirable to retain those who then were with him, to give to his posts increased protection. Whilst measures were adopting in Tennessee to effect this fully, about a thousand volunteers were moving out, to preserve an appearance of opposition, and keep secure what had been already gained. With this force, added to what he already had, if in his power to keep them, he believed he would be able to advance on the enemy, make a diversion in favour of the Georgia army, and obtain other important advantages. With this view, he had addressed this regiment, and brought before them such considerations as might be supposed calculated to excite a soldier's ardour. But they almost unanimously refused to remain beyond the period of their engagement.

As nothing but an unnecessary consumption of supplies was now to be expected from detaining troops so spiritless, orders were given for taking up the line of march to Fort Armstrong, on the 10th; whence they were directed to proceed to Knoxville, and receive orders for their discharge.

Meantime, the volunteers, lately raised, had arrived at Huntsville, where they had been directed to remain until sufficient supplies could be had at head quarters. Could they have proceeded directly on, they would have reached the general suffi ciently early to have enabled him to proceed against the enemy before the period at which the remnant of his troops would have been entitled to a dis charge. His exertions to have in readiness the arrangements necessary to the accomplishment of this end, had been indefatigable. General Cocke had been directed to give instructions to his quarter-master, to forward to Fort Strother such provisions as should arrive at Fort Armstrong ; to proceed thence to Ross's, and make arrangements for the speedy transportation, from that place to De posit, of all the bread stuff which the contractor had been required to collect at that depot; and to have procured a competent supply of that article, as well for the troops then in the field, as for those which had been ordered to be raised. The more certainly to effect this object, he had, on the 20th of December, despatched his own quarter-master and adjutant-general to Deposit and Huntsville, to push on what should be collected at those places ; and had, at the same time, despatched one of the sub-contractors from camp, with directions to examine the situation of the different depots ; and, if found insufficient to meet the requisition he had made, to proceed immediately to the settlements in Tennessee, and procure the necessary supplies. To the contractors themselves he had addressed orders and exhortations almost without number · and, indeed, from every source, and through every channel that the hope of relief could be discerned, had he directed his exertions to obtain it.

On the second of January, Colonel Carroll and Mr. Blackburn arrived at head-quarters, to receive instructions how the volunteers should be organized and brought up. Having reported their strength to be eight hundred and fifty, they were directed to have them formed, as had been desired, into two regiments, under officers of their own choice; and an order was put into their hands, requiring General Coffee, who was then at Huntsville, to march them to Fort Strother, by the 10th instant. That officer, whose feelings had been sufficiently harrowed by the late conduct and defection of his brigade, learning that those troops were unwilling for him to have command of them, had expressed a wish to General Jackson that it might not be assigned him; in consequence of which, and their own request, the latter had determined, after their arrival at his camp, that there should be no intermediate commander over them, between their colonels and himself. With this proposed arrangement, those gentlemen had been instructed to make the troops acquainted; and were particularly requested to use their best endeavours to remove any erroneous impressions that might have been made upon their minds.

General Coffee, having received the instructions of General Jackson, immediately gave orders to Colonels Perkins and Higgins, who had been chosen to the command of the two regiments, to march directly for head-quarters. To his entire astonishment, both these officers refused to obey; alleging, in a written statement they made, that General Coffee had no right to exercise command over them, and that they would disregard any he might attempt to claim. One of them not only refused obedience to the order, but even went so far as to refuse to return it, or permit the brigade-inspector to take a copy; thereby placing it out of his power to make it known to the rest of the brigade.

Unwilling as Coffee was to create any additional perplexities to the commanding general, he felt himself constrained to demand the arrest of those officers.

Notwithstanding the weighty consideratious which had been urged to produce an expeditious movement, it was not until the 13th that those officers, with their regiments, reached head-quarters. Finding they were likely to be noticed, on charges which their better-informed friends advised would not only deprive them of command, but involve them in disgrace, they immediately made an honourable concession, in which they pleaded ignorance of military duty, as an excuse for their misconduct.

The whole effective force consisted, at this time, by the reports, of little more than nine hundred men.

Being addressed by the general, on the 15th, the mounted troops commenced their march to Wehogee Creek, three miles from the fort. Jackson, with his staff, and the artillery company, joined them next morning, and continued the line of march to Talladega, where about two hundred friendly Indians, Cherokees and Creeks, badly armed, and much discouraged at the weakness of his force, were added to his numbers, without increasing much his strength. Seldom, perhaps, has there been an expedition undertaken, fraught with greater peril. Nine hundred new recruits, entirely unacquainted with the duties of the field, were to be marched into the heart of an enemy's country, without a single hope of escape, but from victory, and that victory not to be expected, but from the wisest precaution, and most determined bravery

Although so obviously pregnant with danger, to march was the only alternative that could be adopted. No other could afford a diversion favourable to General Floyd, who was advancing with the army from Georgia, or give favourable results to the campaign, without which it must soon have been abandoned, for want of men to prosecute it. Another reason rendered such a movement indispensable. The officer commanding at Fort Armstrong had received intelligence, that the warriors from fourteen or fifteen towns on the Taliapoosa were about to unite their forces, and attack that place; which, for the want of a sufficient garrison, was in a defenceless situation. Of this General Jackson had been advised. The present movement, hazardous as it was, was indispensable, and could alone prevent the execution of such a purpose. On reaching Talladega, he received a letter from the commandant at Fort Armstrong, confirmatory of the first information. One also from General Pinckney, by express, arrived, advising him that Floyd, on the 10th instant, would move from Coweta, and, in ten days thereafter, establish a position at Tuckabatchee; and recommended, if his force would allow him to do no more, that he should advance against such of the enemy's towns as might be within convenient distance; that, by having his troops employed, he might keep disaffection from his ranks, and be, at the same time, serviceably engaged in harassing the enemy. If, therefore, he could have hesitated before, there was now no longer any room to do so. By an expeditious movement, he might save Fort Armstrong, and render an essential service to General Floyd, by detaching a part of the clans destined to proceed against him.

As he progressed on the march, a want of the necessary knowledge in his pilots, of subordination in his troops, and skill in the officers who commanded them, became more and more apparent; but still their ardour to meet the enemy was not abated.

On the evening of the 21st, sensible, from the trails he had fallen in upon, fresh, and converging to a point, that he must be in the neighbourhood of the enemy, Jackson encamped his little army in a hollow square, on an eligible site, upon the eminences of Emuckfaw, sent out his spies, posted his pickets, doubled his sentinels, and made the necessary arrangements to guard against attack. About midnight the spies came in and reported they had discovered a large encampment of Indians, at about three miles distance, who, from their whooping and dancing, were no doubt apprized of his arrival. Every thing was ready for their reception, if they meditated an attack, or to pursue in the morning, if they did not. At the dawn of day, the alarm-guns of our sentinels, succeeded by shrieks and savage yells, announced their presence. They commenced a furious assault on the left flank, commanded by Colonel Higgins, which was met with great firmness. General Coffee, and Colonels Carroll and Sitler, instantly repaired to the point of attack, and, by example and exhortation, encouraged the men to a performance of their duty. The action raged for half an hour; the brunt of which being against the left wing, it had become considerably weakened. It being now sufficiently light to ascertain the position of the enemy, and Captain Ferril's company having reenforced the left wing, the whole charged, under General Coffee,

and a route immediately ensued. The friendly
Indians joining in the pursuit, they were chased
about two miles, with considerable loss. We had
five killed, and twenty wounded. Until it became
light enough to discern objects, our troops derived
considerable advantage from their camp fires ; these
having been placed at some distance without the
encampment, afforded a decided superiority in a
night attack, by enabling those within to fire with
great accuracy on an approaching enemy, whilst
they themselves remained invisible.

The pursuit being over, Jackson detached Coffee, with the Indians, and four hundred men, to
destroy the enemy's encampment, unless he should
find it too strongly fortified ; in which event, he
was to give information immediately, and wait the
arrival of the artillery. Coffee, having reconnoitred this position, and found it too strong to be
assailed with the force he commanded, returned to
camp. He had not returned more than half an
hour, when a severe fire was made upon the pickets,
posted on the right, accompanied with prodigious
yelling. General Coffee proceeded to turn the left
flank of the assailants. This detachment being
taken from different corps, he placed himself at
their head, and moved briskly forward. Those in
the rear, availing themselves of this circumstance,
continued to drop off, one by one, without his
knowledge, until the whole number left with him
did not exceed fifty. It was fortunate that the
force of the enemy he had first to attack was not
greater. He found them occupying a ridge of
open pine timber, covered with low underwood,
which afforded them many opportunities for concealment. To deprive them of this advantage,

Coffee ordered his men to dismount and charge them. This order was promptly obeyed, and some loss sustained in its execution ; the general himself was wounded through the body, and his aid, Major Donelson, killed by a ball through the head ;—three of his men also fell. The enemy, driven back by the charge, took refuge on the margin of a creek, covered with reeds, where they lay concealed.

The saveges, having intended the attack on the right as a feint, now, with their main force, which had been concealed, made a violent onset on our left line, which they hoped to find in disorder. General Jackson, however, who .had apprehended their design, was prepared to meet it: this line had been ordered to remain firm in its position and, when the first gun was heard in that quarter; he repaired thither in person, and strengthened it by additional forces. The first advance of the enemy was sustained with firmness, and opposed with great gallantry. The battle was now maintained on the part of the assailants, by quick and irregular firing, from behind logs, trees, shrubbery and whatever could afford concealment: behind these, prostrating themselves after firing, and reloading, they would rise and again discharge their guns. After sustaining their fire in this way for some time, a charge, to dislodge them from their position, was ordered: and the whole line under Colonel Carroll, by a most brilliant and steady movement, threw them into confusion, and they fled precipitately away.

In the mean time, General Coffee had been endeavouring to drive the savages on the right from the fastnesses into which they had retired : but, finding that this could not be done without hazard and loss, he began to retire towards the place where he had first dismounted. This expedient, designed for stratagem, produced the desired effect. The enemy, inspirited by the movement, presuming it a retreat, forsook their hiding-places, and rapidly advanced upon him. That officer immediately availed himself of the opportunity thus afforded of contending with them again on equal terms; and a severe conflict commenced, and continued about an hour, in which the loss on both sides was nearly equal. At this critical juncture, when several of the detachments had been killed, many wounded, and the whole greatly exhausted with fatigue, the dispersion of the enemy being effected on the left, a reenforcement was despatched by General Jackson, which, making its appearance on the enemy's left flank, put an end to the contest. General Coffee, although severely wounded, still continued the fight, and, availing himself of the arrival of this additional 'strength, instantly ordered a charge; when the enemy, foreseeing their doom fled in consternation, and were pursued with dreadful slaughter. It is believed that at this place none escaped. Thus drew to a close a day of almost continual fighting.*

Having buried the dead, and dressed the wounded, preparations were made to guard against an at-

---

* The Indians had designed their plan of operations well, though the execution did not succeed. It was intended to bring on the attack at three different points, at the same time; but a party of the Chealegrans, one of the tribes which compose the Creek confederacy, who had been ordered to assail the right extremity of our front line, instead of doing so, thought it more prudent to proceed to their villages, happy to have passed, undiscovered, the point they had been ordered to attack. But for this, the contest might have terminated less advantageously, perhaps disastrously.

tack by night, by erecting a breast-work of timber
around the encampment; a measure the more
necessary, as the spirits of our troops, most of
whom had never before been in collision with an
enemy, were observed visibly to flag, towards the
evening. Indeed, during the night, it was with
the utmost difficulty the sentinels could be maintained at their posts, who, expecting every minute
the appearance of the enemy, would, at the least
noise, fire and run in. The enemy, however, whose
spies were around our encampment all night, did
not think proper to attack us in this position, and
the morning broke without disturbance. The next
day, General Jackson began to think of returning
to the Ten Islands. Many reasons concurred to
render such a measure proper.

Jackson ordered litters to be formed for the
transportation of the sick and wounded, and other
necessary preparations to be made for a return
march. Every thing being ready, it was commenced at ten o'clock the next morning, and continued without interruption until nearly night,
when the army was encamped a quarter of a mile
on the south side of Enotichopco Creek, in the direction to the ford.

As it was evident the enemy had been in pursuit
during the day, a breast-work was thrown up, with
the utmost expedition, and arrangements made to
repel their attempts, should they meditate an attack, in the course of the night, or on the succeeding morning. From a knowledge that they had
been hanging on his rear, during the march of the
preceding day, the general was led to conjecture
that an ambuscade had been prepared, and that an
attack would be made on him whilst crossing the
9 *

creek in his front.   Near the crossing place was
a deep ravine, formed by the projection of two
hills, overgrown with thick shrubbery and brown
sedge, which afforded every convenience for concealment. Along this route, the army, in going out,
had passed; Jackson determined to take a different
route; he secretly despatched, early next morning,
a few pioneers, to designate another crossing place
below. A suitable one was discovered, about six
hundred yards from the old one; and thither the
general now led his army; having, previously to
commencing the march, formed his columns, and
the front and rear guards, that he might be in an
attitude for defence.

A beautiful slope of open woodland led down
to the newly discovered ford, where, except immediately on the margin of the creek, which was
covered with a few reeds, there was nothing to obstruct the view. The front guards, and part of
the columns, had passed; the wounded were also
over, and the artillery just entering the creek,
when an alarm-gun was heard in the rear. The
Indians, unexpectedly finding the route was changed, quitted the defile, where they had expected to
commence the assault, and advanced upon a company, under the command of Captain Russell, which
marched in the rear. Though assailed by superior numbers, it returned the fire, and gradually
retired, until it reached the rear guard, who, according to express instructions given, were, in the
event of an attack, to face about, and act as the
advance; whilst the right and left columns should
be turned on their pivots, so as completely to loop
the enemy, and render his destruction sure. The
right column of the rear guard was commanded by

Colonel Perkins, the left by Lieutenant-Colonel
Stump, and the centre column by Colonel Carroll
Jackson was just passing the stream when the firing
and yelling commenced. Having instructed his
aid-de-camp to form a line for the protection of the
wounded, who were but a short distance in ad
vance, and afterwards to turn the left column, he
himself proceeded to the right, for a similar purpose. What was his astonishment, when, resting
in the hope of certain victory, he beheld the right
and left columns of the rear guard, after a feeble
resistance, precipitately give way, bringing with
them confusion and dismay, and entirely obstruct-
ing the passage, over which the principal strength
of the army was to be re-crossed! This shameful
flight was well nigh being attended with the most
fatal consequences ; which were alone averted by
the determined bravery of a few. Nearly the
whole of the centre column had followed the ex
ample of the other two, and precipitated themselves
into the creek ; not more than twenty remained to
oppose the violence of the first assault. The artillery company, commanded by Lieutenant Armstrong, composed of young men of the first families,
who had volunteered their services at the commencement of the campaign, formed with their
muskets before the piece of ordnance they had, and
hastily dragged it from the creek to an eminence,
from which they could play to advantage. Here
an obstinate conflict ensued; the enemy endeavouring to charge and take it, whilst this company
formed with their muskets, and resolutely defended
    These young men, the few who remained with
   .onel Carroll, and the gallant Captain Quarles·
who fell at their head, with Russell's spies, not ex

ceeding in the whole one hundred, maintained, with the utmost firmness, a contest, for many minutes against a force five times greater than their own and checked the advance of the foe. The brave Lieutenant Armstrong fell at the side of his piece by a wound in the groin, and exclaimed, as he lay, "Some of you must perish; but don't lose the gun." By his side fell, mortally wounded, his associate and friend, Bird Evans, and the gallant Captain Hamilton; who, having been abandoned by his men, at Fort Strother, with his two brothers and his aged father, had attached himself to the artillery company, as a private, and, in that capacity, showed how well he deserved to command by the fidelity with which he obeyed. Perilous as the hour was, this little heroic band evinced themselves cool and collected as they were brave in battle. In the confusion of the moment, the rammer and pricker of the cannon could not be disengaged from the carriage; in this situation, and at such a time, the invention of most young soldiers might have failed. but, nothing fearing, Craven Jackson and Constantine Perkins drove home the cartridges with a musket, and with the ramrod prepared them for the match. In the mean time, while the conflict was thus unequally sustained, General Jackson and his staff had been enabled, by great exertions, to restore something like order, from confusion. The columns were again formed, and put in motion: and small detachments had been sent across the creek to support the little band that there maintained their ground. The enemy, perceiving a strong force advancing, and being warmly assailed on their left flank by Captain Gordon, at the head of his company of spies, were stricken with alarm, and fled away, leaving behind their blankets, and whatever was likely to retard their flight. Detachments were ordered on the pursuit, who, in a chase of two miles, destroyed many, and wholly dispersed them.

In despite of the active exertions made by General Jackson to restore order, they were, for some time, unavailing. In addition to the assistance received from his staff, he derived much from the aid of General Coffee. That officer, in consequence of the wound which he had received at Emuckfaw, had, the day before, been carried in a litter. From the apprehensions indulged, that an attack would probably be made upon them that morning, he had proceeded from the encampment on horseback, and aided, during the action, with his usual deliberate firmness. Indeed, all the officers of his brigade rendered manifest, now, the value of experience. This was not a moment for rules of fancied etiquette. The very men, who, a little time before, would have disdained advice, and spurned an order from any but their own commanders, did not scruple, amidst the peril that surrounded them, to be regulated by those who seemed to be so much better qualified for extricating them from their present danger. The hospital surgeon, Dr. Shelby, appeared in the fight, and rendered important military services. The adjutant-general, Sitler, hastened across the creek in the early part of the action, to the artillery company, for which he felt all the *esprit de corps*, having been once attached to it; and there remained, supporting them in their duties, and participating in their dangers. Captain Gordon, too, contributed greatly to dispel the peril of the moment, by his active sally on the left flank of

the savages. Of the general himself, it is scarcely
necessary to remark, that, but for him, every thing
must have gone to ruin. On him all hopes were
rested. In that moment of confusion, he was the
rallying point, even for the spirits of the brave
Firm and energetic, and, at the same time, perfectly self-possessed, his example and authority alike
contributed to arrest the flying, and give confidence
to those who maintained their ground. Cowards
forgot their panic, and fronted danger, when they
heard his voice and beheld his manner; and the
brave would have formed round his body a rampart with their own. In the midst of showers of
balls, of which he seemed unmindful, he was seen
performing the duties of the subordinate officers,
rallying the alarmed, halting them in their flight,
forming his columns, and inspiriting them by his
example. An army suddenly dismayed, and thrown
into confusion, was thus happily rescued from a destruction which lately appeared inevitable. Our
total loss, in the several engagements, on the 22d
and this day, was only twenty killed, and seventy-
five wounded, some of whom, however, afterwards
died. The loss of the enemy cannot be accurately
stated. The bodies of one hundred and eighty-
nine of their warriors were found ; this, however,
may be considered as greatly below the real number ; nor can their wounded be even conjectured.
The greatest slaughter was in the pursuit. Scattered through the heights and hollows, many of the
wounded escaped, and many of the killed were not
ascertained. It is certain, however, as was afterwards disclosed by prisoners, that considerably
more than two hundred of those who, on this occasion, went out to battle, never returned ; but

those who did return, unwilling it should be known that so many were killed, feeling it might dispirit the nation, endeavoured to have it believed, and so representented it, that they had proceeded on some distant expedition, and would be for some time absent.

The army encamped, on the night of the 26th within three miles of Fort Strother. Thus terminated an expedition replete with peril, but attended with effects highly beneficial. Fort Armstrong was relieved; General Floyd enabled to gain a victory at Autossee, where he would most probably have met defeat; a considerable portion of the enemy's best forces had been destroyed; and an end put to the hopes they had founded on previous delays. Discontent had been kept from the ranks; the troops had been beneficially employed; and inactivity, the bane of every army, had been avoided.

CHAPTER V.

*The volunteers are discharged.—New troops arrive.—Execu
tion of a soldier, and the effect produced.—Want of supplies.—
Mutiny with the East Tennessee brigade.—General Jackson
marches against the Indians.—Battle of Tohopeka.—Returns to
Fort Williams.—Expedition to Hoithlewalee; its failure, and
the causes.—Forms a junction with the Georgia troops, and pro
ceeds to the Hickory Ground.—Indians sue for peace.—Weatherford surrenders himself.—Arrival of General Pinckney at
head-quarters.—Tennessee troops are ordered to be marched
home, and discharged from service.*

THE troops having reached the post whence
they had set out, the general determined to discharge them. The information from Tennessee
was, that there would soon be in the field a considerable force, enlisted for a period sufficient to effect
a termination of the Indian war. He was desirous
of having every thing in readiness by the time of
their arrival, that they might be carried without
delay into active service. Detaining his late volunteers, therefore, a short time, to complete boats
for the transportation of his camp equipage and
provisions down the Coosa, he directed them to be
marched home, and there to be honourably dismissed. The further service of his artillery company was also dispensed with. His parting inter-
view with them was interesting and affecting.

A letter from Jackson to Governor Blount, added
to his own sense of the importance of the crisis,
had induced him to issue an order on the 3d, directing twenty-five hundred of the militia of the second
division to be detached, organized, and equipped,
in conformity to an act of congress of the 6th of

April, 1812. These were to perform a tour of three months, to be computed from the time of rendezvous, appointed to be on the 28th instant. He had also required General Cocke to bring into the field, under the requisition of the secretary of war, the quota he had been instructed to raise. This officer, who had hitherto created so many obstacles, still appeared to desire nothing more ardently than a failure of the campaign. Although many difficulties had been feigned in the execution of the order directed to him, he was enabled to muster into service, from his division, about two thousand men. These, however, as well as those called out from West Tennessee. were but indifferently armed.

The thirty-ninth regiment, under Colonel Williams, had also received orders to proceed to Jackson's head-quarters, and act under his command in the prosecution of the war. It arrived on the 5th or 6th of the month, about six hundred strong. Most of the men were badly armed; this evil, however, was shortly afterwards remedied.

The quarter-masters and contractors were already actively engaged, and endeavouring to procure provisions and the transportations for the army. The failures, in regard to former enterprises, are to be ascribed to these two departments ; to the constant endeavour of the contractors to procure provisions at a reduced price, in order to enhance their profits ; and to fears entertained, lest, if they should lay in any large supply, it might spoil or waste on their hands. The inconveniences in the quarter-master's department, were, indeed, less chargeable to the incumbents than to the causes which they could not control ; for, to the extreme ruggedness of the way over which wagons had to pass, was to be added the real difficulty of obtaining a sufficient number on the frontiers.

About the middle of the month, Jackson ordered the troops to advance, and form a union at head-quarters, then at Fort Strother. Greatly to his surprise, he soon after learned that the contractor from East Tennessee had again failed to comply with his engagement, notwithstanding the ample means which he possessed, and the full time allowed him for that purpose. The troops, however, agree-ably to the order received, proceeded on their march. Those from the second division, under Brigadier-General Johnston, arrived on the 14th; which, added to the force under General Doherty, from East Tennessee, constituted about five thou-sand effectives. Composed, as this army was, o. troops entirely raw, it was not to be expected tha. any thing short of the greatest firmness in its officers could restrain that course of conduct and disorder, which had hitherto so unhappily prevailed.

The execution of a private, (John Woods,) who had been sentenced by a court-martial, on a charge of mutiny, produced, at this time, great excitement. and the most salutary effects. That mutinous spirit, which had so frequently broken into the camp, and for a while suspended all active opera tions, remained to be checked. A fit occasion was now at hand to evince, that although militia, when at their fire-sides at home, might boast an exemp-tion from control, yet in the field those high no-tions were to be abandoned, and subordination ob-served. Painful as it was to the feelings of the general, he viewed it as a sacrifice essential to the preservation of good order, and left the sentence of the court to be inflicted. The execution was productive of the happiest effects; order was produced, and that opinion which had so long prevailed, that a militia-man was privileged, and for no offence liable to suffer death, was, from that moment, abandoned, and a stricter obedience than had been practised afterwards characterized the army.

Nothing was wanting now to put the troops in motion, and actively to prosecute the war, but the arrival of necessary supplies. Remonstrance, entreaty, and threats, had long since been used and exhausted. Every mean had been resorted to, to impress on the minds of the contractors the necessity of urging forward in faithful discharge of their duty; but the same indifference and neglect were still persisted in. To ward off the effects of such great evils—evils which he foresaw must again eventuate in discontent and revolt—Jackson resolved to pursue a different course, and no longer depend on persons who had so frequently disappointed him, and whose only object was the acquirement of wealth. He accordingly despatched messengers to the nearest settlements, with directions to purchase provisions, at whatever price they could be procured. This course, to these incumbents on the nation, afforded an argument infinitely stronger than any to which he had before resorted Unexpectedly assailed in a way they had not previously thought of, by being held and made liable for the amount of the purchases, which by their neglect was rendered necessary, they exerted themselves in discharge of a duty they had hitherto too shamefully neglected. Every expedient had been practised to urge them to a compliance with the obligations they were under to their govern ment; until the present, none had proved effectual. In one of his letters, about this time, the general remarks,—" I have no doubt but a combination has been formed to defeat the objects of the campaign, but the contractor ought to have recollected, that he had disappointed and starved my army once: and now, in return, it shall be amply provided for at his expense. At this point he was to have delivered the rations—and, whatever they may cost, at this place he will be required to pay: any price that will ensure their delivery, I have directed to be given." The supplying an army by contractors, he had often objected to as highly exceptionable and dangerous. His monitor, on this subject, was his own experience. Disappointment, mutiny, and abandonment by his troops, when in the full career of success, and an unnecessarily protracted campaign, were among the evils already experienced, and which he desired, if possible, might be in future avoided. The difficulties, the perplexities, he had met, and the constant dissatisfaction which had rendered his troops inefficient, were wholly to be attributed to those, who, in disregard of the public good, had looked alone to their own immediate benefit. It was high time that the feelings and interest of such men should be disregarded, and a sense of duty enforced, by that sort of appeal which sordid minds best can understand—an appeal to profit and the purse.

Under these and other circumstances, which seemed to involve the most serious consequences, the general had but little time for either repose or quietness. Every thing was moving in opposition to his wishes. The East Tennessee brigade, under the command of Doherty having been instructed

to halt, until adequate supplies should be received
at head-quarters, had already manifested many
symptoms of revolt, and was with difficulty restrained from abandoning the field, and returning
immediately home. Added to their own discontents, pains had been taken by a personage high in
authority to scatter dissension, and to persuade
them that they had been improperly called out, and
without sufficient authority ; that the draft was
illegal, and that they were under no necessity of
remaining. On the morning that General Doherty
was about to proceed to head-quarters, he was
astonished to hear the drums beating up for volun
teers to abandon his camp and return home. Notwithstanding all his efforts to prevent this injurious
measure, one hundred and **eighty** deserted. His
surprise was still greater, on receiving information
in which he confided, that instructions by Major-
General Cocke had been given, that, in the event
any number of the troops should be marched back,
he would take upon himself to discharge them
from all responsibility on their return to Knoxville
The general had previously appeared at the camp
of Doherty, and, by different means, attempted to
excite mutiny and disaffection among the troops.
As a reason for being unwilling to assume the command, and go with them to the field, he stated, that
they would be placed in a situation which he dis-
liked to think of, and one which his feelings would
not enable him to witness ; that they were about to
be placed under the command of General Jackson,
who would impose on them the severest trials, and
where they would have to encounter every imagina-
ble privation and suffering. He represented, that
at head-quarters there was not a sufficiency of pro-

visions on hand to last five days; nor was there a probability that there would happen any change of circumstances for the better; that, should they once be placed in the power of Jackson, such was his nature and disposition, that, with the regular force under his command, he would compel them to serve whatever length of time he pleased. Doherty, who was a brigadier in the first division, was at a loss to know how he should proceed with his own major-general, who, having thus obtruded himself into his camp, was endeavouring to excite mutiny and re volt: he accordingly despatched an express to head-quarters to give information to General Jackson of what was passing in his camp. The messenger arrived, and, in return, received an order to Doherty, commanding him, peremptorily, to seize, and send under guard to Fort Strother, every officer, without regard to his rank, who should be found, in any manner, attempting to incite his army to mutiny. General Cocke, apprehending what was going on, or obtaining intelligence, retired before the order arrived, and thus escaped the punishment due to so aggravated an offence.

About this time, Colonel Dyer was despatched with six hundred men, with orders to proceed to the head of the Black Warrior, and ascertain if any force of the indians was imbodied in that quarter, and disperse them. This detachment, having pro ceeded eight days through the heights along the Cahawba, had fallen in with a trail the enemy had passed, stretching eastwardly, and followed it fo some distance. Apprehending that the army might be on the eve of departing from Fort Strother, and being unable to obtain any certain information of the savages, he desisted from the pursuit, and returned to camp.

That there might be no troops in the field in a situation not to be serviceable, and as supplies were an important consideration, orders were given the brigadiers to dismiss from the ranks every invalid, and all who were not well armed.

General Jackson, at length, by constant and unremitted exertions, obtained such supplies as he believed would be necessary to enable him to proceed. On the 14th he commenced his march, and, crossing the river, arrived on the 21st at the mouth of Cedar Creek, which had been previously selected for the establishment of a fort.* At this place it became necessary to delay a day or two, and await the coming of the provision boats, which were descending the Coosa.

On the 22d of January, the day of the battle of Emuckfaw, General Coffee, as has been already stated, had been detached to destroy the Indian encampment on the Tallapoosa: having reconnoitred their position, and believing them too strongly posted to be advantageously assailed by the force which he then commanded, he had retired without making the attempt. The position they had chosen was at a bend of the Tallapoosa. called by the Indians Tohopeka, which, interpreted into our language, means Horse-Shoe, not far from New Youcka, and near the Oakfusky villages. Fortified by nature and the skill of the savages, no other conjecture was entertained, than that at this place was intended a defence of the most determined kind. Learning that the Indians were still imbodied here, Jackson resolved to make a descent

---

* Fort Williams.

on it, and destroy the confederacy; thence, returning to Fort Williams for provisions, to urge forward
to the Hickory Ground, where he hoped he should
oe able finally to terminate the war.

On the 24th, leaving a sufficient force under
Brigadier-General Johnston for the protection of
the post, with eight days' provisions, he left Fort
Williams for the Tallapoosa, by the way of Emuckfaw.   The whole force now with him amounted
to less than three thousand effective men; being
considerably reduced by the necessity of leaving
behind him detachments for garrisons at the different forts.   At ten o'clock on the morning of the
27th, after a march of fifty-two miles, he reached
the village Tohopeka.   The enemy, having gained
intelligence of his approach, had collected in considerable numbers, with a view to give him battle.
The warriors from the adjacent towns, Oakfusky,
Hillabee, Eufalee, and New Youcka, amounting to
a thousand or twelve hundred, were here collected,
and waiting his approach.   They could have selected no place better calculated for defence ; for, independent of the advantages bestowed on it by
nature, their own exertions had greatly contributed
to its strength.   Surrounded almost entirely by the
river, it was accessible only by a narrow neck of
land, of three hundred and fifty yards width, which
they had taken much pains to secure, by placing
large timbers and trunks of trees horizontally on
each other, leaving but a single place of entrance
From a double row of port-holes formed in it, they
were enabled to give complete direction to their
fire, whilst they lay in perfect security behind.

General Coffee, at the head of the mounted infantry and friendly Indians, had been despatched

early in the morning from camp, with orders to
gain the southern bank of the river, encircle the
bend, and make some feint, or manœuvring, to
divert the enemy from the point where the attack
was intended principally to be waged. He was
particularly instructed so to arrange the force under
his command, that the savages might not escape by
passing to the opposite side in their canoes, with
which, it was represented, the whole shore was
lined. Jackson, with the rest of the army, proceeded to take a position in front of the breast-
work. Having planted his cannon on an eminence,
about two hundred yards from the front of the
enemy's line, with a view to break down his
defence, a brisk fire commenced. The musketry
and rifles, which occupied a nearer position, were
used as the Indians occasionally showed themselves
from behind their works. The artillery was well
served by Major Bradford, and the fire kept up for
some minutes without making any impression ; time,
however, was gained for complete readiness. The
signals having now announced that General Coffee
had reached in safety his point of destination, or,
the opposite side of the river, had formed his line,
and was ready to act, the order was given to
charge. " Never were troops more eager to be
led on than were both regulars and militia. They
had been waiting with impatience for the order,
and hailed it with acclamations. The spirit that
animated them was a sure augury of the success
that was to follow." Between them there was no
difference ; both advanced with the intrepidity and
firmness of veteran soldiers. The thirty-ninth
regiment, led on by their commander, Colonel Williams, and the brave but ill-fated Major Montgomery

and the militia under the command of Colone.
Bunch, moved forward amidst a destructive fire
that continually poured upon them, and were presently at the rampart.   Here an obstinate and
destructive conflict ensued, each contending for
the port-holes, on different sides.   Many of the
enemy's balls were welded between the muskets
and bayonets of our soldiers.   At this moment,
Major Montgomery, leaping on the wall, called to
his men to mount and follow him; he had scarcely
spoken, when, shot through the head, he fell lifeless
to the ground.   Our troops eagerly followed the
example he had set, and scaled their ramparts.
Finding it no longer tenable, the savages abandoned their position, and, retiring from their works,
concealed themselves amidst the brush and timber
that lay thickly scattered over the peninsula;
whence they kept up a galling fire, until they were
again forced back.   Driven to despair, not knowing
whither to flee, and resolving not to surrender,
they saw no other alternative, than an effort to
effect their escape, by passing in their canoes to
the opposite bank of the river; from this they were,
however, prevented, by perceiving that a part of
the army already lined the opposite shore.   Under
these circumstances, the remaining warriors, who
yet survived the severity of the conflict, betaking
themselves to flight, leaped down the banks, and
concealed themselves along the cliffs and steeps,
which were covered by the trees.   Many had betaken
themselves to the west angle of their line of defence, where, under protection of heaps of brush,
a spirited fire was kept up upon those of our troops
who had gained their line, and those who were
advancing on the outer side.   From these secreted

places they would fire and disappear. General Jackson, perceiving that further resistance must involve them in utter destruction, and entertaining a desire that they should yield a contest which now evidently was a hopeless one, ordered the interpreter to advance with a flag, under cover of some trees which stood in front, until he should reach a position sufficiently near to be heard. He did so, and, having arrived within forty yards of the spot where the Indians were concealed, in an audible voice, and in their own language, addressed them; told them of the folly of further resistance, and that he was commanded by General Jackson to say, that, if disposed to surrender, they should be received and treated as prisoners. They waited patiently until he had finished, and heard what he had to say;—a pause ensued; and, at the moment when he was expecting to receive an answer, and to learn that a surrender would be at once made, a fire was opened upon the flag, and the interpreter severely wounded in the breast. Finding they would not yield, orders were given to dislodge them. To accomplish this, the artillery was first turned against them; but, being from its size incapable of producing any effect, a charge was made, in which several valuable lives were lost; it however succeeded, and the enemy were dislodged from their covert place on the right angle of their line of defence. Lighted torches were now thrown down the steeps, which, communicating with the brush and trees, and setting them on fire, drove them from their hiding-places. Still did they refuse to surrender, and still maintained the conflict. Thus the carnage continued until night separated the combatants, when the few misguided savages, who had avoided the havoc and slaughter of the day, were enabled, through the darkness of the night, to make their escape.

Whilst the attack was thus waged in front of the line, the friendly Indians in General Coffee's detachment, under the command of Colonel Morgan, with Captain Russell's company of spies, were effecting much; and, no doubt, to the course pursued by them, on the opposite side, was greatly owing the facility with which the breast-work was scaled, and its possession obtained. The village stood on the margin of the river, and on that part of the peninsula most remote from the fortification. At the line were all their warriors collected. Seve ral of the Cherokees and Russell's spies having swum across, unobserved, and procured their ca noes, a considerable number passed over, entered the town, and fired it. No sooner was this discovered, than their attention was divided, and drawn to the protection of a point where they had not ap prehended an attack. Thus assailed from an unexpected quarter—a force in their rear, and another, still stronger, advancing on their front—the invading army was afforded a much easier and less hazardous opportunity of succeeding in the assault and securing the victory.

This battle gave a death-blow to their hopes; nor did they venture, afterwards, to make a stand. From their fastness in the woods they had tried their strength, agreeably to their accustomed mode of warfare; in ambuscade, had brought on the attack; and, in all, failure and disaster had been me'. None of the advantages incident on surprise, and for which the red men of our forests have been always so characterized, had they been able to obtain. The continual defeats they had received were, doubtless, the reason of their having so strongly fortified this place, where they had determined to perish or to be victorious. Few escaped the carnage. Of the killed, many by their friends were thrown into the river, whilst the battle raged; many, in endeavouring to pass it, were sunk by the steady fire of Coffee's brigade; and five hundred and fifty-seven were left dead on the ground. Among the number of the slain were three of their prophets. Decorated in a most fantastic manner—the plumage of various birds about their heads and shoulders—with savage grimaces, and horrid contortions of the body, they danced and howled their cantations to the sun. Their dependants already believed a communion with Heaven sure, which, moved by entreaty, and their offered homage, would aid them in the conflict, and give a triumph to their arms. Fear had no influence; and when they beheld our army approaching, and already scaling their line of defence, even then, far from being dispirited, hope survived, and victory was still anticipated. Monohoe, one of the most considerable of their inspired ones, and who had cheered and kept alive the broken spirit of the nation by his pretended divinations, fell, mortally wounded, by a cannon shot in the mouth, while earnestly engaged in his incantations.

Three hundred prisoners were taken, most of whom were women and children. That so few warriors should have sought and obtained safety, by appealing to the clemency of the victors, to persons acquainted with the mode of Indian warfare, will not appear a matter of surprise. It seldom happens that they extend or solicit quarter: faithless them-

selves, they place no reliance on the faith of others,
and, when overcome in battle, seek no other protection than retreat affords.   Another cause for it
may be found in a reason already given ; the attack,
by a detachment of General Cocke's division, on
the Hillabee clans, who were assailed and put to the
sword, at a moment when, having asked peace at
discretion, they were expecting it to be given.
This misfortune had alone been occasioned by a
want of concert in the divisions of our army ; but
it was past, and with it was gone, on the part of the
savages, all confidence in our integrity and humanity ; and they looked and trusted for safety now to
nothing but their own bravery.   In this contest
they maintained resistance, fighting and firing from
their covert places, long after the hope either of
success or escape was at an end, and after the proposal had been submitted to spare the further useless waste of blood. • A few, who had lain quiet,
and concealed under the cliffs, survived the severity
of the conflict, and effected their retreat under
cover of the night.

Our loss was small, when compared with that of
the enemy ; the whole estimate, including the
friendly and Cherokee Indians, was but fifty-five
killed, and one hundred and forty-six wounded. Of
the former was Major Montgomery, a brave and en-
terprising young officer, of the thirty-ninth regiment, and Lieutenants Moulton and Somerville, who
fell early in the action.

The object of the present visit being answered
the general concluded to return to Fort Williams.
Having sunk his dead in the river, to prevent their
being scalped by the savages, and made the necessary arrangements for carrying off his wounded, he

commenced his return march for the fort, and in a few days reached it in safety.*

Understanding that the enemy was imbodied, in considerable numbers, at Hoithlewalee, a town situated not far from the Hickory Ground, he was anxious to re-commence his operations as early as possible, that the advantages he had gained, and the impression he had made, might not be lost. The forces under his command, from sickness, the loss which had been sustained in the late battle, and numerous discharges given, had been too much reduced in strength, to permit him to act as efficiently as the importance of the crisis required. It was desirable, therefore, to effect a junction with the southern army as speedily as possible, that, from an increase and concentration of his numbers, greater efficiency might be had. The North Carolina troops, under the command of General Graham, an experienced officer of the revolutionary war, and those of Georgia, under Colonel Milton, were as certained to be somewhere south of the Tallapoosa, and could be at no great distance. To unite with them was an event greatly desired. He had re ceived from General Pinckney strong assurances that all complaints would be at an end, as soon as his and the southern division could unite. No time was to be lost in effecting a purpose so essential. General Jackson accordingly determined to leave his sick and wounded, and the fort, to the care and command of Brigadier Johnston, and to set out again

---

* Sinking them in the river, in preference to burying them, was adopted from the consideration, that these of our troops, who had previously fallen, had been raised, stripped, and scalped. Many of the Indians at Tohopeka were found in the clothes of those who had been killed and buried at Emuckfaw.

for the Tallapoosa. On the 7th, with all his disposable force, he commenced his march, with the double view of effecting a union with the army below, and of attacking on his route the enemy's force which were collected at Hoithlewalee. His greatest difficulty was in conveying to Colonel Milton intelligence of his intended operations. The friendly Indians, who, from their knowledge of the country, had been always selected as expresses. were with difficulty to be prevailed on now for any such undertaking. Believing their nation to be imbodied in larger numbers than any which had been yet encountered, and that, confiding in their strength, they would be better enabled to go forth, searching and spying through the surrounding country, they at once concluded that any enterprise of this kind would be attended with too great peril and danger, and the difficulty of eluding observation too much increased, for them to adventure. This circumstance prevented the arrangement of such measures as were best calculated to bring the different divisions to act in general concert. The necessity, however, of such co-operation, was too important, at this moment, not to be effected, if it were possible.

Having at length succeeded in procuring confidential messengers, Jackson addressed Colonel Milton, and advised him of his intended movement. To guard against any accident or failure that might happen, different expresses were despatched, by different routes. He informed him, that, with eight days' provisions, and a force of about two thousand men, he should, on the 7th, take up the line of march, and proceed directly for Hoithlewalee ; which he expected certainly to reach and attack on the 11th

The point of destination, owing to the rain, he was not able to reach until the 13th. This delay, unavoidable, gave the Indians an opportunity of fleeing from the threatened danger. On arriving at an inconsiderable stream which skirted the town, it was so swollen as to be rendered impassable The savages, gaining intelligence of an approach that was thus unavoidably retarded, were enabled to effect an escape by passing the river in their canoes, and gaining the opposite shore. Had Colonel Milton fortunately made a different disposition of the troops under his command, and, by guarding the southern bank of the river, co-operated with the Tennessee division, their escape would have been prevented, and the whole force, collected, would either have been destroyed or made prisoners. Although Jackson, in his letter of the 5th, had given intelligence that he would reach the enemy on the 11th; and, when prevented by high waters and rotten roads, had again notified him that he would certainly arrive and commence the attack by the morning of the 13th, and urged him to guard the south bank of the Tallapoosa, still was the request disregarded, and the savages permitted to escape. Learning they were abandoning their position, and seeking safety in flight, Jackson filed to the right, and, overtaking the rear of the fugitives, succeeded in making twenty-five prisoners. At this time, nothing was heard of Colone. Milton; but on the same day, having marched about five miles from his encampment at Fort Decatur, and approached within four of Hoithlewalee, he, the next morning, gave notice of an intention to attack the village that day; at this moment the inhabitants and warriors had fled and the town was

11*

occupied and partly destroyed by a detachment from Jackson's army, that had succeeded in passing the creek.

The Georgia army being so near at hand, was a source of some satisfaction, although the escape of the enemy had rendered their presence of less importance than it otherwise would have been. The stock of provisions, with which the march had been commenced from Fort Williams, was now nearly exhausted. Assurances, however, having been so repeatedly given, that abundant supplies would be had on uniting with the southern army, all uneasiness upon the subject was at once dispelled. Colonel Milton was immediately applied to, the situation of the army disclosed, and such aid as he could extend solicited. He returned an answer to the general's demand, observing, he had sent provisions for the friendly Indians, and would, the next day, *lend* some for the remainder of the troops; but felt himself under no obligation to furnish any. Jackson, satisfied of its being in his power to relieve him, and that this apparent unwillingness did not, and could not, proceed from any scarcity in his camp, assumed a higher ground, and, instead of asking assistance, now demanded it. He stated that his men were destitute of supplies, and that he had been apprized of it; and concluded by ordering, not requesting, him to send five thousand rations immediately, for present relief; and for himself and the forces under his command to join him at Hoithlewalee by ten o'clock the next day. "This order," he remarked, "must be obeyed without hesitation." — It was obeyed. The next day, a junction having been effected, the necessary steps were taken to biing down the provisions deposited at Fort Decatur, and, for the first time since the commencement of the Creek war, inconveniences for the want of supplies, and an apprehension of suffering, were removed.

Appearances seemed now to warrant the belief, that the war would not be of much longer continuance; the principal chiefs of the Hickory Ground tribes were coming in, making professions of friendship, and giving assurances of their being no longer disposed to continue hostilities. The general had been met, on his late march, by a flag from these clans, giving information of their disposition to be at peace. In return they received this answer:— that those of the war party, who were desirous of putting an end to the contest, and of becoming friendly, should evince their intention by retiring in the rear of the army, and settling themselves to the north of Fort Williams; that no other proof than this, of their pacific dispositions, would be received. Fourteen chiefs of these tribes had arrived, to furnish still further evidence of their desire for peace. They assured the general that their old king, Fous-hatchee, was anxious to be permitted to visit him in person, and was then on his way, with his followers, to settle above Fort Williams, agreeably to the information he had received by the flag which had lately returned to him.

Detachments were scouring the country to the south, with orders to break up any collection of the enemy that might be heard of in convenient distance. The main body was prepared to advance to the junction of the two rivers, where, until now, it had been expected the Indians would make a last

and desperate stand * Every thing was in readiness to proceed on the march, when it was an
nounced to the geneial, that Colonel Milton's brigade, which had lately united with him, was not in
a situation to move. During the previous night
some of his wagon horses having strayed off, persons had been sent in pursuit, and were expected
shortly to return with them; when, it was reported,
he would be ready to take up the line of march.
To Jackson, this was a reason for delaying the operations of an army, which as yet he had never
learned, and by which he had never been influenced.
IIe had, indeed, been frequently made to halt,
though from very different causes; from murmurs,
discontents and starvation in his camp. He replied
to the colonel's want of preparation, by telling him,
that, in the progress of his own difficulties, he had
discovered a very excellent mode of expediting
wagons, even without horses; and that, if he would
detail him twenty men from his brigade, for every
wagon deficient in horses, he would guaranty their
safe arrival at their place of destination. Rather
than subject his men to such drudgery, he preferred
to dismount some of his dragoons, and thus avoided
the necessity of halting the army until his lost
teams should arrive.

The army continued its march without gaining

---

* The Hickory Ground, or that part of the Creek nation lying
in the forks, near where the Coosa and Tallapoosa unite, was
called by the Iudians *Holy Ground*, from a tradition and belief
prevailing among them, that it never had been pressed by the
foot of a white man. Acting under the influence of their prophets, and a religious fanaticism, it was supposed they would
make greater exertions to defend this than any other portion of
their country

intelligence of any imbodied forces of the enemy ;
and, without the happening of any thing of importance, reached old Toulossee Fort, on the Coosa
river, not far from the confluence, at which another
was determined to be erected, to be called Fort
Jackson, after the commanding general. Here the
rivers approach within one hundred poles of each
other, and, again diverging, unite six miles below.
At this place, the chiefs of the different tribes were
daily arriving, and offering to submit on any terms.
They all concurred in their statements, that those
of the hostile party, who were still opposed to asking for peace, had fled from the nation, and sought
refuge along the coast of Florida, and in Pensacola.
General Jackson renewed the declaration, that
.hey could find safety in no other way than by re-
oairing to the section of the country pointed out
to them, where they might be quiet and free of any
sort of molestation.

To put their friendly professions, which he dis-
trusted, at once to the test, he directed them to
bring Weatherford to his camp, confined, that he
might be dealt with as he deserved. He was one
of the first chiefs of the nation, and had been a
principal actor in the butchery at Fort Mimms.
Justice well demanded retaliation against him.
Learning from the chiefs what had been required
of them by Jackson, he was prevailed upon. as perhaps the safer course, to proceed to his camp, and
make a voluntary surrender of himself. Having
reached it without being known, and obtained ad
mission to the general's quarters, he fearlessly stood
in his presence, and told him he was Weatherford,
the chief who had commanded at Fort Mimms. and
that, desiring peace for himself and for his peop.e

he had come to ask it. Somewhat surprised that one
who so richly merited punishment should so sternly
demand the protection which had been extended to
others, Jackson replied to him, that he was astonished he should venture to appear in his presence; that
he was not ignorant of his having been at Fort
Mimms, nor of his inhuman conduct there, for which
he well deserved to die. "I had directed," con
tinued he, "that you should be brought to me con
fined; and had you appeared in this way, I should
have known how to have treated you." Weatherford replied, "I am in your power—do with me as
you please. I am a soldier; I have done the white
people all the harm I could; I have fought them,
and fought them bravely; if I had an army, I would
yet fight, and contend to the last: but I have none;
my people are all gone. I can now do no more
than weep over the misfortunes of my nation."
Pleased at the firm and high-toned manner of this
child of the forest, Jackson informed him, that he
did not solicit him to lay down his arms, or to become peaceable: "The terms on which your nation
can be saved. and peace restored, have already been
disclosed: in this way, and none other, can you
obtain safety." If, however, he desired still to
continue the war, and felt himself prepared to meet
the consequences, although he was then completely
in his power, no advantage should be taken of that
circumstance; that he was at perfect liberty to retire, and unite himself with the war party, if he
pleased; but, when taken, he should know how to
treat him, for then his life should pay the forfeit of
his crimes; if this were not desired, he might re
main where he was, and should be protected

Nothing dismayed, Weatherford answered, that he desired peace, that his nation might, in some measure, be relieved from their sufferings; that, independent of other misfortunes, growing out of a state of war, their cattle and grain were all wasted and destroyed, and their women and children left destitute of provisions. "But," continued he, "I may be well addressed in such language now. There was a time when I had a choice, and could have answered you: I have none now—even hope has ended. Once I could animate my warriors to battle; but I cannot animate the dead. My war riors can no longer hear my voice: their bones are at Talladega, Tallushatchee, Emuckfaw, and Tohopeka. I have not surrendered myself thoughtlessly. Whilst there were chances of success, never left my post, nor supplicated peace. But my people are gone, and I now ask it for my nation, and for myself. On the miseries and misfortunes brought upon my country, I look back with deepest sorrow, and wish to avert still greater calamities. If I had been left to contend with the Georgia army, I would have raised my corn on one bank of the river, and fought them on the other; but your people have destroyed my nation. You are a brave man: I rely upon your generosity. You will exact no terms of a conquered people but such as they should accede to: whatever they may be, it would now be madness and folly to oppose. If they are opposed, you shall find me amongst the sternest enforcers of obedience. Those who would still hold out can be influenced only by a mean spirit of revenge; and to this they must not, and shall not, sacrifice the last remnant of their country You have told our nation where we might go, and be safe. This is good talk, and they ought to listen to it. They shall listen to it."

The bold independence of his conduct left no doubt of the sincerity of his professions, and full confidence was reposed in his declarations. The peace party became reconciled to him, and consented to bury all previous animosities. In a few days afterwards, having obtained permission, he set out from camp, accompanied by a small party, to search through the forest for his followers and friends, and persuade them to give up a contest in which hope seemed to be at an end, that, by timely submission. they might save their nation from further disasters

The present was a favourable moment for preventing all further opposition. The enemy, alarmed, were dispersed, and fleeing in different directions. To keep alive their apprehensions, and prevent their recovering from the fears with which they were now agitated, was of the utmost importance. If time were given them to form further resolutions, some plan of operation might be concerted; and, although it might not be productive of any alarming consequences, yet it might have a tendency to lengthen out the war, and involve those deluded people in still greater wretchedness. Detachments, sufficiently strong, were accordingly ordered out, to range through the country, prevent their collecting at any point, and to scatter and destroy any who might be found concerting offensive operations. Wherever they directed their course. submission, and an anxious desire for peace. were manifested by the natives. Those who were still resolved upon a continuance of the war, and trusted for relief to the aid which by their British allies was promised. and which they had been for some time expecting, had retired out of the country, towards the sea coast, not doubting but the assistance looked for would shortly arrive, enable them to re-commence hostilities with better hopes of success, and regain their country, which they now considered as lost. Many of the chiefs and warriors, looking to the defeats they had continually met with in all their battles, viewing it as impracticable, with any expectation of better fortune, to resist the numerous forces that were collecting, and anxious to have spared to them a portion of their country, determined to discard all ideas of further resistance, and to throw themselves for safety on the mercy of their conquerors. To this end, the chief men, from the different tribes, were daily arriving, and asking for peace, on condition only that their lives might be spared.

General Jackson was not ignorant of the faithlessness of these people, and how little confidence was to be reposed in the professions of an enemy, who, prompted by fear, could be controlled only by its influence. He well knew they had been too severely chastised for their promises to be relied on, and too much injured not to feel a disposition to renew the conflict with the first flattering hope that dawned. Too many difficulties had been encountered, and too many dangers past, in bringing those savages to a sense of duty, to leave them now with no better security than mere professions. Some arrangement was necessary to be made that should ensure certainty. None seemed better calculated for these ends, than what had been already announced; that those disposed to throw away the war club, and renew their friendly relations with the United States, should retire in the rear of the

12

advance of the army, and occupy the country about
the fort he had established, and to the east of the
Coosa. The effect of such an arrangement he calculated would be this: that, by the line of posts
already established, he would be able to cut them
off from any communication with Florida; while,
by being placed in that part of the nation inhabited
by the friendly Indians, whose fidelity was not
doubted, the earliest intelligence would be had of
their hostile intentions, should any be manifested.
The conditions proposed were most cheerfully accepted; and the different tribes forthwith sat out to
occupy a portion of their country, which alone
seemed to promise them protection and safety
Proctor, the chief of the Owewoha war towns, to
whom this promised security from danger had first
been made, was reported to be still at home, and to
have abandoned all intention of removing, in consequence of permission extended by the United
States' agent to the Creeks, for him and his warriors to remain where they then were residing. On
receiving this information, the general despatched
a messenger with information to him, that whether
he or the agent were to be obeyed, was for him to
decide; but that he should treat as enemies all
who did not immediately retire to the section of
country which he had pointed out. The chief of
Owewoha found no difficulty in deciding the question, and without delay prepared to retire where he
had been previously ordered.

Lieutenant-Colonel Gibson, who had been sent
out with a detachment of seven hundred and fifty
men, returned, and reported, that he had proceeded
a considerable distance down the Alabama River,
and had destroyed several towns of the war party,

sut could gain no intelligence of a force being any
where collected.

By the establishment of Fort Jackson, a line of
posts was now formed from Tennessee and from
Georgia to the Alabama River. The subdued
spirit of the Indians clearly manifesting that they
were sincere in their desire for peace, nothing
remained to be done but to organize the different
garrisons in such a manner, that, should any hostile
intention be hereafter discovered, it might be sup-
pressed. What final steps should be taken, and
what plans adopted, for permanent security, were
to be deferred for the arrival of Major-General
Pinckney, who, being in the neighbourhood, would,
it was expected, on the next day reach Fort Jack
son.

On the 20th General Pinckney arrived, and assumed the command of the army. The course
pursued by Jackson, towards satisfying the Indians,
that to be peaceable was all that was required,
meeting his approbation, and understanding that
the chiefs and warriors of the nation were retiring
with their families, whither they had been directed
he was satisfied hostilities must cease. Independent of their professions, heretofore, much of the
property plundered at Fort Mimms, and along the
frontiers, having been brought in, no doubt was entertained but all further national opposition would
be withdrawn. There being no necessity, therefore, for maintaining an army longer in the field,
orders were issued, on the 21st, for the troops from
Tennessee to be marched home and discharged,
taking care, on the route, to leave a sufficient force
for garrisoning the posts already established.

To troops who had been engaged in such fa

tiguing marches, who had been so often exposed to hardships, and who had, by their exertions in the cause of their country, brought the war to a successful termination, and severely chastised the savages, it was a pleasure to retire to their homes from the scenes of wretchedness they had witnessed, and from a contest where nothing remained to be done.

Whilst these arrangements were progressing, the friendly Creeks were engaged in destroying their fugitive countrymen, with the most unrelenting rigour. To have been at the destruction of Fort Mimms, was a ground of accusation against a warrior, which at once placed him without the pale of mercy. They affected to view this unprovoked offence with sentiments of deeper inveteracy than did even our own troops. Meeting a small party who were on their way to camp, to submit themselves on the terms that had been previously offered, and understanding they had accompanied Weatherford in his attack on this fort, they arrested their progress, and immediately put them to death.

In two hours after receiving General's Pinckney's order, the western troops commenced their return march, and reached Fort Williams on the evening of the 24th. Immediate measures were adopted for carrying into effect what had been ordered; to send out detachments to disperse any collections of the war party that might be found on the route, and within striking distance.

The East Tennessee troops, having a longer period to serve, were, on that account, selected to garrison the different posts. General Doherty was directed to detail from his brigade seven hun

ired and twenty-five men, for the defence of those
points, with a view to an open communication being
preserved with Fort Jackson, and to secure more
effectually a peace, which was, perhaps, not so securely established as that any precautionary measure should be omitted.

General Jackson, being about to separate from
his army, did not omit to disclose to them the high
sense he entertained of their conduct, and how well
they had deserved of their country. "Within a few
days," said he, "you have annihilated the power of
a nation that for twenty years has been the dis-
turber of your peace."

The army proceeded on its march, and, crossing
Tennessee River, in safety reached Camp Blount.
near Fayetteville, where they were discharged
from further service. Johnston, who had previously
fallen in, had destroyed some of the enemy's towns
but had learned nothing of a force being any where
imbodied along the route he had taken.

On parting from his troops, the general again
brought before them the recollection he retained of
their faithful and gallant conduct, and the patience
with which they had borne the privations and hardships of war. On his return, wherever he passed,
the plaudits of the people were liberally bestowed.
The ardent and extraordinary zeal he had manifested in the service of his country, the difficulties
ne had surmounted, with the favourable termination
which, by his exertions, had been given to a contest
that had kept alive the anxieties and fears of the
frontier settlers, excited a general feeling of gratitude and admiration: all were ready to evince the
high sense they entertained of the success with
which every effort had been crowned, and with one
12 *

accord united in manifesting their confidence and
respect for him, who, by his zealous exertions, able
management, and fidelity to the cause in which he
had embarked, had so greatly contributed to the
safety, the happiness, and quiet of the country

CHAPTER VI.

*Jackson is appointed a major-general in the service of the United
States.—Is directed to open a negotiation with the Indians.—
Speech of the Big Warrior, a chief of the nation.—Concludes
a treaty with the Creek Indians.—His views against Pensacola
and Florida.—General Armstrong's letter.—The Spanish
governor is called on for an explanation of his conduct.—His
answer, and General Jackson's reply.—The adjutant-general is
despatched to Tennessee to raise volunteers.—Jackson sets out
for Mobile.—Orders the Tennessee troops to advance to his assistance*

THE celerity with which an army was raised,
and pushed into the heart of the enemy's country,
saved the frontiers. The misfortunes of the misguided Indians may be regretted, but cannot be
considered as unmerited. Great forbearance had
been exercised towards them, as many a parent can
testify, whose heart bleeds at the remembrance of
a child that fell a victim to their sanguinary cruelty.
Cold Water, on the Tennessee, was long a den for
these savages, whence they made inroads, and, by
their inhuman butcheries, kept the frontier inhabitants in perpetual alarm. A descent was made on
this settlement, as early as 1787. which resulted in
its destruction. For causes already detailed, their
towns were once more, in the winter of 1813, assailed, and destroyed.

The war in which the United States were engaged with Great Britain, afforded the Indians,
as they believed, a safe opportunity again to satiate
their angry passions. In addition to former animosities, British emissaries had been among them,
to excite them to opposition. Arms and ammunition
from Pensacola having been liberally furnished.
and a belief strongly inspired, that the American

could be driven off, and the lands possessed by them
regained by the Indians, they at once resolved
upon the course they would pursue. The dreadfu'
and cruel assault made on the settlement of Tensaw
was the first intelligence afforded of the lengths to
which they had determined to proceed. The in-
security of the frontiers requiring that efficient
measures should be taken to defend them, it was
high time for the government to abandon the course
of moderation they had hitherto practised towards
those tribes. The legislature of Tennessee, at the
period of this murderous assault, being in session,
with a promptitude highly honourable, called out the
forces of the state, without giving to the genera
government information of the threatened danger
To protect an extensive country, by erecting garri
sons, and relying on them for defence, did not ap
pear to Jackson a course at all likely to assure its
object. Placed in command, and called on to act
he determined, with the troops he could collect or
so sudden an emergency, to carry the war to their
very doors; and, by giving them employment at
home, to divert them from their plans, and force
them at once into measures of defence. Urging
the contractors, therefore, to be diligent in the dis
charge of their duties, and to forward supplies with
all possible haste, he took his position at Fort Strother, directly in the enemy's country. The battle
of Talladega, which shortly afterwards followed,
gave a severe check to those sanguine hopes they
had indulged, induced them to believe they were
contending with a different kind of people from
what they had expected, and should have convinced
them, too, that the promised safety, offered by their
prophets, through their spells and incantations, was
mere nonsense; yet so deluded were they, and so

confidently confiding in the supernatural powers of their inspired men, that they were ready to attribute a want of success to circumstances over which their prophets could, in future, claim control. when it was discovered that the prophets themselves did not escape that fatality which attended their warriors in battle, they began to think, either that they had never been commissioned, or that the *Great Spirit*, for some unknown cause, had withdrawn his confidence.

The death of Monohoe, at the battle of Tohopeka, is strongly illustrative of the infatuations under which these deluded and ignorant people laboured. They did not at all doubt, but, as their prophets had told them, that, having been spoiled of their hunting-grounds, they were again to re-occupy them through the aid of a new people, who from beyond the great waters were coming to assist in their recovery. A confidence in what those soothsayers disclosed would, also, they believed, produce the effect of protecting and guarding them from wounds and injury when engaged in battle. All those marvellous stories were confided in; but when, at this battle, one of their principal prophets fell, and by a cannon shot received in the mouth, they adopted the opinion, that the character of the wound was a judgment on his false pretensions, and forthwith departed from those visions of faith which previously they had entertained.

The uniform and uninterrupted successes obtained over them, in all our battles, may impress the minds, not only of these, but of the Indians generally within our limits, with a higher reverence for the character of our nation than they have hitherto been disposed to entertain: give protection to our

citizens, and ensure that security to the govern
ment, which the mildness it has practised, and the
tribute it has constantly given them for their *peace*,
has, heretofore, never been able to effect; they
will tend to destroy the influence held over them
by other nations, and bring them to a conviction
that the United States is the only power whose
hostility they should fear, or whose friendship they
should prize.

It was now eight months since General Jackson
had left home, to arrest the progress of the Indian
war; during most of which time he had been in a
situation of bodily infirmity that would have directed a prudent man to his bed, instead of advancing
to the field.   During this period, he had never seen
his family, or been absent from the army, except to
visit the posts in his rear, and arrange with his contractors some certain plan to guard against a future
failure of supplies.   His health was still delicate
and rendered retirement essential to its restoration
but his uniformly successful conduct, and the es
sential advantages he had produced, had brought
him too conspicuously before the public for any
other sentiment to be indulged than that he should
be placed, with an important command, in the service of the United States.

The resignation of General Hampton enabled the
government, in a short time, to afford him an evidence of the respect it entertained for his services and character.   A notice of his appointment as
brigadier and brevet major-general, was forwarded,
on the 22d of May, from the war department.
General Harrison having, about this time, for
some cause, become dissatisfied with the conduct
of the government towards him, refused to be long-

er considered one of her military actors ; to supply this vacancy, a commission of major-general was forwarded to Jackson, which reached him the day after the notification of his first appointment, and before he had been enabled to return an answer whether or not it would be accepted. The important services which he had rendered, added to the rank which, under the authority of his state, he had held, might well induce a doubt whether the appointment first conferred was at all complimentary, or one which, in justice to his own character. he could have accepted. Whatever of objection there might or could have arisen, on this subject, was removed by the subsequent appointment of major-general, made on the resignation of Harrison. and which was accepted.

The contest with the Indians being ended, the first object of the government was, to enter into some definitive arrangement, which should deprive of success any effort that might hereafter be made by other powers, to enlist those savages in their wars. None was so well calculated to answer this end, as that of restricting their limits, so as to cut off their communication with British and Spanish agents in East and West Florida.

No treaty of friendship or of boundary had yet been entered into by the government with the Indians: they remained a conquered people, and within the limits, and subject to the regulations and restrictions, which had been prescribed in March, by General Jackson, when he retired from their country. He was now called upon to act in a different character, and to negotiate the terms upon which an amicable understanding should be restored between the United States and these conquered

Indians. But for the government to proceed on the principles of reciprocal treaty stipulations, was, in reference to the expensive war imposed on them, and the unprovoked manner in which it had been begun, not to be expected. Those Indians had broken without cause the treaty they had made, outraged humanity, and murdered our unoffending citizens. Under such circumstances, by the peace now to be concluded, to negotiate with, and, as heretofore, recognise them as an independent and sovereign people, comported not with propriety, nor was demanded by any of the ties of moral duty. General Jackson, therefore, was directed to treat with them as a conquered people, and to prescribe, not negotiate, the conditions of a peace. Colonel Hawkins, who, for a considerable time past, had been the agent to this nation, was also associated in the mission. With the western people the appointment was not acceptable, and much solicitude was felt from an apprehension of his influence and weight of character amongst the Indians; and a fear that his partialities and sympathies might incline him too much to their interest.

On the 10th of July, the general, with a small retinue, reached the Alabama; and on the 10th of August, after some difficulty, succeeded in procuring the execution of a treaty, in which the Indians pledged themselves no more to listen to foreign emissaries,—to hold no communication with British or Spanish garrisons; guarantied to the United States the right of erecting military posts in heir country, and a free navigation of all their waters. They stipulated also, that they would suffer no agent or trader to pass among them, or hold any kind of commerce or intercourse with their nation. unless specially deriving his authority from the president of the United States.

The stipulations and exactions of this treaty were in conformity with instructions issued from the department of war, and differs in expression from what has been usually contained in instruments of a similar kind. It breathes the language of demand, not of contract and agreement; and hence has General Jackson been censured for the manner after which the negotiation was concluded. The course, however, which was pursued, is readily justified by the expressions of the order under which he acted, and which prevented the exercise of discretion. General Armstrong, who at that time was in the cabinet, and spoke the sentiments of the president, in a letter addressed to Jackson on the 24th of March, uses the following remarks:—"It has occurred to me, that the proposed treaty with the Creeks should take a form altogether military, and be in the nature of a *capitulation;* in which case the whole authority of making and concluding the terms will be in you exclusively, as commanding general." Accompanying this were instructions formally drawn up, and which were to constitute the basis on which the negotiation was to rest.*

---

* In the instructions which issued from the department of war, as the basis on which this treaty was to be concluded, it is enjoined by the secretary to exact,

" 1st. An indemnification for expenses incurred by the United States in prosecuting the war, by such cession of land as may be deemed an equivalent for said expenses.

" 2d. A stipulation on their part, that they will cease all intercourse with any Spanish port, garrison or town; and that they will not admit amongst them any agent or trader who does not derive his authority or license from the United States.

" 3d. An acknowledgment of the right of the United States to

To settle the boundary, defining the extent of territory to be secured to the Creeks, and that which they would be required to surrender, was attended with difficulty, from the intrigues of the Cherokee nation, who sought to obtain such an acknowledgment of their lines as would give them a considerable portion of country never attached to their claim. The Creeks had heretofore permitted this tribe to extend its settlements as low down the Coosa as the mouth of Wills' Creek. It was insisted now, in private council, that, as they were about to surrender their country lying on the Tennessee River, they should, previously to signing the treaty, acknowledge the extension of the Cherokee boundary, which would secure their claim against that of the United States. The only reply obtained from the Creeks was in truly Indian spirit, that they could not lie by admitting what did not in reality exist.

Sufficient territory was acquired on the south to give security to the Mobile settlements, and to the western borders of Georgia, which had often felt the stroke of Indian vengeance and cruelty; while at the same time was effected the important purpose of separating them from the Seminole tribes, and our unfriendly neighbours in Florida. To the frontiers of Tennessee an assurance of safety was given by the settlements which would be afforded on the

open roads through their territory, and also to establish such military posts and trading houses as may be deemed necessary and proper; and

" 4th. A surrender of the prophets, and other instigators of the war, to be held subject to the order of the president.

" You are authorized, in conjunction with Colonel Hawkins, to open and conclude a treaty of peace with the hostile Creeks as soon as they shall express a desire to put an end to the war.

" J. ARMSTRONG

lands stretching along the Tennessee River : whilst
the extent of the cession, west of the Coosa. woulo
effectually cut off all communication with the Chick-
asaws and Choctaws, and prevent, in future, the
passage of those emissaries from the north-western
tribes, who, during the present war, had so industriously fomented the discontents of the Creeks,
and excited them to hostility.

Before being finally acted upon, the treaty had
been fully debated in council, and the voice of tho
nation pronounced against it.　Jackson had already
submitted the views of his government. and now
met them in council, to learn their determination.
He was answered by the Big Warrior, a friendly
chief, and one of the first orators of the nation,
who declared the reluctance that was felt, in yielding to the demand, from a conviction of the consequences involved, and the distresses it must inevita
bly bring upon them.　The firm and dignified eloquence of this untutored orator evinced a nerve
and force of expression, that might not have passed
unnoticed, had it been exhibited before a more
highly polished assembly : the conclusion of his
speech is given, for the satisfaction of such as can
mark the bold display of savage genius, and admire
it when discovered.　Having unfolded the causes
that produced the war, told of their sufferings, and
admitted that they had been preserved alone by the
army which had hastened to their assistance, he
urged, that, although in justice it might be required
of them to defray, by a transfer of a portion of
their country, the expenses incurred, yet was the
demand premature, because the war was not ended,
nor the war party conquered ; they had only fled
away, and might yet return　He portrayed the

habits of the Indians, and how seriously they would be affected by the surrender required of them, and thus concluded:

"The president, our father, advises us to honesty and fairness, and promises that justice shall be done: I hope and trust it will be! I made this war, which has proved so fatal to my country, that the treaty entered into a long time ago, with father Washington, might not be broken. To his friendly arm I hold fast. I will never break that bright chain of friendship we made together, and which bound us to stand to the United States. He was a father to the Muscoga people; and not only to them but to all the people beneath the sun. His talk I now hold in my hand. There sits the agent he sent among us. Never has he broken the treaty He has lived with us a long time. He has seen our children born, who now have children. By his direction cloth was wove, and clothes were made, and spread through, our country; but the *Red Sticks* came, and destroyed all,—we have none now Hard is our situation, and you ought to consider it. I state what all the nation knows: nothing will I keep secret.

"There stands the Little Warrior. While we were seeking to give satisfaction for the murders that had been committed, he proved a mischief-maker; he went to the British on the lakes; he came back, and brought a package to the frontiers, which increased the murders here. This conduct has already made the war party to suffer greatly; but, although almost destroyed, they will not yet open their eyes, but are still led away by the British at Pensacola. Not so with us: we were rational, and had our senses—we yet are so In the war of the revolution, our father beyond the waters encouraged us to join him, and we did so We had no sense then. The promises he made were never kept. We were young and foolish. and fought with him. The British can no more persuade us to do wrong: they have deceived us once, and can deceive us no more. You are two great people. If you go to war, we will have no concern in it; for we are not able to fight. We wish to be at peace with every nation. If they offer me arms, I will say to them, You put me in danger, to war against a people born in our own land. They shall never force us into danger. You shall never see that our chiefs are boys in council, who will be forced to do any thing. I talk thus, knowing that father Washington advised us never to interfere in wars. He told us that those in peace were the happiest people. He told us that, if an enemy attacked him, he had warriors enough, and did not wish his red children to help him. If the British advise us to any thing, I will tell you— not hide it from you. If they say we must fight, I will tell them, No!"

The war party being not entirely subdued, was but a pretext to avoid the demands which were made; presuming that, if the council could break up, without any thing being definitely done, they might, in part, or perhaps altogether, avoid what was now required of them; but the inflexibility of the person with whom they were treating evinced to them, that, however just and well founded might be their objections, the policy under which he acted was too clearly defined, for any abandonment of his demands to be at all calculated upon. Shelocta, one of their chiefs, who had united with our troops

13*

at the commencement of the war; who had march
ed and fought with them in all their battles; and
had attached to himself strongly the confidence of
the commanding general, now addressed him. He
told him of the regard he had ever felt for his
white brothers, and with what zeal he had exerted
himself to preserve peace, and keep in friendship
with them; when his efforts had failed, he had
taken up arms against his own country, and fought
against his own people; that he was not opposed to
yielding the lands lying on the Alabama, which
would answer the purpose of cutting off any intercourse with the Spaniards; but the country west
of the Coosa he wished to be preserved to the nation.* To effect this, he appealed to the feelings
of Jackson; told him of the dangers they had passed together; and of his faithfulness to him in the
trying scenes through which they had gone.

There were, indeed, none whose voice ought
sooner to have been heard than Shelocta's. None
had rendered greater services, and none had been
more faithful. He had claims, growing out of his
fidelity, that few others had: but his wishes were
so much at variance with what Jackson considered
the interest of his country required, that he was
answered without hesitation. "You know," said
he, "that the portion of country, which you desire
to retain, is that through which the intruders and
mischief-makers from the lakes reached you, and
urged your nation to those acts of violence, that
have involved your people in wretchedness, and
your country in ruin. Through it leads the path
Tecumseh trod, when he came to visit you: that

---

* This country west of the Coosa now forms the respectable
state of Alabama, admitted into the Union in the year 1819

path must be stopped. Until this be done, your nation cannot expect happiness, nor mine security. I have already told you the reasons for demanding it: they are such as ought not—cannot be departed from. This evening must determine whether or not you are disposed to become friendly. By rejecting the treaty you will show that you are the enemies of the United States—enemies even to yourselves." He admitted it to be true, that the war was not ended, yet that this was an additional reason why the cession should be made; that then a line would be drawn, by which his soldiers would be enabled to know their friends. "When our armies," continued he, "came here, the hostile party had even stripped you of your country: we retook it, and now offer to restore it;—theirs we propose to retain. Those who are disposed to give effect to the treaty will sign it They will be within our territory; will be protected and fed: and no enemy of theirs, or ours, shall molest them. Those who are opposed to it shall have permission to retire to Pensacola. Here is the paper: take it, and show the president who are his friends. Consult, and this evening let me know who will assent to it, and who will not. I do not wish, nor will I attempt, to force any of you—act as you think proper.'

They proceeded to deliberate and re-examine the course they should pursue, which terminated in their assent to the treaty, and the extension of those advantages that had been insisted on.*

---

* It was agreed that the line should begin where the Cherokee southern boundary crossed the Coosa, to run down that river to Woetum-ka, or the Big Falls, and thence eastwardly to Georgia. East and north of this line, containing upwards of one hundred and fifty thousand square miles, remained to the Indians.

In the progress of this business another *difficul-*
ty arose : the council insisted that there should be
inserted in the treaty a reservation of certain tracts
of land ; one for Colonel Hawkins, in consideration
of his fidelity to them as an agent; and another to
Jackson, because of the gratitude felt towards him
for his exertions in their favour against the hostile
Creeks. To this the general objected. It was
personal as it regarded himself, and he was unwil
ling to appear in any point of view, where suspicion
could attach, that he had availed himself of his
official situation to obtain personal benefits ; fully
aware that, however the facts might be, selfish considerations would be imputed as an inducement to
what was done. He refused, therefore, to have it
inserted ; and for the further reason, that the instructions, under which he was acting, required i
to be a capitulation, not a treaty. The next morning, however, when they met in council to sign the
instrument, the chiefs delivered to the general a
paper, expressing a wish, and disclosing their reasons, that a reservation to himself, Colonel Hawkins, and Mayfield, who, being made a prisoner in
his youth, had always resided in the nation, might
be assented to ; and requested it to be forwarded
on and made known to the government. Jackson
consented to do so, and to recommend its adoption
but that the reservation they had thought proper to
request, if assented to, he would accept of on no
other terms than that their father the president
should dispose of it, and apply the proceeds to those
of the nation on whom distress and poverty had
been brought by the war. Mr. Madison subsequently brought this matter to the consideration of
the senate of the United States, and, in recom-

mending its adoption, highly complimented the delicacy with which the proposition had been met by General Jackson: it was, however never acted on and assented to by the senate.

Every attention had been given, during the negotiation, to impress on the minds of the savages the necessity of remaining at peace and in friendship with the United States ; for, although all apprehensions of their acting in concert as a nation had subsided, yet it was important to leave their minds favourably impressed, lest the wandering fugitives, scattered in considerable numbers towards the Escambia and Pensacola, might, by continuing hostile, associate with them others of their countrymen, attach themselves to the British, should they appear in the south, aid them by their numbers, and pilot them through the country.

This retreat of the savages in East Florida had been always looked upon as a place whence the United States might apprehend serious difficulties. There was no doubt but that the British, through this channel. with the aid of the governor, had protected the Indians, and supplied them with arms and ammunition; nor was it less certain but that, through the art and address practised on them, they had been excited to the outrages which had been heretofore committed. It was an idea entertained by Jackson, at the commencement of the Creek war, that the proper mode of procedure would be to push his army through the nation; gain this den, where vegetated so many evils; and, by holding it, effectually cut off their intercourse, and means of encouraging the war: but the unexpected difficulties, which we have before noticed, had repressed the execution of his well-digested plans, and left him to pursue his course as circumstances, and the obstacles met with, would permit. The assistance which, during the war, had been continually afforded these people from Pensacola, induced him once more to turn his attention there ; and he now strongly urged on government the propriety of breaking down this strong hold, whence so many evils had flowed, and whence greater ones were to be expected. His mind, actively engaged, while employed in settling all differences at Fort Jackson, had sought, through every channel that could afford it, information as to the designs of the British against the southern parts of the Union. The idea had been prevalent, and generally indulged, that, as soon as the severity of approaching winter should put a stop to active operations on the Canada frontier, with all their disposable force, they would turn their attention against the southern states, and there attempt to gain some decisive advantage. New Orleans, with one consent, was fixed upon as the point that most probably would be assailed. The circumstance of there being so many persons there, who have never been supposed to entertain any well founded regard for the country in which they lived, together with a large black population, which, it was feared, might be excited to insurrection and massacre, through the persuasions of an enemy who seemed to disregard all the laws of humanity, were reasons which strongly led to this conclusion.

General Jackson, having understood that that comfort and aid, which heretofore had been so liberally extended, was still afforded by the Spanish governor to the hostile Indians, who had fled from the ravages of the Creek war, cherished the belief that his conduct was such as deservedly to exclude

aim from that protection to which, under other circumstances, he would be entitled, from the professed neutrality of Spain. At all events, if the improper acts of the Spanish agents would not authorize the American government openly to redress
herself for the unprovoked injuries she had received
they were such, he believed, as would justify any
course which had for its object to arrest their continuance, and give safety to the country. In this point
of view he had already considered it, when, on his
way to the treaty at Fort Jackson, he received certain
nformation, that about three hundred English troops
aad landed; were fortifying themselves at the
mouth of the Apalachicola ; and were endeavouring
to excite the Indians to war. No time was lost in
giving the government notice of what was passing,
and of the course most advisable to be pursued.
The advantages to be secured from the possession
of Pensacola he had frequently urged.

On the 17th of January, 1815, after the British
army had been repulsed at New Orleans, and the descent on Florida almost forgotten, through the post
office department, dated at Washington city, the 18th
of July, 1814, he received the following letter from
General Armstrong, then secretary at war:

"The case you put is a very strong one : and, if
all the circumstances stated by you unite, the conclusion is irresistible. It becomes our duty to carry
our arms where we find our enemies. It is believed,
and I am so directed by the president to say, that
there is a disposition, on the part of the Spanish government, not to break with the United States, nor to
encourage any conduct, on the part of her subordinate agents, having a tendency to such rupture. We
must, therefore, in this case, be careful to ascertain

facts, and even to distinguish what, on the part of the Spanish authorities, may be the effect of menace and compulsion, or of their choice and policy. The result of this inquiry must govern. If they admit, feed, arm, and co-operate with the British and hostile Indians, we must strike on the broad princi ple of self-preservation :—under other and differen' circumstances, we must forbear."

That the state of things, here suggested by the secretary, did actually exist ; that the British were favourably received, and every assistance necessary to a continuance of hostilities extended to the Indians, the government had been already apprized, by the frequent communications made to them on the subject.

On arriving at Fort Jackson, his first attention had been directed to a subject which he believed to be of greater importance than making Indian treaties—to establish a plan by which to be constantly advised, during his stay, of those schemes that were in agitation in the south: believing that every passing event might be readily obtained through the Indians, who could go among the British without in the least exciting suspicion, he had required Colonel Hawkins to procure some, who were confidential, and might be certainly relied on, to proceed to the Apalachicola, and towards the coast, and to return as early as they could obtain correct information of the strength, views, and situation of the enemy. In about fifteen days they came back, confirming the statement previously received, that a considerable English force had arrived, and was then in the Bay of St. Rose ; that muskets and ammunition had been given to the Indians, and runners despatched to the different tribes to invite them to the coast.

Satisfied that such permissions, by a neutral power, were too grievous to be borne, he immediately addressed a letter to the governor of Pensacola, apprizing him of the information received; and inquiring why and wherefore it happened that every protection and assistance was furnished the enemies of the United States, within his territory; requesting him to state whether or not the facts were as they had been represented; and demanding to have surrendered to him such of the chiefs of the hostile Indians as were with him. "I rely," continued he, "on the existing friendship of Spain her treaties, and that neutrality which she should observe, as authority for the demand I make." The governor's answer, which shortly afterwards was received, evinced nothing of a conciliatory temper, and left no hope of procuring any other redress than that which might be obtained through some different channel. It was a subject, however, which required to be managed with considerable caution. Spain and the United States were at peace. To reduce any portion of her territory, and take possession of it, in exclusion of her authority, might be construed such an aggression as to induce her into the war. On the other hand, for her, with open arms, to receive our enemies, and permit them to make every preparation, within her ports, for invading our country, were outrages too monstrous to be borne, and, in the opinion of Jackson, required to be remedied, let the consequences in prospective be what they might. Although these things had been earnestly pressed upon the consideration of the war department, no answer to his repeated solicitations on the subject had been received. On his own responsibility, to advance to the execution of a measure, which involved so much, when his government was, and had for some time been, in possession of all the circumstances, was risking too much. Yet, were it delayed longer, every day might give to Pensacola additional strength, and increase the danger attendant on its reduction Undetermined, under considerations like these, he resolved upon another expedient—to despatch a messenger, to lay open to the governor the ground of his complaint—obtain from him a declaration of nis intention, as regarded the course he meant to adopt, and pursue—and ascertain whether he de-signed to make subsisting treaties, between the two nations, the basis of his conduct, or to pursue a con-cealed course, which, under the garb of pretended friendship, cloaked all the realities of war. The propriety of delivering up the hostile Indians, who were with him, to atone for the violation of existing treaties, and the rights of humanity, and the mur-ders they had committed, was again solicited.

A reply was not concluded on by the governor for some time, owing to a very considerable doubt that harassed his mind, whether it would not be more proper to return it without an answer, " in im-'tation of the conduct of General Flournoy, who, acting in conformity to the orders of Mr. Madison, heretofore had omitted to answer a despatch of his." But, having considered the matter quite deliberate-ly, he at length came to the conclusion, to wave the example set him by the president, and, in replying to act in obedience to those " high and generous feelings peculiar to the Spanish character."

To the demand made upon him, that the hostile

Indians should be delivered up. he denied that they were with him, " at that time," or that he could, on the ground of hospitality, refuse them assistance at a moment when their distresses were so great ; nor could he surrender them, without acting in open violation of the laws of nations,—laws, to which his sovereign had ever strictly adhered. and of which he had already afforded the United States abundant evidence, in omitting to demand of them " the traitors, insurgents, incendiaries, and assassins of his cniefs, namely, Guiterres, Toledo, and many others, whom the American government protected and maintained in committing hostilities, in fomenting the revolution, and in lighting up the flames of discord in the internal provinces of the kingdom of Mexico."

To the inquiry, why the English had been suffered to land in his province arms and ammunition, with a view to encouraging the Indians in their acts of hostility, he proceeded with his same " national characteristic," and demanded to be informed if the United States were ignorant, that, at the conquest of Florida, there was a treaty between Great Britain and the Creek Indians, and whether they did not know that it still existed between Spain and those tribes. " But," continued he, " turn your eyes to the island of Barrataria, and you will there perceive that. within the very territory of the United States, p - rates are sheltered, with the manifest design of committing hostilities by sea upon the merchant vessels of Spain ; and with such scandalous notori ety, that the cargoes of our vessels, taken by them have been publicly sold in Louisiana."

It is difficult to discover how, or by what system of logic, it was, that Governor Manrequez was ena

bled to trace any kind of analogy between the
United States affording to a few of the patriots of
South America an asylum from the persecutions
that were threatened to be imposed on them by
Spanish tyranny, and his permitting, within the limits of Florida, comfort, aid, and assistance to be
given the savages, that they might be enabled to
indulge in cruelty towards us. Nor can it be perceived how it was, that the piracies of Lafite and
his party, at Barrataria, and the successful smug-
gling which brought their plundered wealth into
port, in open defiance of our laws, could operate as
a sufficient pretext for giving protection to an enemy entering the territory of Spain, and continuing
there, with the avowed intention of waging war
against a power, with which she not only professed
to be in friendship, but was bound by treaty to be
so, and at the very time, too, when she claimed to
be neutral. Nor can we see the force of the argument, because England had a treaty with the Creek
Indians, which afterwards devolved on Spain, that
the agents of his Catholic majesty were, in consequence, justified in protecting the savages in their
murders, or assisting covertly, as they did, in the
war against us : how the conclusions were arrived
at, the governor can decide at some moment, when,
relieved from those high and honourable feelings
" peculiar to the Spanish character," Reason may
re-assert her empire over him, and point out the
manner in which he was enabled to produce his
strange results.

The governor, however, had evinced rather too
high a state of feeling, and taken his ground without suffering his reflections to go to their full ex
tent. He had placed arms in the hands of the sav

ages " for the purposes of self-defence " many of
them were hastening to him ; more were yet expected. The British had already landed a partial
force, and a greater one was shortly looked for.
Against this expected strength, added to what his
own resources could supply, he believed an Ameri
can general would not venture to advance. These
considerations had led him to assume a lofty tone ;
to arraign the conduct of the United States, in ex-
tinguishing the Indian title on the Alabama ; to ac-
cuse them of violating their treaties, and to point
out the danger to which the restoration of peace in
Europe might expose them. As yet he was ignorant
of the energy of the man already near his borders,
and who, to march against and break down his fancied security, did not desire to be ordered, but only
to be apprized by his country that it might be done.
Jackson, in no wise pleased with the boldness of his
remarks, proceeded again to address him, and exhibited fully the grounds of complaint in behalf of his
country, and in a style at least as courtly as his own.

"Were I clothed," he remarks, " with diplomatic
powers, for the purpose of discussing the topics em-
braced in the wide range of injuries, of which you
complain, and which have long since been adjusted,
I could easily demonstrate that the United States
have been always faithful to their treaties, steadfast
in their friendships, nor have ever claimed any thing
that was not warranted by justice. They have en
dured many insults from the governors and other
officers of Spain, which, if sanctioned by their sovereign, would have amounted to acts of hostility,
without any previous declaration on the subject.
They have excited the savages to war, and afford
ed them the means of waging it : the property of
14*

our citizens has been captured at sea, and, if com
·pensation has not been refused, it has at least been
withheld.   But, as no such powers have been dele-
gated to me, I shall not assume them, but leave
them to the representatives of our respective governments.

"I have the honour of being intrusted with the
command of this district.   Charged with its protection, and the safety of its citizens, I feel my ability
to discharge the task, and trust your excellency
will always find me ready and willing to go forward, in the performance of that duty, whenever
circumstances shall render it necessary.   I agree
with you, perfectly, that candour and polite language should, at·all times, characterize the communications between the officers of friendly sovereign-
ties ; and I assert, without the fear of contradiction,
that my former letters were couched in terms the
most respectful and unexceptionable.   I only requested, and did 'not demand, as you have assert-
ed, that the ringleaders of the Creek confederacy
night be delivered to me, who had taken refuge in
your town, and who had violated all laws, moral
civil and divine.   This I had a right to do, from the
treaty which I sent you, and which I now again en-
close, with a request that you will change your
translation ; believing, as I do, that your former
one was wrong, and has deceived you.   What
kind of an answer you returned, a reference
to your letter will explain.   The whole of it breathed nothing but hostility, grounded upon assumed
facts, and false charges, and entirely evading the
nquiries that had been made.

"I can but express my astonishment at your pro
test against the cession on the Alabama, lying

within the acknowledged limits and jurisdiction of
the United States, and which has been ratified, in
due form, by the principal chiefs and warriors of
the nation. But my astonishment subsides, when
on comparison, I find it upon a par with the rest of
your letter and conduct; taken together, they afford a sufficient justification for any course on my
part, or consequences that may ensue to yourself.
My government will protect every inch of her territory, her citizens, and their property, from insult
and depredation, regardless of the political revolu-
tions of Europe; and, although she has been at all
times sedulous to preserve a good understanding
with all the world, yet she has sacred rights, that
cannot be trampled upon with impunity. Spain
had better look to her own intestine commotions
before she walks forth in that majesty of strength
and power, which you threaten to draw down upon
the United States.

"Your excellency has been candid enough to admit your having supplied the Indians with arms.
In addition to this, I have learned that a British
flag has been seen flying on one of your forts. All
this is done whilst you are pretending to be neutral. You cannot be surprised, then, but on the
contrary will provide a fort in your town for my
soldiers and Indians, should I take it in my head to
pay you a visit.

"In future I beg you to withhold your insulting
charges against my government for one more inclined to listen to slander than I am; nor consider
me any more as a diplomatic character, unless so
proclaimed to you from the mouths of my cannon."

Captain Gordon, who had been despatched to
Pensacola, had been enabled, during the time he

remained there, to obtain much more satisfactory information than it had pleased the governor to communicate. Appearances completely developed the schemes which were in agitation, and convinced him that active operations were intended to be commenced somewhere in the lower country. On his return, he reported to the general, that he had seen from one hundred and fifty to two hundred officers and soldiers, a park of artillery, and about five hundred Indians, under the drill of British officers, armed with new muskets, and dressed in the English uniform.

Jackson directly brought to the view of the government the information he had received, and again urged his favourite scheme, the reduction of Pensacola. "How long," he observed, "will the United States pocket the reproach and open insults of Spain? It is alone by a manly and dignified course, that we can secure respect from other nations, and peace to our own. Temporizing policy is not only a disgrace, but a curse to any nation. It is a fact that a British captain of marines is, and has for some time past been, engaged in drilling and organizing the fugitive Creeks, under the eye of the governor; endeavouring, by his influence and presents, to draw to his standard as well the peaceable as the hostile Indians. If permission had been given me to march against this place twenty days ago, I would, ere this, have planted there the *American Eagle*; now, we must trust alone to our valour, and to the justice of our cause. But my present resources are so limited—a sickly climate, as well as an enemy, to contend with, and without the means of transportation to change the position of my army, that, resting on the bravery of my little phalanx, I can only hope for success."

Many difficulties were presented ; and, although anxious to carry into execution a purpose which seemed so strongly warranted by necessity, he saw that he was wholly without the power of moving, even should he be directed to do so. Acting in a remote corner of the Union, which was thinly inhabited, the credit of his government was inadequate to procure those things essential to his operations , while the poverty of his quarter-master's department presented but a dreary prospect for reliance. But, to have all things in a state of readiness for action, when the time should arrive to authorize it, he was directing his attention in the way most likely to effect it. The warriors of the different tribes of Indians were ordered to be marshalled, and taken into the pay of the government. He addressed himself to the governors of Tennessee, Louisiana, and the Mississippi territory, and pressed them to be vigilant in the discharge of their duties. Information, he said, had reached him, which rendered it necessary that all the forces allotted for the defence of the seventh military district, should be held in a state of perfect readiness, to march at any notice, and to any point they might be required "Dark and heavy clouds hover around us. The energy and patriotism of the citizens of your states must dispel them. Our rights, our liberties, and free constitution, are threatened. This noble patrimony of our fathers must be defended with the best blood of our country : to do this, you must hasten to carry into effect the requisition of the secretary of war, and call forth your troops without delay."

On the day after completing his business at **Fort Jackson**, he had departed for Mobile, to place the country in a proper state of defence. The third regiment, a part of the forty-fourth and thirty-ninth, constituted, entirely, the regular forces he could at this time command. Many reasons concurred to render it necessary that a sufficient force should be brought into the field as early as possible. His appeals to the people of Tennessee had been generally crowned with success ; and he had no doubt but that he might yet obtain from them such assistance as would enable him, should any unexpected emergency arise, to act at least defensively, until the states already applied to should have their quotas ready for .he field. On the citizens of Louisiana and Mississippi he believed he might securely rely, and that their ardour would readily excite them to contend with an enemy at their very doors. Well knowing the delay incident to bringing militia requisitions expeditiously forth, and fearing that some circumstance might arise to jeopardize the safety of the country, before the constituted authorities could act, he had already despatched his adjutant-general, Colonel Butler, to Tennessee, with orders to raise volunteers, and have them in readiness to advance to his relief, whenever it should be required.

Every day's intelligence tended to confirm the belief that a descent would be made,—most probably on New Orleans. Anonymous letters, secretly forwarded from Pensacola, and which found their way into the American camp, suggested this as the point of assault ; and many of the settlers were apprized by their friends of the fears entertained for their safety, and entreated to retire from the gathering storm, which, it was feared, would soon burst.

and entirely involve the lower country in ruin. Where certainly to expect attack, was as yet unknown. The part of the country bordering on Mobile might be assailed; yet, taking into consideration that no very decided advantages could be obtained there, it was an event not much to be apprehended. The necessity, however, of being prepared at all points, so far as the means of defence could be procured, was at once obvious; for, as the general, in one of his letters, remarked, "there was no telling where or when the spoiler might come."

There were now too many reasons to expect an early visit, and too many causes to apprehend danger, not to desire that an efficient force might be within convenient distance. Colonel Butler was accordingly written to, and ordered to hasten forward, with the volunteers he could procure, and to join him without delay. The order reached him at Nashville, on the 9th of September, and he forthwith engaged actively in its execution. He directly applied to General Coffee, to advance with the mounted troops he could collect. A general order was at the same time issued, bringing to view the dangers that threatened, and soliciting those who were disposed to aid in protecting their country from invasion, to unite with him at Fayetteville, by the 28th instant. The appeal was not ineffectual; although the scene of operation was at least four hundred miles from the point of rendezvous, the call was promptly obeyed; and two thousand able-bodied men, well supplied with rifles and muskets, appeared at the appointed time to march with the brave General Coffee, who had so often led his troops to victory and honour. Colonel Butler, with his usual industry, hastened to press forward the militia, under the command of Colonel Lowery which had been heretofore required for garrisoning the posts in the Indian country ; whilst Captains Baker and Butler, with the regular forces lately enlisted, advanced from Nashville to Mobile, where they arrived in fourteen days. By proper exertions every thing was presently in complete readiness : and the troops collected for the campaign, in high spirits, set out for the point to which danger, duty, and their country called them.

CHAPTER VII.

*Colonel Nicholls arrives at Pensacola, and issues a proclamation to
the southern inhabitants.—Attack on Fort Bowyer, and loss of
the Hermes.--Jackson determines to reduce Pensacola.—Demands
of the governor an explanation of his conduct ; his answer —
Enters and takes possession of Pensacola.—Conduct and perfidy
of the governor. Destruction, by the British, of Barrancas
Fort.—Our troops return to Mobile.—Expedition against the
Indians.—General Winchester arrives, and Jackson proceeds to
take command of New Orleans.*

WHETHER a force were thus concentrating to act
defensively against an invading enemy, or were intended to reduce the rallying point of the Indians
and British in the Spanish territory, whence they
had it in their power to make sudden inroads on
any part of our coast, as yet all was conjecture.
It was a trait in Jackson's character to lock closely
in his bosom all his determinations : it was only to
a few, on whom he reposed with unlimited confidence, that the least intimation was at any time giv-
en of his intentions.   The idea could scarcely be
entertained, that, at this time, any hostility was
meditated against Pensacola.

It was impossible he should remain long in doubt,
as to the course best calculated to assure defence,
or to the ulterior objects of the enemy.   Colonel
Nicholls, with a small squadron of his Britannic
majesty's ships, had arrived the latter part of August, and taken up his head-quarters with Governor
Manrequez.   He was an Irishman, sent in advance
by his royal master to sow dissensions among our
people, and to draw around his standard the male-
15

contents and traitors of the country. His proclama
tion, issued to the western and southern inhabitants,
full of well-turned periods, false statements and
high-sounding promises, it was hoped, would lead
them to a belief, that the government under which
they lived was forging for them chains ; that it had
declared war against a power, the freest, the happiest, the most moral and religious on earth. He
stated, that he was at the head of a force amply sufficient to reinstate them in those liberties and en-
joyments, of which they had been bereaved, by the
designs of "a contemptible few." That such as
were disposed to imbrue their hands in the blood
of their countrymen, might not quietly rest, doubting of the assurances proffered them, he concluded
by tendering, as security for all he had said and
promised, "the sacred honour of a British officer."
Perhaps he could have vouchsafed nothing that the
American people would not have sooner relied on
it was a pledge, in which past experience told them
they could not in safety confide. To them it was
a matter of surprise, that a country, from which
they had learned all they had ever known or felt of
oppression, should come to make them freer than
they were ; or that, groaning themselves under a
load of taxes, from which there was scarcely a hope
of being ever relieved, they should come, with such
apparent compassion, and great benevolence, to
take away the burdens of those whom they despised, and on whom, for forty years, they had heaped
nothing but reproach.

He had waited about two weeks, that his proc
lamation might take effectual hold, and prepare the
inhabitants to open their bosoms to receive him,
when this delivering hero aided by his Indian and

Spanish allies, set out to ascertain the effect it had wrought. His first visit was to Fort Bowyer, situated on the extreme end of a narrow neck of land, about eighteen miles below the head of Mobile Bay; the entrance of which it commanded. With the loss of one of his ships and an eye, he had the mortification to learn, that he had been addressing an incorrigible race, who could be neither duped, flattered, nor forced into submission.

Fort Bowyer had been heretofore abandoned: and, until the arrival of General Jackson in this section of the country, was indeed ill calculated for serious resistance. On perceiving its importance, he immediately caused it to be placed in the best possible state of defence. So effectual was its situation in a military point of view, commanding the passes of those rivers which discharged themselves into the bay, that it was with him a matter of surprise it had not been more regarded by the United States, and even better attended to by our enemies.

Major Lawrence had the honour to command this spot, the gallant defence of which has given it celebrity, and raised him to an elevated stand in the estimation of his country. That at Pensacola plans of operation were digesting, which had for their object an invasion of our coast somewhere, was a fact to which Lawrence was not a stranger. A disposition to have his little fortress in such a state of readiness, as would place it in his power, should that be their object, to make a brave defence, had prompted him to the most vigorous exertions. His whole strength was but one hundred and thirty men. By this Spartan band was evinced a confidence in each other, and an unshaken resolution which left their brave commander no room to ap prehend dishonour to his flag, even should defeat result.

The 12th of September determined all doubt of the object which the British had in view. The sen tinels brought intelligence that a considerable force, consisting of Indians, marines, and Spaniards, had landed ; and the same day two brigs and sloops hove in sight of the fort, and anchored.

The next day a demonstration was made, by those who had been landed, to bring on the attack ; but a fire from the fort forced them from their position, and compelled them to retire about two miles whence, attempting to throw up fortifications, they were again made to retreat.

Early on the morning of the 15th, the signals, passing from the ships to the shore, led Lawrence to believe an assault was intended, and would short-ly be made. At half after four o'clock in the even-ing, every thing being arranged, the Hermes, in the van, commanded by Sir W. H. Percy, and the other vessels close in the rear, anchored within musket-shot fire of the fort. From her near posi-tion, supported by the Carron, and brigs Sophia and Anaconda, mounting in all ninety guns, she open-ed a broadside. Colonel Nicholls and Captain Woodbine, at the head of their detachment, com-menced a simultaneous attack by land, with a twelve pound howitzer, at point blank distance ; but from their sand bank fortifications they were so quickly driven as to be unable to produce the slight est injury.

The action raged with considerable violence From the fort and ships was pouring a continual fire The Hermes, having, at length, received a shot through her cable, was driven from her anchorage, and floated with the stream. In this situation she was thrown into a position, where, for twenty minutes, she received a severely raking fire, which did her considerable damage. In her disabled condition, it was no longer possible to control her, whence, drifting with the current, she ran upon a sand bank about seven hundred yards distant, where, until late at night, she remained exposed to the guns of the fort. Her commander, finding it impracticable to be relieved, set her on fire, and abandoned her. She continued burning until eleven o'clock, when she blew up. The Carron, next in advance to the Hermes, was considerably injured, and with difficulty went out to sea.

It may be worth while, to show the difference in battle between the two combatants, to mark the conduct of British and American officers, under cir cumstances precisely similar. Whilst the battle raged, the flag of the van ship was carried away, and at this moment she had ceased to fire. What had caused its disappearance none could tell: no other opinion was, or could with propriety be entertained, than that it had been hauled down, with a view to yield the contest, and surrender. Influenced by this belief, Lawrence, with a generosity characteristic of our officers, immediately desisted from further firing. The appearance of a new flag, and a broadside from the ship next the Hermes, was the first intelligence received that such was not the fact and the contest again raged with renewed violence. It was but a few minutes, however, before the flag-staff of the fort was also carried away ; but, so far from pursuing the same generous course that had just been witnessed, the zeal of the enemy was increased, and the assault more furiously urged

15 *

At this moment, Nicholls and Woodbine, at the head of their embattled train, perceiving what had happened,—that our "star-spangled banner" had sunk,—at once presuming all danger to have subsided, made a most courageous sally from their strong hold; and, pushing towards their vanquished foes, were already calculating on a rich harvest of plunder: but a well-directed fire checked their progress, dissipated their expectations, and drove them back, with a rapidity even surpassing the celerity of their advance.

From the bay, the attack was waged with a force of six hundred men, and ninety guns, of larger caliber than any opposed to them; whilst upwards of four hundred Indians and other troops were on the shore, in rear of the fort. Lawrence's strength was scarcely a tenth of the enemy's. His fort, hastily prepared for defence, with not more than twenty guns, was ill calculated for stubborn resistance: most of these were of small caliber, whilst many, from being badly mounted, were capable of rendering no essential service in the action: yet, with this great inequality, he well maintained the honour of his flag, and compelled the enemy, resting in full confidence of success, to retire, with the loss of their best ship, and two hundred and thirty men killed and wounded; whilst the loss sustained by the Americans did not exceed ten.

Very different were the feelings of the leaders of this expedition, from what had been entertained on setting out from Pensacola, where every thing had been prepared for giving success to their plans, and where scarcely a doubt was entertained of the result. Numerous benefits were expected to arise from a victory, not in expectancy, but already looked to as certain—as an event that could not fail. From it, greater facility would be given to their operations ; while Mobile, it was expected, would fall, of course. This being effected, independent of the strong hold already possessed in Florida, an additional advantage would be acquired, calculated to prevent all intercourse with New Orleans from this section of the country, enable them more easily to procure supplies, and, having obtained their expected re-enforcements, piloted and aided by the Indians to proceed across to the Mississippi, and cut off all communication with the western states. To render the blow effectual was important; that, by impressing at once the inhabitants with an idea of their prowess, the proclamations already disseminated might claim a stronger influence on doubting minds. The force employed was calculated to attain these wished-for results. While the attack should be furiously waged by the ships from the bay and the forces on the shore, the yells of three or four hundred savages in the rear, it was calculated, would strike the defenders of this fort with such panic, as to make them, at the first onset, throw down their arms, and clamour for mercy. This belief was so sanguinely indulged, that obstinate resistance had never been thought of. Different was the reality—instead of triumph, they had met defeat. The only badges of victory they could present their friends, with whom, but a few days before, with flattering promises they had parted, were shattered hulks, that could scarcely keep above the water, and decks covered with the dead and wounded.

The three vessels that retired from the contest were considerably injured, and with difficulty pro ceeded to sea, leaving Nicholls and Woodbine, with their friends and allies, on the shore, to make good their retreat, as discretion should permit.

On the morning of the 14th, Jackson, fearing, from every thing he had learned, that an attack would be made, had set out in a boat from Mobile, to visit Fort Bowyer, examine its situation, and have such arrangements made as would add to its strength, and obtain that security which its re-establishment had been designed to effect. He had proceeded down the bay, and arrived within a few miles of the place, when he met an express from Lawrence, bringing intelligence of the enemy's arrival, and requesting that assistance might be immediately sent to his relief. The general, hastening back, late at night, despatched a brig, with eighty men, under the command of Captain Laval. Not being able to reach his point of destination until the next day, and finding every place of entrance blocked up by the besiegers, he ran his brig to the land, determined to remain there until night, when, under cover of its darkness, he hoped to succeed in throwing into the fort himself and the re-enforcement under his command. The battle, however, having in the mean time commenced, presented new difficulties, and restrained the execution of his purpose, unless he should venture to encounter greater hazard than prudence seemed to sanction. The Hermes, or. being driven from her anchorage, had, at the time of her explosion, floated and grounded in a direction, which, from the position she occupied, placed her immediately in the rear of the fort. This circumstance well accounted for the mistake with which he was impressed, and led Captain Laval to suppose that his brave countrymen had all perished. Believing they would now attempt to carry his vessel, he set sail for Mobile, and report ed to the commanding general the loss. Jackson declared it was impossible ; that he had heard the explosion, and was convinced it was on the water, and not on the shore. Perhaps his great anxiety, more than any reality, had constituted this refined difference in sound. If, however, the disasters were as it was reported, his own situation being thereby rendered precarious, something was necessary to be done to repair the loss, and regain a place for many reasons too important to be yielded. His principal fears were, lest the strength of the enemy should be greatly increased, before his expected re-enforcements could arrive, who would be enabled to extend his inroads, and paralyze the zeal of the country. It was not a time for much deliberation as to the course most advisable to be pursued. He determined, at all hazard, to retake the fort; and to that end a general order was issued for the departure of the troops. Every thing was nearly in readiness, when a despatch arrived from Lawrence, proclaiming the pleasing intelligence, that all was safe, and that the enemy, vanquished, had retired.

The conduct displayed by the officers and soldiers of this garrison is worthy to be remembered. With troops wholly undisciplined, and against an enemy ten times more numerous than themselves, so fearlessly contending, is. a circumstance so flattering, that we cannot wish our country better, than that the future defenders of her honour, and violated rights, may be as sensibly alive to their duty.

The British had now retired to Pensacola, to dispose of their wounded, refit their vessels, and be ready, as soon as circumstances would permit, to

make, perhaps, another descent, on some less guard
ed point.   So long as this, their only place of refuge
on the southern coast, was left in their possession,
it was impossible to calculate on the consequences
that might arise.   The commanding general entertained a suspicion that this was merely a feint, and
that the object of their wishes, so soon as a suffi
cient force should arrive, would be New Orleans.
At this place he believed his presence most material, to guard the important passes to the city, and
to concert some plan of general defence.

Jackson and his government had ever viewed
this subject in very different lights : they were not
willing to risk any act which might involve the possibility of a contest with Spain, for the sake of removing what they considered an unimportant grievance : he thought it of more serious import, and
did not believe it could afford even a pretext for
rupture between the two nations.   If Spain, through
her agents, gave assistance to our enemy, or encouraged a power with whom she was at peace to
be thus annoyed, she deserved to be placed herself
on the list of enemies, and treated accordingly.   If,
however, Great Britain, taking advantage of the
defenceless state of her province, claimed to have
free egress, in exclusion of her authority, she could
have no well-founded cause of complaint against
the injured power, which should claim to hold it
until such time as, by bringing a sufficient force,
she might be in a situation to support her neutra'
ity, and enforce obedience.   Upon either ground,
he believed it might be sufficiently justified.   There
was one, however, on which it could be placed,
where he well knew nothing could result, beyond
his own injury ; and on this issue he was willing to

trust it. If any complaint should be made, his gov
ernment, having never extended to him any author
ity, might, with propriety, disavow the act ; and,
by exposing him to punishment, would offer an
atonement for the outrage ; and Spain, in justice,
could demand no more. The attack on Mobile
Point was a confirmation of his previous conjectures,
as to the views of the enemy ; and from that moment he determined to advance and reduce Pensa
cola, throw a sufficient force into the Barrancas,
hold them until the principles of right and neutrality were better respected, and rest the measure on
his own responsibility. Believing this the only
course calculated to assure ultimate security, he
aecided with firmness, and resolved to execute his
intentions so soon as General Coffee should arrive,
with the volunteers, from Tennessee.

It was now generally accredited, tnat a very
considerable force would shortly sail from England,
destined to act against some part of the United
States ; where, none could tell ; rumour fixed its
destination for New Orleans. The importance of
this place was well known to our enemy ; it was
the key to the entire commerce of the western
country. Had a descent been made a few months
before, it might have been taken with all imagina-
ble ease ; but the British had indulged the belief,
that they could possess it at any time, without difficulty. England and France having ended their
long-pending controversy, it was presumed that
the French people of Louisiana, alive to the great
benefits the English had conferred upon their na
tive country,—benefits that prostrated her liberty
and which have sunk her, perhaps, in eternal sla-
very,—would, on their first appearance, hail their de

liverers, and become their vassals.   Independent of this, they imagined the black population would af ford them the means of exciting insurrection, and deluging the country in blood.   Whether a resort to this kind of warfare, which involves the deepest wretchedness, and equally exposes to ruin the in- nocent as the guilty,—the female as the soldier,— should be sanctioned by a nation professing a high sense of moral feeling ; or whether a nation that adopts such a system merits countenance from the civilized world, are questions on which we should not fear the decision even of an Englishman, could he but divest himself of that animosity which, from .nfancy, he learns to entertain for the Americans.

The expected re-enforcements were announced. General Coffee with his brigade had arrived at the Cut-off, no* far from Fort St. Stephens, on the Mo- bile river.   In addition to the force with which he commenced his march, he had been strengthened by the arrival of others, who had overtaken him at this place ; so that his whole number was now about twenty-eight hundred.   To make the necessary ar- rangements for an immediate march, General Jack- son, on the 26th day of October, repaired to Coffee's camp.   A dependence on himself to further the objects of the government, and the cause of the country, had been his constant lot from the com- mencement of his military career ; and a similar resort, or failure to the enterprise, was now to be assayed.   Money was wanted—the quarter-masters were destitute of funds, and the government credit was insufficient to procure the necessary means to change the position of an army : thus situated, with his own limited funds, and loans effected on his responsibility, he succeeded in carrying his plans into effect, and in hastening his army to the place of its destination.

The difficulty of subsisting cavalry on the route rendered it necessary that part of the brigade should proceed on foot. Although they had volunteered in the service as mounted men, and expected that no different disposition would be made of them, yet they cheerfully acquiesced in the order: and one thousand, abandoning their horses to subsist as they could on the reeds that grew along the river bottoms, prepared to commence the march. Being supplied with rations for the trip, on the 2d day of November the line of march was taken up, and Pensacola was reached on the 6th. The British and Spaniards had obtained intelligence of their approach and intended attack; and every thing was in readiness to dispute their passage to the town. The forts were garrisoned, and prepared for resistance; batteries formed in the principal streets; and the British vessels moored within the bay, and so disposed as to command the main entrances which led into Pensacola.

The American army, consisting of the greater part of Coffee's brigade, the regulars, and a few Indians, in all about three thousand men, had arrived within a mile and a half of this rallying point for our enemies, and formed their encampment. Before any final step was taken, the general concluded to make a further application to the governor, and to learn of him what course at the present moment he would make it necessary for him to pursue. To take possession of Pensacola, and dislodge the British, was indispensable: to do it under such circumstances, however, as should impress the minds of the Spaniards with a conviction, that the invasion of their territory was a measure resorted to from necessity, not choice, and from no disposition to violate their neutral rights, was believed to be essential. It was rendered the more so, on the part of Jackson, because a measure of his own, and not directed by his government. Previously, he determined once more to try the effect of negotiation, that he might ascertain correctly how far the governor felt disposed to preserve a good understanding between the two governments.

Major Piere, of the forty-fourth regiment, was accordingly despatched with a flag, to disclose the objects intended to be attained by the visit, and to require that the different forts, Barrancas, St. Rose, and St. Michael, should be immediately surrendered, to be garrisoned by the United States, until Spain, by furnishing a sufficient force, might be able to protect the province, and preserve unimpaired her neutral character. He was charged by the general with a candid statement of his views, and instructed to require of the governor a decisive declaration of the course intended.

This mission experienced no very favourable result. Major Piere, on approaching St. Michael's, was fired on, and compelled to return. Whether this were done by the Spaniards themselves, or by their allies and friends, was not a material inquiry. The Spanish flag was displayed on the fort, and under it the outrage was committed; though it was a fact well ascertained, that, until the day before, the British flag had been also associated: this, on the arrival of Jackson, had been removed, and the colours of Spain left, which were designed to afford protection to our enemies, and a pretext for every

injury This conduct, so unprovoked, and so directly in opposition to the principles of civilized
warfare, might have well determined the general
to abstain from further forbearance, and to proceed
immediately to the accomplishment of his views
but a consciousness, that although the reduction of
this place was required by circumstances of the
highest necessity, yet, fearing it might be blazoned
to his prejudice, and particularly that it might become a cause of national difficulty, he was prompted
to act with every possible caution. Determining,
therefore, to understand the governor fully, previously to proceeding to extremities, he again despatched
a letter to him, not by any of his officers,—for, after
such perfidy, he was unwilling, and felt it unsafe, to
risk them,—but by a Spanish corporal, who had been
taken on the route the day before. By him it was
required to be known, why the former application
which had been made, instead of being met with a
becoming spirit of conciliation, had been insulted.
In answer, he received from the governor a confir
mation of the opinion he had previously entertained.
that what had been done was not properly chargeable on him, but the English; that he had no agency
in the transaction of which he complained, and
assured him of his perfect willingness to receive
any overtures he might be pleased to make. This
was joyful tidings ; and no time was to be lost in
meeting the offer. If negotiation should place in
his hands the different fortresses, before information of it could be had by the British shipping
lying in the bay, the outward channel would be
effectually stopped, and the means of their escape
entirely cut off. Major Piere was sent off, at a
late hour of the night, to detail to the governor the

reasons which had rendered the present descent proper; and to insist on the conditions already noticed, as alone calculated to assure safety to the United States, and give protection to the provinces of Florida. He was particularly instructed to impress on his consideration the most friendly sentiments, and to assure him that a re-surrender would be made so soon as Spain, by the arrival of a sufficient force, could protect her territory from the inroads of a power at war with the United States; and which, through an opening thus afforded to a violation of the neutrality of Spain, was enabled, and had already done her considerable injury. In his communication to the governor, he remarks, "I come not as the enemy of Spain; not to make war, but to ask for peace; to demand security for my country, and that respect to which she is entitled, and must receive. My force is sufficient, and my determination taken, to prevent a future repetition of the injuries she has received. I demand, therefore, the possession of the Barrancas, and other fortifications, with all your munitions of war. If delivered peaceably, the whole will be receipted for, and become the subject of future arrangement by our respective governments; while the property, laws, and religion of your citizens shall be respected. But if taken by an appeal to arms, let the blood of your subjects be upon your own head. I will not hold myself responsible for the conduct of my enraged soldiers. One hour is given you for deliberation. when your determination must be had."

The council was called, and the propositions made considered, when the conclusion was taken tha they could not be acceded to. As soon as the answer was received. showing that nothing peaceably could be effected, Jackson resolved to urge his army forward; and, immediately commencing his march, proceeded to the accomplishment of his object, determined to effect it, in despite of consequences.

Early on the morning of the 7th, the army was in motion. To foster the idea, that he would march and reach the town along the road on which he was encamped, a detachment of five hundred men was sent forward, with orders to show themselves in this direction, that they might deceive the enemy; while, urging rapidly on, with the strength of his army, he was gaining Pensacola at a different point. This stratagem succeeded: the British, looking for his appearance where the detachment was seen, had formed their vessels across the bay, and were waiting his approach, with their guns properly bearing: nor had they an intimation to the contrary, until our troops were descried upon the beach, on the east side, where they were at too great a distance to be annoyed from the flotilla; and whence, pushing forward, they were presently in the streets, and under cover of the houses.

One company, from the third regiment of infantry, with two field pieces, formed the advance, led by Captain Laval, who fell, severely wounded, while, at the head of his command, he was charging a Spanish battery, formed in the street. The left column, composed of the regular troops, the third, thirty-ninth, and forty-fourth regiments, headed by Majors Woodruff and Pierc, formed the left. next the bay. The dismounted volunteers proceeded down the street, next the regulars: Coffee's brigade next, on their right: the Mississippi dragoons, commanded by Colonel Hinds, and the Choctaw Indians by Major Blue, of the thirty-ninth, advanced

16 *

on the extreme right of all.   Captain Laval's party,
a.though deprived of their leader, moved forward,
and, at the point of the bayonet, took possession of
the battery in their front.   So quickly was this effected, that the Spaniards had it in their power to
make but three fires, before they were forced to
abandon it.   From behind the houses and garden
fences were constant volleys of musketry discharged, until the regulars, arriving, met the Spaniards,
and drove them from their positions.   The governor, trembling for the safety of his city, and remem-
bering the declaration of the general, that, if driven
to extremes, he should not hold himself responsi-
ole for his enraged soldiers, hastened, bearing a flag
in his hand, to find the commander to stay the carnage.   He was met by Colonels Williamson and
Smith, at the head of the dismounted troops, when,
with faltering speech, he entreated that mercy might
be extended, and promised to consent to whatevei
terms might be demanded of him.

General Jackson had stopped for a moment at
the place where Laval had fallen, and was at this
time in the rear.   Receiving information that an
offer had been made by the governor to comply
with every demand heretofore made on him, he hastened to the intendant house, and obtained a confir
mation of what had previously been communicated
to him, that the town arsenals, and munitions of
war, and in fact whatever was required, should immediately be surrendered.

The British vessels remained in the bay: with
the aid of their boats, by which a nearer situation
was obtained, they continued to fire upon our troops,
as, passing along the principal streets, they could
get them in the range of their guns.   Lieutenant

Call, perceiving some of their boats attempting to occupy a more advantageous position, advanced to the beach with a single piece of artillery, where, suddenly unmasking himself from a hill, uncovered, he commenced a brisk and well-aimed fire, which drove them back to a respectful distance.

No time was lost by General Jackson in procuring what was considered by him of vital importance—the surrender of the forts. Although greater benefits would have been derived, had the success of negotiation placed them privately in his hands, without its being previously known to his enemies, yet even now their possession was not to be neglected. Their occupancy was necessary still to his own security—to check any design that might be in agitation. What was the force opposed to him, at what moment re-enforcements might appear off Pensacola, and thereby give an entire change to things, as they at present existed, were matters of which no certain idea could be formed. To possess the Barrancas was a consideration of the first importance ; still, until the town and its fortresses were secured, it was improper to withdraw the army.

Notwithstanding the assurances given by the governor, that all differences would be accommodated, and every thing insisted on agreed to, Fort St. Michael was still withheld. Captain Dinkins was ordered to take post on Mount St. Bernard, form his batteries, and reduce it. He was in a situation to act, when the commandant, Colonel Sotto, ordered his flag taken down, and the fort to be surrendered.

It is curious to observe the treachery of the Spaniards, and the unpardonable method they took to indulge their spleen. Previously to striking his co,ours, the commandant at St. Michael had asked permission to discharge his guns ; to this there could be no objection, and the indulgence was readily extended ; but, faithless and cowardly, he levelled and fired his pieces, charged with grape, at a party of dragoons and Choctaw Indians, who were at a small distance, which killed three horses and wounded two men. Such unpardonable conduct, independent of other injuries already noticed, might have justified any treatment ; the destruction of the garrison would not have been an unmerited chastisement. The general was on his way to Mount St. Bernard, where his artillery was planted, when he received intelligence of what had been done. He determined no longer to confide in persons so faithless, and whose only object seemed to deceive, but at once to make the sword the arbiter between them. His cannon were already turned towards the fort, the resolution taken to batter it down, when it was announced, by the officer he had left in command at Pensacola, that the capitulation had been agreed on, and a surrender would be made in half an hour. Sensible of the delicate situation in which he was placed, he forbore to obey that impulse their unwarrantable conduct had so justly excited and forthwith despatched Captain Dinkins to insist on an immediate delivery ; at the same time giving him directions to carry it by storm if the demand was not instantly complied with.

Difficulties promised thus peaceably to terminate The day was far spent, and the general greatly indisposed : until the next morning, no step could be taken to obtain possession of the Barrancas. On the credit of the governor's promises, made first on

r entrance into the town, the principal part of

the army had been ordered a short distance out. Understanding, at St. Bernard, that what had been required would be done, and that no further delay would be met, the general had set out to the encampment, leaving Major Piere behind, with a sufficient force to preserve every thing in safety and quietness. He was astonished, early in the morning, to learn, that the officer despatched to St. Michael, the preceding evening, had, on his arrival, been threatened to be fired on by Colonel Sotto; who, however, yielded possession, on being made to understand, that, if the fort were not delivered instantly, it would be carried forcibly, and the garrison put to the sword. A capitulation was now agreed on: Pensacola and the different fortresses were to be retained, until Spain could better maintain her authority; while the rights and privileges of her citizens were to be respected.

Every thing was in readiness, on the following day, to take possession of Barrancas Fort. The faithless conduct of yesterday had determined Jackson on the execution of his plans; nor longer to confide in Spaniards' promises, but, on reaching the place, to carry it by force, if it were not immediately surrendered. Major Piere was ordered to give the command of the city to Colonel Hayne, and report himself at camp, to accompany him on the march; previously, however, to retiring, to require of the governor to execute an authority to the commandant of the fort, to deliver it; and, in the event he would not comply immediately, to arrest him, and every public officer, and hold them as prisoners The order for its delivery had been signed, and the line of march ready to be taken up, to receive it peaceably, if the order would effect it, forcibly, if not, when a tremendous explosion in that direction, followed by two others, in quick succession, excited the apprehension that all was destroyed. To ascertain, certainly, whence the noise had proceeded, Major Gales, a volunteer aid, was despatched, with two hundred men, to obtain intelligence. He presently returned, and confirmed what had been previously apprehended, that the fort was blown up, and that the British shipping had retired from the bay.

Although repairing this place might be productive of numerous advantages, yet, as the act was unauthorized by his government, Jackson felt himself restrained from incurring any expense for the re-establishment of what had been thus treacherously destroyed. Though disappointed in the object he had in view, he believed that some of the benefits expected would result. This strong hold, which had so long given protection to the southern hostile savages, and where they had been excited to acts of cruelty, was assailed, and the Indians taught that even here safety was not to be found. The valour of his troops had impressed on the minds of the Spaniards a respect for the character of his country, which, hitherto, they had not entertained ; and the British, by being dislodged, were prevented from maturing those plans, which were to give efficacy to their future operations against the southern section of the Union : but, as the means of maintaining and defending it were destroyed, it was unnecessary to think of attempting to hold it. It was accordingly concluded to re-deliver all that had been surrendered, and retire to Fort Montgomery. Jackson was the more disposed to adopt this course from a belief that the British who had sailed out of the bay, would probably make their way to Fort Bowyer, and, with a knowledge of the principal strength of the army being away, seek to aim a blow somewhere on the Mobile. An express was immediately hastened to Colonel Sparks, who had been left in command at this place, announcing what had transpired, suggesting apprehensions for his safety, and notifying him, in the event of an attack, to endeavour to parry the danger until the regular troops should arrive to support him.

Two days after entering the town, he abandoned it. Previously to retiring, he wrote to Governor Manrequez; and, after stating to him the causes which had induced him, justifiably, as he believed, to enter his territory, he thus concluded : " As the Barrancas and the adjacent fortresses have been surrendered to and blown up by the British, contrary to the good faith I had reposed in your promises, it is out of my power to guard your neutrality, as otherwise I should have done. The enemy has retreated ; the hostile Creeks have fled for safety to the forest ; and I now retire from your town, leaving you to re-occupy your forts, and protect the rights of your citizens."

Our loss in this expedition was quite inconsiderable. The left column alone met resistance, and had fifteen or twenty wounded—none killed. It appears strange, that three heavy pieces of artillery, charged with grape and canister, and three times fired against a column advancing through a narrow street, should not have effected greater injury. Of the number wounded was Lieutenant Flournoy, a promising young man, who, having gone out as a volunteer, was, on account of his merit, promoted to a lieutenancy in the forty-fourth United

States' regiment. By a cannon shot he lost his leg. Captain Laval, being too dangerously injured to be removed, was confided by the general to the clemency of the governor of Pensacola, who humanely gave him that attention his situation required.

The Indian warriors, who had taken refuge in Pensacola, finding themselves abandoned by the British, fled across the country, and sought safety on the Appalachicola : many were afforded shelter on board the shipping, from which they were shortly afterwards landed, to prosecute the war in their own way. Jackson determined they should have no respite from danger, so long as a warlike attitude was preserved. Recent events had shown them, that neither the valour of their allies, nor their own exertions, could afford them protection. He believed it an auspicious moment to pursue them in their retreat ; increase still further their apprehensions ; and effectually cut up that misplaced confidence, which had already well nigh proved their ruin. Understanding that those who had been carried off from Pensacola had been landed on the Appalachicola, and a depot of all necessary supplies there established, Major Blue, of the thirty-ninth regiment, was sent off, on the 16th, at the head of a thousand mounted men, with orders to follow, and destroy any of their villages he might find on his route. General M'Intosh, of the Georgia militia, then in the Creek country, was apprized of the destination, and directed to co-operate, that the savages might be dispersed, before they should have it in their power to attempt hostilities against the frontiers. Having effected this object, they were ordered to repair to Mobile, to aid in its defence.

Shortly after the American army had retired, the Spaniards commenced rebuilding Forts Barrancas and St. Rose. Anxious to regain that confidence they had justly forfeited, the British offered their services to assist in the re-establishment. This offer was refused, and an answer returned by the governor, that, when assistance was in fact needed, he would make application to his friend General Jackson.

There was nothing now so much desired by the general, as to be able to depart for New Orleans where he apprehended the greatest danger. He had already effected a partial security for Mobile, and the inhabitants on its borders ; and such as he believed might be preserved, by proper vigilance in those who were left in command. He determined to set out on the 22d for the Mississippi ; and, by his exertions, seek to place the country in such a situation for defence as the means within his reach would permit. His health was still delicate which almost wholly unfitted him for the duties he had to encounter ; but his constant expectation of a large force appearing soon on the coast impelled him to action. Added to the fatigues incident to his station, he as yet had no brigadier-general in his district to relieve him of many of those duties which he had neither time nor bodily strength to meet General Winchester had been ordered to join him. He had not yet arrived, but was daily looked for. In expectation of his approach, Jackson was making every necessary arrangement for investing him with the command of Mobile, and for his own departure. Colonel Hayne, the inspector-general, was despatched to the mouth of the Mississippi, to examine whether in that direction there

were any eligible site, where, by erecting batteries, the river might be commanded, and an ascent
prevented, if through this route attempted.   General Coffee and Colonel Hinds, with the dragoons
from the territory, were ordered to march with their
commands, and take a position as convenient to
New Orleans as they could obtain a sufficiency of
forage to recruit their horses.   Every thing being
arranged, and intelligence received that General
Winchester had reached the Alabama river, Jackson, on the 22d day of November, left Mobile for
the city of New Orleans, where he arrived on the
1st of December; and where his head-quarters
were, for the present, established.

CHAPTER VIII.

Jackson's correspondence with the governor of Louisiana. -His address to the citizens.—Militia from Tennessee and Kentucky advance ; and general plans adopted for defence.—Plan for fill ing delinquencies in the army.—British shipping arrive on the coast.—Loss of the Sea Horse.—Battle on the lake, and loss of the gun-boats.—Jackson reviews the militia.—His address to them.—Detention of his flag.—Anecdote.—Expresses sent to Generals Coffee and Carroll.—Declaration of martial law at New Orleans.—The British effect a landing, and Jackson prepares to meet them.

GENERAL JACKSON was now on a new theatre : the time had arrived to call forth all his energies. His military career, from its commencement, had been obstructed, but far greater difficulties were now rising. His body worn down by exhaustion, with a mind alive to the apprehension, that the means given him would not satisfy his own wishes and the expecta tions of his country, were circumstances calculated to depress him. He was without sufficient strength or preparation to attempt successful opposition against well-trained troops, which were expected at some unprepared point.

Louisiana, he well knew, was ill supplied with arms, and contained a mixed population, of different tongues, who, perhaps, felt not a sufficient attach- ment for the soil or government, to be induced to defend them. No troops, arms or ammunition had yet descended from the states of Kentucky and Tennessee. His only reliance for defence, if sud- denly assailed, was on a few regulars, the volun- teers of General Coffee, and such troops as the state could furnish. What might be the final re

sult of things was not a matter difficult to conjec
ture. His principal fears at present were, that
Mobile might fall, the left bank of the Mississippi
be gained, all communication with the western states
cut off, and New Orleans be thus unavoidably reduced. Although agitated by such forebodings, he
breathed his fears to none. Closely locking all
apprehensions in his own breast, he appeared constantly serene, and as constantly endeavoured to
impress a general belief, that the country could and
would be defended. ·

While engaged in his operations on the Mobile,
and even while at Fort Jackson, he had kept up a
correspondence with the governor of Louisiana,
urging him to the adoption of such measures as
might give security to the state. From his information, he felt assured, that little reliance was to be
placed on the great body of the citizens; and that,
to gain any decisive advantages from their services,
it would be necessary to abandon temporizing policy, and pursue a course steady and unwavering.
Many of the inhabitants indulging a belief that
Florida would be restored to Spain, had led well
designing men astray; while Englishmen, Spaniards, and other foreigners, feeling no attachment to
the government under which they lived, were ready
to surrender it to any power. The requisition
made had been badly filled; many had refused, after being drafted, to enter the ranks. At so event-
ful a crisis, it was painful to discover so great a
want of union, and disregard of duty .

Governor Claiborne had been addressed on this
subject: "I regret," said Jackson, "to hear of the
discontents of your people: they must not exist.
Whoever is not for us, is against us. Those who are

drafted must be compelled to the ranks, or punish
ed: it is no time to balance: the country must be
defended; and he who refuses to aid, when called
on, must be treated with severity. To repel the
danger with which we are assailed, requires all
our energies, and all our exertions. With union
on our side, we shall be able to drive our invaders
back to the ocean. Summon all your energy, and
guard every avenue with confidential patroles, for
spies and traitors are swarming around. Numbers
will be flocking to your city, to gain information,
and corrupt your citizens. Every aid in your power
must be given to prevent vessels sailing with provisions. By us the enemy must not be fed. Let
none pass; for on this will depend our safety, until
we can get a competent force in the field, to oppose
attack, or to become the assailants. We have more
to dread from intestine, than open and avowed enemies: but vigilance on our side, and all will be
safe. Remember, our watch word is victory or
death. Our country must and shall be defended.
We will enjoy our liberty, or perish in the last
ditch."

He forwarded an address to the people of Louisi
ana, to excite them to a defence of their rights and
liberties, and to raise in their minds an abhorrence
of an enemy. He pointed out the course the present crisis required them to adopt, and entreated
them not to be lured from their fidelity.

" Your government, Louisianians, is engaged in
a just and honourable contest, for the security of
your individual, and her national rights. The only
country on earth, where man enjoys freedom, where
its blessings are alike extended to the poor and

rich, calls on you to protect her from the grasping usurpation of Britain:—she will not call in vain I know that every man, whose bosom beats high at the proud title of freeman, will promptly obey her voice, and rally round the eagles of his country resolved to rescue her from impending danger, or nobly to die in her defence. He who refuses to defend his rights, when called on by his government, deserves to be a slave—deserves to be punished as an enemy to his country—a friend to her foes."

The people of Louisiana were gradually turned to consider the contest, in which it was expected they were to be engaged, that they might be prepared to meet it, when necessary. Preparations for collecting, in sufficient strength, to repel an invasion, when it should be attempted, had been carried actively forward. The fiat of the secretary of war had been issued to the governors of the adjoining states; and ·Jackson had long since anxiously pressed them to hasten the execution of the order, and push their forces to the place of danger The ardour felt by the governor of Tennessee rendered any incentive unnecessary. He was well aware of the importance of activity, and had used all the authority of his office to call the requisition forth, and have it in readiness.

Governor Shelby, of Kentucky, had been no less vigilant. The necessity of despatch in military matters, and the advantages resulting from it, in his youth and more advanced age, he had learned in the field of battle. The troops from his state were immediately organized, placed under the command of Major-General Thomas, and directed to proceed down the Ohio.* It may be esteemed a circumstance of good fortune, that Shelby should have been the chief magistrate of Kentucky ; a state possessing ample resources, and which might have slumbered in inaction, but for the energy of him. He did not remain contented with a discharge merely of those duties which were imposed on him by his office ; but, feeling the ardour of his youth revived, excited his citizens, and inspirited them by his own example. The promptitude with which they crowded to the American standard, at the first danger, enduring cold, hunger, and privation, should be remembered, and entitle her citizens to the gratitude of the country.

William Carroll, who, on the promotion of Jackson in the army of the United States, had been appointed a major-general of Tennessee militia, was to command the requisition intended to be marched from the state. He had issued orders to his division, and, on the 19th of November, twenty-five hundred of the yeomanry of the state appeared at Nashville, and, in eight days, embarked on board their boats for New Orleans. To the industry of General Carroll every respect is due ; for, to his fortunate arrival, as will be seen hereafter, is to be attributed the reason that success did not result to the enemy, in his first assault, or that Louisiana escaped the impending danger.

The militia, now organized, from two states, were respectable for their numbers, and were com-

----

* When this requisition was ready to proceed, the state of the quarter-master's department was discovered to be wholly inadequate to those outfits and supplies necessary to its departure Thus situated, individuals of the state came forward, pledged their funds, and enabled it to advance

manded by officers who carried with them entire confidence In bravery, they were not surpassed ; yet they were without experience or discipline, and indifferently armed. Many had procured muskets and bayonets ; though the greater part of them had arms capable of rendering little or no service ; while some had none at all. To remedy their want of discipline was attended with some difficulty, on account of the slender means afforded for instruction, while, in boats, they were descending the river. Carroll's anxiety, however, for the respectable appearance of his troops, and a still stronger desire entertained, that they might be in a situation for immediate action, if necessity, on his arrival, should require it, led him to seize even on the limited opportunities for improvement.

Although General Jackson had obtained his successes heretofore with troops of this description, yet he was far from entertaining a belief they could be relied on for manœuvring in an open field, against troops inured to war. None knew better the point of exertion to which militia could be strained. In a letter to the secretary of war, of the 20th of November, 1814, he observes, " Permit me to suggest a plan, which, on a fair experiment, will do away or lessen the expenses, under the existing mode of calling militia forces into the field. Whenever there happens to be a deficiency in the regular force, in any particular quarter, let the government determine on the necessary number: this should be apportioned among the different states, agreeably to their respective representations, and called into service for, and during the war. The quota wanted will, in my opinion, be soon raised from premiums offered by those who are subject to militia duty, rather than be harassed by repeated drafts. In the mean time. let the present bounty, given by the government, be also continued. If this be done, I will ensure that an effective force shall soon appear in every quarter, amply sufficient for the reduction of Canada, and to drive all our enemies from our shores."

Such were the course of things, and such the plans in progress for the safety of the country, when the general reached New Orleans.

The legislature of Louisiana had for some weeks been in session; and, through the governor's communication, informed of the situation, condition and strength of the country, and of the necessity of calling all its resources into operation; but, balancing in their decisions, and uncertain of the best course to be pursued, they, as yet, had resolved upon nothing. The arrival of Jackson, however, produced a new aspect in affairs. His activity in preparation, and his reputation as a brave and skilful commander, had turned all eyes towards him, and inspired even the desponding with confidence.

The volunteer corps of the city were reviewed, and a visit, in person, made to the different forts, to ascertain their capacity for defence, and the reliance that might be had on them to repel the enemy's advance. Through the lakes large vessels could not pass: should an approach be attempted through this route, in their barges, it might be opposed by the gun-boats which guarded this passage; but if, unequal to the contest, they should be captured, it would give timely information of a descent, which might be resisted at their landing, and before any opportunity could be had of executing fully their designs. Up the Mississippi, however, was looked upon as the most probable pass,

through which might be made an attempt to reach
the city; and here were in progress suitable preparations for defence.

We have already noticed, that Colonel Hayne
had been despatched from Mobile with directions to
view the Mississippi near its mouth, and report if
any advantageous position could be found for the
erection of batteries; and whether the re-establishment of the old fort at the Balize would command
the river, in a way to prevent its being ascended.
That it could not be relied on for this purpose, the
opinions of military men had already declared
General Jackson was disposed to respect the decisions of those who were entitled to confidence,
yet, in matters of great importance, it formed no
part of his creed to attach his faith to the statements of any, where, the object being within his
reach, it was in his power to look to the fact, and
satisfy himself. Trusting implicitly in Colonel
Hayne as a military man, he had despatched him
thither to examine how far it was practicable to
obstruct and secure this channel. His report was
confirmatory of the previous information received,
that it was incapable, from its situation, of effecting
any such object.

Fort St. Philip was now resorted to as the lowest
point on the river where the erection of a fortification could be at all serviceable. The general had
returned to New Orleans on the 9th, from a visit
to this place, which he had ordered to be repaired.
The commanding officer was directed to remove
every combustible material without the fort; to
have two additional platforms immediately raised;
and the embrasures so enlarged that the ordnance
might have the greatest possible sweep upon their

circles, and be brought to bear on any object within their range, that might approach either up or down the river. At a small distance below, the Mississippi, changing its course, left a neck of land, in the bend, covered with timber, which obstructed the view. From this point down to where old Fort Bourbon stood, on the west side, the growth along the bank was ordered to be cut away, that the shot from St. Philip, ranging across this point of land, might reach an approaching vessel before she should be unmasked from behind it. On the site of Bourbon was to be thrown up a strong work, defended by five twenty-four pounders, which, with the fort above, would be calculated to expose an enemy to a cross fire, for half a mile. A mile above St. Philip was to be established a work, which, in conjunction with the others, would effectually command the river for two miles. At Terre au Bœuf, and at the English Turn, twelve miles below the city, were also to be taken measures for defence; where it was expected by Jackson, with his flying artillery and fire ships, he would be able certainly to arrest the enemy's advance. This system of defence, properly established, he believed, would ensure security from any attack in this direction. Fort St. Philip, with the auxiliary batteries above and below it, would so concentrate their fires, that an enemy could never pass without suffering greatly, and, perhaps, being so shattered that they would fall an easy prey to those defences which were still higher up the river. The essential difficulty was to have them speedily finished. On returning, he hastened to apprize the governor of his views, and of his arrangements, and entreated him to aid in their furtherance. It was proposed to submit it to the consideration of the legislature, and to prevail, if possible, with the planters to furnish their slaves, by whom, alone, such work could, in so insalubrious a climate, be safely executed. "If what is proposed be performed," said he, "I will stand pledged that the invaders of your state shall never, through this route, reach your city." He desired to be informed, early, of the success of the application, and to know how far the legislature would be disposed to extend their fostering care to the objects suggested; that, in the event of failure, he might have recourse to such resources as were within his reach. "But," added he, "not a moment is to be lost. With energy and expedition, all is safe:—delay, and all is lost."

The plans of operation and defence were projecting on an extensive scale. The only objects of fear were the disaffected who infested the city. and to these, after the most incessant exertions, he had well nigh fallen 'a victim.

On Lakes Borgne and Pontchartrain an equally strong confidence was had that all would be safe from invasion. Commodore Patterson, who commanded the naval forces, had executed every order with promptness. Agreeably to instructions from the general, to extend to all the passes on the lakes every protection in his power, he had sent out the gun-boats, under Lieutenant Jones. From their capability to defend, great advantages were calculated to arise; added to which, the Rigolets, the communication between the two lakes, was defended by Petit Coquille Fort, a strong work, under the command of Captain Newman, which, when acting in conjunction with the gun-boats, it was supposed, would be competent to repel any assault Guards

and videttes were also posted in different directions
to give the earliest information of every thing that
passed.   In despite, however, of these precaution
ary measures, treachery opened a way, and pointed
the entrance of the enemy to a narrow pass,
through which they effected a landing, and reached
previously to being discovered, the banks of the
Mississippi.

Such were the measures adopted for the protection of Louisiana against an attack.   Information
of a considerable force having left England filled
with high expectations, the attack on Fort Bowyer, and the inflammatory proclamations already
published, with anonymous letters received from
persons in the West Indies and Pensacola, tended
to unfold the views of the enemy, and to dissipate
every thing of doubt as to their designs.   But the
time was at hand when conjecture was giving
place to certainty; when the intentions of the in
vaders were fully developing themselves, and the
fact fairly presented, that Louisiana must fall, and
her principal city be sacked, unless the brave men
associated to defend her should stand firmly in her
defence.   Certain information was at hand of an
English fleet being off Cat and Ship Islands, and
within a short distance of the American lines,
where their numbers were daily increasing.

Lieutenant Jones, in command of the gun-boats
on Lake Borgne, was directed to reconnoitre, and
ascertain their disposition and force; and, in the
event they should attempt, through this route, to
effect a disembarkation, to retire to the Rigolets.
and there, with his flotilla, contend to the last.
He remained off Ship Island until the 12th o December, when, understanding the enemy's forces
18

were much increased, he thought it advisable to change his anchorage to a position near Malheureux Island This was rendered necessary, because it was a safer position, in the event of being attacked. Whoever looks upon a map of the country will discover the importance of this place if driven into action with a greatly superior force. This, and Chef Menteur, which unite at the entrance to the lake, and form a narrow channel, constitutes the only pass into Pontchartrain. By reaching it, the gun-boats would be enabled to present a formidable opposition.

On the 13th, Jones discovered the enemy moving off in his barges towards Pass Christian. His orders left him no discretion as to the place he should fight them. Indeed, his flotilla, although quite inconsiderable, was of too much consequence to the nation, at this juncture, to be risked at all, unless under circumstances giving a decided superiority. In no other way was this to be obtained, than by reaching the point to which he had been ordered: this he endeavoured to effect, as he became satisfied of what was intended by their movement. Weighing his anchors, with the design of reaching the position referred to in his orders, he discovered it to be wholly impracticable. A strong wind having blown for some days to the east, from the lake to the gulf, had so reduced the depth of water, that the deepest channels were insufficient to float his little squadron. The oars were resorted to, but without rendering the least assistance it was immoveable. Every thing was thrown overboard that could be spared, to lighten them; all, however, was ineffectual. At this moment of extreme peril. the tide coming suddenly in, relieved them from the shoal, and they came to anchor at one o'clock the next morning on the west passage of Malheureux Isle; where, at day, they discovered the pursuit had been abandoned.

At the bay of St. Louis was a small depot of public stores, which had, that morning, been directed, by Jones, to be brought off. Mr. Johnston, on board the Sea Horse, proceeded in the execution of this order. The enemy, on the retreat of Jones, despatched three of their barges to capture him, but, unable to effect it, they were driven back. An additional force now proceeded against him; when a smart action commenced, and the assailants were again compelled to retire with some loss. Johnston, satisfied that it was out of his power to defend himself, and considering it hopeless to attempt uniting, in face of so large a force, with the gun boats off Malheureux Island, blew up his vessel, burnt the stores, and effected his retreat by land, in conformity to the instructions he had received. A prodigious explosion assured Jones of the probable step that had been taken, and of the execution of the order.

Early on the morning of the 14th, the enemy's barges, about nine miles to the east, suddenly weighed their anchors; and, getting under way, proceeded westwardly to the pass, where our gunboats still lay. The same difficulty experienced yesterday was now encountered. Perceiving the approach of the enemy's flotilla, an attempt was made to retreat; but in vain. The wind was entirely lulled, and a perfect calm prevailed; while a strong current, setting to the gulf, rendered every effort to retire unavailing. No alternative was at hand but a single course was left.—to meet and

fight them. At once the resolution was adopted,
to avail themselves of the best position they could
obtain, wait their approach, and defend themselves,
whilst there was a hope of success. The line was
formed, with springs on the cables, and all were
waiting the arrival of a foe, who imagined himself
advancing to an easy conquest. The contest, in so
open a situation, and against such superior force
promised to be very unequal; yet the bravery
which had always characterized our fearless tars
in battle, was, on this occasion, not to be tarnished.

Forty-three boats, mounting as many cannon,
with twelve hundred chosen men, well armed, constituted the strength of the assailants. Advancing
in extended line, they were presently in reach; and,
at half after eleven o'clock, commencing a fire, the
action soon became general. Owing to a strong
current, setting out to the east, two of the boats,
numbers 156 and 163, were unable to keep their
anchorage, and floated about a hundred yards in
advance of the line. This circumstance was unfortunate; for, although it was by no means to be
calculated, that victory could be attendant on a conflict where strength and numbers were so disproportionate, yet, could the line have been preserved
the chances for defence would have been increased,
the opportunity more favourable for inflicting injury
and crippling the foe, while the period of the contest would have been protracted. Every moment
this could have been prolonged would have proved
advantageous; for, soon as the wind should spring
up, which yet continued lulled, the boats would be
more manageable, and an opportunity afforded of
retiring from the battle whenever the result became
disastrous.

The enemy, relying on their numbers, advanced in three divisions. Our gun-boats, formed in a line, were under command of Lieutenant Jones, who, on board No. 156, occupied the centre. No. 162 and 163 rested on his left, under the direction of Lieutenant Spedden and Sailing-master Ulrich; on his right were No. 5 and 23, commanded by Sailing master Ferris and Lieutenant M'Iver. The centre division of the enemy, led by the senior officer of the expedition, Captain Lockyer, bore down on No. 156, the centre of our line, and, twice attempting to board, was twice repulsed with an immense destruction of both officers and crew, and loss of two of their boats, which were sunk: one, a seventy four's launch, crowded with men, went down immediately along-side of the gun-boat. Jones, being too severely wounded longer to maintain the deck, retired, leaving the command with George Parker. who no less valiantly defended his flag, until, badly wounded, he was also compelled to leave his post; and soon after the boat was carried. No. 163, though ably defended, was also taken; and the guns of both turned on No. 162 and 5, which also surrendered; and, last of all, No. 23, commanded by Lieutenant M'Iver. Thus in detail was our little squadron, after a conflict of nearly an hour, lost; a conflict in which every thing was done that gallantry could do, and nothing unperformed that duty required; but it was a disaster which, under all the circumstances, could not be avoided. The calm which prevailed, and the unwieldy condition of the boats, prevented any management by the oars.

The commandant was ably supported by the officers associated with him. Lieutenants Spedden and

18 *

M'Iver were wounded; the former in both arms, and in one so severely as to be compelled to have it amputated; yet this valiant officer to the last continued his orders : nor did the latter quit for a moment his post. Midshipmen Cauley and Reynolds, young men of promise, fell victims to the wounds received in this contest. It is unnecessary to take up the time of the reader in commendation of this Spartan band : their bravery will be long remembered, and excite emotions stronger than language can paint. The great disparity of force between the combatants presents a curious result : that, while the American loss was but ten killed, and thirty-five wounded, that of their assailants was not less than three hundred. The British have never presented any report upon this subject : but, from every information, and from all the attendant circumstances of the battle, it was even believed to have exceeded this number; of which a large proportion was officers.*

The British returned to their shipping, at Cat Island, with their prisoners, with a convincing argument, to do away the belief which they entertained, that, in this section of country, the inhabitants were waiting, with open arms, to receive them.

This disaster was announced to General Jackson while on a visit to the lakes, whither he had gone to examine the situation of the different works

	Boats.	Men.	Guns
* The British had	43	1200	43
The Americans	6	182	23
Difference	38	1018	20

So that the disparity in force of boats, men and guns, was as eight—seven—and nearly two to one.

in progress. He heard it with much concern, for on it important consequences depended.

His fears for the safety of Mobile were much increased. Although he had every confidence in the gallant officer who commanded at Fort Bowyer. he well knew how inefficient were the exertions of a brave man, when assailed by superior strength The security of this place was of great importance. His own apprehensions of an invasion here, as affecting the interest of the lower country, was to him a cause of constant uneasiness. He felt con fident, while this point remained safe, so might the country adjacent; but, if it fell, the Indians would again be excited, the settlements on the Mobile and Alabama rivers become tributary, and New Orleans be involved in the general ruin. Deeply impressed with the importance of defending this place, he had brought to the view of the secretary of war the necessity of adopting such a course as should place it entirely out of the reach of danger. To effect this, he proposed that a large frigate, mounting forty-four guns, which, for some cause. had been left on the stocks, at Tchifonte, in an un- finished state, should be completed. "Let her,' he remarked, "be placed in the Navy Cove, which will protect the rear of the fort, and, my life upon it, ten thousand troops, and all the British fleet, cannot take the place, nor enter the bay. This will be their point of attack; if carried, they will penetrate the Indian nation,—there make a stand, and incite the ravages to war, and the slaves to in- surrection and massacre;—penetrate, if they can, to the left bank of the Mississippi, and arrest all communication. If they succeed in this, the lower country falls of course." No notice, however, was ever taken of his admonition, and nothing done to effect the object proposed. His entire defence and safety rested on the means which he could reach. An express was despatched to General Winchester, apprizing him of what had happened ; that, all communication being cut off, he must look to the procuring supplies for his army from Tennessee River through the posts established in the Creek country "The enemy," he continues, "will attempt, through Pass Huron, to reach you : watch, nor suffer yourself to be surprised ; haste, and throw sufficient supplies into Fort Bowyer, and guard vigilantly the communication from Fort Jackson, lest it be destroyed. Mobile Point must be supported and defended at every hazard. The enemy has given us a large coast to guard ; but I trust, with the smiles of Heaven, to be able to meet and defeat him at every point he may venture his foot upon the land."

Increased vigilance was now required to guard the different routes through which they might make their progress, and reach the object of their visit Major Lacoste, commanding the battalion of coloured troops, was ordered, with two pieces of cannon and a sufficient force, to defend the Chef Menteur road, that led from the head of Lake Borgne to New Orleans. In fact, wherever an inlet or creek, of the smallest size, justified the belief, that through it an entrance might be effected, arrangements were made to prevent approach. Through the Rigolets was presumed the most probable route the enemy would adventure, that, by gaining Lake Pontchartrain, a landing might be made above or below the city, or at Bayou St. John, directly opposite.

This place had been confided to Captain Newman, of the artillery. It was an important point, as well for the purposes already named, as being a position whence any movement on the lakes could be discovered. On the 22d, it was re-enforced by several heavy pieces of cannon, and an additional supply of men. He was advised by the general of the consequence attached to it, and that it was not to be inconsiderately yielded ; but that, in the event of his being compelled to abandon it, every thing being properly secured, he was to make good his retreat to Chef Menteur, where he would be covered by an additional force: "But," added he, " you are not to retreat until your judgment is well convinced that it is absolutely necessary to the very salvation of your command."

On the 16th the militia were reviewed by Jackson. He had perce'ved, on his arrival at New Orleans, such despondency manifested by the people, that to remove it had called forth all his exertions. His incessant endeavours to have defended every accessible point, and a confidence, constantly evinced, that his resources were commensurate with all the purposes of successful resistance, had completely undermined those fears, at first so generally indulged. Lest, from the loss which had lately happened on the lakes, a similar state of doubt might be again produced, was the principal cause of appearing before them to-day on review ; to convince them, by his deportment, that the safety of the city was not to be despaired of. He directed an address to be read to them. It was drawn in lan guage breathing the warmth of his own feelings, and well calculated to inspire the same glow to others. He told them they were contending fo- all that could render life desirable—"for your property and lives ;—for those who are dearer than all, your wives and children ;—for liberty, without which, country, life and property are not worth possessing Even the embraces of wives and children are a reproach to the wretch who would deprive them, by his cowardice, of those inestimable blessings. You are to contend with an enemy, who seeks to deprive you of the least of these—who avows a war of desolation, marked by cruelties, lusts, and horrors, unknown to civilized nations."

That the hour of attack was not distant was confirmed by a circumstance which reflects no considerable honour on the officer in command of the fleet. The day subsequent to the contest on the lakes, Mr. Shields, purser in the navy, had been despatched with a flag to Cat Island, accompanied by Dr. Murrell, for the purpose of alleviating the situation of our wounded, and to effect a negotiation, by which they should be liberated on parole. We are not aware that such an application militated against the usages of war: if not, the flag of truce should have been respected; nor ought its bearer to have been detained as a prisoner. Admiral Cochrane's pretended fear that it was a wile, designed to ascertain his strength and situation, is far from presenting any sufficient excuse for so wanton an outrage on the rules of war. If this were apprehended, could not the messengers have been met at a distance from the fleet, and ordered back without a near approach? Had this been done, no information could have been gained, and the object designed to be secured by the detention would have been answered, without infringing that amicable intercourse between contending armies, which, when disregarded, opens a door to brutal

and savage warfare.   Finding they did not return.
the cause of it was at once correctly divined.

The British admiral resorted to various means to
obtain from these gentlemen information of the
strength and disposition of our army; but so cau-
tious a reserve was maintained, that nothing could be
elicited. Shields was perceived to be quite deaf,
and, calculating on some advantage to be derived
from this circumstance, he and the doctor were
placed at night in the green room, where any conversation which occurred between them could readily be
heard. Suspecting something of the kind, after having retired, and every thing was seemingly still, they
began to speak of their situation—the circumstance
of their being detained, and of the prudent caution
with which they had guarded themselves against
communicating any information to the British admiral. " But," continued Shields, " how greatly these
gentlemen will be disappointed in their expectations! for Jackson, with the twenty thousand troops
he now has, and the re-enforcements from Kentucky,
which must speedily reach him, will be able to destroy any force that can be landed from these ships."
Every word was heard, and treasured ; and, not supposing there was any design, or that he presumed
himself overheard, they were beguiled by it, and at
once concluded our force to be as great as it was
represented.

Early on the 15th, the morning after the battle
on the lake, expresses were sent up the coast; in
quest of General Coffee, to procure information of
the Kentucky and Tennessee divisions, which, it
was hoped, were not far distant. In his communication to Coffee, the general observes, " You must
not sleep until you reach me, or arrive within strik-

ing distance. Your accustomed activity is looked for. Innumerable defiles present themselves, where your services and riflemen will be all-important. An opportunity is at hand, to reap for yourself and brigade the approbation of your country."

In obedience to the order he had received at Mobile to occupy some central position, where his horses could be subsisted, Coffee had proceeded as far as Sandy Creek, a small distance above Baton Rouge, where he had halted. His brigade on its march had been greatly exposed, and many hardships encountered. The cold season had set in; and, for twenty days, it had rained incessantly. The waters were raised to uncommon heights, and every creek and bayou was to be bridged or swam. Added to this, their march was through an uncultivated country, but thinly settled, where little subsistence was to be had, and that procured with much difficulty. He had been at this place eight or ten days, when, late on the evening of the 17th, the express from headquarters reached him. He lost no time in executing the order; and, directing one of his regiments, which, for the greater convenience of foraging, had encamped about six miles off, to unite with him, he proceeded on his march the instant it arrived. In consequence of innumerable exposures, there were, at this time, three hundred on the sick list. These being left, he commenced his advance with twelve hundred and fifty men. The weather continued extremely cold and rainy, which prevented their proceeding with the celerity the exigency of the moment required. Coffee, perceiving that the movement of his whole force, in a body, would occasion delays, ruinous to the object, ordered all, who were able to proceed, to advance with him; while the rest of his brigade, under suitable officers, were left to follow as fast as the weak and exhausted condition of their horses would permit. His force, by this arrangement, was reduced to eight hundred men, with whom he moved with the utmost industry. Having marched seventy miles the last day, he encamped, on the night of the 19th, within fifteen miles of New Orleans, making in two days a distance of one hundred and twenty miles Continuing his advance, early next morning he halted within four miles of the city, to examine the condition of his arms, and to learn, in the event the enemy had landed, the relative position of the two armies

On inspecting their arms, which consisted principally of rifles, two hundred were discovered to be so materially injured by the weather, as to be unfit for service.

The advance of Colonel Hinds, from Woodville, with the Mississippi dragoons, was no less expeditious; an active officer, he was, on this, as on all other occasions, at his post, ready to act as circumstances should require. Having received his orders, he effected, in four days, a march of two hundred and thirty miles.

On the 16th, Colonel Hynes, aid-de-camp to General Carroll, reached head-quarters, with information from the general, that he would be present as early as possible; but that the state of the weather and high and contrary winds, greatly retarded his progress. To remedy this, a steam-boat was immediately put in requisition, and ordered to proceed up the river to aid him in reaching his destination, without loss of time. He was advised of the necessity of hastening rapidly forward; that the lakes were in possession of the enemy, and their arrival daily looked for; " But," continued Jackson, " I am esolved, feeble as my force is, to assail him, on his frst landing, and perish sooner than he shall reach the city."

Independent of the large force which was descending with General Carroll, his approach was looked to with additional pleasure, from the circumstance of his having with him a boat laden with arms, destined for the defence of the country, and which he had overtaken on his passage down the Mississippi. His falling in with them was fortunate ; for, had their arrival depended on those to whom they had been incautiously confided, they might have come too late, and after all danger had subsided ; as was indeed the case with others forwarded from Pittsburg, which, through the unpardonable conduct of those who had been intrusted with their transportation, did not reach New Orleans until all difficulties had terminated. Great inconvenience was sustained, during the siege, for want of arms to place in the hands of the militia. Great as it was, it would have been increased, even to an alarming extent, but for the accidental circumstance of this boat having fallen into the hands of the Tennessee division, which impelled it on, and thereby produced incalculable advantage.

This division left Nashville on the 19th of November. Their exertions entitle them and their commander to every gratitude. But above all is our gratitude due to that benign Providence, who, having aided in the establishment of our glorious independence, again manifested his goodness and power in guarding the rights of a country rendered sacred by the blood of the virtuous, heretofore shed in its defence. It rarely, if ever, happens, that the Cum

berland river admits a passage for boats so early in
the season; but torrents of rain descending swelled
the stream, and wafted our troops safely to the Mississippi, where all obstructions were at an end

While these preparations were progressing, to
concentrate the forces within his reach, the general was turning his attention to ward off any blow
that might be aimed before his expected reenforcements shou'd arrive. Every point capable of being
successfully assailed was receiving such additional
security as could be given. Patrols and videttes
were ranged through the country, that the earliest
intelligence might be had of any intended move
ment. The militia of the state were called out *en
masse ;* and, through the interference of the legis
lature, an embargo on vessels at the port of New
Orleans was declared, to afford an opportunity of
procuring additional recruits for the navy. Gener
al Villery, because an inhabitant of the country, ana
best understanding the several points on the lakes
requiring defence, was ordered, with the Louisiana
militia, to search out, and give protection to the different passes, where a landing might be effected.

To hinder the enemy from obtaining supplies
on shore, a detachment was sent to Pearl River
to prevent any parties from landing until the
stock could be driven from the neighbourhood
The precaution, for some time used, of restricting
the departure of any vessel with provisions, under
the operation of the embargo imposed by the legislature, had greatly disappointed the expectations of
the British, and even introduced distress into Pensacola, whence the Spaniards had been in the habit
of procuring their supplies. The governor had solicited the opening a communication, for the relief

of the suffering inhabitants of his province. Jackson was aware that this appeal to his humanity might be a stratagem, having for its object to aid the enemy. Although the governor, hitherto, had given no flattering evidence, either of his friendship or sincerity, still the statement offered by him might be correct; and, if so, the neutrality of his country established a well-founded claim to the benevolence of the Americans. Balancing between a desire that these people should not be seriously injured, and a fear that the application was intended for a very different purpose, he determined to err on the side of mercy, and, as far as possible, relieve their wants. This he directed General Winchester, at Mobile, to effect, provided his stock of provisions would permit it. It was particularly enjoined on him that the quantity of provisions sent should be small, and be conveyed by water: "For if," said he, "the Spaniards are really in distress, and the supply sent shall be taken by the British, it will excite their just indignation towards them, and erase all friendship, while they will be afforded an additional proof of ours: the supply, too, being inconsiderable, even if captured, will prove of no great benefit to our enemy."

Jackson's arrangements were well conceived, and rapidly progressing; but they were still insufficient; and his own forebodings assured him, that, to obtain security, something stronger required to be adopted. That there was an enemy in the midst of his camp, more to be feared than those who were menacing from abroad, was, indeed, probable. A stranger himself, his conjectures might not have led to the conclusion; but information received, before and soon after his arrival, through different chan

sels, and particularly from the governor of the state,
had awakened a belief, that the country was filled
with disaffected persons.   Although he had been in
possession of data, sufficiently strong to confirm him
in the opinion, no urgent necessity had arisen, rendering a resort to rigid measures essential to the
general safety.   Abundant evidence of prevailing
disaffection had been obtained, through Governor
Claiborne.   In a letter to General Jackson, aftei
his return from Pensacola, he observed, "Enemies
to the country may blame your prompt and energetic measures ; but in the person of every patriot
you will find a supporter.   I am well aware of the
.ax police of this city, and indeed of the whole state,
with respect to strangers.   I think, with you, that
our country is filled ' with traitors and spies.'   On
this subject, I have written pressingly to the city
authorities and parish judges.   Some regulations,
I hope, will be adopted by the first, and greater
vigilance be exercised, in future, by the latter."

Never, perhaps, all the circumstances considered,
did any general advance to the defence and pro
tection of a people, situated in his own country
where greater room was had to distrust the succes.
of the event, and believe all efforts hopeless.   When
General Jackson was informed by the governor
that the legislature, instead of discharging with
alacrity, diligence, and good faith, the duties which
had been confided to them by their constituents,
had, under the garb of privilege, endeavoured to
mar the execution of measures the most salutary,
he might well conclude the country in danger, and
suspect a want of fidelity in her citizens. Upon the
yeomanry alone must every country depend for its
liberty : they are its sinews and its strength. Let
19 *

them continue virtuous, and they will cheerfully nay, fearlessly, maintain themselves against aggression ; but if they become corrupted, or, through the intrigue or misconduct of their rulers, lose confidence in their government, their importance will be impaired. While the people of Rome felt themselves freemen, and proud of the name of citizens, Rome was invincible ; and, to descend to times more modern, the strength of France was an overmatch for combined Europe only while Frenchmen had confidence and regard for their government.

Constitutional resources were attempted, and an effort made to draw out the militia : they resisted the requisition ; and that resistance, so far from being discountenanced by the legislature then in cession, was encouraged by their assuming to themselves the right of declaring the demand to be illegal, unnecessary, and oppressive. Thus supported, the militia, as might have been expected, stood their ground, and resolutely resisted the call to defend their country. The example thus established had already induced the conviction that they were privileged persons, and had reserved to them, on all occasions, when called for, the right of determining if the call were regular, why and wherefore made, where they would prefer to act, and be governed accordingly. When, therefore, the first requisition made by Jackson was attempted to be filled, a number made a tender of their services as volunteers ; but on this condition, that they were not to be marched from the state. The reply made showed they were to act with a general who knew nothing of temporizing policy, and who would go the entire length that safety and necessity required. They were assured his object was to defend the

country, and that he shou'd do it at every hazard ;
that soldiers who entered the ranks with him, to
fight the battles of their country, must forget the
habits of social life, and be willing and prepared to
go wherever duty and danger called ; such were
the kind of troops he wanted, and none others would
he have.

Influenced by these and other considerations,
which were daily disclosed ; sensible of the danger
that surrounded him; and from a conviction which
he felt was founded not upon light considerations,
that the country, without a most decisive course,
could not be saved, he brought to the view of
the legislature the necessity of suspending the writ
of *habeas corpus.* To attempt himself so new and
bold a course, he was satisfied, would draw to him
the reproofs and censures of the orthodox politicians
of the day, and involve him in various reproaches
The legislature had already interrupted the commerce by declaring and enforcing an embargo ; and
the exercise of this subsequent authority, equally
necessary with the first, could involve, he supposed.
no higher exercise of power than the enactment of
an embargo law. He was solicitous, therefore, to
relieve himself of the responsibility, by prevailing
on the legislature to do that which necessity and
the security of the country seemed imperiously to
require. They proceeded slowly to the investiga
tion, and were deliberating, with great caution, upon
their right, authority, and constitutional power to
adopt such a measure, when the general, sensible
that procrastination was dangerous, and might defeat the objects intended to be answered, assumed
all responsibility, and superseded their deliberations

by declaring the city and environs of **New Orleans**
under martial law.

All persons entering the city were required, immediately, to report themselves to the adjutant-general ; and, on failing to do so, were to be arrested
and detained for examination. None were to de
part from it, or be suffered to pass beyond the chain
of sentinels, but by permission from the commanding general, or one of the staff : nor was any vessel
or craft to be permitted to sail on the river, or the
lakes, but by the same authority, or a passport signed by the commander of the naval forces.

The lamps were to be extinguished at nine
o'clock at night ; after which time, all persons
'ound in the streets, or from their respective homes,
without permission in writing, signed as above, were
to be arrested as spies, and detained for examination.

At a crisis so important, and from a persuasion
hat the country, in its menaced situation, could not
be preserved by the exercise of any ordinary
powers, he believed it best to adopt a course that
should be efficient, even if it partially endangered
the rights and privileges of the citizen. He proclaimed martial law, believing necessity and policy
required it ; "under a solemn conviction that the
country, committed to his care, could by such a
measure alone be saved from utter ruin ; and from
a religious belief, that he was performing the most
important duty. By it he intended to supersede
such civil powers, as, in their operation, interfered
with those he was obliged to exercise. He thought
that, at such a moment, constitutional forms should
be suspended, for the preservation of constitutional

rights; and that there could be no question, whether it were better to depart, for a moment, from the enjoyment of our dearest privileges, or to have them wrested from us for ever."

This rigid course, however, was by no means well received. Whether it had for its object good or evil; whether springing from necessity, or from a spirit of oppression in its author, with many, was not a material question: it was sufficient for them to consider it an infraction of the law, to excite their warmest opposition; whilst the long-approved doctrine of *necessitas rei* afforded no substantial argument to induce a conviction of its propriety. Whether the civil should yield to military law, or which should have control, with those whose anxious wishes were for the safety of the state, was not a matter of deep or serious concern ; but to busy politicians it opened a field for investigation : and many a fire-side patriot had arguments at command, to prove it an usurpation of power, an outrage upon government, and a violation of the constitution. During the invasion, and while affairs of major importance impended, no occasion was presented of testing its correctness ; but, soon as the enemy had retired, and before it was ascertained whether, at some more fortunate and less guarded point, they might not return, to renew those efforts which had so lately failed, Dominick A. Hall, judge of the United States' court for this district, determined to wage a war of authority, and to have it decided, if, in any event, the civil power could be deprived of supremacy. Jackson presumed his time of too much importance, at so momentous a period, to be wasted in the discussion of civil matters. He gave to it, therefore, the only attention which he believed it officiousness merited, and, instead of obeying the command, ordered the judge to leave the city. Peace being restored, and danger over, the judge renewed the contest ; and, causing the general to appear before him, on a process of contempt, for detaining and refusing to obey a writ of habeas corpus, which had been directed to him, amerced him in a fine of a thousand dollars. How far he was actuated by correct motives, in exclusion of those feelings which sometimes estrange the judgment, his own conscience can determine : and how far his proceedings were fair and liberal, will appear hereafter, when, in proper order, we examine this prosecution. For the present, we are confident, that, if ever there was a case that could justify or excuse a departure from the law, its features were not stronger than those which influenced General Jackson, on the present occasion, in suspending the rights of the citizens. If Judge Hall were impelled to the course he took, in defence of the violated dignity of the constitution, and to protect the rights of a government, whose judicial powers he represented, whether right or wrong, he deserves not censure ; although it might be well replied, that a fairer opportunity of showing his devotedness to his country had just passed, when he might truly have aided in defence of her honour, nor left even room for his motives to have been unfairly appreciated

Learning the rumours that had been propagated, and fearing lest they might have an injurious tendency, Jackson immediately circulated an address to his troops, in which he sought to counteract the effect, and preserve their ardour and devotion to their country.

"Believe not," he observed, "that the threatened invasion is with a view tr restore the country to
Spain.   It is founded in design, and a supposition
that you would be willing to return to your ancient
government.   Listen not to such incredible tales:
your government is at peace with Spain.   It is your
vital enemy, the common enemy of mankind, the
highway robber of the world, that has sent his hire-
lings among you, to put you from your guard, that
you may fall an easier prey.   Then look to your
liberty, your property, the chastity of your wives
and daughters.   Take a retrospect of the conduct
of the British army at Hampton, and at other places,
where it has entered our country—and every bosom,
which glows with patriotism and virtue, will be inspired with indignation, and pant for the arrival of
the hour when we shall meet and revenge those
outrages against the laws of civilization and hu
manity."

With the exception of the Kentucky troops, all
the forces expected had arrived.   General Carroll
had reached Coffee's encampment, four miles above
the city, on the 21st, and had immediately reported
to the commanding general.   The officers were
busily engaged in drilling, manœuvring, and organizing the troops, and in having every thing
ready for action.   No doubt was entertained, but
the British would be able to effect a landing at
some point: the principal thing to be guarded
against was not to prevent it; for, since the loss of
the gun-boats, any attempt of this kind could only
be regarded as hopeless. but, by preserving a cor.-
stant vigilance, they might be met at the very
threshold.   Small guard-boats were constantly ply
ing on the lakes, to give information of every move

ment. Some of these had come in, late on the evening of the 22d, and reported that all was quiet, and that no unfavourable appearance portended in that direction. With such vigilance, constantly exercised, it is astonishing that the enemy should have effected an invasion, and succeeded in disembarking so large a force, without the slightest intimation being had, until they were accidentally discovered emerging from the swamp, about seven miles below the city. The general impression is. that it was through information given by a small party of Spanish fishermen, that so secret a disembarkation was effected. Several of them had settled at the mouth of this bayou, and supported themselves by fish which they caught, and vended in the market at New Orleans. Obstructions had been ordered to be made on every inlet, and the Louisiana militia were despatched for that purpose. This place had not received the attention its importance merited ; nor was it until the 22d, that General Villery, charged with the execution of this order, had placed here a small detachment of men. Towards day, the enemy, silently proceeding up the bayou landed, and succeeded in capturing the whole of this party but two, who, fleeing to the swamp, endeavoured to reach the city ; but, owing to the thick undergrowth and briers, they did not arrive until after the enemy had reached the banks of the Mississippi, and been discovered.

Bayou Bienvenu, through which the British effected a landing, is an arm of considerable width, stretching towards the Mississippi from Lake Borgne, and about fifteen miles south-east of New Orleans. It had been reported to General Jackson on the 23d, that, on the day before, several strange sail had been descried off Terre au Bœuf. To ascertain correctly the truth of the statement, Majors Tatum and Latour, topographical engineers, were sent, with orders to proceed in that direction, and learn if any thing were attempting there. It was towards noon of the 23d, when they started Approaching General Villery's plantation, and perceiving at a distance soldiers and persons fleeing away, they at once supposed the enemy had arrived. What, however, was but surmise, was presently rendered certain; and it was now no longer a doubt, but the British had landed, in considerable force, and had actually gained, unobserved, the house of General Villery, on the bank of the Mississippi, where they had surprised, and made prisoners, a company of militia, there posted.

Major Tatum, hastening back, announced his discovery. Preparations to act were immediately made by General Jackson. Believing that to act speedily was of the highest importance, the signal guns were fired, and expresses sent forward, to concentrate his forces; resolving that night to meet the invaders, and try his own and their firmness.

20

CHAPTER IX.

General Jackson concentrates his forces, and marches to fight the enemy.—Alarms of the city.—Anecdote.—Mode of attack, and battle of the 23d of December.—British re-enforcements arrive during the action.—Arrival of General Carroll's division.—Our army retires from the field.—Effects of this battle.—Jackson establishes a line of defence.—General Morgan is ordered on the right bank of the Mississippi.—Destruction and loss of the Caroline schooner.—Battle of the 28th December.—Conduct of the legislature of Louisiana ; their deliberations suspended.—Scarcity of arms in the American camp.—Colonel Hinds.

THE hour to test the bravery of his troops arrived. The approach of the enemy, flushed with the hope of easy victory, was announced to Jackson a little after one o'clock in the afternoon. He well knew the greater part of his troops were inured to fatigue, while those opposed to him had just been landed from a long voyage, and were without activity, and unfitted for bodily exertion. Moreover a part only might have arrived from the shipping, while the remainder would be certainly disembarked as early as possible. These circumstances seemed to augment, in his behalf, the chances of victory. He resolved, at all events, to march, and that night give them battle. Generals Coffee and Carroll were ordered to proceed immediately from their encampment, and join him. Although four miles above, they arrived in the city in less than two hours after the order had been issued. These forces, with the seventh and forty-fourth regiments, the Louisiana troops, and Colonel Hinds' dragoons, from Mississippi, constituted the strength of his army, which could be carried into action agains..

enemy whose numbers, at this time, could only be conjectured. It was thought advisable that General Carroll and his division should be disposed in the rear, for the reason that there was no correct information of the force landed through Villery's Canal, and because Jackson feared that this probably might be merely a feint, intended to divert his attention, while a more numerous division, having already gained some point higher on the lake, might, by advancing in his absence, gain his rear, and succeed in their designs. Uncertain of their movements, it was essential he should be prepared for the worst, and, by different dispositions of his troops, be ready to resist, in whatever quarter he might be assailed. Carroll, therefore, at the head of his division, and Governor Claiborne, with the state militia, were directed to take post on the Gentilly road, which leads from Chef Menteur to New Orleans, and to defend it to the last extremity.

Alarm pervaded the city. The marching and countermarching of the troops, the proximity of the enemy, with the approaching contest, and uncertainty of the issue, had excited a general fear. Colonel Hayne, with two companies of riflemen, and the Mississippi dragoons, was sent forward to reconnoitre their camp, learn their position and numbers; and, in the event they should be found advancing, to harass and oppose them at every step, until the main body should arrive.

Every thing being ready, General Jackson commenced his march to meet the veteran troops of England. An inconsiderable circumstance, at this moment, evinced what unlimited confidence was reposed in his bravery. As his troops were marching through the city, his ears were assailed with the screams and cries of innumerable·females, who had collected on the way, and seemed to apprehend the worst of consequences. Feeling for their distresses, and anxious to quiet them, he directed Mr. Livingston, one of his aids-de-camp, to address them in the French language. "Say to them," said he, "not to be alarmed. the enemy shall never reach the city." It operated like an electric shock. To know that he himself was not apprehensive of a fatal result, inspired them with altered feelings; sorrow was ended, and their grief converted into confidence.

The general arrived in view of the enemy a little before dark. Having ascertained from Colonel Hayne their position, and that their strength was about two thousand men,* he immediately concerted the mode of attack, and hastened to execute it Commodore Patterson, who commanded the naval forces on this station, with Captain Henly, on board the Caroline, had been directed to drop down, anchor in front of their line, and open upon them from 'he guns of the schooner: this being the appointed signal, when given, the attack was to be waged simultaneously on all sides. The fires from·their camp disclosed their position, and showed their encampment, formed with the left resting on the river, and extending at right angles into the open field. General Coffee, with his brigade, Colonel Hinds' dragoons, and Captain Beal's company of riflemen, were ordered to oblique to the left, and, by a circui'ous route, avoid their pickets, and endeavour to turn their right wing; having succeed-

---

* This opinion, as it afterwards appeared, was incorrect. The number of the enemy, at the commencement of the action, was three thousand, and was shortly afterwards increased by additional forces: our strength did not exceed two thousand.

ed in this, to form his line, and press the enemy towards the river, where they would be exposed more
completely to the fire of the Caroline. The rest of
the troops, consisting of he regulars, Ploache's
city volunteers, Daquin's coloured troops, the artillery under Lieutenant Spotts, supported by a company of marines commanded by Colonel M'Kee, advanced on the road along the bank of the Mississippi, and were commanded by Jackson in person.

General Coffee with caution had advanced beyond their pickets, next the swamp, and nearly
reached the point to which he was ordered, when a
broadside from the Caroline announced the battle
begun. Patterson had proceeded slowly, giving
time, as he believed, for the execution of those arrangements contemplated on the shore. So sanguine had the British been in the belief that they
would be kindly received, and little opposition attempted, that the Caroline floated by the sentinels,
and anchored before their camp, without any kind
of molestation. On passing the front picket, she
was hailed in a low tone of voice, but, not returning
an answer, no further question was made. This,
added to some other circumstances, confirmed the
opinion that they believed her a vessel laden with
provisions, which had been sent out from New Orleans, and was intended for them. Having reach
ed what, from their fires, appeared to be the centre
of their encampment, her anchors were cast, and
her character and business disclosed from her guns
So unexpected an attack produced a momentary
confusion ; but, recovering, she was answered by a
discharge of musketry, and flight of congreve rockets, which passed without njury, while the grape
and canister from her guns were pouring destruc

20 *

tively on them. To take away the certainty of aim afforded by the light from their fires, these were immediately extinguished, and they retired two or three hundred yards into the open field, if not out of the reach of the cannon, at least to a distance where, by the darkness of the night, they would be protected.

Coffee had dismounted his men, and turned his horses loose, at a large ditch, next the swamp, in the rear of Larond's plantation, and gained, as he believed, the centre of the enemy's line, when the signal from the Caroline reached him. He directly wheeled his columns in, and, extending his line parallel with the river, moved towards their camp. He had advanced scarcely more than a hundred yards, when he received a heavy fire from a line formed in his front; this, to him, was unexpected, as he supposed the enemy lying principally at a distance, and that the only opposition he should meet, until he approached towards the levee,* would be from their advanced pickets. The circumstance of his coming in contact with them so soon was owing to the severe attack of the schooner, which had compelled the enemy to abandon their camp, and form without the reach of her guns. The moon shone, but reflected her light too feebly to · discover objects at a distance. The only means, therefore, of producing certain effect, with the kind of force engaged, which consisted chiefly of rifle-

---

* Banks thrown up on the margin of the river to confine the stream to its bed; and which are extended along the Mississippi on both sides, from the termination of the highlands, near Baton Rouge. Frequently the river, in its vernal floods, rises above the elevation of the plains, and then the security of the country depends on the strength of those levees: they not unfrequent ly break, when incalculable injury is the consequence.

men, was not to venture at random, but to discharge
their pieces only when there should be a certainty
of felling the object.   This order being given, the
line pressed on, and, having gained a position near
enough to distinguish, a general fire was given . it
was well directed, and too destructive to be withstood : the enemy gave way, and retreated,—rallied,—formed,—were charged, and again retreated.
Our gallant yeomanry, led by their brave commander, urged fearlessly on, and drove their invaders
from every position they attempted to maintain.

The enemy, driven back by the resolute firmness
of the assailants, had now reached a grove of orange
trees, with a ditch running past it, protected by a
fence on the margin.   Here they halted, and formed for battle.   It was a position promising securi
ty, and was occupied with confidence.   Coffee's
dauntless yeomanry, strengthened in their hopes of
success, moved on, nor discovered the advantages
against them, until a fire from the entire British
line showed their position.   A sudden check was
given; but it was only momentary; for, gathering
fresh ardour, they charged across the ditch, gave a
deadly fire, and forced them to retire.   The retreat
continued, until, gaining a similar position, the enemy made another stand, and were again driven from
it with considerable loss.

Thus the battle raged on the left wing, until the
British reached the bank of the river; here a determined stand was made, and further encroach-
ments resisted; for half an hour the conflict was
extremely violent on both sides.   The American
troops could not be driven from their purpose, noi
the British made to yield their ground; but al
length, having suffered greatly, the latter were un

der the necessity of taking refuge behind the levee,
which afforded a breast-work, and protected them
from the fatal fire of our riflemen. Coffee, unacquainted with their position, for the darkness had
greatly increased, already contemplated again to
charge them ; but one of his officers, who had discovered the advantage their situation gave them,
assured him it was too hazardous ; that they could
be driven no farther, and would, from the point they
occupied, resist with the bayonet, and repel, with
considerable loss, any attempt that might be made
to dislodge them. The place of their retirement
was covered in front by a strong bank, which had
been extended into the field, to keep out the river,
in consequence of the first being encroached upon,
and undermined in several places : the former, however, was still entire in many parts, which, interposing between them and the Mississippi, afforded security from the broadsides of the schooner, which
lay off at some distance. A further apprehension,
lest, by moving still nearer to the river, he might
greatly expose himself to the fire of the Caroline,
which was yet spiritedly maintaining the conflict,
induced Coffee to retire until he could hear from
the commanding general, and receive his orders.

During this time, the right wing, under Jackson,
had been no less active. A detachment of artillery, under Lieutenant Spotts, supported by sixty marines, constituting the advance, had moved down
the road next the levee. On their left was the
seventh regiment of infantry, led by Major Piere.
The forty-fourth, commanded by Major Baker, was
formed on the extreme left ; while Plauche's and
Daquin's battalions of city guards were directed
to be posted in the centre, between the seventh and

forty-fourth. The general had ordered Colonel Ross, who, during the night, acted in the capacity of brigadier-general,—for he was without a brigadier,—on hearing the signal from the Caroline, to move off by heads of companies, and, on reaching the enemy's line, to deploy, and unite the left wing of his command with the right of General Coffee's. This order was omitted to be executed; and the consequence was confusion in the ranks.

Instead of moving in column from the first position, the troops, with the exception of the seventh regiment, next the person of the general, which advanced agreeably to the instructions that had been given, were formed and marched in extended line. Having sufficient ground to form on at first, no inconvenience was at the moment sustained; but, this advantage presently failing, the centre became compressed, and was forced in the rear. The river, from where they were formed, gradually inclined to the left, and diminished the space originally possessed: farther in stood Larond's house, surrounded by a grove of clustered orange trees; this pressing the left, and the river the right wing to the centre, formed a curve, which presently threw the principal part of Plaucne's and Daquin's battalions without the line. This inconvenience might have been remedied, but for the briskness of the advance, and for the darkness of the night. A heavy fire from behind a fence, immediately before them, had brought the enemy to view. Acting in obedience to their orders not to waste their ammunition at random. our troops had pressed forward against the opposition in their front, and thereby threw those battalions in the rear

A fog rising from the river, which, added to the smoke from the guns, was covering the plain gradually, diminished the little light shed by the moon, and greatly increased the darkness of the night no clue was left to ascertain how the enemy were situated. There was no alternative but to move on in the direction of their fire, which subjected the assailants to material disadvantages. The British, driven from their first position, had retired back, and occupied another, behind a deep ditch, that ran out of the Mississippi towards the swamp, on the margin of which was a wood railed fence. Here, strengthened by increased numbers, they again opposed the advance of our troops. Having waited until they had approached sufficiently near to be discovered, they discharged a fire upon the advancing army. Instantly our battery was formed, and poured destructively upon them; while the infantry, pressing forward, aided in the conflict, which at this point was for some time spiritedly maintained. At this moment, a brisk sally was made upon our advance, when the marines, unequal to the assault were already giving way. The adjutant-general, and Colonels Piatt and Chotard, with a part of the seventh, hastening to their support, drove the ene-my, and saved the artillery from capture. General Jackson, perceiving the decided advantages which were derived from the position they occupied, ordered their line to be charged. It was obeyed and executed with promptness. Pressing on, our troops gained the ditch, and, pouring across it a well-aim-ed fire, compelled them to retreat, and abandon their entrenchment. The plain, on which they were contending, was cut to pieces, by races from the river, to convey the water to the swamp. The

enemy were, therefore, very soon enabled o occupy another position, equally favourable with the one
whence they had been just driven, where they form
ed for battle, and, for some time, gallantly maintained themselves ; but which, after stubborn resistance, they were forced to yield.

The enemy, discovering the obstinate advance
made by the right wing of the American army, and pre
suming perhaps that its principal strength was post
ed on the road, formed the intention of attacking
violently the left. Obliquing for this purpose, an
attempt was made to turn it. At this moment, Daquin's and the battalion of city guards, being marched up, and formed on the left of the forty-fourth
regiment, repulsed them.

The particular moment of the contest prevented
many of those benefits, which might have been derived from the artillery. The darkness of the night
was such, that the blaze of the enemy's musketry
was the only light afforded, by which to determine
their position, or be capable of taking our own to
advantage ; yet, notwithstanding, it greatly annoyed them, whenever it could be brought to bear.
Directed by Lieutenant Spotts, a vigilant and skilful officer, with men to aid him who looked to nothing but a zealous discharge of their duty, the most
important services were rendered.

The enemy had been thrice beaten, and for nearly a mile compelled to yield their ground. They
had now retired, and, if found, were to. be sought
for amidst the darkness of the night. The general determined to halt, and ascertain Coffee's position and success, previously to waging the battle
further ; for as yet no communication had passed
between them. The Caroline had almost ceased

her operations ; it being only occasionally, that the noise of her guns disclosed the little opportunity she possessed of acting efficiently.

The express despatched to General Jackson from the left wing having reached him, he determined to prosecute the successes he had gained no further. The darkness of the night, the confusion into which his own division had been thrown, and a similar disaster produced on the part of Coffee,—all pointed to the necessity of retiring from the field. The bravery displayed by his troops had induced a belief, that, by pressing forward, he might capture the whole British army : at any rate, he considered it but a game of hazard, which, if unsuccessful, could not occasion his own defeat. If incompetent to its execution, and superior numbers, or superior discipline, should compel him to recede from the effort, he well knew the enemy would not have temerity enough to attempt pursuit. The extreme darkness, their entire ignorance of the situation of the country, and an apprehension lest their forces might be greatly outnumbered, afforded sufficient reasons on which to ground a belief, that, although beaten from his purpose, he would yet have it in his power to retire in safety ; but, on the arrival of the express from General Coffee, learning the strong position to which the enemy had retired, and that a part of the left wing had been detached, and were in all probability captured, he determined to retire from the contest, nor attempt a further prosecution of his successes. General Coffee was accordingly directed to withdraw, and take a position at Larond's plantation, where the line had been first formed: and thither the troops on the right were also ordered to be marched.

The last charge made by the left wing had sep
arated from the main body Colonels Dyer and Gibson, with two hundred men, and Captain Beal's company of riflemen. What might be their fate;
whether they were captured, or had effected their
retreat, was, at this time, altogether uncertain; be
.hat as it might, Coffee's command was considerably weakened.

Colonel Dyer, who commanded the extreme left,
on clearing the grove, after the enemy had retired,
was marching in a direction where he expected to
find General Coffee: he very soon discovered a
force in front, and, halting his men, hastened towards
it: arriving within a short distance, he was hailed,
ordered to stop, and report to whom he belonged:
Dyer, and Gibson, his lieutenant-colonel, who accompanied him, advanced, and stated they were of
Coffee's brigade: by this time they had arrived
within a short distance of the line, and, perceiving
that the name of the brigade they had stated was
not understood, their apprehensions were awakened, lest it might be a detachment of the enemy; in
this opinion they were immediately confirmed, and,
wheeling to return, were fired on and pursued.
Gibson had scarcely started when he fell: before
he could recover, a soldier, quicker than the rest,
had reached him, and pinned him to the ground
with his bayonet; fortunately the stab had but
slightly wounded him, and he was only held by his
clothes; thus pinioned, and perceiving others to be
briskly advancing, but a moment was left for deliberation;—making a violent exertion, and springing
to his feet, he threw his assailant to the ground, and
made good his retreat. Colonel Dyer had retreated about fifty yards, when his horse dropped dead;

21

entangled in the fall, and slightly wounded in the thigh, there was little prospect of relief, for the enemy were briskly advancing; his men being near at hand, he ordered them to advance and fire, which checked their approach, and enabled him to escape. Being now at the head of his command, perceiving an enemy in a direction he had not expected, and uncertain how or where he might find General Coffee, he determined to seek him to the right, and, moving on with his little band, forced his way through the enemy's lines, with the loss of sixty-three of his men, who were killed and taken. Captain Beal with equal bravery, charged through the enemy, carrying off some prisoners, and losing several of his own company.

This re-enforcement of the British had arrived from Bayou Bienvenu, after night. The boats that landed the first detachment proceeded back to the shipping, and, having returned, were on their way up the bayou, when they heard the guns of the Caroline; moving hastily on to the assistance of those who had debarked before, they reached the shore, and, knowing nothing of the situation of the two armies, during the engagement advanced in the rear of General Coffee's brigade. Coming in contact with Colonel Dyer and Captain Beal, they filed off to the left, and reached the British lines.

This detached part of Coffee's brigade, unable to unite with, or find him, retired to the place where they had first formed, and joined Colonel Hinds' dragoons, which had remained on the ground where the troops had first dismounted, that they might cover their retreat, in the event it became necessary.

Jackson had gone into this battle confident of success; and his arrangements were such as would have ensured it, even to a much greater extent, but for the intervention of circumstances that were not, and could not be foreseen. The Caroline had given her signals, and commenced the battle, a little too early, before Coffee had reached his position and before every thing was fully in readiness to at tain the objects designed : but it was chiefly owing to the confusion introduced at first into the ranks, which checked the rapidity of his advance, gave the enemy time for preparation, and prevented his division from uniting with the right wing of General Coffee's brigade.

Colonel Hinds, with one hundred and eighty dragoons, was not brought into action during the night. Interspersed as the plain was with innumerable ditches, diverging in different directions, it was impossible that cavalry could act to any kind of advantage : they were now formed in advance, to watch, until morning, the movements of the enemy.

From the experiment just made, Jackson believed it would be in his power, on renewing the attack, to capture the British army : he concluded, therefore, to order down to his assistance General Carroll with his division, and to assail them again at the dawn of day. Directing Governor C'aiborne to remain at his post, with the Louisiana militia, for the defence of an important pass to the city, the Gentilly road, he despatched an express to Carroll, stating to him, that, in the event there had been nc appearance of a force during the night, in the di rection of Chef Menteur, to join him with the troops under his command : this order was executed by one o'clock in the morning. Previously, however, to his arrival, a different determination was made From prisoners who had been brought in, and through deserters, it was ascertained that the strength of the enemy, during the battle, was four thousand, and, with the re-enforcements which had reached them, after its commencement, and during the action, their force could not be less than six :—at any rate, it would greatly exceed his own, even after the Tennessee division should be added. Although very decided advantages had been obtained, yet they had been procured under circumstances that might be wholly lost in a contest waged, in open day, between forces so disproportionate, and by undisciplined troops, against veteran soldiers. Jackson well knew it was incumbent upon him to act a part entirely defensive : should the attempt to destroy the city succeed, numerous difficulties would present themselves, which might be avoided, so long as he could hold the enemy in check. Prompted by these considerations, and believing it attainable in no way so effectually as in occupying some point, and, by the strength he might give it, compensate for the inferiority of his numbers, and their want of discipline, he determined to forbear all further offensive efforts until he could more certainly discover the views of the enemy, and until the Kentucky troops should reach him. Pursuing this idea, at four o'clock in the morning, having ordered Colonel Hinds to occupy the ground he was then abandoning, and to observe the enemy closely, he fell back, and formed his line behind a deep ditch that stretched to the swamp at right angles from the river. There were two circumstances recommending the importance of this place : the swamp, which, from the high lands, at Baton Rouge, skirts the river at irregular distances, and in many places is almost impervious, had here approached within four

nundred yards of the Mississippi, and hence, from
the narrowness of the pass, was more easily to be
defended ; added to which, there was a deep canal,
whence the dirt, being thrown on the upper side, already formed a tolerable work of defence. Behind
this his troops were formed, and proper measures
adopted for increasing its strength, with a determination never to abandon it.

Promptitude in decision, and activity in execution, constituted the leading traits of Jackson's character. No sooner had he resolved on the course
which he thought necessary to be pursued, than with
every possible despatch he hastened to its completion. Before him was an army proud of its name,
and distinguished for its deeds of valour ; opposed to which was his own unbending spirit, and an
inferior, undisciplined and unarmed force. He conceived, therefore, that his was a defensive policy :
that, by prudence, he should be able to preserve
what offensive operation might have a tendency to
endanger. Hence, with activity and industry, bas-
ed on a hope of ultimate success, he commenced his
plan of defence. determining to fortify himself effectually, as the peril and pressure of the moment would
permit. When to expect attack he could not tell ;
readiness to meet it was for him to determine on ; all
else was for the enemy. Promptly, therefore, he proceeded with his system of defence ; and with such
anxiety, that, until the night of the 27th, when his line
was completed, he never slept, or for a moment
closed his eyes. Resting his hope of safety here,
he was every where, through the night, present, encouraging his troops, and hastening a completion of
the work. The excitement produced by the mighty
object before him was such as overcame the demand

21*

of nature, and for five days and four nights he was
without sleep, and constantly employed. His line
of defence being completed on the night of the
27th, he, for the first time since the arrival of the
enemy, retired to rest and repose.

The soldier who has stood the shock of battle,
and knows what slight circumstances oftentimes
produce decided advantages, will be able to appreciate the events of this night.   Although the dreadful carnage of the 8th of January, hereafter to be
told, was in fact the finishing blow, that struck down
the towering hopes of those invaders, yet in the
battle of the 23d is there to be found abundant
cause why success resulted to our arms.   The British had reached the Mississippi without the fire of
a gun, and encamped upon its banks as composed-
ly as if they had been seated on their own soil.
These were circumstances which awakened a be
lief that they expected little opposition, were certain of success, and that the troops with whom
they were to contend would scarcely venture to resist them: resting thus confidently in the expectation of success, they would the next day have moved forward, and succeeded in the accomplishment
of their designs.   Jackson, convinced that an early impression was essential to ultimate success, had
resolved to assail them at the moment of their landing, and " attack them in their first position :" we
have, therefore, seen him, with a force inferior, by
one half, to that of the enemy, at an unexpected
moment, break into their camp, and, with his undisciplined yeomanry, drive before him the pride of
England, and the conquerors of Europe.   It was
an event that could not fail to destroy all previous
theories, and establish a conclusion, which our en-

emy had not before formed, that they were contending against valour inferior to none they had seen;—before which their own bravery had not stood, nor their skill availed them: it had the effect of satisfying them, that the quantity and kind of troops it was in our power to wield, must be different from any thing that had been represented to them; for, much as they had heard of the courage of the man with whom they were contending, they could not suppose, that a general, having a country to defend, and a reputation to preserve, would venture to attack, on their own chosen ground, a greatly superior army, and one, which, by the numerous victories it had achieved, had already acquired a fame in arms; they were convinced that his force must greatly surpass what they had expected, and be composed of materials different from what they had imagined.

The American troops, which were actually engaged, did not amount to two thousand men: they consisted of part of

Coffee's brigade and Captain Beal's company,	648
The 7th and 44th regiments, - -	763
Company of marines and artillery, - -	82
Plauche's and Daquin's battalions, -	488
And the Mississippi dragoons under Colonel Hinds, not in the action, - -	186
	2167*

which, for more than an hour, maintained a severe conflict with a force of four or five thousand, and retired in safety from the ground, with the loss of

---

* This statement may be relied on; it was furnished to the author by Colonel Robert Butler, adjutant-general of the southern division, who assured him it was correct.

but twenty-four killed, one hundred and fifteen wounded, and seventy-four made prisoners ; while the killed, wounded, and prisoners, of the enemy, were not less than four hundred.

Our officers and soldiers executed every order with promptitude, and nobly sustained their country's character. Lieutenant-Colonel Lauderdale, of Coffee's brigade, an officer of great promise, and on whom every reliance was placed, fell at his post, and at his duty : he had entered the service, and descended the river with the volunteers under General Jackson, in the winter of 1812, passed through all the hardships of the Creek war, and had ever manifested a readiness to act when nis country needed his services. Young, brave, and skilful, he had already afforded evidences of a capacity, which might, in future, have become useful; his exemplary conduct, both in civil and military life, had acquired for him a respect, that rendered his fall a subject of general regret. Lieutenant M'Lelland, a valuable young officer of the 7th, was also among the number of the slain.

Coffee's brigade, during the action, bravely supported the character they had established. The unequal contest in which they were engaged never occurred, nor, for a moment, checked the rapidity of their advance. Had the British known they were riflemen, without bayonets, a firm stand would nave arrested their progress, and destruction or capture would have been the inevitable consequence ; but this being unknown, every charge they made was crowned with success. Officers, from the highest to inferior grades, discharged what had been expected of them. Ensign Leach, of the 7th regiment, being wounded through the body, still remained at his post, and in the performance of his duty. Colonel Reuben Kemper, amidst the confusion introduced on the left wing, found himself at the head of a handful of men, detached from the main body, and in the midst of a party of the enemy: to attempt resistance was idle: he sought safety through stratagem. Calling to a group of soldiers who were near, in a positive tone he demanded of them where their regiment was lost themselves, they were unable to answer; but supposing him one of their own officers, they assented to his orders, and followed him to his own line, where they were made prisoners.

The 7th regiment, commanded by Major Piere, and the 44th, under Major Baker, aided by Major Butler, gallantly maintained the conflict, forced the enemy from every secure position he attempted to occupy, and drove him a mile from the first point of attack. Confiding in themselves, and their general, who was constantly with them, exposed to danger, and in the midst of the fight, inspiring by his ardour, and encouraging by his example, they advanced to the conflict, nor evinced a disposition to leave it until the prudence of their commander directed them to retire.

From the violence of the assault, the fears of the British had been greatly excited: to keep their apprehensions alive was considered important, with a view to destroy the overweening confidence with which they had arrived on our shores, and to compel them to act, for a time, upon the defensive. To effect this, General Coffee, with his brigade, was ordered down, on the morning of the 24th, to unite with Colonel Hinds, and make a show in the rear of Lacoste's plantation The enemy, not yet re-

covered of the panic of the preceding evening, be
lieved it was in contemplation to urge another attack, and immediately formed themselves to repel
it ; but Coffee, having succeeded in recovering some
of his horses, which were wandering along the margin of the swamp, and in regaining part of the cloth
ing which his troops had lost the night before, returned to the line, leaving them to conjecture the
objects of his movement.

The scanty supply of clothes and blankets that
remained to the soldiers, from their long and exposed marches, had been left where they dismounted
to meet the enemy. Their numbers were too limited, and the strength of their opponents too well
ascertained, for any part of their force to remain
and take care of what was left behind : it was so
essential to hasten on, reach their destination, and
be ready to act when the signal from the Caroline
should announce their co-operation necessary, that
no time was afforded them to secure their horses ;
—they were turned loose, and their recovery trusted to chance. Although many were regained,
many were lost ; while most of the men remained
with a single suit, to encounter, in the open field,
and in swamps covered with water, the hardships
of camp, and the severity of winter. It is a circumstance which entitles them to much credit, that
under privations so oppressive, complaints were
never heard. This state of things was not of long
continuance. The story of their sufferings was no
sooner known, than the legislature appropriated a
sum of money for their relief, which was greatly
increased by subscriptions in the city and neighbourhood. Materials being purchased, the ladies,
with that warmth of heart characteristic of their

sex, at once exerted themselves in removing their distresses : all their industry was called into action, and, in a little time, the suffering soldier was relieved. Such generous conduct, in extending assistance at a moment when it was so much needed, while it conferred on those females the highest honour, could not fail to nerve the arm of the brave with new zeal for the defence of their benefactresses. This distinguished mark of their benevolence is still remembered ; and often as these valiant men are heard to recount the dangers they have passed, they breathe a sentiment of gratitude to those who conferred upon them such distinguished marks of their kindness.

To keep up a show of resistance, detachments of light troops were occasionally kept in front of the line, harassing the enemy's advanced posts whenever an opportunity was offered. Every moment that could be gained, and every delay that could be extended to the enemy's attempts to reach the city, was of the utmost importance. The works were rapidly progressing, and hourly increasing in strength. The militia of the state were every day arriving, and every day the prospect of successful opposition was brightening.

The enemy still remained at his first encampment. To be in readiness to repel an assault when attempted, the most active exertions were made on the 24th and 25th. The canal, covering the front of our line, was deepened and widened, and a strong mud wall formed of the earth thrown out. To prevent any approach until his system of defence should be in greater forwardness, Jackson ordered the levee to be cut, about a hundred yards below the point he had occupied. The river being very high, a broad stream of water passed rapidly through the plain, of the depth of thirty or forty inches which prevented any approach of troops on foot. Embrasures were formed, and two pieces of artillery, under the command of Lieutenant Spotts, early on the morning of the 24th, were placed in a position to rake the road leading up the levee.

He was under constant apprehensions, lest, in spite of his exertions below, the city might, through some other route, be reached; and those fears were increased to-day, by a report that a strong force had arrived, and debarked at the head of Lake Borgne. This, however, proved to be unfounded: the enemy had not appeared in that direction, nor had the officer, to whom was intrusted the command of this fort, so much relied on, forgotten his duty, or forsaken his post. Acting upon the statement that Major Lacoste had retired from the fort, and fallen back on Bayou St. John, and incensed that orders, which, from their importance, should have been faithfully executed, had been thus lightly regarded, he hastened to inform him what he had understood, and to forbid his leaving his position. "The battery I have placed under your command must be defended at all hazards. In you, and the valour of your troops, I repose every confidence;—let me not be deceived. With us every thing goes on well: the enemy has not yet advanced. Our troops have covered themselves with glory: it is a noble example, and worthy to be followed by all. Maintain your post, nor ever think of retreating." To give additional strength to a place deemed so important, to inspire confidence, and ensure safety, Colonel Dyer and two hundred men were ordered to assist

in its defence, and act as videttes, in advance of the
occupied points.

General Morgan, who, at the English Turn, commanded the fort on the east bank of the river, was
instructed to proceed as near the enemy's camp as
prudence would permit, and, by destroying the levee
to let in the waters of the Mississippi between their.
The execution of this order, and a similar one, previously made, below the line of defence, had entirely insulated the enemy, and prevented his march
against either place. On the 26th, however, the
commanding general, fearing for the situation of
Morgan, who, from the British occupying the intermediate ground, was entirely detached from his
camp, directed him to abandon his encampment,
carry off such of the cannon as might be wanted,
and throw the remainder into the river, where they
could be again recovered when the waters receded ; to retire to the other side of the river, and assume a position on the right bank, nearly opposite
to his line, and have it fortified. This movement
was imposed by the relative disposition of the two
armies. Necessity, not choice, made it essential
that St. Leon should be abandoned.

From every intelligence, obtained through de
serters and prisoners, it was evident that the British
fleet would make an effort to ascend the river, and
co-operate with the troops already landed. Lest
this, or a diversion in a different quarter, might be
attempted, exertions were made to interpose such
defences on the Mississippi as might assure protection. The forts on the river, well supported with
brave men, and heavy pieces of artillery, might,
perhaps, have the effect to deter their shipping from
venturing in that direction, and dispose them to seek
22

some safer route, if any could be discovered. Pass Barrataria was best calculated for this purpose. The difficulty of ascending the Mississippi, from the rapidity of the current, i s winding course, and the ample protection given at Forts St. Philip and Bourbon, were circumstances to which, it was not to be inferred, the British were strangers. It was a more rational conjecture that they would seek a passage through Barrataria, proceed up on the right bank of the river, and gain a position whence, co-operating with the forces on the east side, they might drive our troops from the line they had formed. Major Reynolds was acccordingly ordered thither, with instructions to place the bayous, emptying through this pass, in the best possible state of defence—to occupy the island—to mount sufficient ordnance, and draw a chain, within cannonshot, across, and protect it from approach. Lafite who had been heretofore promised pardon for the outrages he had committed against the laws of the United States, was also despatched with Reynolds. He was selected, because his knowledge of the topography and precise situation of this section of the state was remarkably correct: it was the point where he had constantly rendezvoused, during the time of cruising against the merchant vessels of Spain, under a commission obtained at Carthagena, and where he had become perfectly acquainted with every inlet and entrance to the gulf through which a passage could be effected.

With these arrangements—treason apart—all anxiously alive to the interest of the country, and disposed to protect it, there was little room to apprehend disaster. To use the general's own expression, on another occasion, "the surest defence, and

one which seldom failed of success, was a rampart
of high-minded and brave men." There were some
of this description with him, on whom he could
safely rely, in moments of extreme peril.

As yet the enemy were uninformed of the position of Jackson. They had been constantly engaged, since their landing, in procuring from their shipping every thing necessary to ulterior operations
A complete command on the lakes, and possession
of a point on the margin, presented an uninterrupt
ed ingress and egress, and afforded the opportunity
of conveying whatever was wanted, in perfect safety, to their camp. The height of the Mississippi,
and the discharge of water through the openings
made in the levee, had given an increased depth to
the canal, from which they had first debarked, enabled them to advance their boats much farther, in
the direction of their encampment, and to bring up
their artillery, bombs, and munitions. Thus engaged, during the first three days after their arrival
early on the morning of the 27th, a battery was
discovered on the bank of the river, erected during
the preceding night, and on which were mounted
several pieces of heavy ordnance ; from this position
a fire was opened on the Caroline schooner, lying
under the opposite shore.

After the battle of the 23d, in which this vessel
had so effectually aided, she had passed to the opposite side of the river, where she had since lain.
Her services were too highly appreciated not to be
again desired, in the event the enemy should endeavour to advance. Her present situation was
considered unsafe, but it had been essayed in vain
to advance her higher up the stream. No favourable breeze had yet arisen to aid her in stemming

the current; and towing, and other remedies, had been resorted to without success. Her safety might have been ensured by floating her down the river, and placing her under cover of the guns of the fort, though it was preferred, as a matter of policy, to risk her where she was, hourly calculating that a favourable wind might relieve her, rather than, by dropping her with the current, lose those benefits which, against an advance of the enemy, it might be in her power to extend. Commodore Patterson had left her on the 26th, by the orders of the general, when Captain Henly made a further, but ineffectual effort to force her up the current, near the line, for the double purpose of its defence and for her own safety.

These attempts to remove her being discovered at daylight, on the morning of the 27th, a battery, mounting five guns, opened upon her, discharging bombs and red-hot shot: it was spiritedly answered, but without affecting the battery ; there being but a long twelve pounder that could reach. The second fire had lodged a hot shot in the hold, directly under her cables, whence it could not be removed, and where it immediately communicated fire to the schooner. The shot from the battery were con stantly taking effect, firing her in different places while the blaze, already kindled under her cables, was rapidly extending. A well-grounded appre- hension of her commander, that she could be no longer defended, induced a fear lest the magazine should be reached, and every thing destroyed. One of his crew being killed, and six wounded, and not a glimmering of hope entertained that she could be preserved, orders were given to abandon her. The crew in safety reached the shore, and in a short time she blew up.

Although unexpectedly deprived of so material a dependence, an opportunity was soon presented of using her brave crew to advantage. Gathering confidence from what had been just effected, the enemy left their encampment, and moved in the direction of our line. Their numbers had been increased, and Major-General Sir Edward Packenham now commanded in person. Early on the 28th, his columns commenced their advance to storm our works. At the distance of half a mile, their heavy artillery opened, and quantities of bombs, balls, and congreve rockets, were discharged. It was a scene of terror, which they had probably calculat ed would excite a panic in the minds of the raw troops of our army, and compel them to surrender at discretion. Their congreve rockets, though a kind of instrument of destruction to which our troops, unskilled in the science of warfare, had been hitherto strangers, excited no other feeling than that which novelty inspires. At the moment, therefore, that the British, in different columns, were moving up, in all the pomp of battle, preceded by these insignia of terror, more than danger, and were expecting to behold their "Yankee foes" flee before them, our batteries halted their advance.

In addition to the two pieces of cannon, mounted on our works on the 24th, three others, of heavy caliber. obtained from the navy department, had been formed along the line ; these, opening on the enemy, checked their progress, and disclosed to them the hazard of the project they were on. Lieutenants Crawley and Norris volunteered, and. with the crew of the Caroline, maintained, at the

22*

guns they commanded, that firmness and decision for which they had been so highly distinguished. They had been selected by the general, because of their superior knowledge in gunnery, and, on this occasion, gave a further evidence of their skill, and of a disposition to act in any situation where they could be serviceable. The line, which, from the labours bestowed on it, was daily strengthening, was not yet in a situation effectually to resist; this deficiency, however, was well remedied by the brave men who were formed in its rear.

From the river the greatest injury was effected Lieutenant Thompson, who commanded the Louisiana sloop, opposite the line of defence, no sooner discovered the columns approaching, than, warping her around, he brought her starboard guns to bear, and forced them to retreat: but, from their heavy artillery, the enemy maintained the conflict with great spirit, constantly discharging their bombs and rockets for seven hours, when, unable to make a breach, or silence the fire from the sloop, they abandoned a contest where few advantages seemed to be presented. The crew of this vessel was composed of new recruits, and of discordant materials —of soldiers, citizens, and seamen ; yet, by the activity of their commander, were they so well perfected in duty, that they already managed their guns with the greatest certainty of effect ; and, by three o'clock in the evening, with the aid of the land batteries, had completely driven back the enemy. Imboldened by the effect produced the day before on the Caroline, the furnaces of the enemy were put in operation, and numbers of hot shot thrown from a heavy piece, which was protected by the levee. An attempt was made to carry it off.

In their endeavours to remove it, " I saw," says Commodore Patterson, " distinctly, with the aid of a glass, several balls strike in the midst of the men who were employed in dragging it away."   In this engagement, waged for seven hours, we received little or no injury.   The Louisiana sloop, against which the most violent exertions were made, had but a single man wounded, by the fragments of a shell, which burst over her deck.   Our entire loss did not exceed nine killed, and eight or ten wounded.   The enemy, being more exposed, acting in the open field, and in range of our guns, suffered considerable injury ;   at least one hundred and twenty were killed and wounded.

Among the killed, on our side, was Colonel James Henderson, of the Tennessee militia.   An advance party of the British had, during the action, taken post behind a fence that ran obliquely to our line.   Henderson, with a detachment of two hundred men, was sent out by General Carroll to drive them from a position whence they were greatly annoying our troops.   Had he advanced in the manner directed, he would have been less exposed, and more effectually secured the object intended ; but, misunderstanding the order, he proceeded in a different route, and fell a victim to his error.   Instead of marching in the direction of the wood, and turning the enemy, which might have cut off their retreat, he proceeded in front, towards the river, leaving them in rear of the fence, and himself and his detachment exposed.   His mistake being perceived from the line, he was called by the adjutant-general, and directed to return ; but the noise of the waters, through which they were wading, prevented any communication.   Having reached a knoll of dry ground, he attempted the execution of his order, but soon fell, by a wound in the head. Deprived of their commander, and perceiving their situation hazardous, the detachment retreated to the line. with the loss of their colonel and five men.

While this advance was made, a column of the enemy was threatening our extreme left ; to frustrate the attempt, Coffee was ordered with his riflemen to hasten through the woods, and check their approach. The enemy, greatly superior to him in numbers, no sooner discovered his movement than they retired, and abandoned the attack they had meditated.

A supposed disaffection in New Orleans, and an enemy in front, were circumstances well calculated to excite unpleasant forebodings. General Jackson believed it necessary to his security, while contending with avowed foes, not to be wholly inattentive to dangers at home ; but, by guarding vigilantly, to be able to suppress any treasonable purpose the moment it should be developed. Previously to departing from the city, on the evening of the 23d, he ordered Major Butler, his aid, to remain with the guards, and be vigilant that nothing transpired in his absence calculated to operate injuriously. His fears that there were many of the inhabitants, who felt no attachment to the government, and would not scruple to surrender, whenever, prompted by their interest, it should become necessary, have been noticed. In this belief, subsequent circumstances evinced there was no mistake, and showed that to his energy is to be ascribed the cause the country was saved. It is a fact, which was disclosed on making an exchange of prisoners, that, in despite of all our efforts, the enemy were daily apprized of every

thing that transpired in our camp. Every arrangement, and every change of position, was immediately communicated. "Nothing," remarked a British
officer, at the close of the invasion, "was kept a
secret from us, except your numbers; this, although diligently sought, could never be procured."

Between the 23d and the attack, on the 28th, to
carry our line, Major Butler, who still remained in
the city, was applied to by Fulwar Skipwith, speak-
er of the senate, to ascertain the commanding general's views, provided he should be driven from his
line of encampment, and compelled to retreat
through the city; would he, in that event, destroy
it? It was, indeed, a curious inquiry from one who,
having spent his life in serving his country, might
better have understood the duty of a subordinate
officer; and that, even if, from his situation, Major
Butler had so far acquired the confidence of his
general as to have become acquainted with his designs, he was not at liberty to divulge them, without destroying confidence, and acting criminally.
On asking the cause of the inquiry, Mr. Skipwith
replied, it was understood that, if driven from his
position, and made to retreat upon the city, General
Jackson had it in contemplation to lay it in ruins;
the legislature, he said, desired information on this
subject, that, if such were his intentions, they might,
by offering terms of capitulation, avert so serious a
calamity. That a sentiment, having for its object
a surrender of the city, should be entertained by
this body, was scarcely credible; yet a few days
brought the certainty of it more fully to view, and
showed that they were already devising plans tc
ensure the safety of themselves and property at any
sacrifice. While the general was hastening along

the line, from ordering Coffee against a column of
the British on the extreme left, he was hailed by
Mr. Duncan, one of his volunteer aids, and informed
that it was agitated, secretly, by the members of
the legislature, to offer terms of capitulation to the
enemy, and proffer a surrender; and that Governor
Claiborne awaited his orders on the subject. Poised
as was the result, the safety or fall of the city resting in uncertainty, although it was plainly to be
perceived, that, with a strong army before them, no
such resolution could be carried into effect, yet it
might be productive of evil, and, in the end, bring
about the most fatal consequences. Even the dis
closure of such a wish, on the part of the legislature, might create parties, excite opposition in the
army, and inspire the enemy with renewed confidence. The Tennessee forces, and Mississippi volunteers, it was not feared, would be affected by the
measure; but it might detach the Louisiana militia,
and even extend itself to the ranks of the regular
troops. Jackson was greatly incensed, that those,
whose safety he had so much at heart, should be
seeking, under the authority of office, to mar his
best exertions. He was, however, too warmly pressed at the moment,—for the battle was raging,—to
give it the attention its importance merited; but,
availing himself of the first respite from the violence of the attack waged against him, he apprized
Governor Claiborne of what he had heard; ordered
him closely to watch the conduct of the legislature,
and, the moment the project of offering a capitulation to the enemy should be fully disclosed, to place
a guard at the door, and confine them to their cham-
ber. The governor, in his zeal to execute the command, and from a fear of the consequences involved

in such conduct, construed as imperative an order which was merely contingent; and, placing an armed force at the door of the capitol, prevented the members from convening, and their schemes from maturing.

The purport of this order was misconceived by the governor; or, perhaps, with a view to avoid subsequent inconveniences, was designedly mistaken. Jackson's object was not to restrain the legislature in the discharge of their official duties; for, although he thought that such a moment, when the sound of the cannon was constantly pealing in their ears, was inauspicious to wholesome legislation, and that it would have better comported with the state of the times for them to abandon their civil duties, and appear in the field, yet was it a matter indelicate to be proposed; and it was hence preferred, that they should adopt whatever course might be suggested by their own notions of propriety. This sentiment would have been still adhered to; but when, through the communication of Mr. Duncan, they were represented as entertaining schemes adverse to the general interest of the country, the necessity of a different course of conduct was obvious But he did not order Governor Claiborne to interfere with their duties; on the contrary, he was instructed, so soon as any thing hostile to the general cause should be ascertained, to place a guard at the door, and keep the members to their duty. "My object in this," remarked the general, "was, that then they would be able to proceed with their business without producing the slightest injury: whatever schemes they might entertain would have remained with themselves, without the power of circulating them to the prejudice of any other interest than their own. Claiborne mistook my order, and, instead of shutting them in doors, contrary to my wishes, turned them out."

Before this he had been called on by a special committee of the legislature to know what his course would be, should necessity drive him from his posi tion. "If," replied the general, "I thought the hair of my head could divine what I should do, I would cut it off: go back with this answer; say to your honourable body, that, if disaster does overtake me, and the fate of war drives me from my line to the city, they may expect to have a very warm session." "And what did you design to do," one inquired, "provided you had been forced to retreat?" "I should,' he replied, "have retreated to the city, fired it, and fought the enemy amidst the surrounding flames. There were with me men of wealth, owners of considerable property, who, in such an event, would have been amongst the foremost to have applied the torch to their own buildings; and what they had left undone, I should have completed. Nothing for the comfortable maintenance of the enemy would have been left in the rear. I would have destroyed New Orleans, occupied a position above on the river, cut off all supplies, and in this way compelled them to depart from the country."

We shall not pretend to ascribe this conduct to disaffection to the government, or to treasonable motives. The impulse that produced it was, no doubt, interest—a principle of the human mind which strongly sways, and often destroys, its best conclusions. The disparity of the two armies, in numbers, preparation, and discipline, had excited apprehension, and destroyed hope. If Jackson were driven back,—and little else was looked for,—

rumour fixed his determination of devoting the city to destruction; but, even if such were not his intention, the vengeance of the enemy might be fairly calculated to be in proportion to the opposition they should receive. The government was represented in the person of the commanding general, on whom rested all responsibility, and whose voice, on the subject of resistance or capitulation, should alone have been heard. In the field were persons, enduring hardships, and straining every nerve, for the general safety. A few of the members of their own body, too, were there, who did not despond.*

Additional guards were posted along the swamp, on both sides of the Mississippi, to arrest all intercourse; while on the river, the common highway watch-boats were constantly plying, during the night, in different directions, so that a log could scarcely float down the stream unperceived. Two flat-bottomed boats, on a dark night, were turned adrift above, to ascertain if vigilance were preserved, and whether there would be any possibility of escaping the guards, and passing in safety to the British lines. The light boats discovered them on their passage, and, on the alarm being given, they were opened upon by the Louisiana sloop, the batteries on the shore, and in a few minutes were sunk. In spite, however, of every precaution, Treason discovered avenues, through which to project and execute her nefarious plans, and through them

---

* Only four members of the legislature appeared in the field to defend their country. We regret not knowing the name of one of these persons: those we have ascertained are, General Garrigue Flojack, Major Eziel, and Mr. Bufort, who, abandoning their civil duties for the field, afforded examples worthy of imitation.

2

was constantly afforded information to the enemy carried to them, no doubt, by adventurous friends who effected their nightly passage through the deepest parts of the swamp where it was impossible for sentinels to be stationed

Great inconvenience was sustained for tne want of arms, and much anxiety felt, lest the enemy, through their faithful adherents, might, on this subject also, obtain information; to prevent it, as far as possible, General Jackson endeavoured to conceal the strength of his army, by suffering his reports to be seen by none but himself and the adjutant-general. Many of the troops in the field were supplied with common guns, which were of little service. The Kentucky troops, daily expected, were also understood to be badly provided with arms. Uncertain but that the city might yet contain many articles that would be serviceable, orders were issued to the mayor of New Orleans, directing him to inquire through every store and house, and take possession of all the muskets, bayonets, spades and axes he could find. Understanding too, there were many young men, who, from different pretexts, had not appeared in the field, he was instructed to obtain a register of every man in the city, under the age of fifty, that measures might be concerted for drawing forth those who had hitherto appeared backward in the pending contest.

Frequent light skirmishes, by advanced parties, without material effect on either side, were the only incidents that took place for several days. Colonel Hinds, at the head of the Mississippi dragoons, on the 30th, was ordered to dislodge a party of the enemy, who, under cover of a ditch that ran across the plain, were annoying our fatigue parties. In his advance, he was unexpectedly thrown into an ambuscade, and became exposed to the fire of a line, which had hitherto been unobserved. His collected conduct, and gallant deportment, gained him and his corps the approbation of the command-ing general, and extricated him from the danger in which he was placed. The enemy, forced from their position, retired, and he returned to the line, with the loss of five men.

CHAPTER X.

*Attack of the 1st of January.—General Jackson's line of defence
—Kentucky troops arrive at head-quarters.—British army re-
enforced; their preparations for attack.—Battle of the 8th of
January, and repulse of the enemy.—American redoubt carried,
and retaken.—Colonel Thornton proceeds against General
Morgan's line, and takes possession of it.—Letter of Captain
Wilkinson.—British watch word.—Generous conduct of the
American soldiers.—Morgan's line regained.—General Lambert
requests a suspension of hostilities.—Armistice concluded.—Ex-
ecution of an American soldier by the British.*

THE British were encamped two miles below the
American army, on a perfect plain, in full view.
Although foiled in their attempt to carry our works
by their batteries on the 28th, they resolved upon
another attack, which they believed would be more
successful.   Presuming their failure to have arisen
from not having sufficiently strong batteries and
heavy ordnance, a more enlarged arrangement was
resorted to, with a confidence of silencing opposi
tion.   The interim between the 28th of December
and 1st of January was spent in preparing to execute their designs.   Their boats, had been despatched to the shipping, and an additional supply
of heavy cannon landed through Bayou Bienvenu,
whence they had first debarked.

During the night of the 31st, they were busily
engaged.   An impenetrable fog, next morning, not
dispelled until nine o'clock, by concealing their
purpose, aided them in the plans they were projecting, and gave time for the completion of their works.
This having disappeared, several heavy batteries,
at the distance of six hundred yards, mounting

eighteen and twenty-four pound carronades, were presented to view. No sooner was it sufficiently clear to distinguish objects at a distance, than these were opened, and a tremendous burst of artillery commenced, accompanied with congreve rockets, that filled the air in all directions. Our troops, protected by a defence, which, from their constant labours, they believed to be impregnable, undisturbed, maintained their ground, and, by their skilful management, succeeded in dismounting the guns of the enemy. The British, through the friendly interference of some disaffected citizens, having been apprized of the situation of the general's quarters, that he dwelt in a house at a small distance in the rear of his line of defence, against it directed their first and principal efforts, with a view to destroy the commander. So great was the number of balls thrown, that, in a little while, its porticos were beaten down, and the building made a complete wreck. In this design they were disappointed; for with Jackson it was a constant practice, on the first appearance of danger, not to wait in his quarters, watching events, but instantly to proceed to the line, to form arrangements as circumstances might require. Constantly in expectation of a charge, he was never absent from the post of danger; and thither he had this morning repaired, at the first sound of the cannon, to aid in defence, and inspire his troops with firmness. Our guns, along the line, now opened, to repel the assault, and a constant roar of cannon, on both sides, continued until nearly noon; when, by the superior skill of our engineers, the two batteries formed on the right, next the woods, were nearly beaten down, and many of the guns dismounted, broken, and render

23 *

ed useless. That next the river still continued its fire, until three o'clock; when, perceiving all attempts to force a breach ineffectual, the enemy gave up the contest, and retired. Every act of theirs discovers a strange delusion, and unfolds on what wild and fanciful grounds all their expectations were founded.

That they could effect an opening, and march through the strong defence in their front, was an idea so fondly cherished, that an apprehension of failure had scarcely occurred. So sanguine were they in this belief, that, early in the morning, their soldiers were arranged along the ditches, in rear of their batteries, ready to advance to the charge, the moment a breach could be made. Here, by their situation, protected from danger, they remained, waiting the result. But, their efforts not having produced the slightest impression, nor their rockets the effect of driving our militia away, they abandoned the contest, and retired to their camp, leaving their batteries materially injured.

It occurred to the British commander, an attack might be made to advantage next the woods, and a force was accordingly ordered to penetrate in this direction, and turn the left of our line, which was supposed not to extend farther than to the margin of the swamp. In this way, it was expected a diversion could be made, while the reserve columns, being in waiting, were to press forward the moment this object could be effected. Here, too, disappointment resulted. Coffee's brigade, being extended into the swamp as far as it was possible for an advancing party to penetrate, brought unexpected dangers into view, and occasioned an abandonment of the project. That to turn the extreme left of the line was practicable, and might be attempted, was the subject of early consideration; and necessary precaution had been taken to prevent it.— Although cutting the levee had raised the water in the swamp, and increased the difficulties of keeping troops there, yet a fear lest this pass might be sought by the enemy, and the rear of the line gained, had determined the general to extend his defence even here. This had been intrusted to General Coffee; and surely a more arduous duty can scarcely be imagined. To form a breastwork, in such a place, was attended with many difficulties, and considerable exposure. A slight defence, however, had been thrown up, and the underwood, for thirty or forty yards in front, cut down, that the riflemen, stationed for its protection, might have a complete view of any force, which might attempt a passage. When it is recollected this position was to be maintained night and day, uncertain of the moment of attack, and that the only opportunity afforded our troops for rest was on logs and brush, by which they were raised above the surrounding water, it may be truly said, that seldom has it fallen to the lot of any to encounter greater hardships: but, accustomed to privation, and alive to those feelings which a love of country inspires, they obeyed, and cheerfully kept their position until danger had subsided. Sensible of the importance of the point they defended, that it was necessary to be maintained, be the sacrifice what it might, they looked to nothing but a faithful discharge of the trust confided to them.

Our loss, in this affair, was eleven killed, and twenty-three wounded: that of the enemy was never correctly known. The only certain informa tion is contained in a communication of the 28th instant from General Lambert to Earl Bathurst, in which the loss, from the 1st to the 5th, is stated at seventy-eight. Many allowances, however, are to be made for this report. From the great precision of our fire, their loss was, no doubt, considerable.—The enemy's heavy shot having penetrated our intrenchment, in many places, it was discovered not to be as strong as had been imagined. Fatigue parties were again employed, and its strength daily increased: an additional number of bales of cotton were taken to be applied to defending the embrasures. A Frenchman, whose property had been thus, without his consent, seized, fearful of the injury it might sustain, proceeded in person to General Jackson, to reclaim it, and to demand its delivery. The general, having heard his complaint, and ascertained from him that he was unemployed in any military service, directed a musket to be brought to him, and, placing it in his hand, ordered him on the line, remarking, at the same time, that, as he seemed to be a man possessed of property, he knew of none who had a better right to fight, to defend it.

It was understood by Jackson, that the enemy were in daily expectation of re-enforcements; though he rested with confidence in the belief, that a few more days would also bring to his assistance the troops from Kentucky. Each party, therefore, was constantly engaged in preparation, the one to wage a vigorous attack, the other to oppose it.

The position of the American army was in the rear of an intrenchment formed of earth, which extended in a straight line from the river to a cor. siderable distance in the swamp. In front was a deep ditch, which had been formerly used as a mill-race. The Mississippi had receded, and left this dry, next the river, though in many places the water still remained. Along the line, at unequal distances, to the centre of General Carroll's command, were guns mounted, of different caliber, from six to thirty-two pounders. Near the river, in advance of the intrenchment, was a redoubt, with embrasures, commanding the road along the levee, calculated to rake the ditch in front.

General Morgan was ordered, on the 24th of December, to cross to the west bank of the Mississippi. From apprehension that an attempt might be made through Barrataria, and the city reached from the right bank, the general had extended his defence there: in fact, unacquainted with the enemy's views,—not knowing the number of their troops, he had carefully divided out his forces, that he might be able to protect, in whatever direction an assault should be waged. His greatest fears, and hence his strongest defence, next to the one occupied by himself, was on the Chef Menteur road, where Governor Claiborne, at the head of the Louisiana militia, was posted. The position on the right was formed on the same plan with the line on the left,—lower down than that on the left, extending to the swamp at right angles with the river Here General Morgan commanded.

To be prepared against every possible contingency, Jackson had established another line of defence, about two miles in the rear of the one at present occupied, which was intended as a rallying point, if driven from his first position. With the aid of his cavalry, to give a momentary check to the advance of the enemy, he expected to be en

abled, with inconsiderable injury, to reach it; where
he would again have advantages on his side, be in
a situation to dispute a farther passage to the city,
and arrest their progress.   To inspirit his own
soldiers, and to exhibit to the enemy as great a
show as possible of strength and intended resistance, his unarmed troops, which constituted no
very inconsiderable number, were here stationed.
All intercourse between the lines, but by confidential officers, was prohibited, and every vigilance employed, not only to keep this want of preparation
concealed from the enemy, but even from being
known on his own lines.

Occasional firing at a distance, which produced
nothing of consequence, was all that marked the
interim from the 1st to the 8th.

On the 4th of this month, the long-expected re-
enforcement from Kentucky, amounting to twenty-
two hundred and fifty, under Major-General Thomas,
arrived at head-quarters; but so ill provided with
arms, as to be incapable of rendering any considerable service.   The alacrity with which the citizens
of this state had proceeded to the frontiers, and
aided in the north-western campaigns, added to the
disasters which ill-timed policy or misfortune had
produced, had created such a drain, that arms were
not to be procured.   They had advanced, however,
to their point of destination, with an expectation of
being supplied on their arrival.   About five hundred of them had muskets; the rest were provided
with guns, from which little or no advantage could
be expected.   The mayor of New Orleans, at the
request of General Jackson, had drawn from the
city every weapon that could be found; while the
arrival of the Louisiana militia, in an equally un

prepared situation, rendered it impossible foɪ the evil to be effectually remedied.   A boat, laden with arms, was somewhere on the riʋer, intended for the use of the lower country ; but where it was, or when it might arrive, rested alone on conjecture. Expresses had been despatched up the river, for three hundred miles, to hasten it on; still there were no tidings of an approach.   That so many ꝺrave men should be compelled to stand w:th folded arms, unable to render the least possible service to their country, was an event, which did not fail to excite the sensibility of the general.   His mind, prepared for any thing but despondency, sought relief in vain.   No alternative was presented, but to place them at his intrenchment in the rear, conceal their actual condition, and, by the show they might make, add to his appearance, without at all increasing his strength.

Information was received, that Major-General Lambert had joined the British commander-in-chief, with a considerable re-enforcement. It had been announced in the American camp, that additional forces were expected, and something decisive might be looked for, so soon as they should arrive.   This circumstance, with others, had led to the conclusion that a few days more would, in aɪl probability, decide the fate of the city.   It was more than eveɪ necessary to keep concealed the situation of his army ; and, above all, to preserve as secret as possible its unarmed condition.   To restrict all communication, even with his own lines, was now, as danger increased, rendered more impurtant.   None were permitted to leave the line, and nʋne from without to pass into camp, but such as were to be implicitly confided in.   The line of sentinels wɜ strengthened in front, that none might pass to the enemy, should desertion be attempted: yet, notwithstanding this precaution, his plans were disclosed. On the night of the 6th, a soldier from the line, by some means, succeeded in eluding the vigilance of our sentinels. Early next morning his departure was discovered: it was at once correctly conjectured he had gone to the enemy, and would, no doubt, afford them all the information in his power. He unfolded to the British the situation of the American line; the late re-enforcements we had received, and the unarmed condition of many of the troops; and, pointing to the centre of General Carroll's division as a place occupied by militia alone, recommended it as the point where an attack might be most safely made.

Other intelligence received was confirmatory of the belief of an impending attack. From some prisoners, taken on the lake, it was ascertained the enemy were busily engaged in deepening Villery's Canal, with a view of passing their boats and ordnance to the Mississippi. During the 7th, a constant bustle was perceived in the British camp. Along the borders of the canal, their soldiers were continually in motion, marching and manœuvring, for no other purpose than to conceal those who were busily engaged at work in the rear. To ascertain the cause of this uncommon stir, and learn their designs, as far as was practicable, Commodore Patterson had proceeded down the river, on the opposite side, and, having gained a favourable position, in front of their encampment, discovered them to be actually engaged in deepening the passage to the river. It was no difficult matter to divine their purpose. No other conjecture could be entertained,

than that an assault was intended to be made on
the line of defence commanded by General Mor
gan; which, if gained, would expose our troops on
the left bank to the fire of the redoubt erected on
the right; and in this way compel them to an
abandonment of their position.   To counteract this
scheme was important; and measures were immediately taken to prevent the execution of a plan,
which, if successful, would be attended with incalculable dangers.   An increased strength was given
to this line.   The second regiment of Louisiana
militia, and four hundred Kentucky troops, were
directed to be crossed over, to protect it.   Owing
to some delay in arming them, the latter, amounting, instead of four hundred, to but one hundred
and eighty, did not arrive until the morning of the
8th.   A little before day, they were despatched to
aid an advanced party, who, under the command
of Major Arnaut, had been sent to watch the movements of the enemy, and oppose their landing.
The hopes indulged from their opposition were not
realized; and the enemy reached the shore.

Morgan's position, besides being strengthened by
several brass twelves, was defended by a strong
battery, mounting twenty-four pounders, directed
by Commodore Patterson, which afforded additional
security.   The line itself was not strong, yet, if
properly maintained by the troops selected to defend it, was believed fully adequate to the purposes
of successful resistance.   Late it night, Patterson
ascertained the enemy had succeeded in passing
their boats through the canal, and immediately
communicated his information to the general.   The
commodore had formed the idea of dropping the
Louisiana schooner down, to attack and sink them

This thought, though well conceived, was abandoned, from the danger involved, and from an apprehension lest the batteries erected on the river, with
which she would come in collision, might, by the
aid of hot shot, succeed in blowing her up. It was
preferred to await their arrival, believing it would
be practicable, with the bravery of more than fifteen
hundred men, and the slender advantages possessed
from their line of defence, to maintain their position.

On the left bank, where the general in person
commanded, every thing was in readiness to meet
the assault when it should be made. The redoubt
on the levee was defended by a company of the
seventh regiment, under the command of Lieutenant Ross. The regular troops occupied that part
of the intrenchment next the river. General Carroll's division was in the centre, supported by the
Kentucky troops, under General John Adair ; while
the extreme left, extending for a considerable distance into the swamp, was protected by the brigade
of General Coffee. How soon the attack would
be waged was uncertain. General Jackson, un-
moved by appearances, anxiously desired a contest, which he believed would give a triumph
to his arms, and terminate the hardships of his
soldiers. Unremitting in exertion, and constantly
vigilant, his precaution kept pace with the zeal and
preparation of the enemy. He seldom slept: he
was always at his post, performing the duties of
both general and soldier. His sentinels were
doubled, and extended as far as possible in the direction of the British camp ; while a considerable
portion of the troops were constantly at the line,
with arms in their hands, ready to act when the
first alarm should be given.

For eight days had the two armies lain upon the same field, and in view of each other, without any thing decisive on either side. Twice, since their landing, had the British columns essayed to effect by storm the execution of their plans, and twice had failed, and been compelled to relinquish the attempt. It was not to be expected that things could long remain in this dubious state.

The 8th of January at length arrived. The day dawned; and the signals, intended to produce concert in the enemy's movements, were descried. On the left, near the swamp, a sky-rocket was perceived rising in the air; and presently another ascended from the right, next the river. They were intended to announce that all was ready, to carry by storm a defence which had twice foiled their utmost efforts. Instantly the charge was made, and with such rapidity, that our soldiers, at the outposts, with difficulty fled in.

The British batteries, which had been demolished on the 1st of the month, had been re-established during the preceding night, and heavy pieces of cannon mounted, to aid in their intended operations. These now opened, and showers of bombs and balls were poured upon our line; while the air was lighted with their congreve rockets. The two divisions, commanded by Sir Edward Packenham in person, and supported by Generals Keane and Gibbs, pressed forward; the right against the centre of General Carroll's command, the left against our redoubt on the levee. A thick fog, that obscured the morning, enabled them to approach within a short distance of our intrenchment. before they were discovered. They were now perceived advancing with firm, quick. and steady pace, in column, with

a front of sixty or seventy deep. Our troops, who
had for some time been in readiness, gave three
cheers, and instantly the whole line was lighted
with the blaze of their fire. A burst of artillery
and small arms, pouring with destructive aim upon
them, mowed down their front, and arrested their
advance. In our musketry there was not a moment's intermission; as one party discharged their
pieces, another succeeded; alternately loading and
appearing, no pause could be perceived,—it was
one continued volley. The columns already perceived their dangerous situation. Battery No. 7,
on the left, was ably served by Lieutenant Spotts,
and galled them with an incessant fire. Batteries
No. 6 and 8 were no less actively employed, and no
less successful in felling them to the ground. Notwithstanding the severity of our fire, which few
troops could for a moment have withstood, some of
those brave men pressed on, and succeeded in
gaining the ditch, in front of our works, where they
remained during the action, and were afterwards
made prisoners. The horror before them was too
great to be withstood; and already were the British
troops seen wavering in their determination, and
receding from the conflict. At this moment, Sir
Edward Packenham, hastening to the front, endeavoured to inspire them with renewed zeal. His
example was of short continuance; he soon fell,
mortally wounded, in the arms of his aid-de-camp,
not far from our line. Generals Gibbs and Keane
also fell, and were borne from the field, dangerously wounded. At this moment, General Lambert,
who was advancing at a small distance in the rear,
with the reserve, met the columns precipitately retreating, and in great confusion. His efforts to

stop them were unavailing,—they continued retreating, until they reached a ditch, at the distance
of four hundred yards, where, a momentary safety
being found, they were rallied, and halted.

The field before them, over which they had ad
vanced, was strewed with the dead and dying
Danger hovered still around; yet, urged and encouraged by their officers, who feared their own
disgrace involved in the failure, they again mo ed
to the charge. They were already near enough to
deploy, and were endeavouring to do so; but the
same constant and unremitted resistance that caused
their first retreat continued yet unabated. Our
batteries had never ceased their fire; their constant
discharges of grape and canister, and the fatal
aim of our musketry, mowed down the front of the
columns as fast as they could be formed. Satisfied
nothing could be done, and that certain destruction
awaited all further attempts, they forsook the field
in disorder, leaving it almost entirely covered with
the dead and wounded. It was in vain their officers endeavoured to animate them to further resistance, and equally vain to attempt coercion. The
panic produced from the dreadful repulse they had
experienced; the plain, on which they had acted
being covered with innumerable bodies of their
countrymen; while, with their most zealous exer
tions, they had been unable to obtain the slightest
advantage,—were circumstances well calculated to
make even the most submissive soldier oppose the
authority that would have controlled him.

The light companies of fusileers, the forty-third
and ninety-third regiments, and one hundred men
from the West India regiment, led on by Colone
Rennie, were ordered to proceed under cover of

24 *

some chimneys, standing in the field, until having cleared them, to oblique to the river, and advance, protected by the levee, against our redoubt on the right. This work, having been but lately commenced, was in an unfinished state. It was not until the 4th, that General Jackson, much against his own opinion, had yielded to the suggestions of others, and permitted its projection; and, considering the plan on which it had been sketched, it had not yet received that strength necessary to its safe defence. The detachment ordered against this place formed the left of General Keane's command. Rennie executed his orders with great bravery; and, urging forward, arrived at the ditch. His advance was greatly annoyed by Commodore Patterson's battery on the left bank, and the cannon mounted on the redoubt; but, reaching our works, and passing the ditch, Rennie, sword in hand, leaped on the wall, and, calling to his troops, bade them follow; he had scarcely spoken, when he fell by the fatal aim of our riflemen. Pressed by the impetuosity of superior numbers, who were mounting the wall, and entering at the embrasures, our troops had retired to the line, in rear of the redoubt. A momentary pause ensued, but only to be interrupted with increased horrors. Captain Beal, with the city riflemen, cool and self-possessed, perceiving the enemy in his front, opened upon them, and at every discharge brought the object to the ground. To advance, or maintain the point gained, was equally impracticable for the enemy: to retreat or surrender was the only alternative; for they already perceived the division on the right thrown into confusion, and hastily leaving the field.

General Jackson, being informed of the success of the enemy on the right, and of their being in possession of the redoubt, pressed forward a re-enforcement to regain it. Previously to its arrival they had abandoned the attempt, and were retiring. They were severely galled by such of our guns as could be brought to bear. The levee afforded them considerable protection ; yet, by Commodore Patterson's redoubt, on the right bank, they suffered greatly. Enfiladed by this, on their advance, they had been greatly annoyed, and now, in their retreat, were no less severely assailed. Numbers found a grave in the ditch, before our line ; and of those who gained the redoubt, not one, it is believed, escaped ;—they were shot down as fast as they entered. The route, along which they had advanced and retired, was strewed with bodies. Affrighted at the carnage, they moved from the scene in confusion. Our batteries were still continuing the slaughter, and cutting them down at every step : safety seemed only to be attainable when they should have retired without the range of our shot, which, to troops galled as severely as they were, was too remote a relief. Pressed by this consideration, they fled to the ditch, whither the right division had retreated, and there remained until night permitted them to retire.

A considerable portion of our troops were inactive for the want of arms to place in their hands. If this had not been the case—had they been in a situation to have acted efficiently, the whole British army must have submitted.

Colonel Hinds was very solicitous, and in person applied to the commanding general for leave to pursue, at the head of his dragoons, the fleeing columns of the enemy: Jackson, however, would not permit it. "My reason for refusing," he remarked, "was, that it might become necessary to sustain him, and thus a contest in the open field be brought on: the lives of my men were of value to their country, and much too dear to their families to be hazarded where necessity did not require it; but, above all, from the numerous dead and wounded stretched out on the field before me, I felt a confidence that the safety of the city was most probably attained, and hence, that nothing calculated to reverse the good fortune we had met should be attempted."

The efforts of the enemy to carry our line of defence on the left were seconded by an attack on the right bank, with eight hundred chosen troops, under the command of Colonel Thornton. Owing to the difficulty of passing the boats from the canal to the river, and the strong current of the Mississippi, the troops destined for this service were not crossed, nor the opposite shore reached, for some hours after the expected moment of attack. By the time he had effected a landing, the day had dawned, and the flashes of the guns announced the battle. Supported by three gun-boats, he hastened forward, with his command, in the direction of Morgan's intrenchment.

Some time during the night of the 7th, two hundred Louisiana militia had been sent off, to watch the movements of the enemy, and oppose him in his landing: this detachment, under the command of Major Arnaud, had advanced a mile down the river, and halted; either supposing the general incorrect, in apprehending an attack, or that his men, if refreshed, would be more competent to exertion, he directed them to lie down and sleep. one man only was ordered to be upon the watch, lest the enemy should approach them undiscovered. Just at day, he called upon his sleeping companions, and bade them rise, for he had heard a considerable bustle a little below. No sooner risen, than confirmed in the truth of what had been stated, they moved off in the direction they had come, without even attempting an execution of their orders. The Kentucky troops, having reached Morgan at five o'clock in the morning, were immediately sent to co-operate with the Louisianians. Major Davis, who commanded, had proceeded about three quarters of a mile, and met those troops hastily retreating up the road; he ascertained from them that the enemy had made the shore; had debarked, and were moving rapidly up the levee. He informed them for what purpose he had been despatched,— to oppose an approach as long as practicable, and, with their assistance, he would endeavour to execute his orders.

The two detachments, now acting together, formed behind a saw-mill-race, skirted with a quantity of plank and scantling, which afforded a tolerable shelter. Davis, with his two hundred Kentuckians, formed on the road next the river, supported by the Louisiana militia on the right. The enemy appearing, their approach was resisted, and a spirited opposition for some time maintained. The British again advanced, and again received a heavy fire At this moment, General Morgan's aid-de-camp, who was present, perceiving the steady advance of the enemy, and fearing for the safety of the troops, ordered a retreat. Confusion was the consequence —order could not be maintained. and the whole fled, in haste, to Morgan's line. Arriving in safety though much exhausted, they were immediately directed to form, and extend themselves to the swamp; that the right of the intrenchment might not be turned.

Colonel Thornton, having reached an orange grove, about seven hundred yards distant, halted, and, examining Morgan's line, found it to "consist of a formidable redoubt on the river," with its weakest and most vulnerable point towards the swamp. He directly advanced to the attack, in two divisions, against the extreme right and centre of the line; and, having deployed, charged the intrenchment, defended by about fifteen hundred men. A severe discharge, from the field-pieces mounted along our works, caused the right division to oblique, which, uniting with the left, pressed forward to the point occupied by the Kentucky troops. Perceiving themselves thus exposed, and having not yet recovered from the emotions produced by their first retreat, they began to give way, and very soon abandoned their position. The Louisiana militia gave a few fires, and followed the example Through the exertions of the officers, a momentary halt was effected; but a burst of congreve rockets falling thickly, and setting fire to the sugar-cane, and other combustibles around, again excited their fears, and they moved hastily away; nor could they be rallied, until, at the distance of two miles, having reached a saw-mill-race, they were formed, and placed in an attitude of defence.

Commodore Patterson, perceiving the right flank about to be turned, had ceased his destructive fire against the retreating columns on the opposite shore and turned his guns to enfilade the enemy next the swamp; but, at the moment when he expected to witness a firm resistance, and was in a situation to co-operate, he beheld those, without whose aid all his efforts were unavailing, suddenly thrown into confusion, and forsaking their posts. Discovering he could no longer maintain his ground, he spiked his guns, destroyed his ammunition, and retired from a post where he had rendered the most important services.

In the panic that produced this disorderly retreat, at a moment when resistance was expected, are to be found circumstances of justification, which might have occasioned similar conduct even in disciplined troops. The weakest part of the line was assailed by the greatest strength of the enemy : this was defended by one hundred and eighty Kentuckians, who were stretched out to an extent of three hundred yards, and unsupported by any pieces of artillery. Thus openly exposed to the attack of a greatly superior force, and weakened by the extent of ground they covered, it is not to be wondered at, or deserving of reproach, that they should have considered resistance ineffectual, and forsaken a post, which they had strong reasons for believing they could not maintain. General Morgan reported to General Jackson the defeat, and attributed it to the flight of those troops, who had also drawn along with them the rest of his forces. It is true, they were the first to flee; and equally true, that their example may have had the effect of producing general alarm ; but in point of advantageous situation, the troops materially differed : the one party were exposed, and enfeebled by the manner of their arrangement; the other, though superior in numbers, covered no greater extent of ground, and were de

fended by an excellent breastwork, and several
pieces of cannon: with this difference, the loss of
confidence of the former was not without sufficient
cause. Of these facts Commodore Patterson was
not apprized; General Morgan was: both, however,
attributed the disaster to the flight of the Kentucky
militia. Upon their information General Jackson
founded his report to the secretary of war, by
which those troops were exposed to censures
they did not merit. Had all the circumstances, as
they existed, been disclosed, reproach would have
been prevented. At the mill-race, no troops could
have behaved better: they were well posted, and
bravely resisted the advance of the enemy, nor, until an order to that effect was given, had entertain-
eu a thought of retreating.

The heart-felt joy at the glorious victory achieved on one side of the river was clouded by the disaster witnessed on the other. A position was gained which secured to the enemy advantages the
most important ; and whence our whole line, on the
left bank, could be severely annoyed. But for the
precaution of Commodore Patterson, in spiking his
guns, and destroying the ammunition, it would have
been in the power of Colonel Thornton to have completely enfiladed our line of defence, and rendered
it untenable. Fearful lest the guns might be un-
spiked, and brought to operate against him, General
Jackson hastened to throw detachments across, with
orders to regain the position at every hazard. To
the troops on the right bank, he forwarded an address, with a view to excite them to deeds of valour, and inspirit them to exertions that should wipe
off the reproach they had drawn upon themselves.
Previously, however, to their being in readiness to

act, ne succeeded by stratagem in re-obtaining his lost position, and thus spared the effusion of blood.

The loss of the British, in the main attack on the left bank, has been variously stated. The killed, wounded, and prisoners, ascertained, on the next day after the battle, by Colonel Hayne, the inspector-general, places it at twenty-six hundred. General Lambert's report to Lord Bathurst makes it but two thousand and seventy. From prisoners, however, and information derived through other sources, it must have been even greater than is stated by either. Among them was the commander-in-chief, and Major-General Gibbs, who died of his wounds the next day, besides many of their most distinguished officers; while the loss of the Americans, in killed and wounded, was but thirteen.*

It appears to have been made a question by the British officers, if it would not be more advisable to carry General Morgan's line, and refrain from any attempt on this side the river. It was believed, that, if successful in this attack, they would be able to force General Jackson from his intrenchment, and pass with the main body of the army to the city. A letter found in the possession of Captain Wilkinson, a British officer, who fell in the battle, to a friend at home, in the war department, speaking on this subject, shows that a difference of opinion pre-

---

* Our effective force, at the line on the left bank, was three thousand seven hundred; that of the enemy at least nine thousand. The force landed in Louisiana has been variously reported; the best information places it at about fourteen thousand. A part of this acted with Colonel Thornton; the climate had rendered many unfit for the duties of the field; while a considerable number had been killed and wounded in the different contests since their arrival. Their strength, therefore, may be fairly estimated, on the 8th, at the number we have stated; at any rate, not less

25

vailed, and confesses his own as being decidedly in favour of a vigorous attack on both sides. It bears date late on the night of the 7th, nor does it appear, although he was a captain and brigade-major, that he, at that time, knew whether an assault was seriously intended against Jackson's line, or was designed as a feint, to aid the operations of Colonel Thornton. With the true spirit of a British officer, however, he indulged a hope of success,—entertained no fears for the result, nor doubted but that the Americans would at once retire before their superior skill and bravery. A general order, which must have been communicated after he had written. disclosing the manner of attack, on the left, where he acted, was also found with the letter. In that the fusileers and light troops were instructed, after reaching our line, to act as a pursuing squadron and keep up alarm, while the army on the right should press closely in the rear and support them. It breathes an assurance of success, and shows with what anxiety they looked to the approaching morning, as likely to bring with it a successful termination of their labours, and a triumph over a foe whose advantages, more than bravery, they supposed, had so long baffled their efforts.

Let it be remembered of that gallant but misguided general, who has been so much deplored by the British nation, that, to the cupidity of his soldiers, he promised the wealth of the city, as a recompense for their gallantry ; while, with brutal licentiousness, they were to revel in lawless indulgence, uncontrolled, over female innocence. Scenes like these, our nation, insulted, had already witnessed ; she had witnessed them at Hampton and Havre-de-Grace : but it was reserved for her yet to learn that an officer of the standing of Sir Edward Packenham, polished, generous, and brave, should, to induce his soldiers to acts of daring valour, permit them, as a reward, to insult and injure those whom all mankind, even savages, respect. The facts which were presented at the time of this transaction left no doubt on the minds of our officers, but that " *Beauty* and *Booty*" was the watch-word of the day. The information was obtained from prisoners, and confirmed by the books of two of their orderly-sergeants taken in battle, which contained record proof of the fact.

A communication, shortly after, from Major-General Lambert, on whom, in consequence of the fall of Generals Packenham, Gibbs, and Keane, the command had devolved, acknowledges that he had witnessed the kindness of our troops to his wounded. He solicited of General Jackson permission to send an unarmed party to bury the dead, lying before his lines, and to bring off such of the wounded as were dangerous. The request to bury the dead was granted. General Jackson refused to permit a near approach to his line, but consented that the wounded, who were at a greater distance than three hundred yards from the intrenchment, should be relieved, and the dead buried : those nearer were, by his own men, to be delivered over, to be interred by their countrymen. This precaution was taken, that the enemy might not have an opportunity to inspect, or know any thing of his situation.

General Lambert, desirous of administering to the wants of the wounded, and that he might be relieved from his apprehensions of attack, proposed, about noon, that hostilities should cease until the same hour the next day. General Jackson, cherishing

the hope of being able to secure an important advantage, by his apparent willingness to accede to
the proposal, drew up an armistice, and forwarded it to General Lambert, with directions for it to
be immediately returned if approved. It contained a stipulation to this effect—that hostilities, on
the left bank of the river, should be discontinued
from its ratification, but on the right bank they
should not cease; and that, in the interim, under
no circumstances were re-enforcements to be sent
across by either party. This was a bold stroke at
stratagem; and, although it succeeded, even to the
extent desired, was attended with considerable hazard. Re-enforcements had been ordered over to
retake the position lost by Morgan in the morning,
and the general presumed they had arrived at their
point of destination; but, at this time, they had not
passed the river, nor could it be expected to be retaken with the same troops who had yielded it the
day before, when possessed of advantages which
gave them a decided superiority: this the commanding general well knew; yet, to spare the sacrifice of his men, which, in regaining it, he foresaw
must be considerable, he was disposed to venture
upon a course, which, he felt assured, could not fail
to succeed. It was impossible his object could be
discovered: while he confidently believed the British commander would infer, from the prompt manner in which his proposal had been met, that such
additional troops were already thrown over, as
would be fully adequate to the purposes of attack,
and greatly to endanger, if not wholly to cut off,
Colonel Thornton's retreat. General Lambert's
construction was such as had been anticipated. Although the armistice contained a request that it

should be immediately signed and returned, it was neglected to be acted upon until the next day; and Thornton and his command were, in the interim, under cover of the night, re-crossed, and the ground they occupied left to be peaceably possessed by the original holders. The opportunity thus afforded of regaining a position on which, in a great degree, depended the safety of those on the opposite shore, was accepted with an avidity its importance merited, and immediate measures taken to increase its strength, and prepare it against any future attack that might be made. This delay of the British commander was evidently designed, that, pending the negotiation, and before it was concluded, an opportunity might be had, either of throwing over re-enforcements, or removing Colonel Thornton and his troops from a situation so extremely perilous. Early next morning, General Lambert returned his acceptance of what had been proposed, with an apology for having failed to reply sooner: he excused the omission, by pleading a press of business, which had occasioned the communication to be overlooked. Jackson was at no loss to attribute the delay to the correct motive: the apology, however, was as perfectly satisfactory to him as any thing that could have been offered; beyond the object intended to be effect ed, he felt unconcerned, and, having secured this, rested perfectly satisfied. It cannot, however, appear otherwise than extraordinary, that this neglect should have been ascribed by the British general to accident, or a press of business, when it must have been, no doubt, of greater importance, at that moment, than any thing which he could possibly have had before him.

25 *

The armistice was this morning (9th of January) concluded, and agreed to continue until two o'clock in the evening. The dead and wounded were now removed from the field, which, for three hundred yards in front of our line of defence, they almost literally covered. For the reason already suggested, our soldiers, within the line of demarcation between the two camps, delivered over to the British, who were not permitted to cross it, the dead for burial, and the wounded on parole, for which it was stipulated, an equal number of American prisoners should be restored.

It has seldom happened that officers were more deceived in their expectations than they were in the result of this battle, or atoned more severely for their error: their reasoning had never led them to conclude, that militia would maintain their ground when warmly assailed: a firm belief was entertained, that, alarmed at the appearance and orderly approach of veteran troops, they would at once forsake the contest, and in flight seek for safety. At what part of our line they were stationed, was ascertained by a deserter, on the 6th; and, influenced by a belief of their want of nerve, and deficiency in bravery, on this point the main assault was urged. They were indeed militia; but the enemy could have assailed no part of our intrenchment where they would have met a warmer reception, or where they would have found greater strength: it was indeed the best defended part of the line. The Kentucky and Tennessee troops, under Generals Carroll, Thomas and Adair, were here, who had already won a reputation that was too dear to be sacrificed These divisions, alternately charging their pieces, and mounting the platform, poured forth a constant fire, that was impossible to be withstood, repelled the advancing columns, and drove them from the field with prodigious slaughter.

There is one fact told, to which general credit seems to be attached, and which clearly shows the opinion had by the British of our militia, and the little fear which was entertained of any determined opposition from them. When repulsed from our line, the British officers were fully persuaded that the information given them by the deserter, on the night of the 6th, was false, and that, instead of pointing out the ground defended by the militia, he had referred them to the place occupied by our best troops. Enraged at what they believed an intentional deception, they called their informant before them, to account for the mischief. It was in vain he urged his innocence, and, with the most solemn protestations, declared he had stated the fact truly. They could not be convinced,—it was impossible that they had contended against any but the best disciplined troops; and, without further ceremony, the poor fellow, suspended in view of the camp, expiated, on a tree, not his crime, for what he had stated was true, but their error, in underrating an enemy who had already afforded abundant evidences of valour. In all their future trials with our coun trymen may they be no less deceived!

CHAPTER XI

Bombardment of Fort St. Philip.—British army return to their shipping.—General Jackson, with his troops, returns to New Orleans.—Day of thanksgiving.—Reduction of Fort Bowyer. —Legislature of Louisiana re-commence their session.—Discontents fomented among the American troops.—Arrest of Louaillier ; of Judge Hall.—Peace announced.—General Jackson is prosecuted for contempt of court ; his appearance in court.— Speech at the coffee-house.—His own opinion of martial law.— Troops are discharged, and the general returns to Nashville.— Reduction of the army.—Jackson's commission as general annulled.— Treaty with Spain.—He is appointed governor of the Floridas.—Transactions there.—His resignation.—He is appointed minister to Mexico ; declines the mission ; his reasons ; is elected a senator of the United States ; resigns the office.—His person and character.—Anecdotes.—Conclusion

THE conflict had ended, and each army occupied 'ts former position.   The enemy were visibly altered : menace was sunk into dejection, and offensive measures yielded to those which promised safety They were perceived to be erecting partial defences, to guard against expected attack.   It had been announced, that a considerable force had succeeded in passing the Balize—made prisoners of a detachment, and was proceeding up the Mississippi, to cooperate with the land forces : it was intended to aid in the battle of the 8th.   The enemy, it seemed probable, might again renew the attack, on the arrival of this force, and every preparation was in progress to be again in readiness.

Of this formidable advance no certain intelligence was received until the night of the 11th, when a heavy cannonading, supposed to be on Fort St. Philip, was distinctly heard.   Jackson entertained no fears for the result.   The advantages in de fence, which his precaution had early extended to this passage to the city, added to an entire confidence in the skill of the officer to whom it had been confided, led him to believe there was nothing to be apprehended. The enemy's squadron, consisting of two bomb vessels, a brig, sloop, and schooner, were discovered by the videttes, from Fort Bourbon, on the morning of the 9th, directing their course up the river; signals were made, information communicated, and every thing was in readiness to receive them. About ten o'clock, having approached within striking distance, an assault was commenced on the fort, and an immense quantity of bombs and balls was discharged against it. A severe and well-directed fire from our water battery soon compelled them to retire about two miles. At this distance, the enemy was possessed of decided advantages,—having it in their power to reach the fort with the shot from their large mortars, while they were entirely without the range of ours. The assault continued without much intermission, from the 9th until the night of the 17th. They had hitherto lain beyond the effective range of our shot, and although, from their large mortars, the fort had been constantly reached, and pierced in innumerable places, still, such an effect had not been produced, as to justify a belief, that they could now, more than at the moment of their arrival, venture to pass. A heavy mortar having been turned against them on the 17th, the security they had hitherto enjoyed was taken away: their vessels could now be reached with considerable effect. This circumstance, and an ineffectual bombardment, which, though continued for eight days, had secured no decided advantage, induced them to suspend all further efforts; and, on the morning of the 18th, they retired.

Major Overton, who commanded at this place, his officers and soldiers, distinguished themselves. To arrest the enemy's passage up the river, and prevent them from uniting with the forces below the city, was of great importance; and to succeed in this was as much as could be expected. So long, therefore, as they kept at a distance, nor attempted a final accomplishment of their object, no other concern was felt than to watch their manœuvres, and adopt such a course as should afford safety to the troops in the garrison: for this purpose, pieces of timber and scantling were used, which formed a cover, and gave protection from their bombs. The store of ammunition was also divided, and buried in different places in the earth, that, in the event of accident, the whole might not be lost. During the period of the bombardment, which lasted with little intermission for nine days, sleep was almost a stranger in the fort. The night was the time when most of all it was feared the enemy, aided by the darkness, and some fortunate breeze, would have it in their power to ascend the river, in despite of every opposition: the constant activity, which was necessary, prevented all opportunities for repose. On a tempestuous night, the wind setting fair to aid them, an attempt was made to pass: to divert the attention of the fort, and favour the chances for ascent, their boats were sent forward to commence an attack. In this they were disappointed, and compelled to abandon the undertaking. At length, after many fruitless efforts, and an immense waste of labour and ammunition, they retired without effecting their purpose, or producing, to us, a greater injury than the loss of nine of the garrison, who were killed and wounded.

The failure of this squadron to ascend the river, perhaps, determined General Lambert in the course which he immediately adopted. His situation before our line was truly an unpleasant one. Our batteries, after the 8th, were continually throwing balls and bombs into his camp; and wherever a party of troops appeared in the field, they were greatly annoyed. Thus harassed,—perceiving all assistance through this channel had failed, and constantly in apprehension lest an attack should be made upon him,—he resolved on availing himself of the first favourable opportunity to depart, and forsake a contest where every effort had met disappointment, and where an immense number of his troops had found their graves. The more certainly to effect a retreat in safety, detachments had been sent out to remove every obstruction that could retard their progress through the swamp. To give greater facility to his departure, strong redoubts were erected on the way, and bridges thrown across every creek and bayou that obstructed the passage. Every thing being thus prepared, on the night of the 18th, General Lambert silently decamped, and, proceeding towards the lake, embarked for his shipping, leaving, and recommending to the clemency of the American general, eighty of his soldiers, who were too severely wounded to be removed. With such silence was this decampment managed, that not the slightest intelligence was communicated, even to our sentinels occupying the out-posts. Early on the next morning, the enemy's camp was perceived to be evacuated; but what had become of them

and whither they had gone, could only be conjectured : no information on the subject was possessed.
To ascertain the cause of this new appearance of
things, detachments were in readiness to reconnoitre their camp, when Surgeon Wadsdale, of the
staff, arrived at our line, with a letter to General
Jackson, from the British commander, announcing
his determination to suspend, "for the present, all
further operations against New Orleans," and requesting his humanity towards the wounded he had
left, whom necessity had compelled him to abandon.

Detachments were sent out to ascertain the cause
of this unexpected state of things; with orders to
harass their rear, if a retreat were really intended.
But the precaution taken by the enemy, and the
ground over which they were retreating, prevented
pursuit in sufficient numbers to secure any valuable result.

Thus, in total disappointment, terminated an invasion from which much had been expected. Twenty-six days before, flushed with the hope of certain
victory, had this army erected its standard on the
banks of the Mississippi. At that moment, they
would have treated with contempt an assertion, that
in ten days they would not enter the city of New
Orleans. How changed the portrait from the expected reality! But a few days since, and they
were confident of a triumph, and a termination of
their labours : now, vanquished and cut to pieces,
at midnight, under the cover of its darkness, they are
found silently abandoning their camp,—breaking
to pieces their artillery,—fleeing from an enemy,
whom, but a little while before, they had held in utter contempt, and submitting their wounded to his
clemency.

The enemy had indeed retired, and, "for the present, relinquished all further operations against New Orleans;" but of what continuance their forbearance would be, whether they might not avail themselves of the first flattering opportunity to renew the struggle, and wipe off the stain of a defeat so wholly unexpected, could not be known. The hopes and expectations indulged in England, of the success of this expedition, had inspirited the whole army; and failure had never been anticipated. They had now retired; yet, from their convenient situation, and having command of the surrounding waters, it was in their power, at a short notice, to re-appear, at the same, or some more favourable point, cause a repetition of the hardships already encountered, and, perhaps, succeed in the accomplishment of their views. These considerations led General Jackson to conclude, that, although, for the present, there was an abandonment of the enterprise, still it behooved him not to relax in his system of defence; but be in constant readiness to maintain the advantages he had gained; and not to risk a loss of the country by a careless indifference, growing out of the belief that danger had subsided.

The enemy being again at their shipping, with an entire control of the lakes and gulf, it could not be known at what point they might venture on a second attack. General Jackson determined to withdraw his troops from the position they had so long occupied, and place them about the city, whence, to repel any further attempt that might be made, they could be advanced wherever it should become necessary. The seventh regiment of infantry remained to protect the point he was leaving,

while, farther in advance, on Villery's Canal, where
a landing had been first effected, were posted a detachment of Kentucky and Louisiana militia. To
secure this point more effectually, orders were giv-
en, on the 22d, to throw up a strong fortification at
the junction of Manzant and Bayou Bienvenu ; which
order was again attempted to be executed on the
25th. On both occasions failure was the result,
from the circumstance of the enemy having, on
their retreat, left a strong guard at this place,
which, from its situation, defied approach by a force
competent to its reduction. Their occupying this
position was looked to as a circumstance which afforded strong evidence that further hostilities were
not wholly abandoned. To counteract, however,
any advantages which might thence be derived, different points along the swamp, and in the direction
of Terre au Bœuf, were occupied, and strong works
erected.

These arrangements being made, calculated, if not
to prevent, to give intelligence of an approach in
time to be resisted, on the 20th of January, General Jackson, with his remaining forces, commenced
his march to New Orleans. The general glow excited at beholding his entrance into the city, at the
head of a victorious army, was manifested by all
those feelings which patriotism inspires. The win-
dows and streets were crowded, to view the man
who had preserved the country It was a scene
well calculated to excite the tenderest emotions.
Fathers, sons, and husbands, urged by the necessity
of the times, were toiling in defence of their wives
and children. A ferocious soldiery, skilled in the
art of war, and to whom every indulgence had been
promised, were straining to effect their object. The

tender female, relieved from the anguish of sus-
pense, no longer trembled for her safety and her
honour: a new order of things had arisen: jcy
sparkled in every countenance; while scarcely a
widow or an orphan was seen, to cloud the general
transport. The general, under whose banners every thing had been achieved, deliberate, and sparing of the lives of the brave, had dispelled the storm
which had so long threatened the ruin of thousands;
and was now restoring, unhurt, those who had with
him maintained the contest. His approach was
hailed with acclamations. All greeted his return,
and hailed him as their deliverer.

The 23d having been appointed a day of prayer
and thanksgiving for the happy deliverance effected by our arms, Jackson repaired to the cathedral.
The church and altar were splendidly decorated,
and more than could obtain admission had crowded
to witness the ceremony. A grateful recollection
of his exertions to save the country was cherished
by all; nor did the solemnity of the occasion, even
here, restrain a manifestation of their regard, or induce them to withhold the honour he had so nobly
earned. Children, robed in white, and representing the different states, were employed in strew-
ing the way with flowers; while, as he passed, a
flattering ode, produced for the occasion, saluted
his ears :—

> Hail to the chief! who hied at war's alarms
> To save our threatened land from hostile arms:
> Preserved, protected by his gallant care,
> Be his the grateful tribute of each fair :
> With joyful triumph swell the choral lay—
> Strew, strew with flow'rs the hero's welcome way.
> Jackson, all hail !—our country's pride and boast
> Whose mind's a council, and his arm a host·

> Welcome, blest chief! accept our grateful lays,
> Unbidden homage, and spontaneous praise;
> Remembrance long shall keep alive thy fame,
> And future infants learn to lisp thy name.

When the general reached the church, Dubourg the reverend administrator of the diocess, met him at the door. Addressing him in a strain of pious eloquence, he entreated him to remember, that his splendid achievements, which were echoed from every tongue, were to be ascribed to Him to whom all praise was due. "Let the votary of blind chance," continued he, "deride our credulous simplicity. Let the cold-hearted atheist look for an explanation of important events to the mere concatenation of human causes : to us, the whole world is loud in proclaiming a Supreme Ruler, who, as he holds the destiny of man in his hands, holds also the thread of all contingent occurrences : from his lofty throne, he moves every scene below,—infuses his wisdom into the rulers of nations, and executes his uncontrollable judgments on the sons of men, according to the dictates of his own unerring justice." He concluded his impressive address, by presenting the general with a wreath of laurel, woven for the occasion, and which he desired him to accept as "a prize of victory."

General Jackson accepted the pledge, presented as a mark of distinguished favour by the reverend prelate, and returned him a reply no less impressive than the address he had received. He was now conducted in, and seated near the altar, when the church ceremonies were commenced, and inspired every mind with a solemn reverence for the occasion. These being ended, he retired to his quarters, to renew a system of defence, which should ensure entire safety. and ward off any future danger that might arise. The right bank of the Mississippi was now strengthened by additional re-enforcements, and a strong position taken on La Fourche, to prevent any passage in that direction. Suitable arrangements for security having been already made below the city, Generals Coffee and Carroll were instructed to resume their former encampment, four miles above. The rest of the troops were arranged at different points, where necessity seemed most to require it.

Previously to General Lambert's departure, articles of agreement had been entered into by the commanders of the two armies, for an exchange of prisoners; in pursuance of which, sixty-three Americans, taken on the night of the 23d, had been delivered up: the remainder, principally taken at the capture of our gun-boats, were afterwards surrendered by Admiral Cochrane, and an equal number of British prisoners sent off to be delivered at the Balize.

The enemy had now withdrawn from the shore the troops which had been landed, and occupied their former position at Cat and Ship Islands. Mortified at their unexpected disaster, they were projecting a plan, by which it was expected a partial advantage might, perhaps, be secured, and the stigma of defeat be somewhat obliterated.

Fort Bowyer had been once assailed, with a considerable force, by land and water, and failure had resulted. This post, the key to Mobile, of infinite consequence, had been retained under the command of him, who, heretofore, had defended it so valiantly. The British commander, turning from those scenes of disappointment, and anxious to re-

trieve his fortunes, before, with his shattered and
diminished forces, he should retire, perceived no
place against which he might proceed with better
founded hopes of success

On the 6th of February, the British shipping appeared off Dauphin Island, fronting the point on
which stood the fort, garrisoned with three hundred
and sixty men. Having made the necessary arrangements, on the 8th an attack was commenced,
both from the land and water. The fleet was formed in two divisions, and approached within one and
two miles, bearing south and south-west from it.
But the principal attack, and that which compelled
a surrender, was from the shore, where Colonel
Nicholls and Woodbine had carried on their operations in September. Five thousand troops, aided by
pieces of heavy ordnance, secured from the fire of
our guns by large embankments, urged the assault.
Under cover of the two succeeding nights, redoubts
had been thrown up, and trenches cut through the
sand, which enabled them to approach gradually,
without being exposed to the fire of our guns.
Twice, on the 8th, were detachments sent out, to
effect by storm the accomplishment of their purpose ; but the fire from the fort compelled an abandonment of their course, and drove them to the necessity of approaching by trenches, protected by
strong redoubts. To demolish these from the fort
was impracticable from their strength ; and to attempt to prevent their erection by any sortie, with
so weak a force, would have been imprudent. Thus
situated, and every thing being ready to attack the
fort, if opposition were still intended, about ten
o'clock on the 11th the enemy hoisted a flag: Major
Lawrence raised another. Hostilities ceased, and

General Lambert required a surrender. The offi
cers, being convoked, with one consent agreed that
further resistance would be ineffectual, and could
only lead to the unnecessary loss of many valuable
lives. A capitulation was agreed on, and the fort
forthwith yielded to the enemy.

General Winchester, who commanded at Mobile,
having received intelligence of what was passing
at the point, ordered a detachment of a thousand
men, under Major Blue, to proceed down the bay,
and aid in its defence. This auxiliary force was too
late : having surprised and captured one of the en
emy's out pickets, consisting of seventeen men, and
ascertained that a surrender had already taken
place, they returned. Had this detachment reach
ed its destination, our loss would have been more
severe. The enemy's forces were too numerous,
and their means of attack too effectual, for any
different result to have taken place, even had the
detachment arrived in time.

It had early been the wish of General Jackson
for the large frigate, lying at Tchifonte, to be completed, and placed in defence of Fort Bowyer. We
have before remarked the confidence entertained
by him, that, with the aid of this vessel, no force
brought against the place would be competent to
its reduction. Near it is the only channel a vessel
of any size can pass. This frigate, occupying the
passage, would have presented as strong a battery
as could be brought against her, and, with the aid
of the fort, defied any assault from the water ·
while her position would have enabled her to have
thrown her bombs and shot across the narrow neck
of land, in the rear of the point, and arrested the ad
vance of any number of troops, which, in this direc

tion, might have attempted an approach. Yet more money had been disbursed by the government ir erecting shelters, to protect the frigate from the weather, than would have been sufficient for her completion.

The legislature of Louisiana had re-commenced their session. Some of the members, during the past struggle, had forsaken their official duties, and repaired to the field, where more important services were to be rendered, and where they had manifested a devotion to the country worthy of imitation. A much greater part, however, had pursued a very opposite course, and stood aloof from the impending danger. The disposition they had shown, on the 28th of December, to propose a capitulation, has been adverted to : how far it was calculated to estrange the public sentiment from that conviction, which the commanding general had endeavoured to impress, " that the country could and would be successfully defended," can be easily imagined But with them he had sinned beyond forgiveness. The course he had adopted—his arresting their proceedings, and suspending their deliberations, by placing an armed force at the door of the capitol were viewed as intolerable infringements upon legislative prerogative, denounced as an abuse of power, and hence the first opportunity was seized to exhibit their resentment.

No sooner had the members resumed the exercise of their legislative duties, than their first concern was to pass in review the incidents of the last month. To those who had acted vigilantly in the defence of the state, and who, by their toils and exertions, had contributed to its safety, they officially tendered their thanks. In pursuance of their reso-

lutions, the governor addressed the principal offi
cers; but of Jackson nothing was said. We are
not disposed to censure, or even call in question, the
conduct of this body, though the circumstances present no very favourable appearance. When danger threatened, they were disposed to make terms
with the enemy, by a surrender of the city: from
this they were prevented by a decision of character that compelled legislative to yield to military
authority. Greatly incensed at being thus unexpectedly restrained in the execution of their designs, no sooner did they resume the duties of their
station, than they became lavish in the praise of
those who pursued a course directly contrary to
their own; while in that commendation they inten-
tionally neglected the very man, to whom their section of the country was indebted for its salvation.

Appearances in the American camp were about
this time assuming an unfavourable aspect: present
danger being removed, confusion was arising, and
disaffection spreading through the ranks. Pretexts
were sought after to escape the drudgery of the
field. Many naturalized citizens, who had been
brought into the service, to aid in the general defence, were seeking exemption from further control,
and claiming to be subjects of the king of France.
Some were indeed foreigners; but most of them
had, by naturalization, become citizens of the United States. Notwithstanding this, as French subjects, they were actually procuring exonerations
through Monsieur Toussard, the consul resident at
New Orleans. No applicant ever went away un-
supplied, and hundreds, for the price of a consular
certificate, obtained protections which were to relieve them from the drudgery of the field, and the

ties due to their adopted country A flag was displayed from the consul's residence, and rumour circulated, that under it every Frenchman would find protection. Five dollars, the price of the certificate, was all that was required of any applicant to assure, through the consel, the protection of the French government. Harassed by such evils, every day increasing, and having satisfactory reasons to believe the enemy, then within a few hours' sail of the shore, were constantly advised of his situation, Jackson determined to adopt such measures as would at once put down the machinations of the designing. Toussard, thus manifesting—what could be considered in no other light—a warmth of attachment to the English, and a desire to aid them, for the services, perhaps, which they had given in the restoration of his monarch, was ordered to leave the city, retire to the interior of the country, nor venture to return, until peace was restored. His countrymen, also, who were disposed to claim his protection, and abandon the service, were ordered to follow him, and, at their peril, not to appear again about New Orleans. The general did this with a view to his own security, from a conviction that those who could thus shamefully seek to avoid a contest, threatened against a country which they had adopted, would not scruple, if an occasion offered, to inflict any injury in their power.

Our own citizens, too, were giving rise to difficulties, and increasing the danger of the moment. Mr. Livingston had arrived, on the 10th, from the British fleet, whither he had gone to effect a general cartel: through him, Admiral Cochrane had announced the arrival of a vessel from Jamaica, with news, that a treaty of peace had been agreed on, and signed by the two countries. This information was immediately caught at by the news-mongers, and, either from intention or want of correct intelligence, it suddenly appeared in the Louisiana Gazette, in an entirely different shape : it stated the arrival of a flag at head-quarters, which announced the conclusion of a peace, and requested a suspension of hostilities. It was evident the effect of such a declaration would be to introduce lassitude, or perhaps disaffection, among the troops, and induce a belief that their accustomed vigilance was no longer necessary. Sensible of this, General Jackson sent for the editor, and instructed him to alter what he had stated, and exhibit the facts, which he now communicated to him, truly as they were. He adopted this course from fear of the consequences to be produced to himself. One thing he well knew, that the enemy had retired under circumstances of mortification at their complete discomfiture ; nor was it an improbable conjecture that they might yet seek an accomplishment of their views through any channel a hope of success could be discerned. Might not this annunciation of peace, and request for the suspension of hostilities, introduced through the public journals, be a device of the enemy to induce a relaxation in his system of operation ; to divert his officers and soldiers from that activity so essential to security ; to excite discontents, and a desire to be discharged from the further drudgery of a camp? All these dangers he saw lurking beneath it, if false ; and, whether true or false, it was foreign to his duty to be influenced by any thing, until it should be officially communicated by his government. Fearful of the effect it might produce, he lost no time in addressing his army·

"How disgraceful," he remarked, " as well as disas
trous, would it be, if, by surrendering ourselves
credulously to newspaper publications, often pro·
ceeding from ignorance, but more frequently from
dishonest design, we should permit an enemy, whom
we have so lately and so gloriously beaten, to regain the advantages he has lost, and triumph over
us in turn !" A general order, at the same time, an
nounced that no publication relating to, or affect
ing the army, was to be published in any newspaper, without permission first obtained.

Notwithstanding this prohibition, shortly afterwards an anonymous publication appeared in the
Courier, calculated by its inflammatory character
to excite mutiny among the troops, and afford the
enemy intelligence of the disposition of the army.
It was high time, the general believed, to act with
decision, and prove, by the rigid exercise of authority, that such conduct militated against the police
and safety of his camp, and required not to be passed with impunity.   The enemy had heretofore effected a landing without opposition ; and, although
beaten, might again return.   If spies were to be
nestled in his camp, and permitted to go forth to the
world with the gleanings of their industry, it was
folly to believe the enemy would not profit by the
information.   Martial law still prevailed in New
Orleans, and he resolved to put it in execution
 gainst those who manifested such an evident dis-
.egard of the public good.   The editor was immediately sent for to the general's quarters ; he stated the author of the piece to be ————— Louaillier,
a member of the legislature, and he was thereupon
discharged.

Louaillier was arrested, and detained for trial. This circumstance afforded civilians a fair opportunity of testing if it were in the power of a commanding general to raise the military above the civil authority, and render it superior by any declaration of his. Application was made to Judge Hall for a writ of habeas corpus, which was immediately issued. The general, to render the example as efficacious as possible, and from information that the judge had been much more officious than his duty required, and believing, in fact, that it was a measure of concert to test his power, determined to arrest him also, and thereby at once to settle the question of authority.

Instead of surrendering Mr. Louaillier, and acting in obedience to the writ which had issued for his relief, he seized the person of the judge, and, on the 11th of the month, sent him from the city, with these instructions—" I have thought proper to send you beyond the limits of my encampment, to prevent a repetition of the improper conduct with which you have been charged. You will remain without the line of my sentinels until the ratifica tion of peace is regularly announced, or until the British shall have left the southern coast."

The spirit of discontent had become extensively diffused. The different posts, which had been established, could with difficulty be maintained. The Kentucky troops, and two hundred of the Louisiana militia, stationed in defence of Villery's Canal, had abandoned their post. Chef Menteur, too, a point no less important, had been forsaken by one hundred and fifty of the Louisianians, in despite of the exertions of their officers to detain them. Governor Claiborne had been heard to declare, in words

27

of mysterious import, that serious difficulties would
be shortly witnessed in New Orleans. For the
commanding general, at a time like this, when disaffection was spreading like contagion through his
camp, patiently to have stood and witnessed muti
ny fomented and encouraged by persons, who, from
their standing in society, were calculated to possess a dangerous influence, would have been a crime
for which he never could have atoned. He thought
it time enough to relax in his operations, and ground
his arms, when the conclusion of peace should be
announced through the proper authorities. Until
then, believing that imperious duty required it, he
resolved to maintain his advantages, and check opposition, at every hazard. To have obeyed the writ
would have been idle. He had declared the existence of military authority, and thereby intended to
supersede all judicial power. If he had obeyed the
mandate, it would have been an acknowledgment or
civil supremacy, and a virtual abandonment of the
course he had adopted. It was not an improbable
event, that the petitioner would be discharged, on a
hearing, because guilty of no offence cognizable by
the civil courts.

On the 13th of the month, two days after the
departure of Judge Hall from the city, an express
reached head-quarters, with despatches from the
war department, at Washington, announcing the
conclusion of a peace between Great Britain and the
United States, and directing a cessation of hostilities. A similar communication from his govern
ment was received by General Lambert shortly af
terwards, and on the 19th military operations, by
the two armies, entirely ceased. The aspect of af
fairs was now changing: the militia were discharg

ed from service; bustle was subsiding; and joy and tranquillity every where appearing. A proclamation, by the direction of the president of the United States, was issued, extending pardon and forgiveness for past offences.

Judge Hall, being restored to the exercise of those functions, of which he had been lately bereaved by military arrest, proceeded, without loss of time, to an examination of what had passed, and to become the arbiter of his own injuries. Accordingly, on the 21st, he granted a rule of court for General Jackson to appear, and show cause why an attachment for contempt should not be awarded, on the ground that he had refused to obey a writ issued to him, detained an original paper belonging to the court, and imprisoned the judge.

On the 24th, his appearance being entered, he stood represented at the bar by John Reid, his aid-de-camp, and Messrs. Livingston and Duncan. Major Reid, addressing himself to the court, remarked, that he appeared with the general's answer, supported by an affidavit, which went to show, that the rule should be discharged, and no further proceeding had against him. A curious course of judicial proceeding was now witnessed. Cause why the rule should not be made absolute was to be shown, and yet the judge would determine whether the reasons were exceptionable or not, previously to their being heard or seen. The counsel urged in vain the propriety of his hearing first, before he decided, if the answer were consonant with propriety. This was over-ruled. He would first determine what it should be. If within any of the rules laid down, it should be heard,—not else.

"If," remarked the judge, "the party object to the jurisdiction, he shall be heard.

"If it be a denial of facts, or that the facts charg ed do not amount to a contempt, he shall be heard

"If it be an apology to the court, or an intention to show, that by the constitution and laws of the United States, or in virtue of his military commission, he had a right to act as charged, the court will hear him."

"Hear what it does contain, and you can then decide if it come under any of the general rules laid down," was replied and argued at length by his counsel, as the correct and proper course.

After a debate of considerable length, Major Reid was permitted to read the answer. He had gotten through the exceptions reserved as to the jurisdiction, and was proceeding with the respondent's reasons, manifesting the necessity, and the consequent propriety, of declaring martial law, when he was again interrupted by the judge, because coming within none of the rules which he had laid down. The ears of the court were closed against every thing of argument or reason, and, without hearing the defence, the rule against him was rendered absolute, and the attachment sued out.

This process was made returnable the 31st; and on that day the general appeared. Public feeling was excited, and the crowd, on the tiptoe of expectation, were anxiously waiting to know what punishment the judge would think due to acts, which all agreed had contributed to the success of our cause. Jackson, apprized of the popular fervour towards him, and solicitous that nothing on his part should be done calculated to give it impulse, practised more than usual caution; and now, when it had be-

come necessary to appear in public, to ward himself
from crimes imputed, he threw off his military cos-
tume, and, assuming the garb of a citizen, the bet-
er to disguise himself, entered alone the hall where
he court was sitting. Undiscovered amidst the
concourse which was present, he had nearly reached the bar, when, being perceived, the room instantly rung with the shouts of a thousand voices.
Raising himself on a bench, and moving his hand
to procure silence, a pause ensued. He then addressed himself to the crowd ; told them of the duty
due to the public authorities ; for that any impropriety of theirs would be imputed to him ; and urged,
if they had any regard for him, that they would, or
the present occasion, forbear those expressions of
opinion. Silence being restored, the judge rose
from his seat, and, remarking that it was impossible
to transact business under such threatening circumstances, directed the marshal to adjourn the court.
The general immediately interfered, and requested
that it might not be done. "There is no danger
here ; there shall be none ; the same arm, that protected from outrage this city, will shield and protect this court, or perish in the effort." This dec
laration had the effect to tranquillize the feelings of
the judge ; and the business of the court was proceeded with. It was now demanded of him to answer nineteen interrogatories, drawn up with much
labour, and in studied form, which were to determine as to his guilt or innocence. He informed the
court he should not be interrogated ; that, on a
former occasion, he had presented the reasons
which had influenced his conduct, without their
producing an effect, or being even listened to.
You would not hear my defence, although you

27 *

were advised it contained nothing improper, and
ample reasons why no attachment should be awarded. Under these circumstances, I appear before
you, to receive the sentence of the court, having
nothing further in my defence to offer.

"Your honour will not understand me as intending any disrespect to the court ; but as no opp rtu-
nity has been afforded me of explaining the reasons and motives by which I was influenced, so is
it expected, that censure or reproof will constitute
no part of that sentence which yo1 may imagine it
your duty to pronounce."

The judge proceeded to a final discharge of what
he conceived was due to the offended majesty of
the laws, and fined the general a thousand dollars.

The hall in which this business was transacted
was greatly crowded, and excitement every where
prevailed. No sooner was the judgment of the
court pronounced, than again were sent forth shouts
of the people. He was forcibly hurried from the
hall to the streets, amidst reiterated cries of " Huzza
for Jackson !" from the immense concourse that surrounded him. They presently met a carriage in
which a lady was riding, when, politely taking her
from it, the general was made, spite of entreaty, to
occupy her place : the horses being removed, the
carriage was drawn on, and halted at the coffee-
house, into which he was carried, and thither the
crowd followed, huzzaing for Jackson, and menacing violently the judge. Having prevailed on them
to hear him, he addressed them with great earnestness ; implored them to run into no excesses ; that,
if they had the least gratitude for his services, or
regard for him personally they could evince it in
no way so satisfactorily, as y assenting as *he* most

freely did, to the decision which had been pronounced against him ; "that the civil was the paramount and supreme authority of the land. He had never pretended to any thing else, nor advocated a different doctrine. He had departed from its rules, because that they were too feeble for the state of the times. By a resort to martial law, he had succeeded in defending and protecting a country, which, without it, must have been lost; yet under its provisions he had oppressed no one, nor extended them to any other purpose than defence and safety; objects which its declaration was intended alone to effect." "I feel," continued he, "sensible for those marks of personal regard, which you have evinced towards me; and with pleasure remember those high efforts of valour and patriotism, which so essentially contributed to the defence of the country. If recent events have shown you what fearless valour can effect, it is a no less important truth to learn, that submission to the civil authority is the first duty of a citizen."

Being at length relieved from this warm display of regard manifested towards him for the exertions he had made in their defence, Jackson retired to his quarters, and, giving a check to his aid-de-camp sent him to discharge the fine imposed, and to terminate his contest with the civil authority. He was greatly consoled at learning, through various respectable channels, that all was tranquil, and that against the judge nothing of indignity or unkindness was longer meditated.

So riveted was the impression, that the course pursued by the general was correct, and the conduct of Judge Hall more the result of spleen than any thing else, that the citizens of New Orleans

determined to ward off the effect of his intended
injury, by discharging themselves the fine imposed.
It was only necessary to be thought of, and it was
done. So numerous were the persons entertaining the same feelings on the subject, that in a short
time the entire sum was raised by voluntary con-
tribution. The general, understanding what was in
agitation, to spare his own and their feelings, had
despatched his aid-de-camp to seek the marshal,
and thereby avoided the necessity of refusing a
favour intended to be offered, and which he could
not have accepted. Without, however, any knowledge of his wishes, or consulting at all his feelings
on the subject, they proceeded in the arrangement,
and, by subscription, the entire amount was in a
short time raised, and deposited to his use in the bank,
and notice thereof given. But it was not accepted ; though refused in a manner the most delicate.
In reply, he declared 'the obligations felt for this renewed evidence of regard ; and, although he could
not accept of it, yet, as it was the result of the most
generous feeling, he solicited that the amount might
be applied to the relief of those whose relatives
had fallen in battle. The proposition was acceded
to, and the amount subscribed expressly for his re
lief was disposed of for the benefit of the widow
and the fatherless.

Jackson once, concerning the declaration of martial law, expressed himself after the following manner : " I very well knew the extent of my powers,
and that it was far short of that which necessity
and my situation required. I determined, therefore,
to venture boldly forth, and pursue a course corre-
spondent to the difficulties that pressed upon me.
I had an anxious solicitude to wipe off the stigma

.ast upon my country by the destruction of the cap-
.tal. If New Orleans were taken, I well knew that
new difficulties would arise, and every effort be made
to retain it; and that, if regained, blood and treas
ure would be the sacrifice. My determination,
therefore, was formed, not to halt at trifles, but to
lose the city only at the boldest sacrifice, and to
omit nothing that could assure success. I was well
aware that calculating politicians, ignorant of the
difficulties that surrounded me, would condemn my
course; but this was not material. What became
of me was of no consequence. If disaster did
come, I expected not to survive it; but, if a successful
defence could be made, I felt assured that my country, in the objects attained, would lose sight of, and
forget the means that had been employed."

The war being now ended, it was necessary to
relieve from the toils of the field those brave men,
who had so long been struggling in their country's
defence. The necessary measures to effect this
were adopted. The Tennessee, Kentucky, and
Mississippi troops had taken their departure. General Gaines being invested with the command, in a
few days General Jackson left New Orleans for
Nashville. The good wishes and friendship of the
people followed him: there were a few, however,
who rejoiced at his departure; but they were those
who, in moments of peril, had stood aloof from
danger, or sought to increase it, and who, in the reproaches to be cast upon him, expected to palliate
their own misdeeds. Previously to breaking up
his encampment, he addressed his army, and declared the high sense he entertained of those valiant
men, who, with him, had toiled in the field, and, by
perseverance and fidelity, had obtained safety

for their country, a id distinguished honour for them
selves.

On his return, the respect of all was manifested
in his behalf: all evinced a partiality for the man,
whose signal achievements had raised his country
to a high and dignified standing, and whose unremitting exertions had closed the war with a lustre
that enlightened even the blots of its commencement.

The annunciation of the triumphant defence of
New Orleans was, in every section of the country,
hailed with acclamation; illuminations and fêtes
followed it into all our cities and principal towns;
and in all was it agreed, that none other than the
decided course adopted by Jackson could have attained so auspicious a result. The legislatures of
many of the states voted to him their thanks for
what he had done. The congress of the United
States did the same,.and directed a gold medal to be
presented to him, commemorative of the event. Ad-
dresses from numerous societies and meetings of the
people were forwarded, expressive of their great
regard, and proclaiming him the deliverer and second saviour of his country.

A tedious journey of eight hundred miles brought
him to Nashville, where he was gratified with a mani
festation of the regard of his fellow townsmen. An
immense concourse was collected, to welcome his
arrival. They had long known him as among the
number of their best and most respectable citizens;
but curiosity had a new incentive: until now, they
had not beheld him as one, who, to protect his country, knew no difficulty too great to be encountered—
who, by his firmness and unconquerable perseverance, amidst surrounding dangers, had saved her
from foreign and intestine foes. An address, deliv

ered at the court-room, in behalf of the citizens, welcomed his return. Relieved from this further display of public confidence, the more grateful, because from those who were his acquaintances, neighbours, and friends, he retired home, to repair a broken constitution, and to enjoy that repose, to which, for eighteen months, he had been a stranger.

Early in the congressional session of 1820, several propositions were made for the reduction of the army, which, however, were not decided upon. On the 9th of January, 1821, the subject was again revived; and on the 5th of March, following, by an act of congress, approved by the president, the reduction was effected. By this law, only one major-general was retained, and, as General Jackson was not the senior commissioned general, his commission was annulled, and by courtesy his senior was retained. All commissioned officers were allowed three months' pay, after their commissions were returned. Previous to this, as early as the preceding January, the news of the ratification of the Florida treaty, by the Spanish cortes, had been received. On the 3d of January, Mr. Stanbury, the diplomatic agent, arrived at Philadelphia, in the Pleiades, with an authenticated copy of the treaty, for the re-ratification of the senate, which had become necessary, as the time allowed to Spain to signify her acceptance of the instrument had expired before this acceptance was declared. The senate, on the 9th of February, 1821, considered the subject, and gave their sanction anew to the instrument, which was finally confirmed on the 22d. By this advantageous treaty, East and West Florida were ceded to the United States, and provision made for indemnifying American citizens for Spanish spoliations by paying five millions of dollars, the amount agreed upon as the purchase money, directly to the claim ants.

On the 1st of March, 1821, a bill passed, autho rizing the president to take possession of the newly acquired territory. Three days after this, March 5th Mr. Monroe was sworn to his second term of office, and one of the earliest and most important duties that devolved upon him was the appointment of a person suitably qualified to take possession of the Floridas. Various conjectures were abroad, in relation to the individual upon whom this honour would be conferred. Mr. Monroe very judiciously fixed his eye on the man whose patriotic exertions had been so instrumental in bringing the war in that very region to a successful termination. On the 15th of March, therefore, General Jackson's appointment, as governor of the Floridas, with a salary of five thousand dollars a year, was official ly announced.

Soon after being notified of his appointment, he commenced his journey towards his place of destination.

On the 23d of April, he left New Orleans for Pensacola, having received the greatest attention from the municipal authorities in the very theatre of his former warlike exploits. The hospitality of individuals, and the general expression of the people of New Orleans, were calculated to call forth the liveliest feelings of gratitude.

There was considerable delay, on the part of the Spanish authorities, in delivering up the territories. This resulted from their prejudices against the United States, and their disapprobation of the treaty requiring the transfer.

On the 7th of July, 1821, Governor Croppinger, by proclamation, formally delivered East Florida to Colonel Robert Butler, the properly authorized commissioner. General Jackson, though not present, was in the vicinity, making the necessary arrangements for the government of both. Ten days after this, July 17th, West Florida was delivered to Governor Jackson in due form. Thus the whole of the newly-acquired territory was placed under his control as governor-general. When the proper course had been adopted for the happiness of all classes, he issued a proclamation of a paternal character, defining the policy of the government, and pointing out the duties of the people in their new relation.

After the satisfactory termination of the great business of receiving the Floridas, he made an excursion to New Orleans, and, on the 11th of August, delivered a valedictory address to the remainder of the conquering army, then on the point of being disbanded. In this speech, which breathed the sentiments of affectionate regard towards those brave men, who had aided him in the accomplishment of so many perilous undertakings, for the glory and honour of their country, he made known that his career, as commander in chief of the southern division of the American army, was then terminated. Again we find him, at the close of August, at St. Augustine. On the 1st day of September, Governor Jackson promulgated the names of those whom he had appointed for the civil government of East Florida. There was much contention, about this time, relative to the Spanish archives, which resulted in some unpleasant personal feelings between the governor and Judge Fromentin. Urgent measures, on the part of Governor Jackson,

28

were highly necessary, and hence he issued a proclamation, which obliged the Spanish officers to leave
the territories at a specified period. Against this
Governor Croppinger, together with the offended
officers, made a remonstrance. Croppinger, particularly, protested against the seizure of the public
papers, &c. The details of this occurrence our
limits will not permit us to narrate. It is certain,
however, that there were intriguers in the territories, and various misrepresentations, touching the
administration of the newly-formed government,
which, probably, induced Governor Jackson to resign a power, which could not contribute to his
own happiness, or increase his sphere of useful-
ness.

On the 8th of September, Governor Jackson,
then at Pensacola, made known his intention of visiting Tennessee with his family. This was no
sooner understood, than he was invited to a public dinner by the inhabitants. On that occasion,
every demonstration of respect was shown to the
distinguished and successful warrior. To the surprise and regret of an increasing circle of friends,
who knew how to appreciate his talents, he made a
farewell address to the people of the Floridas. In
the course of his speech, he remarked that he
should not return again, unless some unexpected
event should render it necessary.

Soon after the meeting of the seventeenth congress, on the 29th of the following December, Governor Jackson, having discharged with fidelity and success the duties of his appointment, tendered to the
president his resignation.

Scarcely thirty days had elapsed from the time of
his resignation of the government of the Floridas,

before he was honoured by Mr. Monroe with another appointment of higher political consequence. January 23d, 1823, General Jackson was appointed envoy extraordinary and minister plenipotentiary to the government of Mexico. As an evidence that he had no knowledge of the intentions of the executive, we find, on the 1st of the following March, in a respectful manner, he declined the offered mission. It has been generally understood that this was in consequence of the unsettled and distracted state of Mexico, then under the control of Iturbide, who had declared himself emperor. The true motive, however, for declining the proffered honour, is to be found in the general's own words : " From the present revolutionary state of Mexico, the appearance of an *American* envoy, with credentials to the *tyrant* Iturbide, might add to his strength, and thereby aid him in *riveting the chains of despotism* upon that country, which of right ought to be free. To be the instrument of *tyranny,* however innocent on my part, I could not reconcile to my feelings. With these views, and other reasons, which I have communicated to Mr. Monroe, I have declined accepting the mission to Mexico." But a short time after, May 13th, the Mexican emperor abdicated his throne, and made the best of his way from a country, which he had brought to the verge of ruin.

General Jackson now retired to the quietude of private life, and, in the circle of his own family, sought that rest from the fatigues and countless anxieties of a military life, which his exhausted frame and spirits so obviously required. The confidence, however, which the citizens of Tennessee had in his talents and wisdom, was again manifested in electing him a senator to the eighteenth congress, which assembled in December, 1823 and once more he resigned the endearments of home to mingle in the councils of the nation. On his route from Nashville to Washington, he was greeted by the most enthusiastic applause. The citizens of Knoxville, in a special manner, honoured their celebrated guest with a public dinner, and exhibited, in the strongest language, and in the most unequivocal hospitality, that they considered him a man of extraordinary talents, whose past services entitled him to the admiration and confidence of his country.

During the session of congress, he entered with spirited interest into the general business of the nation, and was frequently on some of the most important committees. As indefatigable in the senate as in military command, he found that such unremitted attention to public affairs, as his duty required, to sustain the dignity of the station, was altogether too severe for the delicate state of his health. The political horizon, also, now began to present a different aspect, and the circumstance of his being a candidate for the presidential chair, without doubt, influenced him, to a considerable extent, in resigning his seat in the senate. Soon after the close of the session, he made known to his constituents the determination, and, in a few weeks, it was announced, to the sincere regret of all who knew the integrity of his character.

In the person of General Jackson is perceived nothing of the robust or elegant. He is six feet and an inch high, remarkably straight and spare, and weighs not more than a hundred and forty-five pounds. His conformation appears to disqualify him for hardship; yet, accustomed to it from early

..fe, few are capable of enduring fatigue to the same extent, or with less injury. His dark blue eyes, with brows arched and slightly projecting, possess a marked expression .at when, from any cause, excited, they sparkle with peculiar lustre and penetration. In his manners he is pleasing—in his address commanding ; while his countenance, marked with firmness and decision, beams with a strength and intelligence that strikes at first sight. In his deportment there is nothing repulsive. Easy, affable, and familiar, he is accessible to all. Influenced by the belief, that merit should constitute the only difference in men, his attention is equally, bestowed on honest poverty as on titled consequence. No man, however inconsiderable his standing, ever approached him on business, that he did not patiently listen to his story, and afford him all the information in his power. His moral character is without reproach, and by those who know him most intimately he is most esteemed. Benevolence in him is a prominent virtue. He was never known to pass distress without seeking to assist and to relieve it.

It is imputed to him, that he derives from his birth a temper irritable and hasty, which has had the effect to create enemies, and involve him in disputes. In Jackson, however, these defects of character exist to an extent as limited as with most men ; and the world is in error in presuming him under a too high control of feeling and passion. A fixed devotion to those principles which honour sanctions, renders him scrupulously attentive to his promises and engagements of every description Preserving system in his moneyed transactions, his fiscal arrangements are made to correspond with his resources, and hence his every engagement in

28 *

relation to such subjects is met with **marked punc-**
tuality, not for the reason that he is a man of extraordinary wealth, but rather because he has method, and with a view to his resources, regulates
properly his *balance of trade.*

No man has been more misconceived in charac
ter. Many, on becoming acquainted with him, have
been heard to admit the previous opinions which
they had entertained, and how great had been their
mistake. Rough in appearance, positive and over-
bearing in his manner, are what all, upon a first in-
troduction, expect to find ; and yet none are pos
sessed of milder manners, or of more conciliating
address. The public situations in which he has
been placed, and the circumstances which surrounded him, are doubtless the cause that those opinions
have become so prevalent ; but they are opinions
which an acquaintance with him tends to remove.
The difficulties under which he laboured at **New Or-**
leans were such as might well have perplexed, and
thrown the mind aside from every thing of mildness.

Light and trifling pleasantries often mark character as distinctly as things of consequence. General Jackson, one day during the siege of **New Or-**
leans, was approached by an officer of the militia,
who stated his desire to leave the service, and return home ; for that he was made *game of,* and
called by the company *Pewter Foot.* He manifested great concern, and an anxious desire to be relieved from his unpleasant situation. The general,
with much apparent sympathy for him, replied, that
he had ascertained there was a practice in the camp
of giving nick-names ; and had understood, too,
that very many had dared to call him *Old Hickory:*
"Now," said he, "if you prefer mine, I am willing

to exchange; if not, remain contented, and perform your duty faithfully, and, as soon as we can get clear of those troublesome British, our wrongs shall be inquired into by a court-martial, and the authors punished; for then, and not till then, shall we have an end of those insults." The effect was happy, and induced the complaining officer to retire, perfectly satisfied to learn, that his grievance would be united with the general's, and both ere long be effectually redressed

General Jackson possesses ambition, but it rests on virtue; an ambition, which, regulated by a high sense of honourable feeling, leads him to desire " that applause which follows good actions—not that which is run after." No man is more ready to hear and to respect the opinions of others, and none, where much is at stake, and at conflict with his own, less disposed to be under their influence. He has never been known to call a council of war, whose decisions, when made, were to shield him from responsibility or censure. His council of war, if doubting himself, was a few officers, in whom he fully confided, whose advice was regarded, if their reasons were conclusive; but, these not being satisfactory, he at once adopted and pursued the course suggested by his own mind.

At the battle of Tohopeka, an infant was found pressed to the bosom of its lifeless mother. This circumstance being made known to General Jackson, he became interested for the child, directed it to be brought to him, and sought to prevail on some of the Indian women to take care of and rear it. They signified their unwillingness to do so, stating that, inasmuch as all its relations had fallen in battle, they thought it best it should be killed. The

General, after this disclosure, determined he would
not intrust it with them, but became himself the
protector of the child. Bestowing on the infant
the name of Lincoier, he adopted it into his family,
and has ever since manifested the liveliest zeal to-
waras it, prompted by benevolence, and because,
perhaps, its fate bore a strong resemblance to his
own, who, in early life, and from the ravages of war,
was left in the world forlorn and wretched, without
friends to assist, or near relations to direct him on
his course.

CONCLUSION.

WE have said before that one of the reasons that
induced General Jáckson to resign his seat in the
Senate was the circumstance of being a candidate
for the Presidential chair. As long as he remained
in the military service of his country, little was ever
said about bringing him out for the presidency. It
was only after he had become a private citizen that
the eyes of his fellow-countrymen were turned
towards him, as having eminently entitled himself,
by his brilliant and patriotic services, to the highest
honors within the gift of a free and enlightened people. His friends in Tennessee first, in good earnest,
took the necessary steps to place his name prominently before the country. It is true that some
four or five candidates were already in the field;
but so confident were they of General Jackson's
strength and popularity with the people, on account
of his great public services, that they entertained

no fears for the result. On July 20, 1822, the State
Legislature adopted a preamble and resolutions
which placed the General before the country as a
legitimate candidate for the presidency, and from
this moment his friends in every section of the
Union entered into the contest with increased
vigor and energy.

Our space does not permit us to here give any
detailed account of the spirited and exciting contest which took place during this campaign, which
resulted, after all, in there being no election, Andrew Jackson having received a plurality, but not
a majority, of the votes cast. The vote stood as
follows: Wm. H. Crawford, 41; Henry Clay, 37;
Mr. Adams, 84; Andrew Jackson, 99.

The people, therefore, having failed to elect a
President, it devolved upon the House of Representatives, voting by States, each State having one vote,
to elect one from the three candidates who had
received the highest number of electoral votes.
The great question was decided on the 9th of
February, 1825. A long contest had been expected, and the friends of Crawford were present
in great force, hoping that the House, after weary-
ing itself by repeated ballots, would turn to their
candidate and end the affair by giving him the
election.

The result, when announced by the tellers, surprised almost every one; surprised many of the
best-informed politicians who heard it. Upon the
first ballot Mr. Adams received the vote of thirteen
States, which was a majority. Crawford received
the vote of four States, and General Jackson, for
whom eleven States had given an electoral major-

ity, received the vote of but seven States in the House.

That General Jackson was not only disappointed at the result, but indignant, is well known; but he loftily acquiesced in his defeat, and was prominent among the congratulatory throng on the occasion of the inauguration of the new President. A few days afterwards General Jackson returned to his home, and was welcomed by his native State as conquerors are welcomed.

From the moment that the result of the election in the House of Representatives was known, the Jackson party resolved to make General Jackson a candidate for renomination for 1829. In October, 1825, only seven months after the inauguration, the Legislature of Tennessee passed a resolution "recommending him to the freemen of the United States, to be elected to the office of the Chief Magistrate of this Union, at the next Presidential election." In May, 1826, the nomination was indorsed by an immense public meeting in Philadelphia, and in November of the same year a powerful movement in his behalf was begun in Georgia. Long before the usual time of beginning the quadrennial agitation, he was placed before the people in most of the States as the candidate for the presidency, in opposition to the re-election of Mr. Adams.

During the next three years General Jackson, who had resigned his seat in the Senate of the United States, was the central figure in an extraordinary number of receptions and public dinners. He could hardly stir abroad without finding a committee lying in wait for him, who would take possession of him bodily, convey him to some public hall, and get him to make a speech.

We must now go back a little to touch briefly upon the reasons that had induced General Jackson to leave Washington after the election in the House of Representatives, which had ended so disastrously for his expectations. It was well known that the influence of Henry Clay, which he wielded in the House, derived from his long connection with it, from his winning cast of character, from his strenuous will, and his eloquence, placed it in his power to give the election to whichever of the candidates he preferred. Mr. Clay was not on cordial terms with either of the two highest candidates. The considerations that ought to have influenced his decision should have been purely founded on the principles of his party and of the Constitution, and not on the comparative fitness of the candidates. The one that had come nearest to an election by the people was obviously the one for whom a truly Democratic member of Congress would have given his vote. This republic was set up on a certain principle, and the spirit of that principle required that Andrew Jackson should have been elected President. The principle may. be wrong, but the Republican party obtained power, and for twenty-five years retained the supremacy, because it thought the fundamental principle of the government right, feasible, and safe. But Mr. Clay did not think so. Though he acknowledged that "he would never have selected Mr. Adams, if he had been at liberty to draw from the whole mass of our citizens for a President," he declared to confidential friends, before the result of the popular election was known, that under no circumstances whatever would he vote for General Jackson. The appointment of Mr. Clay as Secretary of State, after his inauguration, at once raised the suspicion that there had been a corrupt understanding between Mr. Clay and Mr. Adams, to the effect that Clay should make Adams President on condition that Adams should appoint Clay Secretary of State. General Jackson, whose failing it was to be always too prone to believe evil of those who opposed him, was fully convinced that this was true, and this "bargain and corruption cry" was the most telling card of the Jackson party in the campaign of 1828. And they kept it ringing, too. Yet no cry however telling, no enthusiasm however wild and general, ever carried a presidential election, nor ever will. The union of a powerful Southern interest with a respectable Northern one, or *vice versâ*, has always been deemed essential to success by knowing politicians. General Jackson, as a candidate for the presidency, was nothing, in 1824, till Pennsylvania took him, and he would have been elected then, if New York had only joined Pennsylvania. It was now necessary to get New York into line for the campaign of 1828.

Martin Van Buren was the man on whom the question of securing New York rested. He was a Senator of the United States, and was elected to a second term, in 1827, by a large majority. The sudden death of Governor Clinton, in 1828, removed from the scene the only man in New York that could be considered Mr. Van Buren's competitor, and left him undisputed master of the situation.

Mr. Van Buren had early taken sides against the administration of Mr. Adams, and maintained the attitude of opposition to the end. This, of course, involved the support of General Jackson in 1828, for there was no other man in the country who had the remotest chance of carrying the day against the administration.

The resolution of Mr. Van Buren to support General Jackson was formed, it is said, as early as the year 1825; but he kept that resolution to himself, and enjoined the same reticence upon his confidants. After the re-election of Mr. Van Buren to the United States Senate, more freedom was tolerated in the expression of opinions favorable to Jackson and adverse to Adams; but it was not until late in 1827 that the Democratic party came out plainly for General Jackson. Then all the machinery, the construction of which had for two years put in requisition the skill and ingenuity of Mr. Van Buren and his friends, was suddenly put in motion, and the effect was prodigious.

The friends of the administration were not alarmed; Mr. Clay was not, and Mr. Adams expected a re-election. The campaign of 1828 opened with a stunning flourish of trumpets. Louisiana, like New York, was a doubtful and troublesome State. It was highly desirable that its scattering vote of 1824 should be concentrated in 1828, and this could only be managed by getting up an enthusiasm. In 1827, the Legislature of Louisiana invited him to visit New Orleans, and unite with them in the celebration of the 8th of January, 1828, on the scene of his great victory. General Jackson accepted, and his reception was

the most stupendous thing of the kind that **had**
ever, up to that time, occurred in the United States.
Delegates of States as distant as New York were
sent to New Orleans to swell the *eclat* of the demon·
stration.

The campaign had now fairly set in. During the
rest of the year, the country rang, from one end
to the other, with the names of JACKSON AND CAL-
HOUN, and ADAMS AND RUSH. The contest during
this final year became chiefly one of personalities.

Against Mr. Adams, every possible change was
rung of bargain and corruption. He was accused
of federalism, haughtiness, selfishness, and extravagant expenditures. General Jackson was accused
of every crime, offence, and impropriety that man
was ever known to be guilty of, not even sparing
the peculiar circumstances of his marriage, nor the
memory of his mother; then resting in her grave.
We have not space here to give any account of the
electioneering tactics on both sides; but the following characteristic paragraph, written by one who
was then commencing his literary career, and who
subsequently became known far and wide in con·
nection with the *New York Herald*,—James Gordon
Bennett,—will give a good idea of the attacks that
were made on General Jackson.

"The impotency of the attacks which have been
made on General Jackson during the campaign
by the Adams party, reminds us of an anecdote.
'Mother,' bawled out a girl, one day, 'my toe
itches!' 'Well, scratch it then!' 'I have; but
it won't *stay* scratched.' 'Mr. Clay, Mr. Clay,'
cries out Uncle Toby, 'Jackson's a-coming—Jackson's a·coming!' 'Well, then, anti-tariff him in

the *Journal*.' 'I have; but he won't *stay* anti-tariffed.' 'Mr. Clay, Mr. Clay,' bawls out Alderman Binns, 'the old farmer's a-coming.' 'Well, then,' says Clay, 'coffin-hand-bill him.' 'I have, I have; but he won't *stay* coffin-hand-billed.' 'Mr. Adams, Mr. Adams,' says John Pleasant, 'the hero's a-coming, actually a-coming.' 'Well, then,' says Mr. Adams, 'Burr him, and traitor him.' 'I have; but he won't *stay* Burred or traitored.' 'Mr. Clay, Mr. Clay,' calls out the full Adams, slandering chorus, 'we have called Jackson a murderer, an adulterer, a traitor, an ignoramus, a fool, a pretender, and so forth; but he won't *stay* any of these names.' 'He won't?' says Mr. Clay; 'well, then, I sha'n't *stay* at Washington, that's all!'"

The result of the election was, that out of the two hundred and sixty-one electoral votes cast in 1828, one hundred and seventy-eight were given to General Jackson, and eighty-three to Mr. Adams.

The people of Nashville, greatly elated by the success of their General, resolved to celebrate it by a banquet, to come off on the 23d of December, the anniversary of the Night Battle below New Orleans. General Jackson accepted an invitation to be present.

But the banquet never took place. Mrs. Jackson, whose health had been for four or five years very precarious, was taken suddenly very ill on the 17th of December, and died on the night of the 22d, the day before the time appointed for the banquet. The sad news reached Nashville early on the 23d, when the committee of arrangements were busied with the preparations for the General's reception; of course, everything was at an end to the proposed manifestation, and the most heartfelt and general mourning pervaded the entire community.

General Jackson never recovered from the shock of his wife's death, and was never quite the same man afterwards. It subdued his spirit and corrected his speech. Except on occasions of extreme excitement, few and far between, he never again used what is commonly termed "profane language."

He was, however, not allowed much time for mourning, for, in the middle of January, he started for Washington. The journey was one ovation the whole way through, for the whole country appeared to more than acquiesce in the result of the election, and joined in the cry: "Hurrah for Jackson!" The day of the inauguration was one of the brightest and balmiest of the spring, and there had never been known to be such vast crowds as were present on that memorable occasion. Half the nation seemed to have rushed to the capital. His inaugural address was an acceptance of the leadership of the party which had elected him.

Little was known of General Jackson's intentions with regard to Cabinet appointments except by the chosen few. In distributing the six most important offices, he assigned two to the North, two to the West, and two to the South. Van Buren, of course, was appointed Secretary of State, resigning the governorship of New York, after holding it only seventy days. S. D. Ingham, of Pennsylvania, Secretary of the Treasury; John H. Eaton, Secretary of War; John Branch, of North Carolina, Secretary of the Navy; John McPherson Berrien, of Georgia, Attorney-General; Wm. T. Barry, of Kentucky, Postmaster-General. Such, then, was the Cabinet of the new President. With the exception of Mr. Van Buren, its members had no great influence over the measures of their chief and play no great part in the general history of the times. There were other individuals who stood nearer to the President than they did, and who exerted over him a far more powerful influence. Major W. B. Lewis, of Nashville, to whom, more than to any other, General Jackson owed his election to the presidency, one of his oldest and stanchest friends, had accompanied the General to Washington, and remained a member of his family, being appointed to an Auditorship of the Treasury. General Duff Green, Editor of the *United States Telegraph*, St. Louis; Editor Isaac Hill from New Hampshire, and Amos Kendall, late an editor of a Jackson paper in Kentucky, all of whom had been most indefatigable and zealous in their support of General Jackson during the campaign, were all three much about the person of the President during the first months of his administration, and were supposed to have most of his confidence. These four — Lewis, Green, Hill, and Kendall — were in consequence stigmatized by the opposition as the Kitchen Cabinet.

Among the powers entrusted to the honor of President of the United States was the power of removing from office, without trial or notice, the civil employees of the Government. In the civil service of the country, every man holds his place at the will of the head of the Government. The early Presidents disposed of the places in their

29 *

gift with a scrupulous conscientiousness which is most delightful to observe. Washington set a noble example. During his administration of eight years, he only removed nine persons from office, all for good and sufficient cause, with which politics had nothing whatever to do. The example of Washington was followed by his successors, and up to the hour of the delivery of General Jackson's inaugural address, it was supposed that he, too, would act upon the principles of his predecessors. But the sun had not gone down upon the day of his inauguration when it was known in all official circles that there would be a removal from office of all who had conspicuously opposed, and an appointment to office of those who had conspicuously aided, the election of the new President. The work was promptly begun, and soon there was a reign of terror all over Washington. The great body of officials awaited their fate in silent dread, and so numerous were the removals that the business of the place became paralyzed. In fact, the old system of appointments and removals was changed, from the accession of General Jackson, to the one in vogue ever since, which has been aptly described as "to the victor belong the spoils." It is not our intention here to enter into any discussion regarding the evils of this system, which are but too apparent to every one — a system which renders pure, decent, and orderly government almost impossible.

The course of the administration with regard to removals caused so loud and general a clamor as to inspire the opposition with new hopes. The old Federalists who had supported General Jackson were especially shocked, and occasionally the officers who were so summarily removed did not submit to the process without protesting. It must be here mentioned, as a matter of justice to his friend Major Lewis, that the latter was most strenuously opposed to this fatal removal policy from begining to end, but without avail. At the meeting of Congress on December 7th, 1829, General Jackson's first Message was delivered, and was a most important paper, marked with a calm deliberateness of tone, characteristic of the General. It was full of brief, pregnant paragraphs, the most prominent and important of which was one which sounded the first note of war against the United States Bank, and two others defending the course of the Government in its removals and appointments, the leading ideas of which were that a long tenure of office is almost necessarily corrupting; that an office-holder has no more right to his office than an office-seeker; and that if any one had a right to complain of a removal from office, it was not the luckless individual who had been suddenly deprived of the means of subsistence without cause.

The Message was, upon the whole, a candid and straightforward document, announcing plainly a policy of the administration, which was carried out with a consistency and a resolution rarely pai alleled. The debates began, and were most carefully watched by President Jackson. The proceedings of the Senate were the first to kindle his wrath. The Senate was not so disposed to confirm as the President had been to appoint. A large number of his nominations were opposed, and several on which he had set his heart were rejected. The

most remarkable case was that of Isaac Hill (one of
the Kitchen Cabinet before referred to). It was the
one that gave the President the deepest offence, and
which he avenged most promptly and strikingly.
The term of Senator Woodbury, for New Hampshire, was about to expire, and through the influ
ence of the President and his party, Isaac Hill was
taken up by the Jackson men with prompt enthusiasm for the seat, and he was elected by an unu-
sual majority, thus coming back to Washington a
member of the body that had deemed him unworthy
of a far less elevated post.

The removal and appointment question was ably
discussed in both Houses, and many plans were suggested for restricting the dread power of removal,
but of course nothing could be, or was done, against
so powerful an administrative majority in the House.

The Bank of the United States enjoyed two tri-
umphs during the session. The Committee of
Ways and Means, to which had been referred that
part of the President's Message that related to the
bank, reported strongly in favor of the existing
bank, and as strongly against the bank proposed
by the President. Later on in the session other
resolutions, which were introduced adverse to the
bank, were laid upon the table by a vote of eighty-
nine to sixty-six. But notwithstanding these tri-
umphs, the bank was a doomed bank. This was
the session of Congress which was remarkable for
the great debate between Mr. Hayne and Mr. Webster, the preliminary debate on Nullification, a new
and distinct doctrine in the United States, embracing such questions as State-Rights, Liberty before Union, Inequality of Burdens and Benefits.

Of this party Mr. Calhoun was regarded by Southern extremists as their predestined chief, and they were in the habit of giving utterance to sentiments regarding the Union which thrilled with horror the patriotic spirits of those days. The Nullifiers evidently expected that the President, having been elected by the aid of the extreme Southern or State-Rights party, would have given them some show of acquiescence and support. But in this they were quickly deceived, as he took occasion, on the birthday of Thomas Jefferson (April 13th), to give the toast which electrified the country and has become historical,

" Our Federal Union: It must be preserved,"

intended by him as a proclamation from the President to announce a plot against the Union, and to summon the people to its defence.

Congress adjourned on the thirty-first of May, and shortly after a most serious rupture took place between General Jackson and the Vice-President, Mr. Calhoun. General Jackson's antipathy to Mr. Calhoun was of long standing,—so far back as December, 1829,—and it now broke out, so far as the President was concerned, into avowed and irreconcilable hostility. In reviewing the whole affair, at once so trivial and yet so important in its effect upon the course of political events, there is no evidence, that we can see, that Mr. Calhoun was guilty of the duplicity towards General Jackson of which the latter accused him. Not only was he not bound to communicate to General Jackson the transactions of the Cabinet Council, but he was bound *not* to reveal them. Nor does it appear that he ever professed, publicly or privately, to **General Jackson**, or to any one else, that he approved *all* of the General's proceedings in Florida. He admitted and believed that General Jackson's motives had been patriotic, and if he disapproved of some of them, the General surely had no right to make that a ground of offence. Mr. Calhoun's only mistake was in his replying to the General's first letter in any other way except to civilly decline giving the desired information. Had he done this, General Jackson might still have hated him, but he could never have despised him. A manly defiance General Jackson liked next to complete submission.

One result of this feud between the President and Vice-President was the defection of one of the oldest and stanchest friends of the former, Duff Green, whose paper, the *United States Telegraph,* was the organ of the administration, and on which they depended for aid in the contest with the Bank of the United States, which they saw impending. Duff Green began to take the side of Calhoun, it being, as he said, "the side of truth and honor;" so the administration determined to establish another organ, and the man selected as being the best fitted for the editorship of the proposed organ was Francis P. Blair, of Kentucky, one of the most decided opponents of the bank in the Union and also of Nullification. Like Jonah's gourd, the *Globe*, the new organ, sprang into existence almost in a single night, and it soon, by getting more than its share of departmental printing, was on a paying basis. Being recognized as the administration organ, subscribers poured in by hundreds in a day, office-holders seeing that it was to their interest to take it.

Congress again met on December 6th, 1830, and the second Message of the President was read, one of the most carefully elaborated documents ever presented to Congress, touching upon the leading topics then agitating the public mind with great skill and powerful argument. It concluded with a second and louder warning to the United States Bank. Only one event in this short session of Congress, ending March 3d, 1831, was Colonel Benton's first formal attack upon the bank, which was a very able and effective speech, and which roused the people; the instant it was delivered, a vote was called for and taken, resulting in a strong vote against the bank — twenty to twenty-three — enough to excite uneasiness.

Towards the close of this brief but uneventful session of Congress, Mr. Calhoun published his "book," containing his late correspondence with the President, and a mass of letters and statements illustrative thereof. This pamphlet was discussed in a strictly partisan spirit—all the opposition papers applauding it, and all the Jackson organs condemning it as an attack upon the President. The President's retort was prompt, adroit, and overwhelming. By a series of skilful movements he shelved the three members of his Cabinet — Ingham, Branch, and Berrien — who were Calhoun's friends and political allies. A dissolution of the Cabinet was the expedient hit upon. Mr. Van Buren and Major Eaton were to resign and to be provided for—the former going to England in place of Mr. McLane, who was recalled to be Secretary of the Treasury, and the latter it was intended to appoint to a seat in the Senate. The obnoxious

three were asked for their resignations, which of
course they tendered. The dissolution, its causes
and consequences, and the many scandals it gave
rise to, of which we cannot here speak, were the
newspaper topic of the whole summer. Mr. Webster
took a very serious view of the prospect before his
— the opposition — party. He wrote to Mr. Clay,
in October, urging his return to the Senate. " We
are to have an interesting and arduous session.
Everything is to be attacked. An array is preparing, much more formidable than has ever yet assaulted what we think the leading and important
public interests. Not only the tariff, but the Constitution itself, in its elementary and fundamental
principles, will be assailed with talent, vigor, and
union. Everything is to be debated, as if nothing
had ever been settled."

This was true. Nullification hung like a dark
cloud over the Southern horizon. South Carolina
was in a ferment, and, unless the tariff was rectified
at the next session, she might do such things as
then she knew not of.

The next session was the great session of Jackson's
administration. Illustrious names, great debates,
extraordinary incidents, momentous measures, all
combined to make it a memorable one in the history of the country.

The Message was, strange to say, one of the
quietest and shortest ever presented to Congress
by General Jackson. Without delay, and without
even a debate, the Senate confirmed the nominations of the new members of the Cabinet. Not so
the nomination of Mr. Van Buren to the post of
British Ambassador. The leaders of the Senate

had resolved upon his rejection, and after preliminary manœuvres, lasting fifty-one days, and a debate of two days, the nomination of Mr. Van Buren
was rejected.

The rejection secured Mr. Van Buren's political
fortune. His elevation to the presidency, long
before desired and intended by General Jackson,
from that hour became one of his darling objects.

The two great topics of the session were the
tariff and the bank. As it wore on, the all-important question was "Shall the Bank of the
United States be rechartered, or shall it not?"

On January 9th, 1832, a memorial was presented
from the President and Directors of the Bank,
asking a renewal of their charter, — a memorial
couched in language most modest and respectful.
It was a prominent subject of debate during all the
winter and spring of 1832. January, February,
March, April, May, and June passed away before
the final passage of the bank bill was voted upon;
and never was exhibited so striking an illustration
of the maxim that will, not talent, governs the world.
The will of one man, General Jackson, operating
upon the will of one other man, Thomas H. Benton, carried the day against the assembled talent
and the interested capital of the country.

The bill rechartering the bank passed the Senate, on June 11th, by a vote of 28 to 20, and the
House, on July 3d, by a vote of 109 to 76. It was
presented to the President on July 4th, and by him
returned to Congress, vetoed, on the 10th of the
same month.

There was rare speaking in the Senate on the
reception of the veto message. Mr. Webster

opened the debate by predicting the direst consequences to the country, unless the people, at the approaching election, reversed the President's decision. Mr. Clay followed, and so the discussion was kept up until Congress adjourned on July 16th.

The result of the election of 1832 astonished everybody. Not the wildest and most enthusiastic Jackson man had anticipated so overwhelming a victory. The total number of electoral votes in 1832 was 282. General Jackson received 219, and Mr. Van Buren, for the Vice-Presidency, received 189.

How can such a result be explained? Only that General Jackson was right in all his leading public measures, excepting his appointment and removal policy, and that he was supported by the masses of the people.

We now come to the topic of Nullification, which was one of the most momentous during the administration of General Jackson. This word Nullification was first introduced into American politics as early as 1798, when the passage of the alien and sedition laws prompted the Legislatures of Virginia and Kentucky to adopt what are known as the "Resolutions of '98," of which Madison and Jefferson were the authors. The interpretation put on these resolutions by the Nullifiers of 1832 was this: Any single State may nullify any act of Congress which it deems unconstitutional. The extreme Nullifiers even boldly avowed that the Resolutions of 1798 meant *that any State of the Union may secede from the Union whenever it likes.* The language of Mr. Calhoun amounted to this, and nothing short of that. He proposed a nullification of a revenue law, and a revenue law must be universal in its operation, or it cannot anywhere be obeyed. The comment of General Jackson on this reasoning was forcible and about the best the discussion elicited. "If this thing goes on," he said, "our country will be like a bag of meal with both ends open. Pick it up in the middle or endwise, it will run out."

The contrast between the slow and limited prosperity of the South and the swift and marvellous progress of the North, was never so remarkable as it was during the administration of General Jackson. The North was bounding forward on a bright career; but the South was paralyzed and desolate. As the first years of General Jackson's administration wore away without giving the South that relief which they had hoped from it, the discontent of the Southern people increased. Circumstances gave them a new and telling argument. In 1831, the public debt had been so far diminished, as to render it certain that in three years the last dollar of it would be paid. The government had been collecting about twice as much revenue as its annual expenditures required. In three years, therefore, there would be an annual surplus of twelve or thirteen millions of dollars. The South demanded, with almost a united voice, that the duties should be reduced so as to make the revenue equal to the expenditure, and that, in making this reduction, the principle of protection should be, in effect, abandoned.

The case was one of serious difficulty. To reduce the revenue at one swoop thirteen millions of

dollars, would be disastrous to all the manufactur-
ing interests of the country. At this juncture, Mr.
Clay returned to the Senate in December, 1831,
and, after an able and exhaustive discussion, proposed that "the duties on articles imported from
foreign countries, and not coming into competition
with similar articles produced in the United States,
be forthwith abolished, except the duties on wines
and silks, and that those be reduced." A bill in
accordance with this was passed by both Houses,
and signed by the President, preserving the pro-
tective principle intact, and reducing the income
of the government about three millions of dollars.
A month after Congress adjourned, the Vice-President went home to South Carolina, and the discontent of the South was inflamed to such a degree,
that the Legislature of the State of South Carolina
called a convention of its citizens to take into consideration the late action of Congress. The convention met on November 19th, 1832, and a committee of twenty-one appointed, the result of whose
labors was the celebrated *Nullifying Ordinance* of
November 24th, 1832. The people of the State accepted this ordinance, and the Legislature passed
the act requisite for carrying it into practical effect.
The Governor was authorized to accept the services
of volunteers, and the State resounded with the
noise of warlike preparations. Medals were struck
bearing the inscription, "John C. Calhoun, First
President of the Southern Confederacy." Mr. Calhoun was selected to fill the vacancy created in the
Senate of the United States by the election of Mr.
Haynes to the governorship, and resigning the vice-

presidency, he began his journey to Washington, leaving his State in the wildest ferment.

General Jackson at this time was at his home, the Hermitage; but he kept an eye on South Carolina, and General Scott was quietly ordered to South Carolina. Other changes were made by the President in the disposition of naval and military forces, so resolved was he to preserve intact the authority with which he had been entrusted.

Congress met on the 3d of December. The President's Message was an unusually quiet and business-like document; but it was followed, a few days after, by another of a very different tenor — that remarkable proclamation refuting one by one the leading positions of the Nullifiers, which electrified the North, as it irritated the excited feeling of South Carolina. This proclamation was answered by a counter-proclamation from the Governor of the latter State, calling upon his fellow-citizens to "disregard the menaces of military force, which, if the President was tempted to employ, it would become their solemn duty to resist." When this reached Washington, the President asked Congress for an increase of power adequate to the impending collision, which was granted him.

The collision, however, fortunately, was averted by the passage of what was called a compromise bill, introduced by Mr. Clay, for the regulation of the tariff, proposing a gradual reduction of duties, and intended to postpone further action until a more auspicious day. To this bill Mr. Calhoun agreed, and even voted for, and it was passed by a vote of 119 to 85. General Jackson disapproved

30 *

of this hasty and, as it proved, unstable compromise; but he signed it.

As soon as it was passed, Mr. Calhoun left Washington, and travelling night and day reached Columbia in time to meet the convention before they had taken any further steps. His explanation satisfied them, and so the storm, which at one time had seemed so threatening and imminent, passed over.

General Jackson passed his sixty-sixth birthday in the spring of 1833. He stood then in the zenith of his career, opposition being for the moment almost silenced, and the whole country, except South Carolina, looking up to him as to a saviour. Had he only gone on quietly during the remaining years of his term, making no new issues and provoking no new controversies, it would have been better for him; but going on quietly was not his forte.

Hardly had the Nullification question been settled, as it were, than war was again renewed upon the Bank of the United States. General Jackson had recommended to Congress, in his Message of December, 1832, to sell out the stock held by the United States in the bank, and to investigate its condition, with a view to ascertain whether the public deposits were safe in its keeping. Congress, however, voted down these propositions by immense majorities; but this did not divert the President from his fixed purpose. He believed that the bank was insolvent, and that unless he could cripple the institution before Congress again met, the bank would certainly attain a two-thirds majority. The idea occurred to him then "to remove the deposits," not in the actual sense of removing what deposits there were then in the bank, but to *cease depositing* the public money in its vault, and to draw out what was there as the public service required. It was proposed, instead of depositing the public money in the Bank of the United States and its twenty-five branches, to deposit it in a similar number of State Banks.

This measure was strongly opposed by every member of the Cabinet but two, and a large majority of the President's best friends from the beginning to the end. The Secretary of the Treasury, Mr. Duane, positively refused to sanction any such measure, and desired the whole subject presented in the clearest light before Congress, being fully confident that they would correct the abuses and avert the mischief apprehended by the President. General Jackson then caused to be read to the Cabinet the paper known to history as " The paper read to the Cabinet on the 18th of September." In this he takes upon himself the sole responsibility of the removal, and names the first day of October next as the day the deposits would be removed. Two days later, the President announced in the *Globe* that the Government would cease to deposit the public money in the Bank of the United States after October 1st. The Secretary of the Treasury refused to order the change in the fiscal system announced in the financial newspaper, and remaining firm in his refusal, the President removed him from the Secretaryship, and appointed Mr. Roger B. Taney, then Attorney-General, in his place.

When Congress met on December 2d, the President, in his Message, again avowed the measure of the removal of the deposits to be his own measure. This question was the topic of the day from the first week in December, 1833, to the last day of June, 1834. Indeed, it was the great topic from 1833 to 1842. It lived through the panic of 1834, the inflation of 1835, the madness of 1836, the crash of 1837, the depression of 1838 to 1842, and only received its quietus in 1844. The result of the whole discussion was the Sub-treasury — a result which might have been reached just as well in 1834 as in 1838.

The 8th of January, 1835, was the day which General Jackson esteemed as the most glorious of his presidency. It was the anniversary of the battle of New Orleans, and was seized as the occasion to celebrate the payment of the last instalment of the public debt. The parties made the most of this auspicious event by a banquet of more than ordinary magnificence, given at Washington on the 8th of January, 1835. On the 30th of the same month, his life was twice attempted by a lunatic named Lawrence, but luckily both times the pistol missed fire.

The Message of 1835, the last but one of General Jackson's annual communications to Congress, demands a moment's notice from us. The country seemed to be prosperous beyond example. The national debt was paid, and there was a surplus in the treasury of eleven millions. The President's love of a hard currency appeared conspicuously in this Message.

One of the most important acts passed by this Congress was the State Deposit Act of 1836. Congress sat until the 4th of July, and adjourned without introducing any measure to put a stop to the land speculations, such as compelling purchasers of public lands to pay for them in specie only. One week after Congress adjourned, President Jackson, who saw the ruin that threatened the country, if these speculations continued, issued the famous "Specie Circular" on his own authority, against the known will of Congress, but it came too late. It could only now precipitate the crash which had become inevitable. The pressure in the money market increased steadily from May, 1836, until it ended in the stupendous ruin of May, 1837.

In November, 1836, General Jackson's most cherished hope of the election of Mr. Van Buren to the presidency was realized, a result for which, for seven years, he had schemed and labored. It was a signal triumph, for it was one which secured all the objects nearest his heart, dismayed the opposition, and deprived the bank party of its last hope. During the last session of Congress, at the close of General Jackson's administration, the most notable act was the rescinding by both Houses of the Specie Circular of 1836, which, however, the President killed by not acting upon it.

The inauguration of Mr. Van Buren took place on the 4th of March, 1837, and on the third day after General Jackson began his homeward journey. He was seventy years of age when he retired from the presidency — an infirm old man, seldom free from pain for an hour, never for a day, and poor. He said himself that he returned home "with only ninety dollars" in his pocket. During the next few years he lived the life of a planter, enjoying the society of his adopted son and his amiable and estimable wife. They and their children were the only consolation of his old age. Surrounded by an affectionate circle of friends, he passed many happy days, and most of his latter days would have been happy had it not been for his being frequently reduced by illness to the condition of a helpless invalid.

The Hermitage was still, as ever, the seat of hospitality, and was visited not only by his numerous friends, but by many strangers, who came to see the "General." All were welcomed cordially, whether they were friends or strangers.

The ex-President took as lively an interest as ever in the fortunes of his party after his retirement from public life. When, in 1840, General Harrison was re-nominated, General Jackson exerted himself powerfully to secure his friend Mr. Van Buren's re-election, even to the extent of making personally a considerable tour in the western part of Tennessee to aid his cause.

In 1842 General Jackson became sadly embarrassed through the misfortunes of his son, and, as a last resource, he applied to his fast friend, Mr. Blair, of the *Globe*, who was then in affluent circumstances. Ten thousand dollars was the sum needed, and Mr. Blair not only resolved on the instant to lend the money, but to lend it on the General's personal security, and to make the loan as closely resemble a gift as the General's delicacy would permit it to be. Upon reading Mr. Blair's letter, the old man burst into tears, but would accept the money only on conditions which secured his friend against any possibility of loss.

We come now to the closing scenes of the life of

General Jackson. Inheriting a constitution that was never strong, he had been for thirty-one years a diseased man. During the first six years after his retirement from the presidency his health was not much worse than it had usually been in Washington. The attacks of hemorrhage, to which he was still subject, left him weaker than he had ever been before, and during the last two years of his life he never really rallied from these attacks, and knew few, and those very brief, intervals of relief from pain. A cough harassed him day and night, and he had all the symptoms of consumption. Six months before his death dropsy set in, and he was alternately swollen by dropsy and prostrated by diarrhœa.

The patience which he displayed during these months of dissolution was sublime. No pain, however severe, ever wrung from this naturally most irascible of men a fretful or complaining word.

On Sunday, May 24th, 1845, the last Sunday but two of his life, General Jackson partook of the communion in the presence of his family. He conversed freely of the consolation of religion, and declared that he was fully prepared for the final summons. "Death," said he, after the solemn ceremony was over, "has no terrors for me. When I have suffered sufficiently, the Lord will take me to himself; but what are my sufferings compared with those of the blessed Saviour who died on the accursed tree for my sake? Mine are nothing."

On the Friday before he died, in an interval of comparative relief, he expressed to his daughter his

desire to be buried without pomp or display of any
kind — only in a plain, unostentatious manner.
Even at this supreme moment his thoughts were
directed to the affairs of his beloved country, and
he dictated a letter to the President, Polk, expressing confidence in his judgment and patriotism, and
urging him to act promptly and resolutely in the
affairs of Texas and Oregon. This was his last
letter.

He saw the light of another Sunday morning --
June 8th — a brilliant, hot day. He lingered all
the day, lying tranquil and without pain, at intervals recognizing his children and friends who surrounded his death-bed, and sending farewell mes-
sages to others who were not present. At six in
the evening he passed away quietly, without a
struggle or a pang.

Two days after he was laid to rest in the grave,
by the side of his beloved wife. All Nashville and
the surrounding country were present at the fu-
neral — not less than three thousand persons, it was
estimated — and the ceremonies were of the most
impressive and touching character. The tablet
which covers the remains of the aged warrior bears
the following inscription :

GENERAL ANDREW JACKSON.

Born on the 15th of March, 176;

Died on the 8th of June, 1845.